JUMPERS

A.C. HESSENAUER

ISBN 979-8-218-70366-0

Jumpers Playlist

1. Big Dreams-The Score
2. Australia-The Shins
3. Up Jumped the Devil-Nick Cave And The Bad Seeds
4. Street Fight-Adam Jensen
5. Beast- Nico Vega
6. Railroad Track- Willy Moon
7. Friend of the Devil-Adam Jensen
8. hunter- Paris Paloma
9. Trouble-Adam Jensen
10. Wild Horses- Bishop Briggs
11. Not Your Fault- AWOLNATION
12. labour- Paris Paloma
13. Stronger- The Score
14. Dizzy- MISSIO
15. Feed the Machine- Poor Mans Poison
16. Stay- The Score
17. Bang Bang (My Baby Shot Me Down)- Nico Vega
18. Jailbreak-AWOLNATION
19. More To This- Marc Scibilia

To every girl who has dreamed of flying;
this one's for you.

Trigger Warnings:

Jumpers contains few trigger warnings, but I will list those I can think of here. Mild gore. Smut. If you're not a fan of open-door romance or are in any way related to the author, maybe (please, for the love of God) choose a different book. The characters swear frequently, including taking the Lord's name in vain, as the author has been known to do (see above).

If you dislike love triangles, witty banter, and enemies-to-lovers vibes, this may not be the book for you. If you hate paranormal aspects in your thrillers, please reconsider (your opinions, not whether you should read this).

All joking and snarking aside, there is a scene that may be triggering, which involves attempted SA, which occurs in chapter 19.

If you've gotten this far and haven't rolled your eyes (too hard) or added me to your cancelled list, welcome. I hope you find entertainment, meaning, and most importantly, hope, within these pages.

"He who fights with monsters might take care, lest he thereby become a monster."

-Friedrich Nietzsche

"The world is violent and mercurial--it will have its way with you. We are saved only by love--love for each other and the love that we pour into the art we feel compelled to share: being a parent; being a writer; being a painter; being a friend. We live in a perpetually burning building, and what we must save from it, all the time, is love."

-Tennessee Williams

Prologue

It started like every other assault he'd ever taken part in. Ward stood there in the hangar of *The Beagle* with his men as they waited for the transport pod to open. The young ones, especially, he would need to keep an eye on today. Two of them were a liability; this would be their first time under fire. He didn't envy them that: they weren't broken yet.

He clapped one of them, Stowell, on the back and gave him a reassuring smile. "You hit the ground running. Follow Command. Follow orders. We'll get you where you need to be. Get you through this. Okay?" Stowell swallowed, nodding nervously, but his eyes looked less wide now. Less panicked. The others were listening, too. Ward noted several men nodding at his words.

The door of the transport pod fell open. "Move out!" Ward turned, calling over their heads, waving an arm, "Let's go!"

The men started moving, shuffling past him and onto the pod, the other units down the line all doing the same. Captain Harris stood behind them, back against the wall of the hangar, hands on his hips, scanning the crowd. He caught Ward's eye and beckoned him over.

Ward pushed through the crowd to get to his captain. "Sir." He stood at attention, saluted.

"At ease, Ward," Harris muttered, resting a hand on his shoulder blades. He pulled Ward closer, "We're the final wave; they're not sending B Company in after us as planned."

"Sir?" Ward ducked nearer, frowning, trying to make sure he was hearing him correctly over the din and bustle of the busy hangar.

Harris sighed, "Things are rough down there. And we're getting some... odd reports, from the ground. They're sending us down to provide cover fire. Captain Swan's company is pinned down, just past the bridge. I'll be debriefing everyone over the comms as we go."

Ward nodded, wondering why he'd been called over then. "What sort of odd reports, Sir?"

Harris paused, frowning for a moment as he watched the men filing onto the pods. "I'm not quite sure, son. There's been chatter over the comms. Strange men who move too fast.

They sound like they're... deformed, or something. Something's wrong with them."

Ward's eyebrows rose, and he turned to face Captain Harris directly. "Deformed, Sir?"

Harris just nodded. "Look, son, I don't know what kind of shit we're heading into." He sighed again. "I'm taking point. If anything happens to me," he clapped Ward on the back, "the company is yours."

Ward just stared back at his captain. He realized he probably looked about as wide-eyed as Stowell had moments ago. Ward snapped to attention. "Sir, yes Sir!" He swallowed thickly. "It would be an honor, Sir."

Harris nodded, his smile half-grimace. "Get going," he nodded towards the pod with Ward's men inside. Ward turned and went to join them at a light jog.

"What'd the Captain want?" MacMillan called out to him. He was standing on the ramp, hands on his hips, his brows creased with concern, blue eyes locked onto Ward. Ward shook his head, shooting him a dark look back. He addressed his men, gathering around the pod door.

"He's going to brief us over the comms on the way down. Just stay close, keep your eyes peeled. We'll be providing cover fire for the company pinned down past the bridge."

That was all he elected to tell them, for the moment. Vague rumors about men who 'moved too fast' would do nothing but terrify them more than they already were.

MacMillan stared at him for several seconds, but Ward only shook his head once more, his lips pressed into a thin line. MacMillan shrugged, then sighed, and turned to enter the pod.

They were headed into the thick of it. Their recent skirmishes had been on a smaller scale, on the sidelines of the main action. Up until recently, the Northern Alliance had avoided sending troops directly into the heart of the Southern territories. But today, they were heading for Texas. Houston. They were walking straight into the mouth of the beast. All of that was nerve-wracking enough, without throwing in some sort of deformed super soldiers.

Ward gritted his teeth, holding onto the railing over his head as the transport pod launched from the Carrier. Riding the transport pods always felt a little like rattling around in a tin can.

Thankfully, the ride down was smooth enough; they avoided hitting any major turbulence banks. Captain Harris popped over the comm, as promised, but there was no mention of the 'odd reports' as he had called them. The men sat there silently, stoic, after he finished his briefing. As they began to slow, nearing the surface, Ward watched as Stowell leaned over and puked his guts up on the floor of the pod.

Ward nodded grimly at Stowell as he wiped his mouth with the back of his hand. *Best to get it out now.* He wasn't the first to lose his lunch on a transport pod, and he wouldn't be the last.

The pod landed with a thud, rising back into the air momentarily, before coming down again, skipping and hovering over the ground like a stone on water, its stabilizers hissing, until it finally came to a sliding, shuddering halt.

The anticipation didn't last long. The pod door shuddered as it yawned open, the wall to Ward's left falling away to form a ramp. Their first glimpse of Houston was of the hazy sky above, dotted with rolling grey clouds. Below, was carnage.

Ward called out to his men, urging them forward as they streamed off the pod and ran down the ramp. They hit the ground, boots squishing and squelching in the damp earth.

Ward led his unit toward the bridge. They stepped over bodies as they went. Almost immediately, a stray bullet took out the man running beside him. A headshot: the round managed to pierce straight through his metal helmet, causing his head to snap to the side just before he fell face down in the mud.

Stowell stopped in his tracks, gaping down at the body of his fellow soldier, eyes wide as saucers. Ward moved forward and rolled the soldier over. It was Smith. His eyes were frozen. Lifeless. He cursed under his breath and ordered two of his men to help drag Smith's body back towards the pods. They would have to retrieve him on the way out. *Jesus Christ.* Ward cursed again to himself as they continued forward at a running crouch.

They moved as fast as they could, crossing the expanse that stretched before them—a field of death, littered with bodies, discarded in the mud. Ward communicated using hand signs when possible and yelled through the comms over the din of battle when necessary.

The sun was starting to sink low on the horizon behind them, coloring the skyline red. Ward scanned the bodies on the ground as they scrambled over them, heading for the bridge. Nearly all were dressed in blue Northern Alliance uniforms, although they came upon pockets of men in the brown fatigues of the South. *How had things gone this badly? What the hell happened down here?*

They wove between ruts dug into the ground, dark holes that led below the surface. "Watch out for foxholes!" Ward called out over the comms. Two of the men beside him jumped, leaping over the foxhole to his right. The enemy had been dug in here. The NA had managed to rout them, but clearly at great cost.

His men found what cover they could as they neared the bridge, crouching down behind the rubble of fallen buildings and overturned cars.

When they finally managed to get into position, they lay into the opposite bank, providing suppressing fire as directed. The company below was pinned by the terrain and surrounded on three sides by the enemy, but why hadn't they retreated? The riverbed was nearly dry. The water pooled at the bottom looked filthy, but it couldn't be more than a foot or two deep. Why hadn't they moved past the bridge and back to their transport pods? Was the objective to stand their ground?

Ward turned, scanning the field behind them warily. He squinted through the hazy, smoky air, but could see nothing but their pods in the distance. *Why hadn't they retreated?* Perhaps they were just outnumbered and couldn't risk sprinting back to their pods; decided to hunker down to wait, since help was on its way.

Ward eyed the bodies again. A wave of blue stretched out over the field at their backs. He felt a tide of grief and despair that threatened to swallow him, and he replaced it with anger. Rage. Letting it build in his chest. *What a goddamn waste.* He breathed in deeply, trying to remind himself why they were here—the camp, at GITMO.

They came for the foreigners first. Undocumented. Claimed they were all criminals. But they were just regular people.

Those poor men and women, trapped there. Children, growing up in that slum. A whole generation of children who knew nothing but suffering and fear. It filled him with a blind sort of rage. Made him see red.

Those bastards had tortured them, starved them half to death. Ward remembered how they'd fallen to their knees in the dirt, squinting up at the sun.

He'd never forget the sight of the bodies. Humans, thrown like garbage in a pile, their bodies so thin and wasted that they looked more like skeletons with skin stretched over.

So, more men had to die. To fight. Become monsters. Because they would never let something like that happen again. Never again. They'd hammer the South until it was laid to waste. They'd throw their own lives away, down here, in the mud.

Ward had walked away from Guantanamo a different person. He'd changed after that. Learned to bury his humanity. Because that was what was necessary. To fight back. To survive. He'd sell his soul to the devil, if that was what it took. It wasn't worth all that much anyway. Not anymore.

Harris called out over the comms, directing the units to spread out. Ward clenched his fist harder around his rifle and called out to his men, leading them further down along the bridge, using the rubble for cover.

They moved into position and continued to hammer the far bank. There were snipers up in the buildings on the other side, picking off men, one at a time. Ward moved among his men, calling out to them by name. He kept an eye on Stowell, glad to see he was still with them, and he kept another eye on that field behind them, his gut twisting with dread.

They must have been down there, waiting. Though waiting for what, he didn't know. Some said afterward that they were waiting for it to get dark. But Ward didn't think so.

It was dusk, the sun just disappearing below the horizon, when they began to crawl out of the foxholes.

Ward turned to see just a half dozen or so—solitary dark figures, silhouetted against the red sky. For a moment, he thought they were NA men, but he knew Harris had said they weren't sending B company down after all. And besides, there were too few of them.

Then he spotted them crawling. Coming up from the ground. The first one, Ward figured, had tripped, fallen over a body, and was getting back up. But he watched in horror as an arm shot out of the ground, reaching up and scrambling for purchase in the damp earth. The man swiftly moved to his feet, joining the others. They moved strangely, hunched over, almost as though they were injured. But at some signal within them, they began to run. They moved as a unit, sprinting towards the bridge. And they were fast. Too fast.

Ward tapped his helmet twice, hitting the officer's comms link. "We've got company at our rear; they are *not* friendlies. I repeat, *not* friendlies. Hostiles coming in hot!"

He was aware of the other officers responding as he switched back to his unit's comm, directing half of them to turn and fire towards the incoming figures running through the field. The rest maintained suppressing fire on the far bank. A band of men in the pinned company below had finally started to make their way under the bridge.

Harris's voice boomed over the comms. "Take those fuckers out!" He shouted. "I need heavy artillery on the bank. Hostiles coming out of the foxholes to our rear. Repeat–"

His voice was cut off with a garbled cry. Ward turned to see a wave of brown coming down the far bank. They were swarming the company below as they began to retreat. The Southern Coalition soldiers on the left flank had already managed to route around the men, attempting to cut them off.

Ward scanned their side of the bank, searching for Captain Harris, hoping he hadn't been hit. But he couldn't see him, and he couldn't hear anything through the chaos of the comms; everyone shouting over each other at once, bullets from the far bank whizzing past, a buzzing whine in his ears.

"Is Harris down?" Ward called out over the comms in frustration, before remembering to switch to the officer's channel. He strained to see down the line to where Harris had stood. "Lieutenant Powers! Can you confirm, is Harris down?" He prayed Powers was still with them and able to respond. Ward's heart thundered now in his chest, in his ears. He turned back to the field to their rear. More of the strange figures were clambering out of the ground. They were going to be trapped. Pinned down on either side.

"Confirmed, Ward," he heard Powers' voice crackle through the comms. "Harris is down." He heard Powers cough, then sputter, "I repeat, Harris is down. The company is yours, Ward."

Ward swallowed thickly, muting his comms for a moment as he scanned the field again, and the wave of NA men coming towards them from behind the bridge.

Ward paused, wracked with indecision. He didn't know what the orders from Command had been. *Fuck.* Were they supposed to stand their ground? Was Harris given the order not to retreat? *Goddamn it.* Why hadn't he told him more?

"Ward?" Powers' voice rang out over the officer's comm.

Ward watched as one of the strange men moved closer. Patches of white, what looked like cobwebs, stretched over the man's face. He was wearing the brown fatigues of the South, but they were frayed and ripped, torn half off his body.

More white patches were visible on the man's exposed ribs. He dropped down on all fours, legs splayed out to the side; his movements animalistic, almost like a– "Ward? Goddamn it, Ward, are you hit?" Powers' voice rang out shrilly in his ear. "Ward, confirm you have the Company. Over."

They had to leave. Now. While they still had the chance. Before the field was flooded with those... things. A group of them had already reached the line, crashing over the men like a wave.

Ward took a breath and tapped his helmet to unmute. "This is First Lieutenant Ward. Confirmed. I have the Company." He heard a muttered chorus of confirmation from his fellow officers. He took a deep breath. *Fuck it.* "Lieutenant Powers, relay orders to *The Beagle*. Repeat, relay orders to *The Beagle*; prepare for incoming pods." Ward paused, surveying the men. "Tell them to put Med Bay on alert."

"Yes, Sir." Powers called back. The relief in his voice was audible. Ward lifted his rifle and aimed. He shot the thing sprinting towards him and his men on all fours. He hit it repeatedly in the head until it went down.

He turned to survey the far bank. The wave of brown uniforms was reaching their rear now on the left flank, mixing with the swath of blue below. "Lieutenant Johnson!" Ward called out over the comms, "contact our friends past the bridge and relay my orders to them. Tell them we're preparing to retreat, and I advise them to do the same. We're about to be pinned down on this side."

Ward spun back to the field. He watched in disbelief, and then horror, as the man he had downed seconds before began to rise from the pile of bodies. He was about ten yards away, and for a moment, Ward wasn't sure. Then the man staggered to his feet, revealing the ripped uniform and the strange white cobwebs over his ribs. *What the fuck?*

The man's face was missing. Half his head blown apart, blood flowing freely down his mangled neck. But he stood there, teetering back and forth for a moment, before continuing forward, advancing directly towards Ward and his men.

Ward tapped his helmet twice, rapidly, switching back to the general comms link. "This is First Lieutenant Ward. Harris is down, I repeat, Harris is down." Ward paused, giving the announcement a moment of silence. "Unfortunately for me, I'm now in command of your sorry asses." Several men sniggered at that.

"I want the right and left units on our flanks to continue to lay down suppressing fire for as long as possible. I'm ordering a full retreat. Keep up the pressure from our flanks. Let's give these men a chance to cross over up the middle."

Chatter ensued over the comms. Ward continued, "Listen up: We've got hostiles to our rear. I want suppressing fire on both fronts—heavy artillery on the opposite bank. Let's get our boys the hell out of here! Move it!" He yelled into the comms, "We take every man still breathing with us. Drag them behind you if you have to. Fall back to the pods! Move out!"

Ward peppered the thing in ripped fatigues, still moving towards him, with another couple of rounds. This time, he aimed for his chest. It went down again, and he swallowed and turned to grip Stowell by the arm. "Let's go, son, move it!"

The men nearby were starting to realize now that something wasn't right with the figures sprinting through the field. Several that had been brought down had gotten back up, and Ward registered for the first time, with a jolt of surprise, that none of them seemed to be carrying weapons. Screams began to drift across the field as the men in the middle of the formation surged forward. More figures were climbing out of the foxholes to meet them. They launched themselves onto the surging crowd. Voices called out over the comms in terror. A rising tide of panic was spreading amongst the ranks.

Ward watched as one of the men in ripped brown fatigues leapt onto an NA soldier, taking him down. The soldier landed on his back. The deformed enemy soldier crouched on his chest, heaving forward, that strange, white substance spewing from his open mouth, as he heaved again and again, splattering the man below him. Ward recoiled, panting, as he paused and surveyed the field. He fought to keep his own panic down.

"D Company!" Ward barked into the company wide comm, "These bastards climbing out of the foxholes are all manner of fucked. And some of them like the taste of our lead so much, they keep coming back for more." Some of the men nearby laughed, scanning the fields ahead. Ward continued, "I don't care how many times those fuckers in the field get back up, you take them down again, and you keep going. Keep moving. Do not stop. I repeat, do not stop. Let's show these Southern fucks what we're made of."

The men surged forward, shouts and cries, bullets flying, the boom of heavy artillery at their backs. A vibration shook the ground beneath their feet whenever the payload hit home. More figures swarmed grotesquely out of the darkness below as they ran.

Ward surveyed the chaos surrounding him as he moved forward, half-dragging Stowell along with him, rifle raised at the deformed figures in brown that rushed towards them at breakneck speed.

Ward's band of men made it across the field, for the most part. Martin was hit in the gut about halfway across. Ward had Molton and Sully drag him the rest of the way, with the others forming up around them to provide cover.

The strange men crawling out of the ground seemed to have no fear. They threw themselves headlong towards the soldiers, straight into oncoming fire. Some of them sported what looked like talons, ripping into his men, clawing at their chests, their faces. Their features were malformed, appearing more alien than human. Their dark, beady eyes were devoid of life, pitch-black and fathomless.

A shot to the chest, in the heart, seemed to take them down permanently, while headshots did little to deter them; merely slowing them down momentarily, until they were able to get back up again.

Ward watched as one of them up ahead dropped to all fours and was shot promptly between the eyes. Its head jerked backwards, and it slumped to the ground.

Ward glanced back as they moved past the prone figure, trying to mark the spot where its body had fallen, waiting to see if it would get back up. But it was nearly impossible in the failing light. He lost sight of it in the chaos of battle; just another body amongst those that already littered the ground.

They made it to the transport pods, and he had the men carry Martin aboard, along with Smith's body, still slumped near the pod.

Ward directed Powers' and Johnson's units to form a skirmish line at the transport pods, shooting strategically to cover the men that still streamed towards them. He joined them with a few volunteers from his own unit.

Ward waited as long as possible before giving the final order to board the pods and prepare for take-off. His pod was one of the last to leave. He fired from the door, aiming at the figures in the field until it slammed shut with a final shudder, the pod rising into position to take off.

MacMillan clapped Ward on the back as he turned, his blue eyes wide, his chest still rising and falling rapidly. "You did everything you could, Ward," he murmured, "you got us out."

Ward scowled at his words. He felt sick. He scoffed, keeping his voice low. "Did you see how many men were still down there? I just... left them behind." Ward's voice came out hoarse.

"They may still make it to their pods," MacMillan said. "Don't beat yourself up; you got us out of there. You got as many out as you could." MacMillan patted him again on the back. "No one could have done anything differently."

Ward hung his head, nodded once. He stood there, staring at the floor of the pod for several seconds.

Then he turned, and his fist shot out, slamming into the door. Once. Twice. His knuckles stung, but he hit the door a third time. MacMillan lunged forward, grabbing his arm, pulling it back. "Goddamn it, Ward. Stop."

Ward stayed silent and still until they were back on *The Beagle*.

The pod doors slid open in the hangar to reveal more chaos; wounded men were being rushed to Med Bay, their screams of pain echoing through the hangar.

Ward walked silently through all of it, MacMillan trailing behind him. He went straight for the Bridge, entered it, and approached the desk. He slammed a hand on the keyboard to bring the screen to life on the right-hand wall.

He took his helmet off, setting it on the desk, and lifted the headset, sliding it over his ears. Then, he selected the comms to Command and hit the transmit button. "This is First Lieutenant Ward, D company, over." he paused for a moment.

"Go ahead, Lieutenant, over," a voice responded.

Ward cleared his throat. "Captain Harris fell at approximately 1800 hours. I was given the Company." He swallowed thickly. "I ordered a full retreat." No response, just the low hum that told him the comms link was still open.

"This is Admiral Martinez." The Admiral's voice rang out over the comm. "Well done, Lieutenant."

Ward shook his head, pinched the bridge of his nose, and took a deep breath. MacMillan stood on the other side of the desk, along with the other men who had trailed behind them. Molton and Johnson, a few of the others. They watched him, their eyes wide, faces streaked with mud and sweat. "Sir, we took heavy casualties…" Ward paused again, unable to find the right words. "And Sir, there was... something, down there, that I think you need to know about. It's urgent, Sir."

A prolonged silence this time. "Son, report back to base. See me in my office. Now." The Admiral cleared his throat. "In the meantime, I want a full containment on Med Bay. Post an armed guard outside the doors." A heavy silence fell in the room as the men stilled.

Ward swallowed, hitting the mute button briefly. He paused, staring down at the floor. Then he flicked the mic back on. "Sir, yes Sir. Over." He barely registered the response back. Ward raised his eyes to find MacMillan and the other men staring at him.

"Sir," one of them started, then paused, "What the fuck were those things?"

1.

It will never get old. Flying. I started out running in the fields at night, on my grandparents' farm. I'd run with the wind, moonlight shining on my upturned face, damp grass between my toes, arms stretched wide, sure that if I ran fast enough, and leapt into the air, I would continue to rise, until I was airborne. I would swoop low over buildings, skimming the tops of trees, until I was part of the sky, part of the night, something dark and mysterious, and free.

There was always that moment, that split second, when my feet left the ground, and I wasn't falling yet. A split second of hope. Of freedom.

I'd flop down eventually, exhausted, landing on my back in the field, nothing but me and the open sky above. I would stare up at the stars, barely visible through the overburdened ozone, and just below, the twinkling lights on the Northern Alliance Base, beckoning me to join them.

I went downtown on my 18th birthday. I enlisted the moment I was old enough. My family was less than thrilled. A song and dance. A story about doing my duty, protecting the North. But it was only partially about all that.

It was true that I believed in the ideals of the Northern Alliance and all it stood for. The mentality of the South terrified me. But more than anything, I wanted to be airborne. I craved the freedom of the sky like it was my own secret holy grail, mysterious and elusive, and forever just out of reach. I pictured myself flying a dog fighter. Fantasized it was me, behind the glass, whenever they swooped low over the fields. I imagined living up on that space station, staring down at the Earth far below. I would do anything to feel that freedom. I told myself I would risk dying for it, for just a taste. Well, I got my chance. And then some.

My aptitude tests, and, let's face it, discrimination, which was still present even in the North, had placed me in Intelligence. I spent a year and a half in training. It wasn't that the work bored me. I actually enjoyed it, for a while. But it wasn't flying. I spent my free time making inroads with the Air Force officers whenever the opportunity arose. I'd gone to my Captain at the time, and I'd practically begged him for a chance at Flight School. He'd been furious. But he must have seen something in my eyes. Or maybe he just felt sorry for me.

Eventually, he managed to put in for a transfer to the Air Force on my behalf. I'd risen quickly through the ranks once

I got my bearings. I got my feet wet in skirmishes over the coast. Babysitting the shipping lanes. The Carolinas. Then dog fights over Florida. And while flying in a fighter wasn't the same as flying on my own, it was close enough. As close as I figured I could get.

But now I'd been given my first ground assignment, and the flight suit to go with it. I bent my knees and leapt into the air, twin blasters whirring away on my back, as I took off into the night sky.

My heart lodged in my throat as I continued to climb higher. The blood in my veins thrummed with joy; that secret magic that I'd longed for as a child was finally mine. I soared higher, skimming over the treetops below. Pine and maple; their branches reaching out to embrace me, waving in the wind as I sped past. I felt like I was finally home.

My lashes were damp with tears. But I kept quiet, trying to keep my breathing under control as I blinked rapidly. This assignment was different than any I'd been given previously. A squadron of fighter pilots had been assembled into a new rapid response force, and my wing had spent the last week or so training with our flight suits. There'd been odd reports on the ground recently. Sightings. We were here to investigate local claims of activity out in the woods.

I banked and turned, twisting and spinning mid-air. I went a little off kilter for a moment but managed to right myself. *God damn.* A rush of exhilaration flooded my body, every nerve

21

on fire. *Fuck.* I would never get over this feeling. But I forced myself to try to focus. I could play later. We were here for a reason.

Dark shapes followed behind me, swooping low, mimicking my flight path. "Nice move, Lieutenant." One of the men chuckled in my ear. "Now you just need a Gatling gun, and The Crimson Reaper can go full stealth mode."

That had been Anderson. "Damn right," I murmured into the comms, grinning at his reaction. But all good things come to an end, and I forced myself to slow and straighten until my feet were aimed at the ground below me once again. "Fan out. Positions."

I watch as the dark shadows around me, black against the dark blue sky, spread out in all directions as one by one, we lower to the ground.

I move into position, hitting the switch on my helmet to cycle through to the map we'd drawn up in advance of the area. I locate the underground chamber and move forward, an outcropping of stone visible up ahead.

I stand on the precipice for a moment, attempting to peer over the edge. I crouch down, lowering my center of gravity, as I start to tilt forward. But it does me no good. I can't see anything except dirt below. And while my scanner indicates there should be a way through, some sort of opening in the rock beneath me, I can't glimpse any signs of it from this angle.

I crouch lower and jump, springing forward and landing solidly on my feet with a thud. It takes time to adapt to the alloy suit, but thankfully, after a week or so of training, I'm finally starting to feel like I've spent enough time in mine to feel comfortable. I can't say my movements are completely natural, but they're close enough, and getting better all the time.

I lift my arm, aiming straight ahead, and spin 180 degrees, turning towards what I expect to be a wall of rock behind me, maybe with a cave opening hidden in its face. But instead, I find two pillars, carved out of the rock face itself, framing a dark tunnel.

I tap my helmet on the left side, switching my viewing mode until it's optimal for dim lighting. I move forward slowly, one foot in front of the other, my right arm still pointing straight ahead, my hand in a fist. I could grab my rifle, but the little blaster in my suit does well enough for situations like this. I can always switch if needed. The weight of my rifle is reassuring on my shoulders.

A squawk of static in my ear, before Binson's voice rings out in my helmet. "Nothing on this side," he's somewhat breathless. "Fuck this shit. This place is giving me the creeps."

I can't help but chuckle back a little. "Just keep your eyes peeled; I'm sure it's just another case of raiders. Probably more scared of us than we are of them."

"This far north?" McCullough's voice chimes in next. "Hardly seems likely."

I sigh, "That's what the locals made it sound like, okay? Let's just be quiet and get this over with."

"I thought Detroit was a massive city," Binson whines. "Looks like we're in the goddamn middle of nowhere."

"It was, you idiot," McCullough huffs a laugh. "Besides, we're miles outside of Detroit. Didn't you look at the map during briefing?"

"Enough chatter," I bark, an edge to my voice this time. The comm falls silent, and I turn my attention back to the pathway in front of me. This space is shrouded in shadows, but the far end of the underground room is open to the sky. I approached from the right and didn't realize it was exposed. That might have been a better place to enter. At least now I have another option for an exit.

I take another few steps into the void, as the beam of light from my suit sweeps over something lying on the ground to my left. I realize with a little jolt of surprise that it's a dead body. A woman. She's wearing a dress and a worn wool coat. She's beautiful, even in death, despite the waxy cast to her skin, her blonde hair falling in waves, spread out over the dirt. An overturned basket lies on the ground next to her. Some sort of pale substance has dribbled out of her mouth to pool on the ground beside her.

I lean forward, squinting. It's definitely not blood. It looks white and thick. Vomit? Had she been out here foraging and eaten something poisonous? Maybe the wrong kind of mushroom.

I catch a flash of movement out of the corner of my eye. I freeze, my breath coming faster now, as I drop instinctively down to a crouch.

A shuffling, sliding, then a low sound, almost a moan. "I've got movement here," I murmur into the comms. "Going in for a closer look."

I move around crumbled rock, piles of dirt, and stone mixed together. I crouch behind what used to be a table, half buried in the rubble. I grip my rifle, pulling it swiftly into position and flicking the safety off.

A scurrying sound, and out of nowhere, large bugs that look like some type of beetle come scrabbling over the mound of dirt ahead. They skitter over my feet in the dark, emitting a low chittering sound. I jump back, a small gasp leaving my throat.

"Kessler?" McCullough's voice, apprehensive in my ear. "You okay?" I don't respond, eyes on the shadows moving up ahead, as I crouch back down, raising my rifle. "Position?" McCullough's voice sounds more urgent now.

"I've just entered the underground building through the front entrance. Roof's caved in in the back," I manage to murmur, "there's something in here, hiding in the dark..."

I realize my flashlight's gone dark. I must have switched it off somehow by accident. I tap my right arm again, angling it forward, squinting at the spot where I'd last seen the shadowed figure moving.

"*Fuck! Fuck, fuck!*" Binson. His voice rings shrilly over the comms, sparking a barrage of commentary. McCullough's deep voice barking out, demanding his location. "What the hell is that? What the *fuck* is that thing?" The clatter of gunfire, Binson panting in my ear. "It's... he's all fucked up. We need to get out of here, Lieutenant –" his voice is cut off in a yelp.

"Binson!" I hiss into the comms unit. "McCullough, get to his location. Now." I take a step back, still in a crouch, eyes wide, scanning the surrounding darkness. But there's nothing there. I can't locate the shadow I thought I saw earlier.

I don't risk turning my back, but I begin to move backward, in controlled, shuffling steps, rifle still raised, at the ready. I hear it then. A low hiss to my left. Then an odd chittering sound. More beetles? I swing to the left, bringing the end of my rifle around.

It's a person. A man, moving towards me through the shadows. My light's somehow gone out again on its own. I mutter a curse under my breath and pause, readying myself, I aim at his chest. He moves closer, passing beneath a hole in the ceiling where the moonlight above streams into the dark, cavernous room. I hear a gasp leave my throat as the light hits his face.

His pale features are disfigured, mouth gaping open in a snarl. He's covered in more of that white substance. It looks wet.

Sticky, like cobwebs or mold. Strands stretch over his lips, into his mouth. An open, dark maw, framed by jagged, elongated slivers. He's bent at an odd angle, his back hunched, arms raised, fingers splayed in a menacing sort of stance. But he's unarmed.

The comm is flooded with chaos now. I can hear my men, some of them crying out, screaming in terror. In pain. More. There must be more of them. Binson is right. We need to get out of here. The man moves closer to me, his body now illuminated by the moonlight, revealing more of the white substance in patches all over him. He turns his head, and his ear is missing; just the stub of a pinna remains. His jaw moves oddly, shuffling back and forth, and it's barely audible, but it almost seems like he's making some sort of sound, with those odd movements. His pitch-black eyes are fixed in my direction. The corners of his mouth rise, stretching, and he releases more of those odd noises, louder now.

I watch as a figure drops from the sky, in the far corner of the room, landing in the shadows. Then another. Two more. At first, I think they're my men, but the dark figures are oddly bent, hunched over. More follow, landing one or two at a time. A low chittering echoes throughout the space, interspersed with squeals, and my blood runs cold. *How many are there?*

I don't wait to find out. A shuffling and scrabbling, a mass moving towards me from the far corner. Some appear to be down on all fours now, moving swiftly across the room. I have enough time to register their speed. They're fast. Much faster than this one that stands before me.

Then I turn, and I run.

2.

He's distracting, this officer. A First Lieutenant, if I had to guess, although his insignia appears to be missing. I chose a seat in the back corner of the room on purpose, against a wall, as far from the raucous as possible. But my eyes keep being drawn back to him.

I adjust my sweater, patting down the scarf around my neck, flinging my hair over my shoulder. It's getting too long again. I rarely wear it down, but I decided to tonight. I'd chosen this dive bar on the far side of the base on purpose, far from where anyone from my unit would be on a night like this.

I fold my arms across my chest for a moment as I stare down at my notes, the worn notebook splayed open on the table. I take a deep breath, scanning over the last page, then I down a large gulp of whiskey.

I look up to find his eyes on me again. And I quickly look away. This is the last thing I need.

But is it? Isn't that why I came here? My eyes stray back to the band, the dark-haired drummer, specifically. Head thrown back and arms splayed, a wicked grin on her face. If I ever forget that I'm not entirely straight, all I need to do is come to this bar and watch her play. She's a welcome distraction. But him... he's something else.

He's boisterous, clearly at least halfway on his way to being solidly drunk. But that's nothing new. Half the men in the bar are the same. There's something dark– something different about him.

The song ends, and he jumps up onto the stage at his men's insistence, as they push him forward. Someone takes the drink out of his hand before it spills. He's laughing, shaking his head at them.

He turns to the band, and after a short exchange, they're playing an old marching tune. One of the bawdy, lewd ones. What a surprise. I roll my eyes and focus back on my scribbled notes, picking up my pen once more.

His voice isn't bad. Not great. But it's not bad. I find myself watching as the men crowd around the small stage, laughing and cheering. He catches me staring at him, a smirk on my face, and I immediately drop my eyes.

They're off duty, but, given the circumstances down below, surely just for the night. And for some of them, I know it will be their last. I sigh deeply, and his eyes meet mine again, sending a jolt of fire through my midsection. *Don't.*

I bend over the tattered notebook, and I start to write. I'm supposed to be going over my notes from our mission outside of Detroit, making sure I have every last detail down. I'm to be brought before Admiral Martinez, but I don't know when exactly, and the wait is killing me.

My pen starts to slide, dancing across the page before I know it. And I'm writing their expressions. Their laughter. The sounds of the bar. The men, all in uniform, enjoying one last night of freedom. Of being alive.

It's frivolous, I know, but I can't help myself. Not tonight. And besides, I know every detail. I could recite the facts I'd gathered so far in my sleep. And I probably do. I'd jolted awake last night once again, covered in a sheen of sweat, a cry on my lips.

The song ends. And I'm only half aware, lost in the words I'm writing so fast that it will be a challenge to read these scribbles on another day. Ink scrawled across the page in an illegible mix of cursive and print.

The Lieutenant is stepping down off the stage now, as his men clap him on the back. Someone puts his drink back in his hand. He holds it aloft as he approaches me, raising the glass towards me in a salute as he catches my eye. *Fuck.*

He sets his glass down on my table with a thud. "What are you writing about?" He asks, his voice pitched low. The men take their cue and drift back over towards the bar.

I shrug, sliding an arm over the opposite page, covering my notes. I tilt my head, indicating the room behind him. "Just what I see."

An eyebrow raised, "Oh?" He studies me more closely, rather than turning around. "And what's that?"

I shrug again, gripping my whiskey glass and taking another sip. "Life." I should leave it there. Make him go away. But my lips keep moving. "Desperation."

"Desperation?" He repeats, his dark eyes intense, locked on mine.

I nod, meeting his gaze, setting my glass down, empty. "The desperation to live."

He stares at me openly, silent for several heartbeats, his own glass forgotten in his hand. Then he swallows, scoffing, looking away. "But you're not a reporter." He murmurs. "You can't be, not in here." His brows furrow for a moment, then he shrugs. "Did you make sure you got down I'm an amazing singer?"

I chuckle slightly, leaning back against the worn seat behind me, careful to keep one arm over the notebook as he glances at it.

"Don't forget to describe how handsome I am." He indicates the notebook with his glass, giving me a wide smile that makes my heart race. He's handsome, all right. And cocky.

I clear my throat, peering down at the cursive scribbles on the right-hand page, "'The tall, dark, and handsome... First

Lieutenant?'" I pause, eyebrows raised, glancing up at him. He grins and laughs again. "Did I get that right?"

"What gave it away?" He asks, leaning over the table now, propped on both hands.

I clear my throat again, "...with a general air of debauchery and a reckless disregard for peril, which only a First Lieutenant in the Northern Alliance can cultivate," he lets out a full-bellied laugh, "took to the stage, at the insistence of his men, half-drunk on whiskey, half-drunk on fear," my eyes flick up to his, gauging his reaction, "...on the eve of battle."

His expression is serious now, and he eyes me with a faint distaste. I can't say I blame him. I lean back again, shrugging. "That's as far as I got," I say coolly.

He nods, taking another sip of his whiskey. "Let me finish it for you." He clears his throat, looking down at the table for a moment, then back up at me. "The handsome First Lieutenant looked up, and saw the most beautiful woman he'd ever seen in his life." I feel my cheeks start to flush before I can control my reaction. He's a smooth talker, I'll give him that.

"He went over and talked to her..." he trails off for a moment, grinning wickedly, "...managed to seduce her. And she took him home."

"And why would she do that?" I hear myself ask.

He smiles, more of a grimace than anything else. "Maybe she took pity on him." His smile disappears, "On the eve of battle." He downs the rest of his drink, his eyes never leaving mine.

I take a deep, even breath, looking away. *Fuck.* I've been propositioned how many times before? From my own goddamn men. And never, not once, have I felt tempted to say yes. I feel slightly sick suddenly. The room is too hot. Stifling, as he waits for me to respond.

I look down at the notebook, picking up my pen again, I write in his words, the best that I can recall them, as he watches me, still grinning. Then I clear my throat and continue, "But the woman didn't think that was a good idea."

He chuckles, "And why's that? I think it's a great idea."

I look up at him briefly, from under lowered lashes, "She didn't think it was a good idea at all. And she told him so." I pause for a moment, licking my lips. I keep my eyes on the page as I write. "Because she liked him. And this was the eve of battle, after all. And she doesn't like saying goodbye." My eyes flicker back to his, from my words on the page. His expression is dark, dangerous, and my pen stills.

"That sounds a lot like cowardice," he murmurs. My cheeks flush deeper as I set my pen down on the notebook.

"This is war," I say simply, "we're all afraid." He shakes his head, eyes narrowing, "Everyone is afraid of dying–" I continue, but he cuts me off.

"Sounds like you need to decide whether it's dying or living, that you're actually afraid of." His voice has dropped an octave, so deep it's almost a growl. A purr. His words, his voice, reverberate through me, and I tense as we stare each other down.

"Just because I choose to turn you down, because I don't want to get to know you, only to have to say goodbye, doesn't mean I'm not living." I retort, through clenched teeth. "It doesn't mean I'm *afraid* of living."

He smirks, shrugging slightly. "Sure sounds like you're afraid. The only question is, of what?"

I duck my head, turning back to my notebook, as though it's some sort of barrier between us, and begin to write again. "The Lieutenant was persuasive, but he was also cocky..." I pause, tapping the end of the pen against my lips for a moment as I think, his eyes following it, "no... that's not the right word... arrogant!" I say, holding up the pen. "The Lieutenant was persuasive, but arrogant."

"And the..." he pauses, waiting for me to insert my title, but I don't. I just wait for him to continue. "Woman," he continues, "was too afraid. Too fragile," my eyebrows lift, and I shoot him an icy stare, as my pen pauses its scratching against the page, "to take a risk. Too afraid that she might end up caring about the Lieutenant. So, she rejected him."

"That's not why," I begin, "it's because he was an abrasive, self-centered—"

"That's not what you said," he holds up a finger, "your first answer was the true one; you're afraid," he quips. Then he shrugs, "Either that, or you're a liar."

35

I arch an eyebrow at him, in a warning glare. "You were either lying then, or you're lying now..." a slow, wicked sort of grin spreads over his features, a bloom of warmth flooding my core, "... so which is it?"

I sigh and pick up the pen again, poised over the paper. I open my mouth to speak, to give some sort of retort, but nothing but silence falls from my lips, and my pen remains still against the page. I can't remember the last time I was at a loss for words. I feel my cheeks flush hot again as he slides into the seat next to me. He stays a comfortable distance away, doesn't get too close, but my gut twists, just the same. I look up to find him watching me intently.

"And the woman had no answer. No response..." he leans forward, "so he asked her, what's the point, then?" He murmurs, leaning closer to me, his voice dropping low. "What's the fucking point? Of this?" He sweeps an arm, indicating the bar. "Of fighting. Of dying. What's the fucking point? If you aren't going to live?"

My breath catches in my throat as our eyes meet again. My heart is pounding in my chest. "If you aren't going to really live, while you can, then what's the goddamn point of anything?" He swallows, a muscle ticking in his jaw, as he watches me. Waiting for an answer. But I don't have one.

My heart thunders in my chest, almost painfully now, and I still haven't taken a breath. It's the oddest thing, but I feel an overwhelming wave of emotion flooding through me at his words. It's as though he's reached into my mind and pulled out my secret fears. Gave them a voice. A name.

What was the point? The point of all of this? The suffering. The dying. The struggle to live. To stay alive. Just one more day. One more flight. One more fight. I look into his eyes and know that I feel the same desperation. That desperation to live. And not just to live, but to live fully. I want to experience everything. All of it, all at once. I crave life like only the dying can. And I can feel it; I'm actually going to say yes. I'm going to break my only rule.

I stare up at him, eyes wide, lips parted. I shake my head, blinking, and attempt to recover my composure. "I..." I start, then trail off.

One of his men runs over, a mop of curly blonde hair, and striking blue eyes. He's followed by two others. The man claps a hand on his back and leans in to whisper something in the Lieutenant's ear.

"Captain..." his lips continue moving, but the words are lost to my ears, as he eyes me and my notebook suspiciously. *Captain?*

The captain slides out of the seat with an air of reluctance and stands, straightening his jacket. He nods to me, jaw tight. "We have to go," he says, his voice clipped. "Maybe I'll see you around–"

He waits for a name. But I don't have one to give him.

I nod back to him. "Maybe you will." I give him the ghost of a smile. A suggestive one, my eyes locked on his. I can't help it.

The corner of his mouth twitches, and he nods again. Then he leaves with them, rounding up the others as they go. He looks back once, to find me still watching him, drinking in every second, before he disappears through the door.

3.

My comms unit squawked loudly, startling me from sleep. It felt as though it had only been an hour, maybe two, since I'd finally drifted off, but somehow it was already morning; the reminder I'd set the night before clanging loudly beside my head.

I groaned and forced myself to get up. I got the message late last night. I was to report to the Admiral at 0800 this morning. I'd expected to feel wracked with nerves upon waking, but I felt only drained. Oddly numb.

I showered clumsily. Twisted my long black hair into one thick braid down my back, and donned my dress uniform, fingers fumbling over the buttons.

I grabbed my worn notebook, clutching it in one hand against my thigh as I walked out of my quarters, and made my way down the corridor in the direction of the Admiral's office.

I don't know what I expected, exactly. Perhaps, an audience one-on-one, behind closed doors. But I was admitted after a brief wait to find the Admiral at the head of a long conference table, with five or six high-ranking officers in attendance. They stood as I entered, and I saluted smartly. They saluted back in response.

"At ease. Have a seat, Lieutenant." The Admiral nodded to me. His salt and pepper hair was buzzed short, just like always. His warm, dark brown eyes twinkled slightly. He chuckled. "Make that Captain."

I glanced up at him as I sat, eyebrows raised. "Sir?"

He grinned slightly at my expression. "You're being promoted, as part of this assignment. You won't have a full company beneath you for this mission; you'll select two of your best men to join you, but you'll be afforded the rank. And we trust you'll earn it." My gut twisted a little at the thought of leaving my men behind. But I knew it would only be temporary.

He nodded at the notebook, still gripped in my hand. "I've already received the preliminary report from your superiors. And we've been briefed on your accomplishments thus far." He chuckled again, waving a hand. "Not that it was necessary. Everyone in the fleet has heard *of* The Crimson Reaper."

I nodded briskly, keeping my expression flat. I'd never feel comfortable with the accolades, and I hadn't had any say in my call sign. But I wouldn't deny it gave me a sick little twist of pleasure to hear it on the Admiral's lips. "It's an honor, Sir. I won't let you down."

He nodded grimly at me and gestured with both palms open. "Let's hear it, Captain. Like I said, we've all been briefed, and nothing said here leaves this room." He pointed at the table, tapping the surface for emphasis. "Any details you'd like to go over with us?"

I cleared my throat. I had briefed my superior officers, half to death, on what I had found so far. But I couldn't be sure how much detail they had already gone over with the Admiral. Clearly, it had been enough. Enough that they were taking this seriously.

"Sir, I have my notes here; I can certainly expand on any area that might be of interest. Or if there are any questions as far as what's already been discussed." I paused briefly, but no one spoke up. "But the main synopsis is pretty straightforward," I cleared my throat, "my crew set down in the Northern Provinces, just outside the city of Detroit, to be exact. There had been reports of unusual activity in the area, mainly taking place at night. We figured it was likely just rumors... raiding parties drifting farther North than they might typically." I shrugged. "Maybe dressed in some sort of... crude... costumes," I added, for lack of a better term. "Trying to scare the locals."

"But that wasn't the case, Sir." I paused and surveyed the men around the table, their eyes locked on me. "This was something else. Something I've never seen before." I took a deep breath. "I think they were raiders, at one point. But what they are now... I don't have a clear explanation. They were... deformed. Grotesque. Based on their... abnormalities, I understand the theory is that this is some sort of disease."

The Admiral nodded, his expression grim. "We need to know what type of disease we're dealing with, exactly. And how contagious it is. From the reports we've been receiving, the fear is that this thing, whatever it is, is spreading."

I nodded, taking another breath. "Yes, Sir."

"We need samples, so we can run tests, to know for sure what it is we're dealing with." The Admiral said grimly.

I shook my head slightly, sighing. I was still kicking myself for not having the foresight to try to gather samples that night. The Intelligence training I'd received meant I should have known better. And, knowing what I knew now, I couldn't forgive myself for it. But we had been close to a bloodbath. My men and I had been lucky to get out of there alive, much less with samples. "I regret, Sir," I said evenly, "that I wasn't able to retrieve any samples that night."

The Admiral nodded grimly. "Well, that's why we're here." He nodded to the man next to him, who stood and moved over to the projector, and hit the lights. The room dimmed, and the projector came on, displaying an image on the large screen across the room—a map of North America.

Dotted grey lines indicated the old State lines. The continent was split in half, overlaid by two outlines, in blue and red: the Northern Alliance and Southern Coalition.

To the North, Canada appeared outlined in a paler shade of blue, identifying them as our ally. I realized, with a twist of dread in my gut, that the South was littered with black circles, some larger than others. Only one black dot appeared in the North, just outside of Detroit.

"I can only say that this has gotten away from us for so long, because of the location. Whatever this is, it seems to have spared us, thank God, and has been primarily wreaking havoc in the South." He turned back to me, voice rough, "I won't deny, Captain, that this thing has been working to our advantage. Or at least it was, at first." He shook his head. "The enemy was being affected by... something. We didn't know what, but it was distracting them, slowing them down, allowing us to swoop in and take out strategic sites. It hadn't affected us much, otherwise." He nodded at the map. "Until Texas. Houston."

I stared at the black circle over Houston, the largest one on the map. "It was a fucking bloodbath. Excuse my French." He sighed, rubbing his right temple. "Our boys were slaughtered. Not just by the enemy, that was bad enough. But by whatever those... things, are." He sighed, then nodded to the man at the projector. The image disappeared with a click, and the room flooded with light. I closed my eyes momentarily, opening them again, and squinting over at the admiral.

I'd heard. We all had. The battle of Houston was immediately infamous among the ranks. The rumors had run rampant in the days that followed. That had been nearly a week and a half ago now. The atmosphere on base had escalated since then. The men were desperate. Afraid. Waiting anxiously for orders to put boots on the ground. Even the fighter pilots were terrified. Sure, there was always that underlying level of fear that never left you. But this was different. This was something no one understood. This was terrifying on a whole new level.

I'd been forced to write up two of my best men for disorderly conduct, that next evening, after news about the battle of Houston spread. They'd beaten the shit out of each other. Things were starting to get out of hand.

I nodded grimly at the Admiral as he continued. "Congress has ordered an investigation. They want to know how this thing spreads, and whether we can prevent it. Treat it." He cleared his throat. "Intelligence is obviously already working hard on this. Hacking into their communications and gathering whatever data they can. But we need someone on the ground. We need samples."

The Admiral sighed. "Boots on the ground. Tonight. As I'm sure you're already aware. We're heading to Florida. We've intercepted intelligence. We'll stage two separate coordinated attacks tonight. We need to take out a local weapons factory; it's out in the boondocks. And we're also sending troops into Gainesville, a city nearby."

The Admiral paused, quieted for a moment as though he were considering his next words carefully. "We are close, Captain. So close. Closer to holding the advantage in this war than we have ever been before, at least in my career. I believe we are at a tipping point." He waved his hand, "In the meantime, we can't afford to have this thing spreading out of control. We can't risk it crossing over the border." I nodded again. "We have no idea how it got to Detroit. How it got so far north…" his voice trailed off. "They must have traveled by air… on some raider transport. Either way," he pointed at me, "this has to end. Sooner, rather than later. We need to know exactly what it is we're dealing with, and how to stop it."

"Sir." I nodded. I understood. I understood it better than anyone. Other than those who had been in Houston. The ones who had made it out alive.

"You'll have a lab crew, a team to help you, to run tests on the samples and analyze the results." I sat up straighter, nodding my understanding. "You take the time that you need to get this done right. But Captain, we need answers, fast."

I nodded my understanding again. "Yes, Sir."

A rap at the door interrupted us, and the door swung inwards. A soldier held the door open as a man in dress uniform entered the room. The men around the table stood, and I joined them a fraction of a second later, my stomach lurching.

It was the captain from the bar. He stood at attention, saluted the Admiral. "At ease." Arms falling to his sides, then tucked behind his back, legs spread a foot apart as he waited.

The Admiral, who had remained seated, waved his hand and gestured at the chair in front of the captain. "Have a seat," he murmured, "This is Captain Ward. Of *The Beagle*. He'll be your transport for the mission." My brows furrowed. Grant Ward. I'd heard of him. *Jesus Christ.* He scanned the room, his gaze falling on me, and I saw his eyebrows raise imperceptibly. My heart pounded in my throat.

He recovered quickly, moving over to the chair at the end of the table, he pulled it out and took a seat as the Admiral continued. "Captain Ward, you were already briefed on your orders yesterday; D Company will be part of the coordinated attack in Florida. In addition, you'll be transporting The Crimson Reaper. This will be a reconnaissance mission for research purposes. Highly Classified, on a need-to-know basis." He let silence fall in the room for a moment. "There will be several fighters brought aboard to allow the Reaper's team to travel down to the surface as needed. I expect you to do everything you can to assist them; provide an armed escort when needed and accommodate the need to gather intelligence and samples."

Captain Ward nodded briskly, "Yes, Sir." He scanned the men around the table with a raised brow, a slow smile on his face. "The Crimson Reaper, Sir? Where is he?"

I felt a jolt of satisfaction seeing the corners of the Admiral's mouth twitch. He raised a hand and gestured towards me. "*She's* right there, Captain."

Ward turned to me, one eyebrow raised. The muscle in his jaw ticked as he nodded to me. His voice came out clipped. "It's an honor, Lieutenant." I nodded stiffly back to him.

"It's captain, now," the Admiral corrected. "Captain Kessler. You, Ward," he clarified, "will remain the commanding officer on board *The Beagle*. But Kessler has just been promoted." The Admiral turned to me. "Captain Ward was recently promoted as well. He was on the ground in Houston. In the last wave. His commanding officer, Captain Harris, was killed in action. The company was pinned down, cornered on all sides by the SC, and those... things." He glanced at Ward briefly before his gaze shifted back to me. "Ward took over command, managed to save most of his men."

I'd heard of Ward all right, even before Houston, and the rumors had been circulating since. I nodded, swallowed, and risked a glance over at Ward. His eyes were down on the table, glazed and staring, seeing something that wasn't there. I could guess what it was.

I turned my attention back to the Admiral as a grim silence fell. He stared at Ward for several seconds, something in his expression that I couldn't put a finger on. "I can't overstate the importance of this mission, Ward."

Ward's jaw clenched, that muscle ticking again. "Sir." His eyes lifted to the admiral as he pulled his gaze away from the table, back to the present. "Sir, I would like to request that Captain Kessler... be placed on another ship." His words echoed dully through the room. My eyes widened as they sunk in. *What the hell?*

The Admiral froze, frowning at Ward. "Ward... I just said this mission is crucial to–"

"I understand the importance of the mission, Sir." Ward interrupted the Admiral mid-sentence, and I felt the room freeze. Ward swallowed, taking a breath. "And with all due respect, Sir. I'd like to request that the captain be transferred to another Carrier."

The Admiral's brows were drawn down over his dark eyes, his voice dangerously quiet. "*The Beagle* is the fleet's premier research vessel. It's the only Carrier already equipped with the proper Biohazard facilities to handle this mission."

Ward seemed to consider this for a moment, then nodded. "If it has to be *The Beagle*, then I'd like to request a different officer be assigned to the mission."

The Admiral's eyebrows went up, and he folded his hands in his lap, one over the other, leaning back in his chair, studying Ward. I refused to look in his direction. My heart was pounding in my chest, and I could feel the flush creeping over my cheeks. What was Ward's problem? This was the biggest moment of my career. And he was going to request that I be reassigned? Taken off the mission? For what possible reason? He knew nothing about me. So, we'd met briefly. We'd spoken for what, ten minutes? Probably less.

"I don't have time for this, Ward." Admiral Martinez said softly, his voice pitched dangerously low. "Your request is denied."

I still refused to look at Ward, eyes straight ahead, on the blank wall across from me.

"Sir," Ward said, "permission to speak with you in private, Sir." I felt a stab of apprehension in my gut. What could he possibly have to say to the Admiral about me that needed to be said in private? I waited, body rigid, hardly daring to breathe.

"Denied, Captain." The Admiral snapped after a moment. He got to his feet, and we all rose as well. My cheeks were on fire now. I didn't need to look in a mirror to know they were probably bright red. I held myself stiffly, muscles taut, practically trembling with rage. He had no idea. No idea what I'd gone through. What I'd endured to be here. To be sitting in this chair. I had earned this, and he was trying to take it away from me. Over what?

"You're to report to *The Beagle* by 1400 hours, Captain Kessler." The Admiral snapped.

I nodded. Still standing at attention, I brought my hand up in a swift salute, eyes forward. "Sir, yes sir!" I managed to respond.

"Dismissed," the Admiral barked back. I moved instinctively, falling at ease, remembering to grab my notebook at the last second.

I eyed Captain Ward darkly as I turned and fled the room. He stood at attention, but his eyes flickered over me, dark and cold, no doubt taking in my inflamed cheeks.

I blinked rapidly, out in the corridor, as I rushed back to my quarters. Tears of rage fighting to be released. That bastard. He'd seemed thrilled at first, when he heard The Crimson Reaper was going to be on board. When he was expecting a man. He'd quickly changed his tune. Well fuck him. If that was the case, he didn't deserve to be a captain in the Northern Alliance; he belonged down there, fighting for the South. And I wouldn't give him the time of day. Or the satisfaction of seeing he'd affected me. Not again. Never again.

4.

I reported to *The Beagle* promptly at 1400 hours, just as I'd been ordered. I would be on my game. I wouldn't give him any quarter. He would have nothing on me. Nothing he could report to the Admiral. He'd have to lie, make something up, if he wanted ammo to kick me off his rig.

I'd chosen McCullough and Binson to join me. We managed to merge with the ranks as they boarded the vessel, falling in line inconspicuously. It appeared that the crew was gathering down in the hangar of the massive Carrier.

We followed the crowd and found a spot off to the side, near the far wall of the hangar, surveying the company. I spotted two or three female soldiers amongst the men. That was pretty typical, numbers-wise, I admitted begrudgingly to myself. I'd been curious to see if there were any women on board. Most Captains didn't have full control over who got assigned to their crew, but they had some sway at least. Although Ward was new, he'd only taken over about a week ago. Given time, maybe these women would be quietly transferred to another company.

It wasn't common, at least not out in the open, but I'd heard of such things happening before, even in the North. It was far worse in the South. Multiple Southern territories didn't allow women to enlist at all. It was illegal, in certain parts. I'd heard rumors that a few managed to sneak through, but I figured they were mostly just that: rumors.

Ward appeared eventually, climbing onto the wing of my fighter. *My* fighter. I felt my hands clenching into fists as I watched him, standing there on the wing, like he owned it. *Bastard.*

What I'd taken as mild cockiness the other night, or confidence, was clearly arrogance. He was just another blowhard asshole who thought he could do whatever he wanted. Have, anyone he wanted. Well, he'd lost his chance with me, that was for sure. I thanked my lucky stars we'd been interrupted before I had a chance to make a fool of myself and take him back to my quarters. My cheeks blazed at the memory.

But I remembered his expression, his eyes, burning into mine, and his voice, heavy with emotion, when he asked me what the point was. What was the point of fighting, of dying, if we weren't really living?

There was a darkness to him, and a depth that I felt I'd only seen the edge of. Wasn't that what had drawn my eyes back to him, over and over? Sure, he was handsome enough; thick brown hair falling in casual waves over his brow, piercing dark eyes. He was tall. And built. He carried himself with an air of authority, an easy confidence. But there was something about him. Something that made my gut twist. He had a look of cunning to him. An almost cruel, suggestive curve to his smile, that made me squirm. I narrowed my eyes, staring him down, as he stood there on my fighter, and addressed his men.

He was going with the standard inspirational speech. I'd heard them how many times, over the years. For our homes. For liberty. Freedom. Freedom from tyranny. From subjugation. From racism. From misogyny. I had to snort at that one, drawing a few sideways glances from the men nearby. We would fight for the truth. For hope. For love. For everyone to have the freedom to love who they love, without fear. I felt my gaze soften at that last part, my fists loosen at my sides. I watched him suspiciously as he went on. But most of all, we would fight for the man beside us. For our brothers. We would leave no one behind.

It was working; whatever depth of feeling, of meaning, lay behind his words, they were working. I could hear the men calling out. Cheering. Feel the nervous buzz of energy in the air shifting towards that fever pitch of battle.

The speech ended abruptly, and someone reached out to help him down. But he jumped, landing easily, and was lost in the crowd as men began to move, readying for take-off.

I sighed deeply to myself. Right. I had no clue what to do next. I'd been told to report to the ship. That was it. I felt my jaw clench. I guess that meant I should report to the commanding officer. *My* commanding officer, I reminded myself.

While I'd been promoted to the rank of Captain, it would likely be several days before my papers came through. And besides, the Admiral had made it clear who was in charge on this ship. I took a deep breath, steeling myself, and turned to my men, nodding at them, and we moved towards the fighter.

Ward hadn't made it very far, stuck in a clump of officers, they muttered amongst themselves, occasionally interrupted by a private asking for orders, or clarification. I watched them for a moment, recognizing one of the men beside Ward as the blue-eyed man who had pulled him away at the bar.

Ward's eyes found me in the crowd eventually. My men and I were the only ones standing still, after all. The only ones without orders. Without a place.

He nodded to me, and I made my way over to him. He turned to the blonde man beside him, tapping him on the arm as I approached. "First Lieutenant MacMillan, this is Captain Kessler; you know her as The Crimson Reaper." He paused for dramatic effect, as every head in the general vicinity swiveled towards me. I didn't like to advertise my identity. I preferred to keep it a secret, especially amongst other companies. The dog fighters knew exactly who I was, but that couldn't be helped. I sighed. So much for anonymity. I forced myself to stay still. Not to roll my eyes. "She'll be joining us for the time being."

Lieutenant MacMillan's eyes flickered from my men back to me, then travelled up and down my body. Nothing I wasn't used to. But his gaze didn't come off as lewd or disrespectful, at least. He just looked surprised. He stood at attention, saluting me sharply. "Captain Kessler. It's an honor."

"Holy crap." Another man beside him murmured. He had short brown hair, brown eyes, currently wide, as he stared at me. He seemed to realize I was staring back at him, and he snapped me a salute as well. "Excuse me. First Lieutenant Powers, Sir." A few of the men sniggered while I returned the salute. But Lieutenant Powers seemed unfazed. He grinned openly at me, his smile somewhat lopsided. "*The Crimson Reaper*. No freaking way. I heard you shot down 40 enemy fighters in one afternoon."

A few of the men gathered around moved forward, all starting to talk at once. "I heard–" someone else started. But Ward cut them off.

"Yeah, yeah, you'll all get your chance to fanboy later. Let's get going. We don't have time to waste." Ward grinned slightly as the men dispersed, grumbling and looking back in my direction.

Lieutenant MacMillan moved forward, reaching out a hand to me, his blonde curls falling over one eye. I took it, shaking it firmly. "Call me Wren, Captain." He grinned at me, white teeth framed by twin dimples, blue eyes sparkling. "I mean, if you want to. Everybody else does."

I nodded, smiling back. "It's nice to meet you, Wren." His grin widened, but his eyes flickered back to Ward, who stood there with his arms crossed over his chest, staring him down. "I'll see ya around," Wren muttered hastily, and he took off, disappearing through the hangar door.

"You're going to be quite the celebrity on board," Ward said dryly, moving closer to me. "I hope you're ready for it."

"Yeah, thanks to you." I quipped back, unable to keep the edge from my voice. His eyebrows went up. "There was no need to tell them, you know. You could have kept that part to yourself."

He thought for a moment, and looked away, sighing, slipping his hands into his pockets. "Right." He shrugged, looking back at me with an eyebrow raised, "Well, it's too late for that now, isn't it?"

"I'd say so." I glared at him until the grin was wiped off his face. I didn't think he was funny. Or charming. Not anymore. "Look, Captain," I moved closer to him, until I was only several inches away. I could sense McCullough and Binson, standing a few feet behind me, edging closer as well, and I dropped my voice lower. "You've made it abundantly clear that I'm not wanted on this ship, but allow me to make something else clear: I won't let you, or anyone, or anything, get in my way of completing this mission." I paused, eyes flickering back and forth over his, all hints of humor now gone from his expression. "So how about this: I stay out of your way, and you stay out of mine." I waited for a response, but he didn't move a muscle. "Fair enough?"

He refused to break eye contact, and we stared each other down for several excruciating seconds. I could feel the men moving around us slowing as they passed, watching us. Ward licked his lips, eyes never leaving mine. "How about this: as the commanding officer aboard this vessel, *I* tell *you* how it's going to be. Otherwise, we're going to have a problem." His eyes narrowed. "Do I make myself clear, *Captain*?" He practically spat my title at me, his voice dripping with derision.

I wanted to tell him to fuck off. I could feel my fists clenching again. I took a deep breath, but he continued, "I want you in your private quarters until 1700 hours, at which point, you will report to me directly. On the bridge." I didn't move a muscle, frozen, as his mouth twitched in the slightest of smiles. He could tell he'd gotten to me. And he was enjoying it. "That's an order, Captain. Got it?"

I forced myself to answer through clenched teeth. "Yes."

"Yes, what?" He murmured, one eyebrow raised, and he leaned in even closer.

"Yes, Sir," I murmured back, my voice barely a whisper, my cheeks beginning to flush.

Ward nodded, "That's right. Yes, *Sir*." He gave me his charming, slightly wicked grin, making my stomach flip. "You and I are going to get along just fine, *Kessler*, as long as you remember who's in charge here." He winked at me as he backed away, his gaze shifting over to my men, still standing behind me. My gut clenched, churning with rage.

"Private Wilkins," Ward called out, "come show Captain Kessler to her quarters." I forced myself to stay calm and take a step back, tearing my gaze away from him. "Your men will bunk with the Lieutenants." He called out to me, smiling at them, as they shot daggers back at him. "If there's room," he shrugged, "if not, they'll bunk down with the Privates." He shot us one last smug grin and turned and walked away.

I swiveled stiffly, nodding to McCullough and Binson. They nodded back, Binson's hands clenched in fists.

"We'll catch you later, Captain," McCullough murmured.

I nodded again and turned to follow a nervous-looking Private Wilkins out of the hangar.

I'm sure my obviously foul mood did nothing to help Private Wilkin's nerves, as I practically stalked down the corridor beside him. Men moved out of our way naturally, clearing a pathway through the crowded, busy corridors, probably partially due to the expression on my face, and partially due to the sight of a woman in an officer's dress uniform. I noticed several men eyeing me up and down. Several lewd gazes and the occasional muted catcall trailed in our wake.

At least they waited until well after I'd gone past. This was going to be fun.

It was like starting all over again, in a way. I'd earned respect, earned my spot, the hard way, amongst the fighter pilots. But here, I was an unknown. An oddity at best, and a target at worst. That thought gave me pause. I didn't know now if it had been for the best that Ward had outed me. Maybe the men would think twice about messing with The Crimson Reaper, once word got around.

Of course, my prowess as a fighter pilot did me little good inside locker rooms and dark corridors. But I was in the habit of carrying my sidearm with me, minimally, at all times, along with a knife that I kept sharpened, strapped to my thigh. And I would certainly continue to do so here.

Private Wilkins brought me eventually to a doorway down a narrow corridor and came to a halt. "This is the officer's wing," he announced to me, stiff-backed. "These are your private quarters here; the scanner's already been programmed to only open for you." He indicated the large scanner set into the wall beside the door. "And your Flight Suit's been brought aboard as ordered." I lifted my right palm and placed it over the scanner. A green line swept down the screen, and a beep sounded as the door slid open. "Do you–" he stopped abruptly, "will you," he corrected, "need help, finding the bridge?" His eyes flickered nervously over mine.

I gave him a tight-lipped smile. "Thank you, Private. I think I can manage. I've been on a Carrier before. The layout is pretty much always the same." He nodded, standing even straighter than before. "But I appreciate it." He snapped to attention, and I saluted him back. "At ease, Private." He relaxed slightly, nodding gratefully, and he turned and fled back down the hallway, turning back with a nervous expression, to see me still watching him as he turned the corner. I grinned to myself as I stepped into my private quarters. This was all going to take some getting used to.

While I was used to the layout of our Carriers, this was a much nicer space than I'd ever stayed in before. I had been just a private myself back when I had last been transported on one; I slept in the rows of narrow cots set into the wall down in the lower level back then, where conversations were practically drowned out by the constant hum emanating from the engine room.

Now it seemed I would have a large living space all to myself. A massive window set in the far wall overlooked the vastness of space, and the Earth below, with what looked like at least a queen-sized bed nestled directly beneath the window. I was sure the window must have a screen that shuttered over it; otherwise, you'd feel like you were falling out into space, lying in that bed.

There was a circular seating area, set low into the floor to the right, facing a large screen on the wall. To my left, a mini kitchen area, with a small table and two chairs. The coffee dispenser actually looked like it was functional. My eyebrows went up in surprise. Apparently, there were some perks to being a Captain, after all.

I sighed, shrugging my bag off my shoulders and setting it on the floor next to the bed. I'd unpack later. I had no clue how long I would be aboard *The Beagle*, and I had shoved as many clothes as I could in my kit. My notebook, of course, and a personal book I'd brought along as well, my tattered old copy of *1984*. It was falling apart, but it was invaluable. Most copies had been burned in the mass book burnings, shortly before the Northern states began declaring independence.

I slumped down onto the couch, facing the screen on the wall. As though it sensed my eyes on it, the screen woke up, the symbol for the NA rotating in the middle. "Greetings, Captain Kessler! Welcome aboard!" A man's voice exploded into the room. "I am TODD; I'll be your personal assistant aboard *The Beagle*. When you want to speak to me, you can say 'Hello, TODD' or you may program your own unique voice command. Would you like to do this now?"

The AI voice paused, waiting for an answer. I sighed deeply. "No, TODD, thank you, though."

"You are very welcome, Captain Kessler."

"Just Kessler is fine, TODD."

A long pause. "I'm sorry, did you want to tell me you are fine, or that I should refer to you as *'Kessler'* from now on, rather than *'Captain Kessler'*?"

I sighed deeply, leaning forward and massaging my temples. "Yes, TODD, you may refer to me as *'Kessler'* from now on. Thank you, but I won't be needing any further assistance at the moment."

"Yes, Sir. *Kessler.*" I scoffed slightly and stood to check out the rest of the space. There was a small private bathroom as well, a true luxury. I breathed deeply and stood there in the middle of the room, staring through the window out into the vast void of space.

Things would be different back on base, too. I would move to the captain's quarters, located in a different rung of the endlessly rotating space station. But I needed to get through this mission first.

I paced idly for a while and ended up splayed out on the couch, asking TODD to pull up recent reports from the last few skirmishes, just prior to the battle of Houston. There wasn't much there that I didn't already know. A few references to odd activity. Strange encounters with deranged soldiers were mentioned in several reports. I wasn't able to find any new information that might be relevant.

I had too much time, with nothing to do, until I was due to report at the bridge. I was tempted to go walk the corridors of the rig and get my bearings. But Ward had specifically ordered me to my private quarters. I frowned, biting my lip as I stood again and began to pace back and forth. Was there a reason for that beyond the obvious? Other than acting like a jerk, and trying to establish who was in control?

I decided to make a coffee. I didn't know what lay in store for us tonight, but it was probably a safe bet that it would involve a late night and lack of sleep.

I stood there for a moment, coffee in hand, considering. With a small smirk to myself, I turned and strode out of my quarters and headed down to the bowels of the ship.

I knew, from my limited experience onboard a Carrier, that the lower level would likely be practically empty. Typically, soldiers had little reason to travel below the level of the ship that held the hangar and Med Bay.

My luck held out, as I found a stairwell at the end of a nearby corridor. It appeared to be empty, as I swiftly made my way to the bottom, managing not to spill my full mug of coffee.

When I exited at the bottom of the stairwell, I found myself on the Engineering floor, just as I'd anticipated. There was something about the constant background hum of the engines that I found soothing.

I wandered idly as I sipped my coffee, feeling some of the restless, nervous, pent-up energy I couldn't seem to contain begin to dissipate as I walked.

I practically jumped when a loud voice called out behind me, "Hey! What are you doing down here?"

I turned to see an older man glaring at me from beneath bushy eyebrows. I moved over closer to him, with what I hoped was a winning smile.

"Hi! I'm sorry if I disturbed you." I held out my hand to him. "Captain Kessler. I've been assigned to *The Beagle* for a reconnaissance mission." I shrugged when he didn't take my hand immediately and kept talking. "I just wanted to walk about a bit, get to know the ship." I glanced around at the massive machinery. "I've always loved it down in the engine room; there's something about hearing all that machinery running, keeping the ship going."

I couldn't tell if he was smiling now or grimacing, but he finally lifted his hand to mine and shook it briefly. "Curtis," he said gruffly, his gaze dropping to my coffee. "Next time you come down here, make sure you bring me a cup of coffee." He raised an eyebrow at me, as though he was skeptical I was listening. "From the Mess Hall– you understand? It's better. The coffee down here," he waved his hand dismissively, "it isn't the same." He grimaced in earnest this time, and I grinned back.

"I can do that," I said, still smiling. "How do you take it?"

Curtis huffed, a sort of laugh, maybe? "Strongest coffee they have, one cream. No sugar."

I nodded, filing the info away for later. "Well then, I'll see you again, soon," I smiled, starting to drift away, assuming I now had his blessing. "And next time, I'll have two cups with me."

Curtis only grunted, eyeing me slightly less suspiciously than before, as he continued on his way.

I spent another twenty minutes or so walking around in Engineering before deciding not to overstay my welcome. I returned to my room and made a second cup of coffee, for good measure. I brought it over to the couch and ended up grabbing my tattered copy of *1984*. The corner of the cover was ripped off, so it looked like the title was only *'198'*. I ran a thumb over the familiar, cracked cover, and I settled in to read, to pass the remainder of the time.

5.

I reported to the bridge promptly at 1700 hours to find Captain Ward already assembled with a small contingent of his men. I assumed the men gathered were all First Lieutenants, each in charge of their own unit, which made up D Company.

MacMillan, *Wren*, I reminded myself, was seated to Ward's right at the large table on the left side of the bridge. He gave me a wry smile as I strode through the doors. I recognized Powers as well, seated on the far side of the table. He grinned widely at me as I entered the room.

I'd stopped down in the hangar on my way and put on my flight suit. It was lightweight enough that I didn't mind changing early. I had no clue what time we would be leaving, and I'd rather be overprepared than risk Ward claiming I somehow held them up.

"Kessler!" Ward called out as he stood. "You're almost late." He eyed my suit with a raised brow, a slight smirk on his lips. The room quieted as the men watched me approach.

"Almost, doesn't count, Sir," I replied in a clipped tone.

Ward's eyes narrowed. "It does in battle."

I raised an eyebrow at him. "Is that what this is?" I added, "Sir?" After a slight pause, allowing my voice to hold the barest undertone of sarcasm.

Several of the men stifled their laughter. I kept my eyes on Ward. He stared at me for several seconds, then he stood, clearing his throat, and pointed to an empty seat at the table. "Have a seat, Captain. We were just going over our battle plans. Boots on the ground at 1900."

I sighed internally. "I'd prefer to stand, thanks." I crossed my arms over my chest. He may be the commanding officer aboard, but I wasn't going to let him dictate my movements. Best to establish from the beginning that I didn't take to that level of micromanagement.

Ward stared at me. I waited to see if he would back down. "Fine." He shook his head briefly and turned back to the table. "TODD, bring up the terrain map."

The top of the table was an encased screen; it lit up from within with a green glow, and a projection appeared, floating above the table, displaying a detailed map of the terrain somewhere far below us.

"The munitions factory is out in the middle of nowhere, thankfully. We won't be coming close to any major cities." Ward said, the glow of the map below throwing his features into strange shadows.

"Why aren't we just bombing it then?" I asked, eyebrows raised, as I surveyed the map. "Why not send in some drones, even? Seems like that would be far more efficient."

Ward glanced up at me briefly with annoyance. "True. That would have been. Unfortunately, they have the factory nearly as protected as a city. That means there's an EMP shield above," Ward tapped the controls on the edge of the screen, and a giant dome appeared above the factory. "No way a drone is getting anywhere close to that building. They also have anti-aircraft munitions located to the north, ready to take out any incoming bombers."

Ward cleared his throat before continuing. "This whole area is going to be a swampy mess, but boots on the ground is the only way to take out the target. At least, if we want to do this quietly, that is. The other option is a full-scale assault, putting Intelligence on the task of trying to hack their anti-aircraft and EMP shield generator to put them off-line. By the time all that would be accomplished, the enemy would know we were here and would have time to fully mobilize. The goal is to go in quickly and quietly. Get charges laid and get out."

His explanation made sense. I was used to being part of those full-scale assaults; flying in once Intelligence had gotten their job done. I didn't have exposure to these sorts of stealth ground missions.

The terrain did look pretty swampy in several places. Ward zoomed in on the anti-aircraft munitions, located in a thick copse of tropical-looking trees, momentarily, as though to reiterate his point. He continued, as I took in the terrain. "We'll land here," he zoomed out, then swiped over, and zoomed in on another position on the map, south of the factory, "and we'll have a trek in. We'll follow this path; try to avoid the thickest parts of the swamp. We can't risk the road; no clue what sort of tech they have on that road. We'll cross the train tracks, here," he indicated on the map, "just before we reach the factory."

Ward stopped and looked around the room. "Any questions so far?"

I sighed deeply. I had one, although I thought I knew the answer already. I'd never tried setting down a fighter this close to an EMP shield. "I'm assuming this means my men and I won't be able to land anywhere in the vicinity?"

Ward grinned up at me, "You assume right. That's why we use our tin cans and land at a distance. They're low tech. Your fighters might be able to land out here," Ward zoomed in on an area further from the factory, "But you'd still risk triggering their system, putting them on high alert."

I nodded. "So, we'll join you. Stick to our flight suits." I didn't love the idea, but clearly, that was our only option.

Ward's grin broadened. He leaned back in his chair and shrugged. "You could. Normally, you might be able to get away with it, out in the boondocks. But those flight suits are useless in any heavily patrolled area. I wouldn't be surprised at all if they have EMP guns out here. Whatever's at that factory, is pretty important to them."

I frowned at him. "What are EMP guns?"

Ward scoffed, grinning at me. "You haven't heard of EMP guns?" He raised an eyebrow, smirking at his men.

"I'm a fighter pilot, Ward. When exactly do you think was the last time I spent significant time on the ground?"

Ward shrugged. "My point exactly. That's another good argument for why Martinez should have sent someone else."

My eyes narrowed, and I could feel my fists clenching, my shoulders tensing, and inching towards my ears. Ward stared me down, his eyes daring me to speak.

"Oh yeah?" I said, voice pitched low. "And what were the other ones?" I moved closer to the table. "I know the Admiral wouldn't give you the time of day, but I'd love to hear what you planned to say to him."

Ward took a deep breath. "Yeah, I don't think so, Kessler." He shrugged. His act of fake nonchalance was getting old. "Let's just say the arguments involved are tactical. Strategic. I don't think you'd handle it well, hearing what I had to say." His eyes narrowed on mine. "Too fragile."

Fuck. Him. I forced myself to stay calm, lowering my arms to my sides, forcing my shoulders to relax. "Oh, I'm sure. I'm sure they were all profound, coming from you. You must be a master tactician." My voice was ice cold as I moved in slow steps around the table. "After all, you assumed command, what, a week and a half ago?" I thought for a moment, one hand on my chin, "You retreated. Lost the battle. And managed to lose nearly a third of your company." I shook my head. "I'm shocked the Admiral didn't want to hear your brilliant ideas."

Ward's jaw clenched tight, that muscle ticking, and he stared me down, his dark eyes dangerously cold. I noticed his chest was heaving slightly. Wren's bright blue eyes were wide next to him. He met my gaze and shook his head.

Ward stood and moved slowly past me, over to the circular desk off to the right. He slid a drawer open and pulled out a grey handgun, holding it aloft. "This, is an EMP gun. You run into one of those Southern fuckers, and he's carrying this... he doesn't need to worry all that much about aiming. This goes off anywhere within a three-foot radius of your flight suit, and you're dead in the water. He'll disable you completely with one shot. You won't be able to do a thing to stop him."

I eyed the inconspicuous-looking handgun with a raised brow. "We'll see about that." I shrugged. "Our suits are shielded." But I wasn't so sure. He certainly seemed to know what he was talking about. Why on earth we hadn't been briefed on this, was beyond me.

Ward grinned at me, head cocked to the side. "Care for a demonstration?" Before I could respond, he flicked the gun, almost lazily, in an upward motion, in my direction.

The gun went off with a loud crack, echoing in the enclosed space; the blast sounded just like any handgun I'd ever heard. I felt a jolt of abject terror go through me as the force of it hit me in the chest. I was slammed backwards, landing flat on my back on the floor, the air knocked out of my lungs. My entire body went numb, as I choked and gasped for air.

"Jesus Christ, Ward!" I heard one of the men yelp, as general commotion ensued. I thought it was Wren speaking. "Are you nuts? You could have taken out our tech. You can't fire a fucking EMP gun on the goddamn bridge."

Ward only laughed in response. *Hilarious.*

I couldn't move. At all. My limbs were frozen in place. It was like the suit had locked up; the EMP blast had effectively taken out my suit's electrical functions and managed to stun me somehow in the process. I assumed the EMP gun must emit some type of charge that seizes up muscles, along with delivering an electromagnetic pulse, knocking out anything electronic.

I heard Ward, closer now, off to my right, his voice coming from too low to the ground, like he was crouching down beside me, but I couldn't turn my head to look at him. "You feeling the tingling now, Captain?" He moved closer to my ear as he spoke, his voice dropping to a deeper, gravelly pitch. Something in my core shifted, at the sound of his voice. And I managed to grit my teeth. My entire body was tingling now, sure enough. Pins and needles, like I was on fire.

He continued, now at a normal volume, "You're correct, Captain, the flight suits are shielded, in a sense. They're designed to detect the EMP, milliseconds before it hits, but the only way to prevent permanent damage is for the suit to power off completely. It'll recover its full functionality, once it's able to reboot and get back online. But EMP guns are effective either way. They'll still render you completely helpless. They've managed to combine it somehow with some sort of taser-like pulse. That'll knock you on your ass for a few minutes as well. You'll recover, though. Eventually."

I was starting to get some sensation back in my arms and legs now, but the suit was still locked tight. I was able to wiggle my fingers and toes inside the suit. It was now a prison. I wouldn't be able to get it off until it powered back on. Not without help. That bastard. At least he hadn't actually shot me. I wasn't dead, like I had thought I was for a split second when the gun went off. Just embarrassed. In front of all his officers.

Wren's face appeared, floating above mine, accompanied by sniggering in the background. "Hang on, Captain. We'll get you out of there. It'll just take a minute."

He managed to remove me from the suit, with help. I could feel my cheeks flushing as they struggled to pull my weak limbs out of the suit, one at a time. Captain Ward stood there with his arms folded, watching the whole thing with an amused, shit-eating grin on his face.

I eventually managed to get to my feet with Wren's help. I stood, attempting to hide my limbs trembling as I brushed strands of hair that had come loose off my face. I wanted to have it out with him, right here, and right now. But I cringed a little. I'd had time to rehash my words to him as they were pulling me out of the suit. What I'd said had been pretty awful, to be fair. I was furious at him, but I couldn't say that I didn't deserve it. Maybe just a tiny bit.

I tried to keep my breathing under control. Stop my chest from heaving, as I regained some of my composure. "Why the fuck weren't we briefed on those things?" I heard myself asking out loud. "They sent my crew down, just outside of Detroit. We were all in our flight suits. We would have been taken out, picked off one by one, if they'd had these." I gestured towards the gun. "Does Command not know about them?" I couldn't fathom that being the case, but it didn't make any sense.

Ward looked down at the gun, lying on the desk now. He shrugged, frowning a little. "I mean, Detroit's a ghost town, right? And you were out in the country nearby, from what I've heard. I can't imagine you'd encounter any hostiles in that area that would be carrying one of these. Seems unlikely, especially that far north." He looked up at me, considering. "We've only run into them in major cities so far, or close to strategic targets, and it seems only the higher-ranking officers carry them."

I raised an eyebrow at him. He cleared his throat, picking up the EMP gun once more. I willed myself not to flinch. But he wasn't paying any attention to me. He stared down at the gun in his hand. "I took this one off of an officer." He set it back in the desk drawer and slid it shut. His eyes met mine. "They aren't standard issue. Yet." I licked my lips, brushing another stray hair off my face, as Ward studied me. "You said you hadn't spent much time on the ground yet. Maybe they were planning on briefing you soon."

I felt an uncomfortable twisting in my gut. But when? The Admiral knew where we were headed next. Why hadn't he briefed me before this mission? But I nodded, still trying to brush off what had just happened and my growing sense of unease. My body still felt off, my limbs weak and shaky.

Wren stood at my side, reaching an arm out to me as I tilted slightly, unsteady on my feet. I shifted my gaze to him as I felt him grip my left arm, and I grabbed onto him, clutching his chest as my left leg gave out completely beneath me.

I gritted my teeth, trying to force my legs to hold, but my left couldn't seem to bear any weight at the moment, and my right was barely holding on, weak and shaking. I didn't want to show any weakness, not in front of the men, and especially not in front of Ward. Not after he had called me *fragile*. For a second time. But I'd have fallen over, if Wren hadn't been there.

"Thanks," I murmured to him. His eyes were so blue, fixed on mine, they looked almost unnatural.

He didn't blink, meeting my gaze steadily, "No problem," he nodded once, adding "Captain," as an afterthought. There wasn't a trace of sarcasm in his tone. I decided I liked Wren. Even if he did seem to be Ward's right-hand man.

Ward cleared his throat, and we looked over to see him fixing us with an icy glare. "If you're feeling too weak to stand, *Captain*, why don't you take a seat?" He nodded towards the empty chair he'd offered me earlier. "That is, unless you're above sharing a table with my men."

I looked up at Wren and nodded silently, and he helped me limp over to the table. I sank into the chair gratefully, avoiding Ward's gaze. Wren stood there, awkwardly, for a moment, watching me. As though he was reluctant to leave my side.

"Well," Ward said, moving back to his seat on the far side of the table, "I think we've established your flight suits and fighters won't be the best options on this mission. I suggest you join us in the tin cans." He clapped his hands, then rubbed them together, grinning. A few of the men chuckled. "We'll be doing this the old-fashioned way; set down on the other side of the swampy area, out in the fields to the south of the target. We'll make our way in on foot. The only electronics we'll carry will be our standard comm units. Radio transmission only. For obvious reasons. They'll likely have the entire vicinity bugged for any significant electrical activity." I stared down at the table. I refused to look at him. But I nodded to show my agreement.

"Good," he said, voice clipped. "We don't know what we'll be walking into, exactly. There's limited intelligence gathered on the security forces inside the factory. We can assume an armed guard. But how many... that's up for debate." He sounded tired, suddenly. I squirmed uncomfortably in my own skin, for a moment. I knew what it was like to lead a Unit. That was difficult enough. I had yet to experience leading a whole Company. Being the one in charge, on a mission like this, on any mission, couldn't be easy. But I shoved any shred of compassion I felt for him down deep, below the resentment that burned in my core.

"Wren, where are we with our pod count?" Ward asked, turning to Wren, who had taken his seat again at his side. I glanced over to find Wren watching me still, an odd expression on his face. He pulled his gaze away from me and focused back on Ward for a moment, seeming unsure of what he'd been asked. "Pod count?" Ward asked him again, his voice clipped.

Wren shook his head as though to clear it, and leaned forward, pulling up a schematic on the tabletop, lists and charts rising into the air.

Ward studied me through the thin lines, his face bathed in blue light. His gaze flickered swiftly, shifting from me, back to Wren, then back to me again, before he focused on Wren's response. A cold, calculating look in his eyes.

God damn it. My gut clenched with something like apprehension. I needed to get off this rig. I didn't belong here. The faster I could gather the intelligence the Admiral needed, the faster I could get out of here. Back to my own men.

6.

Once Ward had finished briefing everyone, he dismissed the men, asking Wren and me to stay behind. I stood there, feeling uneasy, my legs having finally recovered enough to bear my weight, waiting for the men to file out of the bridge. Wren stayed seated at the table, eyes still roving over the floating map of the factory below.

Once the doors had slid shut, I turned and spoke to Ward's back. "I'd like to have some time to brief my team before departure." *Two men hardly constitute a team.* The thought flitted through my mind as I spoke.

"That's what I wanted to talk to you about," Ward sighed, moving back over to the table. "Are you sure you want to join us this time? I'm not sure exactly what we're getting into down there. You won't have the benefit of your flight suits, unless you'd like to risk wearing them anyway." He shrugged.

"Maybe it's best to sit out for this one, wait until tomorrow to do a reconnaissance. I'm not sure it'll be worth it."

I paused for a moment, unsure how to respond. "I thought you said there were reports of activity nearby?"

Ward nodded, moving over to the table. He manipulated the controls and pulled up a map of the larger region. He pointed as I oriented myself to the new map. "Here. Closer to Gainesville. There were reports of activity." I glanced over at Wren as he spoke, and Ward waved his hand dismissively. "He already knows everything." I nodded thoughtfully as Wren watched my response.

"I don't envy the boys dropping into Gainesville tonight. It's going to be brutal." Ward shrugged again. "But that's a ways away from where we're headed. Like I said, I'm not sure it'll be worth it."

"Worth what, exactly?" I asked, crossing my arms over my chest.

"The risk," he said, leaning forward, hands propped on the table. "I can't guarantee your protection—" he started. That was as far as he got.

"I'm not asking you to." I spat back at him. "I'm an officer of the Northern Alliance, just the same as you. What makes you think I need your protection?" I was steaming now. Livid. I could practically feel the heat rising off my face.

Ward's brows raised, eyes narrowing. I was vaguely aware of Wren sighing, resting his chin in his hands. "What makes you think we're the same, Captain?" Ward asked, his tone incredulous. "I have years of combat training. I've done this more times than I can count. Can you say the same?" He stood and held his hands out. "Look, you want to get in a dog fight, you'll have the upper hand, no question. But down there, on the ground? You don't know what it's like down there." He shook his head. "You'll be as bad as a new recruit."

Wren groaned softly, sliding his face into his hands. I took a deep breath. "Listen, I get where you're coming from. You're right, I don't have the same experience with hand-to-hand combat, not like you do. But I am still an officer. I went through basic boot camp; I know how to fight. I've gone through specialist training since then. You don't need to treat me any differently than you would any other soldier assigned to your Company." I stood there, hands on my hips, chest rising and falling more rapidly than I would have liked. But I had managed to keep my anger under control. "Just because I'm a woman, doesn't mean–"

Ward cut me off this time. "That has absolutely nothing to do with it." He said emphatically. His tone was firm, and he didn't look away, meeting my gaze. I stared back at him. "Is that what you think–"

"Yes." I barked at him, my emotions getting the best of me. "That is exactly what I think. What I know," I amended. "I told you," I pointed at him, "I won't let you stand in my way of completing this mission. So, you can forget your bullshit excuses, whatever they may be. I don't care if you're motivated by spite, misogyny, or some warped, misguided sense of benevolent sexism. I don't need it. I don't need any of it. What I need, is for you to let me do my job." I'd taken several steps towards him as I spoke, my voice rising in volume.

Ward stared at me, a look of something so close to hatred in his eyes that I could think of no other word for it. He glanced at Wren briefly and moved past me, towards the doors leading out of the bridge.

"MacMillan!" Ward barked out over his shoulder. "Would you be so kind as to show Captain Kessler down to the lab? She may want to meet the rest of her team before we leave." He didn't wait for a response. I heard the doors slide shut behind him as he left.

I stood staring at the floor for a moment, taking deep breaths. When I looked up, I found Wren watching me, leaning back casually in his chair, arms crossed over his chest.

"Well, you certainly have a way with words, don't you, Captain Kessler?" He smirked slightly.

I sighed, feeling my body go suddenly limp. I was already exhausted, and we had a long night ahead of us.

Wren nodded towards the doors. "He's still beating himself up, you know. About Houston." He shook his head. "He did the best he could. He saved us, ordering the retreat when he did. But that's just how he is. He's too hard on himself. Always has been." He shrugged, my gut twisting a little.

His eyes dropped to the map, still rotating slowly over the table. "I've been with him from the beginning. Since boot camp. He's saved my life, more than once." He paused, his eyes flickering back to find mine. "He's not what you think he is." He said quietly. Then he stood up and sighed. "Come on; I'll take you down to the lab. Your team's already gotten cozy down there."

7.

The lab was a dimly lit space. Long tables stretched into shadows in a wide, yawning cavity, almost as large as the hangar below us.

I squinted, peering across the room, at a figure that seemed oddly familiar. She was removing something from a large box on the floor, and nearly dropped whatever it was when I shouted out, "Lindsay?"

She turned towards me and laughed, turning to set the item carefully down on the table beside her, before heading our way.

Wren watched, a grin spreading across his face, pushing two dimples into existence, as Lindsay reached us and threw her arms around me. "I can't believe it!" I exclaimed, pulling back to look at her more closely. "God, I thought they had you assigned to a lab out in California?"

She smiled, nodding, pushing her glasses back up her nose. Her hair was pulled back in a bun, exposing an undercut. "This is new," I grinned, gesturing to her hair. I'd always envied her thick blonde hair, somehow streaked with natural highlights. She tended to wear it cropped short; too annoyed to deal with it in the outdoor conditions she typically worked in.

Lindsay grinned back. "Yeah, it was too hot in Cali, I needed to get some of the weight off my neck." She shrugged, "It keeps me cooler."

"And now they've managed to tuck you away on a Carrier?" I raised an eyebrow at her.

"Oh, I volunteered." She sighed, smiling grimly.

"Really?" I asked, eyebrows stretching higher. "I have to say that surprises me a little."

She shrugged again, grinning. "I may have heard that a certain someone was in charge of this thing... although," she shrugged again, "that's not the main reason I volunteered." Her expression shifted. "We need to figure out what the hell this thing is. And how it's spreading."

I met her eyes, nodding solemnly. Lindsay and I met during my initial stint in Intelligence. She and I were never assigned to the same unit, and hadn't worked together directly. She was a biologist. A good one. I felt some of the weight I didn't realize I was carrying ease slightly off my shoulders.

"That's why we're here," I said quietly. "You tell me what you need. Whatever it is, I'll find a way to get it."

She nodded solemnly back, then gestured us over to the table she had been working on. She continued to unpack supplies as we watched. "Starting with the basics. Anything you can get is better than the nothing we have right now. Tissue samples, blood samples... ideally, we want multiple vials of each type of sample you gather. The process for DNA splicing is extremely wasteful, in a way. We'll take what we have and amplify the DNA first, but we need a lot of raw source material to do so. More than you might think. Sometimes samples get corrupted, don't run correctly... we need redundancy. Running multiple samples at once and comparing them will give us the most accurate data. Ideally, from there, I'd eventually like a full specimen."

I swallowed thickly, one eyebrow arching. "A specimen? You mean, like a body?"

Lindsay nodded, "That's the best way to get the full picture. To be sure of what we're dealing with. We're interested in finding out how this thing can make such sweeping changes to our morphology. It's fascinating. We've never seen anything like it." She shrugged, "I doubt anything like it has ever existed before. At least not on this planet."

I took a deep breath at her words and nodded, peering around the lab as she spoke. "Who's we?" I asked, frowning. "It's not just you in here, is it?"

Lindsay grunted slightly, lifting what looked like a particularly heavy and ancient-looking machine from a large crate and setting it on the metal lab table with a thunk. "No, thank God... they've assigned two lab techs; James and Isla. I'll introduce you later. There's also Topher." She nodded further into the darkness of the lab. "He's a hacker."

She grinned up at us. "You heard about the DC hack, back in April?" I nodded, and she inclined her head towards the far side of the lab. "That was him." She shrugged. "I'm sure he'll be useful when it comes to the actual data analysis. Who knows what all we'll need in terms of running computer simulations, programming, that type of thing, in the meantime. So," her voice became thick and muffled as she leaned halfway into another crate, her upper body disappearing for a moment. "We'll have our own tech support, right in-house."

I nodded again, gazing over at the far shadows of the lab. "Wow, it's like they're finally taking this seriously." Wren chuckled behind my back.

I turned to him. I'd forgotten he was there; I was too caught up. "Lindsay, this is First Lieutenant MacMillan," I gestured towards him. "Second-hand man to Captain Ward."

Lindsay paused long enough to shake Wren's hand. "Call me Wren," he said, grinning at Lindsay. "Have you met Ward yet?" I heard him ask. I frowned as they chatted, biting down on my lip, I strolled up the aisle between tables, Wren's words echoing in my mind.

I was grateful they had sent Lindsay; that had been a stroke of serendipity. And it did sound like this Topher character would be useful. But something about Wren's comment had struck me. Were they? Taking this seriously? Two Intelligence assets, one biologist, one techie. Two lab techs. Me. And only two of my men.

I felt an odd pit forming in my stomach as I wandered the huge, practically empty lab. It was a small operation, all things considered. Given the scope of this threat, its potential, it honestly didn't feel like they were taking it seriously enough.

Wren made his excuses and turned to leave, nodding once in my direction. I nodded back, watching him weave between tables and step swiftly through the sliding double doors.

"There he is," Lindsay said. I turned to see her nodding towards the back of the lab.

A man with a shock of shaggy-looking brown hair approached us, carrying what looked like an ancient brick of a laptop raised in one hand, like a waiter might carry a serving tray. He approached me directly, as Lindsay stood and wiped her hands on her green fatigues. The pockets jingled as she did so.

"You must be Captain Kessler," Topher said, throwing me a lazy salute, tilting his head down and peering at me over the top of his wire-framed glasses, his green eyes flickering up and down. "It's a pleasure, Captain." He nodded briskly at me, seeming to find me satisfactory after his brief inspection. "I'm getting acquainted with the software installed on the rig." He jerked his head back toward the large screen, taking up most of the far wall, casting the room below in a blue glow. "Getting everything updated, at the moment. That'll take a while." He surveyed the lab. "Doesn't seem like anyone's been in here in ages."

I nodded in approval, then pointed at the laptop in his hands. "What's with the brick? If you don't mind me asking."

Topher grinned; his smile was wide, but brief. There, then gone just as quickly. He scurried around the table next to him and set the laptop down gently. "This?" He nodded down at the laptop, fingers moving swiftly over the keys, clacking away. He typed so fast, it seemed almost fake. Like a child on his parents' computer, pretending to write a manuscript. I suppressed a chuckle. I had a feeling he did everything fast. "This, is Lucy." He paused briefly to grin up at me. "She's fully locked down; no one's hacking into her. She may be a brick, but she's secure."

I felt my lips curve up in an answering grin. "Nice," I replied simply. "Well, I think this operation will be in good hands. I'm excited to get started." I cleared my throat, looking back and forth between the two of them. "We'll be putting boots on the ground shortly. We'll do the best we can to gather as many samples as possible."

Lindsay nodded, waving me over as she moved across the room. "Let's get you set up with some supplies; go over how to collect the samples."

Topher followed us, picking up Lucy, and moving closer, but he stayed focused on the screen, eyes down, as Lindsay went over how to gather samples safely and put together little kits for McCullough, Binson, and me to carry with us.

"I heard you've seen them, in person," Topher spoke up suddenly.

I swallowed, nodding. "I have. Not an experience I'm likely to ever forget."

He nodded back, raising his eyes to peer over at me briefly, as he continued to type. "I'd like to see them. See how they move, how they behave. Samples are all well and good, but visuals, in real-time, or better yet, a recording we can analyze later, would give us useful data as well."

I pursed my lips, thinking for a moment, then nodded. "I don't see why not, right? If you have the gear we'd need, I don't see why we couldn't."

Topher nodded, not looking up. "Oh, I have the gear. With a simple adjustment, we can set it up so you can patch us into a video feed in real time. That'll be no problem. We'll plan to record it as well."

"We heard all about the white substance on them, but how would you describe it? Some sort of foam? Or is it more like saliva, or pus?" Lindsay asked. "We definitely want samples of that."

I shook my head slowly. "No, I don't think it's foam. It looks like it's a different texture. More slippery and wet, but also, it's like, stringy, almost."

I frowned, thinking back to that woman I'd found; the body I'd stumbled across before running into them. At first, I thought the white substance might have been vomit, from eating something poisonous. It had been thick and wet-looking, but it had also been oddly strand-like in appearance.

"There are visible strands," I said slowly, recalling the image of the white threads stretching out of the mouth of that first one, almost like they had been growing there, taking root deep in its maw... down its throat. Snaking tendrils reaching out towards the sunlight. "I almost wondered if it was vomit when I first saw it. But then... I wasn't so sure. It looked sort of like it was... growing on them. Some had strands coming out of their mouths, but other places too. Almost like it was growing from inside of them." I shook my head with a grimace of disgust. "I'm not sure what it is."

Lindsay nodded, a thoughtful expression on her face. "Is it possible it's some sort of fungus?" She said slowly.

"A fungus?" I asked, brows wrinkling. "Growing on a living thing like that?"

Topher's curved fingers paused in their frantic typing. "I was thinking the same thing." He said flatly.

"Zombie-ant fungus," Lindsay murmured, more to herself than to us. We both turned towards her. She stared off into the distance. "Or *Gibellula attenboroughii...*" she murmured, trailing off.

"What's–" I attempted to reproduce the syllables she had just uttered and found myself incapable. "What's that?" I frowned.

Lindsay moved back to the sample kits, fingers moving swiftly as she assembled them. "While there are an unknown number of microscopic fungi species, maybe even millions, there are certain species that are known as macro fungi, think mushrooms, molds, things of that nature, that are easily visible to the naked eye. In terms of growing on a living host, like what you might be describing, two main well-known species of fungal infections are considered parasitic. They are primarily known to infect insects and cause... aberrant behavior, in the host."

Topher cleared his throat, "TODD, pull up data on Zombie-ant fungus." A secondary, smaller bank of screens off to our left came to life.

"Here's what I was able to find, *All-Powerful-Master*." Lindsay and I paused, turning to Topher. He stood there grinning, and I smirked, snorting a little.

"Really? All-powerful master?" Lindsay raised an eyebrow at him and shook her head.

"What?" Topher grinned back, shrugging. "Might as well have a little fun."

Lindsay just shook her head again and moved closer to the screen. "We'd already suspected from our briefing that this might be some sort of parasite, versus a viral infection. The changed behavior of the host is fascinating. And certainly, reminiscent of the Zombie-ant fungus, as well as the lesser-known *Gibellula attenboroughii,* which affects certain species of spiders."

Topher peered up at the screen, swiping quickly back and forth, too fast for my eyes to follow.

Lindsay continued, "These types of fungal infections infect the host, causing changes in the brain itself, which lead the host to behave erratically. In ants, the fungus ends up controlling the ant, forcing it to move to an area where it's more likely to spread its spores to others, just before it dies."

I frowned, staring at the images flashing on the screen. Topher zoomed in on an image of an ant, infected with what was clearly some type of fungus, growing in white tufts all over its body. It perched on a stick, limbs spread into the air.

"Their reported swarming behavior is similar to how ants behave." Lindsay went on, sounding excited now, turning back to me. "Ants communicate via pheromones. They release alarm pheromones when they feel threatened, which can draw dozens or even hundreds of other ants in the vicinity towards them, to attack a threat." Lindsay shrugged. "The data we have so far is limited, of course, but it's hard to ignore the possible implications."

I shook my head slowly, trying to take in what she was saying. "But... you're talking about two different things. A fungus, of some type, that acts as a parasite, that might change the host's behavior... but why would that cause people, humans, to behave like insects? Even if the fungus that infects ants, or spiders, somehow was able to jump to human beings, wouldn't it just... have the same sorts of effects in humans? Not necessarily change us to act like ants..."

I frowned deeply, thinking back to that night, outside Detroit. Those things had swarmed us, alright. Flocking out of nowhere, emerging from the shadows beneath the trees, coming in wave after wave. I recalled the odd, twittering sounds they made. The strange jaw movements. They were certainly reminiscent of insects. I shuddered involuntarily, pushing away the memories from that night.

I looked up to find Lindsay and Topher glancing at each other, an almost wary expression on their faces. "It wouldn't," Lindsay said, her voice pitched low. "If one of these fungal infections, or a similar one we haven't discovered yet, were to cross over to humans, it wouldn't make us behave like insects. Not unless it underwent significant mutations. Combining somehow, merging with the host DNA..." her voice trailed off.

My eyes narrowed. "So, that could happen, though? In theory? It's possible?"

Lindsay frowned for a moment, then nodded. "In theory, yes, it's possible." She murmured, "It's possible some sort of mutation occurred naturally. It could be that's what we're dealing with..."

"Or," Topher said, clearing his throat, eyes wide and fixed on me, expression solemn, "if it was designed to." I felt myself go cold at his words, a little shiver starting at the base of my neck. "It could also occur... unnaturally. If it were specifically designed to." He glanced over at Lindsay again, but she didn't look at him. She was watching me closely, gauging my reaction.

Clearly, they'd already discussed this before. At length, would be my guess. I felt myself stand up straighter, my shoulders dropping. I met Lindsay's gaze, trying to read what was beneath them. "And the samples would tell us that?" I said slowly. "The samples would tell you, if that were the case?"

She broke eye contact, looking briefly at Topher, then back at me. Topher sighed, flopping down into the chair that sat before the computer screens, turning slightly away from us as it spun in a circle with his momentum.

"You get us the samples we need, and we'll figure out the rest," Lindsay said softly.

I swallowed, nodding, feeling my fists clenching slightly at my sides, at the thought of this possibility. "I'll get you what you need," I said quietly. "And this stays between us. Everything that happens here, everything you learn, stays inside this room." I could feel my heart thumping away in my chest, as though it was knocking against my rib cage. Beating against my sternum.

Lindsay's expression darkened, and Topher stopped spinning. "And by that, I mean the three of us, specifically. I'll share only what I need to, with McCullough and Binson. They'll be helping me gather the samples. But I don't want anyone else involved." My cheeks flushed slightly, "Not even Captain Ward."

Lindsay and Topher both nodded, and Topher kicked off the floor, spun around once, and then slid the chair over to the table, grabbing onto the corner and pulling himself back over to Lucy. "You don't need to tell us twice." He murmured, fingers clacking away again on the keys. He shot me a solemn glance. "We've got you, Captain." He didn't bother to raise his eyes again from the screen as I murmured my goodbyes and turned to leave.

Lindsay's expression was grim as she walked me back to the entrance of the lab. She grabbed my arm, just as I went to move through the wide double doors, sliding open with a rush of air. "Jordan, just be careful, down there." She whispered, then smiled slightly. "I know that goes without saying, but..." she trailed off, "we don't really know what this thing is. We don't know exactly how it spreads yet. Be careful what you touch, especially when gathering samples. Gloves, at all times. Remove them carefully, the way I showed you. Okay?"

I nodded solemnly. "I will," I managed. She gave me a small, tight-lipped smile as I turned and left.

I'd be careful, all right. Careful to keep what we learned a secret, while I was being careful not to get myself or my men killed, and not to somehow get infected by those things. I felt a shudder travel down my spine once more.

I'd had plenty of practice hiding my emotions. I knew not to betray any outward signs, keeping my expression blank and my shoulders relaxed as I passed a group of men in the narrow hallway, nodding briskly back as they saluted me in their passing. My expression remained calm, but my pulse and my mind were racing.

8.

Now I understood why the men called them tin cans. We held onto whatever we could, as we rocketed down to Earth. My body jolted, heels stinging from the impact, as the transport pod touched down on the surface. I pitched forward, smashing into the soldier next to me. Ward witnessed my discomfort with a self-satisfied smirk that I didn't care for.

He hadn't spoken a word to me since the bridge, hardly glancing in my direction as we prepared to leave. I, in turn, was making a point of ignoring him, looking away, my expression neutral, as I struggled to maintain my balance.

The pod finally shuddered to a halt, and one wall creaked open, falling to the ground with a crash. It revealed a lush, green landscape.

I moved slowly off the pod, pausing on the ramp, following the flow of bodies, eyes on the tall, tropical trees stretching overhead, oddly shaped leaves swaying lazily. A warm breeze kissed my skin, and I could feel the humidity hit me instantly, the air heavy with moisture. A low fog hung over the ground. This place felt alien, like another world completely.

Ward had given us a short briefing on the local wildlife and terrain before we'd boarded the pods. He'd also warned the men that there may be "Jumpers" in the vicinity, as the men were starting to call them. McCullough, Binson, and I were to stay together, assigned to Wren's unit.

As this was meant to be a stealth mission, the men were all in black. The three of us didn't have standard issue battle fatigues, but it had been easy enough to find a set in black for McCullough and Binson.

They'd given me a small, but I was still swimming in it. I'd refused to wear the shirt; it would have only gotten in my way. I donned a tight black long-sleeved shirt instead. Tucking it into the black pants and turning the waistband over several times made the pants wearable, at least. I slipped on a lightweight chest plate with attached shoulder pads over the shirt, which was far too big as well, but it would have to do, for now. Wren told me he'd see what he could do to get me something better for next time.

The men painted their faces with black camouflage paint. I'd wanted to refuse at first. The paint, whatever it was, stunk of chemicals. But I decided I would do whatever they did. I wouldn't be the one to risk the mission over my bare face. So,

I stuck my hand into the cold slop and spread it all over, careful not to get any in my eyes.

"You alright, Reaper?" Powers grinned at me as he moved past. I almost didn't recognize him with his cheeks covered in streaks of black camo paint.

I shot him a weak grin back and nodded. "That was quite a landing."

"You get used to it," he shrugged, throwing me a wink before continuing on.

Binson nodded to me, as I turned back to find him, his teeth and eyes blazing white in the darkness of the pod. "Let's fucking go." He murmured. I was glad someone was jacked up over the evening's itinerary. I certainly wasn't.

While I'd meant every word I'd said earlier to Captain Ward, I was now feeling nervous as hell. The foreign, jungle-like atmosphere and the fact that it was foggy did nothing to help ease my anxiety. My conversation with Lindsay and Topher had left me feeling vaguely unsettled as well, and I felt practically naked now, standing here in the open. Exposed. I was used to being tucked into my fighter jet, or minimally, in the flight suit. This felt dangerous. And stupid.

We moved out at some silent signal. Ward had ordered us to stay off the comms as much as possible, to keep quiet, and stick to the plan. I gripped my rifle tightly in both hands and moved off at a slight crouch, following the man in front of me.

We were traveling on the edge of the nearby wetlands. The ground was swampy. Boggy in places. My boots were soaked before I'd taken a dozen steps. I could feel my clothes sticking to me, the humidity taking over. Little flies, some type of gnat, hung in clouds randomly. Binson got a mouthful as we wove between trees, sputtering as he spat them out. I moved forward, chuckling, waving a hand in front of my face, trying to clear a path.

"God damn it. I'd take flying any day over this shit." McCullough grumbled next to me. I couldn't help but grin. I had to say I agreed with him.

"Shh!" One of Wren's men turned, a finger held over his mouth. McCullough and I looked at each other, and he rolled his eyes.

We spread out a bit, moving through the trees. I heard a crackle over the comms. "This is Nathan. We've got movement on our six." I whipped my head around instinctively, but I saw nothing but figures all in black, moving silently through the trees, and the low-hanging fog beyond them. The fog was too dense here, and we were too far towards the front of the pack to see anything.

"How many?" Came Ward's clipped reply. "Hostiles or Jumpers? Over."

"Hard to say," Nathan replied. "They're off a ways. We can't get a clear view, with the fog, but I think it's safe to say we're being followed. Over."

"We'll know what they are if they start shooting. Over." Wren's voice squawked over the comms.

I tapped my comms unit. "Sir, shouldn't my men and I hang back? Over."

"You stay where you are, Captain Kessler. Stick to Wren. Over." I sighed loudly, not caring who heard me. If those were Jumpers back there, it made no sense for us to keep going. That was the entire point of us being here.

"Nathan," Ward chimed back in, "you and your men stay at our rear, form a perimeter, and hunker down out of sight. Stevens, you join them. Over." I was somewhat reassured by his orders, feeling my shoulders relax down from my ears a bit. At least we'd be covered at the rear. Hopefully, that would leave us an avenue to retreat when we were ready.

We finally made it to the train tracks that Ward had pointed out earlier on the map. The men paused there, heads swiveling up and down the tracks, peering through the fog, as they crossed into the open in twos and threes, running swiftly for the other side, back to the cover of the trees. I stepped on a branch underfoot, and it snapped with a loud crack. I jumped, my heart racing.

About five minutes later, we came to the edge of the woods. The factory loomed ahead. We kept back a good ten feet from the perimeter and hunkered down for a moment, waiting for orders.

"Nathan, update? Over." Ward's voice came through the comms.

"Nothing yet, Sir. We can still see movement here and there. Dark shapes in the trees. Not sure what they're planning. Over."

"Hold your position." Ward hissed back. "We're going to head for the rear of the building, as planned. Fall in and follow your squad commander. One unit at a time. Let's get in and lay those charges and get the fuck out of here."

We waited until it was our unit's turn, which didn't take long. I listened to the low level of chatter over the comms as they breached the door to the factory. We stilled, waiting for an alarm to go off. But there was only silence. The men began to stream inside, and we followed, our unit pushing forward.

"Why is it so goddamn quiet?" Someone muttered off to my right.

"I don't know, but this place is giving me the creeps." Another voice responded.

"Can it, Stowell," Wren's voice barked through the comms. "Just keep your eyes peeled."

We'd made it into the building and started to fan out through the first floor, all without encountering a soul. I smirked slightly to myself. Maybe this wouldn't be so bad, after all.

We passed down a corridor, our footfalls landing as softly as possible on the faded carpet. This building was old;

how old was hard to say exactly. The overhead lights gave off a warm golden glow that didn't quite penetrate the shadows in corners. Large posters hung on the wall to my right. I studied them as we moved swiftly past. The faces of their leaders, in once bright shades of red and blue, now faded. I recognized most of them. Starting with the one who first plunged our country into chaos. Stamped out democracy like it was a disease, to be eradicated, all for his lust for power.

The men in our unit seemed to know exactly where they were going, which I was grateful for. We trailed at the tail end of the group, as we headed up to the second and then the third floor. The munitions teams laid down charges, working in pairs as we went.

The third floor was filled with large wooden crates. We moved quietly between them. Wren stood there, frowning at the crates. He reached up and began to try to open one. A few of the men pitched in, and they managed to pry it open as quietly as possible.

Wren reached in and pulled out a grey handgun. It looked similar enough to the EMP gun that Ward had used on me, that I moved closer, approaching Wren. "Is that an EMP gun?" I hissed at him.

He looked up, nodding slowly. "Yeah, I think it is…" he trailed off, leaning over the top of the crate. "This crate's full of 'em."

The men waved us forward, and we continued on. I moved past the open crate, managing to reach up on my tiptoes, I snaked a hand in and grabbed hold of one of the EMP guns. Wren caught me, but he just grinned at me, shaking his head. I tucked the gun into my waistband at the small of my back. They'd just finished laying another charge when all hell broke loose.

I don't know who shot first, or where they came from, but next thing I knew, bullets were flying, whining and whizzing past our heads. I ducked, my hands flying over my head, and the ridiculous metal helmet they made me wear, as though that would somehow prevent my brains from being splattered all over the floor.

McCullough shouted something to me. I felt his hand on my back as he turned to look for Binson. But there was no time to worry about trying to stay together. I watched as a red, gaping gash opened up in a man's neck to my right. He attempted to close it with his own hand; blood spurting in a geyser through his fingers as he crumpled to the floor.

A string of rounds hit the wooden crates next to us, right beside our heads, and we scattered.

I ran in between the rows of crates, which seemed to be never-ending. Sprinting as best I could at a crouch, keeping my head low, attempting to stay lower than the top of the crates.

I made it to the corner of the room, bullets flying around me as I went. This corner seemed to be away from the thick of the action. The comms were going nuts; voices screaming and calling out. Names and voices jumbled together.

"We've got Jumpers, I repeat, we've got Jumpers!" I heard what I recognized as Nathan's voice, rising out of the din, from his location back in the woods at our rear. "For fuck's sake. *Goddam kamikazes...*" Nathan sputtered.

"Nathan, hold your position the best you can; you're our escape route. We're taking heavy fire." Ward's familiar voice rang out over the comms.

I spied a doorway up ahead, leading maybe to a stairwell, maybe to another room. Another round whined right past my ear, and I ducked, turning to see a man in brown fatigues behind me, down the row of crates, running straight towards me at a crouch.

I ran for it, as another barrage of rounds whizzed past my head. I ducked around the crate beside me just in time, the rounds spattering the wall past where I had just been standing. The man appeared, sprinting past the last crate, gun sweeping in my direction, as I ducked into the doorway, through the black pit ahead of me, and hoped it was the right move.

I realized with a plunging dismay that this was a stairwell, after all. No way I wouldn't encounter hostiles on the stairs. I pulled in a breath and began to make my way down the first set of stairs, pausing to pull my rifle off my back, where it still hung on its strap. I continued forward, while keeping an eye on the doorway behind me, rifle sweeping above and below.

The stairwell seemed miraculously empty, for the moment. I made it down the first flight before I heard voices echoing up from down below, followed by rounds flying up in my direction. Footsteps echoed now on the stairs above as well. I turned and ducked through the doorway to my right, shooting a volley down the stairwell as I went.

I found myself facing a hallway, branching out ahead of me and to my right. I chose the right at random, moving swiftly. Voiced drifted from behind me, as I turned and pushed open the first door to my right, ducking into the room.

I moved through what looked like an office. A large radio sat on a desk against the wall, bathed in a pool of warm light from a small desk lamp. I nearly fell, stumbling over my own feet for a moment, and bumping into a trash can. It tipped back and forth; I shot my hand out, grabbing it, and righting it quietly.

"Shh," I heard a voice hiss, just as I hit a cubicle wall, sliding down it into a crouch, I froze, listening, but heard nothing further for a few seconds. Then a low groan, followed by a grunt of pain.

I peeked slowly around the far wall of the cubicle, rifle raised. A man in brown fatigues lay there. He had been shot in the thigh. From the amount of blood, it didn't look good.

An older man knelt beside him, holding a towel loosely over the wound. The injured man's eyes went wide as he locked onto me, and he lifted a hand weakly, pointing with a trembling finger. The man next to him gasped, jumping back slightly, one hand raised.

"Please," he murmured, "we're unarmed." He gestured at the soldier. "He's been injured." His voice shook. "I... I'm just a radio operator." I don't..." He shook his head again. "Please."

I lowered my rifle slowly. The injured man had blue eyes, brown hair worn short, but what looked like a week's worth of stubble on his face. He looked young. Too young. I sighed internally. *Fuck.*

I moved over to them. "Here, you're doing it wrong." I grabbed the older man's hands, although he shied away from me, and pressed them down firmly over the towel. The young soldier cried out in pain. "You need to apply firm pressure; try to stop the bleeding." I reached into the pocket of my fatigues, pulling out my kit. "I'm going to apply a tourniquet; we need to try to slow blood flow to the leg as much as possible."

I pulled out the tourniquet I carried and made quick work of securing it, the young man grunting when I jostled him too roughly. It was done, and I swiped my forehead with the back of my hand, sweat dripping into my eyes. My hands were covered in blood.

"Why are you helping me?" He asked weakly, his head tipping back against the wall. I heard the cries of pain and fear, rattling in my ears over the comms unit. Men hurt. Dying. I felt sudden, overwhelming despair sweep over me. A deep certainty that we would never leave this building. I studied the young man, silently. Then I reached out and took his hand in mine, squeezing it.

"I've seen enough death to last me a lifetime," I told him, his blue eyes locked on mine. "I don't care what color your fatigues are; none of this is your fault." I swallowed, voice thick with unshed tears. "Not any more than it's mine."

The man next to me, the radio operator, let out a shaky sob. "You need to get out of here– they're sweeping the building." I hadn't heard orders to retreat yet. I'd been trying to keep an ear out. I turned to him, his eyes wide with fear, damp behind his thick glasses. The oddity of the situation struck me then. I'd never been this close to a Southerner before, never talked to one.

"Thanks," I murmured to him, "I appreciate it." I shook my head slowly. I'd been on missions gone FUBAR before. And this was definitely one of them. It wasn't going well, out in the woods either, from the sound of it. I doubted I would make it out of the building though, much less out of the woods. "I don't think it matters, at this point," I said quietly. The man just stared back at me, his hands going loose again. I held my hands over his and pressed down firmly.

"God," he murmured, his eyes glazing over, "we're all going to hell for this. All of us. Killing women... what's next..." his voice trailed off.

I heard a click behind me and jumped back, reaching for my rifle, lying on the floor next to me. Three men stood there, all aiming directly at me.

"Don't!" The man next to me cried out. "Don't shoot."

The man in the lead didn't move a muscle, eyes locked onto mine. Then lowered the muzzle of his gun imperceptibly. "Put the gun down," he demanded, his voice gruff.

I swallowed. *Fuck.* I was beyond fucked. I let my grip on the rifle go slack, and it clattered back to the floor, but I kept one hand hovering over it. My heart thundered in my chest as I breathed heavily, chest rising and falling rapidly.

"You're a woman." He murmured. I felt my gut twist with a stab of fear, and a wave of panic swept over me as I took in the man standing before me. He was middle-aged, clean-shaven. His blue eyes were unsettling; they reminded me of Wren's. He had short salt and pepper hair. A deep frown on his face, as he studied me back.

I'd heard things, about what they did in the South to women they came across in combat positions. I'd been hearing about how they mistreat women, in general, in the South, my entire life. There had been a note of disbelief, in his voice, but not necessarily hostility. He took in my bloody hands, my right still hovering over the soldier's wound. "Are you a medic?" He asked, frowning.

I shook my head once. I wouldn't lie. I doubted it would save me, either way. "No," I said simply, "I'm not."

He shook his head, and the tip of his rifle fell another inch. "Why are you helping him?" His eyes narrowed as he spoke.

I looked over at the soldier, head still back against the wall, eyelids fluttering as he watched me. He was practically a boy. "How old is he?" I turned back to the man standing over me, a note of accusation in my tone. I tried to curtail it, swallowing and taking a deep breath. "I'm not going to sit here, watching a man suffer in front of me, while I do nothing." I hissed at him. "I'm not a monster."

The room went still once more. Voices called out over the comms, the vibrations of their screams causing the comms unit to rattle, tickling my ear. I winced as Nathan called out desperately for backup. Ward's voice rang out in response. Wren jumped on the comms a few seconds later, calling out to me, "Kessler, report? Location? Kessler, come in!"

"Goddamn it, Wren, she isn't with you?" I heard Ward's immediate response.

"We lost her somewhere on the third floor," came Wren's staticky response.

"For *fuck's sake*," Ward murmured. They were about to retreat. I could tell. They were going to leave me here. "*Goddamn it*. Kessler; report! Over."

I focused back on the trio before me. The man in front was staring out the darkened window, a distant look in his eyes.

I reached up and tapped my comms unit as inconspicuously as possible, and the cacophony of voices cut off abruptly.

"There'll be a lot more men suffering tonight," he said slowly. "Your pals have stirred up those things, out in the woods. Fucking monsters. You'll be lucky if any of you make it out alive." He turned back to me. "We don't even really need to pursue you. We can just let 'em finish the job for us."

I stared up at him, my heart racing. "We didn't do anything to stir them up—" I started.

"You sure as hell did," the man next to him interjected. "You need to stay off your goddamn comms. They're attracted to it. They—"

"Jesus Christ, Pratchett. Why don't you just hand our enemy the fucking—" the third man chimed in.

"She's not our enemy," the man in front, clearly their leader, cut him off, "she's just a person." He lowered his weapon fully, the end of his rifle hanging nearly to the ground. "Those things, out there; they're our enemy. They're mindless fucks. They have no fear, and they never stop. Not a shred of humanity left in them."

I moved my hand away from my rifle, and slowly got to my feet, both hands held up, palms out. They moved back a step. The man on the right twitched his gun at me, but he didn't shoot.

"I've seen them, on the ground," I murmured, "they leapt at us, ran right into the line of fire. They took out almost half of my men."

The man nodded grimly at me. "Stay off your damn comms next time, like he said." He shot the soldier behind him a weary glance.

I took a tentative step towards him. "I'm Captain Kessler, Air Force." I extended a shaking hand out to him.

He didn't move, staring down at my hand, still covered in blood. I hastily wiped it on my pant leg, then held it back out to him. He reached out and grasped it. His hand was warm, his grip sweaty in mine.

"Captain?" He said, eyebrows raised. "Well, you ain't exactly in the air, Captain Kessler. What're you doing all the way down here?" I just smiled back at him, treating it as a rhetorical question.

He touched his forehead with two fingers, as though he were tipping an imaginary hat towards me. "I'm Captain Williams. It's nice to meet you, Ma'am." His voice had an odd twang to it. The corners of my mouth twitched, and I saw the ghost of a smile appear on his lips.

"It's nice to meet you, too, Captain Williams. I'd love to hear more," I said, tilting my head to the side. "Anything you know, about those monsters out there."

"Boy, I betchu you would," his grin broadened. He looked over at the older man, still crouched against the wall beside the wounded soldier. "Old Billy here's a radio expert. Knows everything there is to know about radio waves. Rumor is, staying off the comms, is key. We're still trying to figure out the rest."

He shrugged under my skeptical glance. "What? You can't expect me to just give away all our secrets now, can you?" I smiled, taking a deep breath as he eyed me up and down. "But how about I let you walk out of here? Would that be good enough?"

I nodded swiftly. "Thank you, Captain," I said, my eyes on his, "I won't forget this."

He nodded solemnly back to me, turning to the side. "Grab your rifle, and let's get going. Your men are already on the run."

I ducked down and scooped up my rifle. As I stood, I found Billy moving towards me. He held out his hand, and I took it, shaking it firmly. "Thank you, for helping us, Captain Kessler." He shrugged, "And for not killing us." He gave me a lopsided grin. "I nearly wet myself when I saw you crouched there."

I grinned back at him. "It was no problem. Really." I turned to leave. "Take care of yourself," I said to the wounded soldier, nodding in his direction. He nodded weakly back.

"You too, Captain," Billy called back to me.

I followed Captain Williams towards the doorway, his men trailing behind me, keeping an eye on me, no doubt. I was careful not to make any sudden movements. My gaze fell on the radio, sitting on the desk. I scanned it, noticing a large brass dial, I squinted at it as I passed. It was set to 750 MHz.

"Wait," I murmured, pausing mid-step. "You said they're attracted by the comms transmissions," I turned back to Billy, "how is it you're able to man the radio up here? Doesn't it draw them to the building?"

Billy slipped his hands in his pockets, nodding towards the radio. "Well, we think the EMP shield over the building may help. They tend to stay out of the major cities, possibly for the same reason. But the secret, is in the frequency. Stick to the lower range of GSM frequencies. They don't like it."

"*Billy*," Captain Williams murmured, his voice dangerously low. "That's enough."

I inclined my head towards Billy, thanking him. And I turned and followed the captain out into the now quiet hallway.

9.

Captain Williams and his men stayed true to his word. They saw me safely through the building and down to the back entrance, calling for a medic to head to the comms center, as we went.

We moved past silent, staring men, as they tracked our movements, their eyes going wide as they realized I was female. No one made a move to stop us or ask where I was being taken. Although I could tell from the expression on some of their faces that they were less than thrilled to see me being escorted past, with my rifle still in my hands.

The captain even held the door open for me, the humid air and scent of the swamp hitting me in the face as it swung open. But that was where his courtesy ended. He tipped his imaginary hat to me once more, "You take care of yourself, Captain Kessler." And then he swung the door shut behind me, already calling out orders to his men inside.

There seemed to be no one outside, at least in the immediate vicinity. Although the thick fog hid everything below the trees from my view. I felt a little fissure of surprise at that. He'd said they were going to let the Jumpers finish the job. I guess he'd been serious. Unless more of his men were busy out in the woods, hastening our retreat. I eyed the wall of primitive looking trees before me warily. Lifting my rifle, I moved forward at a crouch, not daring to breathe until I hit the treeline.

On our way out of the factory, we had passed the bodies of Ward's men. Splayed figures in black littered the hallways. I had spied perhaps half as many wearing brown. There were more bodies in black, scattered out here in the woods. I nearly tripped over one as I moved at a low crouch. My heart was in my throat. I could hear voices, pitched low, and sense movement up ahead. Further in the distance, the peppered crackling of gunfire came sporadically.

I prayed I'd make it back to the pods before they left. I debated for a moment whether I should risk using the comms. The last thing I wanted was to alert the soldiers nearby of my presence, or draw the Jumpers to me, but I decided it was worth the risk to let them know I was heading their way. I wondered how that all worked, assuming it was even true. Had they just been fucking with me? Could I trust anything they'd said?

I tapped my comms unit to unmute the audio and then tapped again to unmute myself. I waited for a pause in the chatter before muttering as loudly as I dared, "This is Kessler.

I'm behind enemy lines, past the train tracks. Looking to cross over to your position. Over."

"Goddamn it, Kessler," Ward's voice came over the comms. Was there a shred of relief in his tone? Or purely anger?

"Where have you been?" Wren asked incredulously.

"Don't worry about that now," I heard Binson pipe in. "Head for their left flank, Captain, it's clearer in that direction. We'll try to meet up with you."

"Don't you dare," I hissed back. "Sit tight. I'm coming to you. That's an order."

"Yes, Sir," Binson and McCullough muttered practically in unison. My heart leapt a little hearing both of their voices.

I focused on moving carefully forward, my eyes peeled for any sign of movement up ahead. I managed to reach the train tracks and paused in the shadows for a moment. The tracks stretched out before me, and for as far as I could see in the fog, both directions looked clear, at the moment. But I could hear voices floating to me from uncomfortably close, off to my right, along with the occasional gunshot. Clearly, Captain Williams had left at least a unit or two of his men outside, after all. I took a deep breath and darted across the tracks.

Just as I reached the far side, a round ricocheted off the track behind me, voices calling out. I shot forward, moving faster now, through the underbrush. They were heading my way. The sound of footsteps crunching on gravel told me they were running along the tracks. I crouched low, taking cover in a thicket, and waited. I wasn't going to try to outrun them. Hopefully, the fog would help provide some cover.

Suddenly, they were almost even with me. I aimed, taking out the first soldier, then the second, before he had a chance to turn his head. A third lagged behind, aiming wildly in my direction. I got him in the chest. I waited a moment, then turned to leave. But a rustling stopped me in my tracks. I spun just as a dark shape rushed towards me from behind. A bullet whizzed past my head, and a flame of fire licked my shoulder.

I had just enough time to aim my rifle at him, peppering him with several rounds, as his momentum carried him into me. I fell back with a thud, the air knocked out of my lungs for the second time today, crushed beneath the weight of his body on top of me.

I managed to slide out from under him, staring at his wide eyes, pupils fixed, his mouth gaping open. I paused, listening, as I scrambled to my feet. But only the panting of my own breath and the distant gunfire drifted to my ears.

I turned, and a hand clapped over my mouth, stifling a scream. "Shh, it's okay, it's me." I recognized Ward from his voice, more than his face. He was still mostly coated in the thick black camouflage paint, now marred with tracks of sweat. The whites of his eyes seemed to float before me as I blinked.

"Ward?" I hissed, pulling his hand off my mouth. "What the hell are you doing here?"

"Quiet," he hissed back, "let's move, we need to get out of here, now."

"You think?!" I whisper-screamed back at him. "You're the goddamn Captain, what are you doing right now?"

He moved closer to me. "What am I doing?" The whites of his eyes appeared extra wide, standing out starkly in contrast to his face paint. "I'm following my goddamn orders, that's what I'm doing. Maybe you should try it sometime." He grabbed me by the wrist, pulling me forward. "We're wasting time. Move out."

I scrambled after him, managing to keep on my feet. "We're going to run into the Jumpers on our way back, as we get closer to the pods. Don't stop to gawk at them, keep moving." I rolled my eyes, watching as he tapped his left ear. "We're headed in, boys, get ready to provide cover. On your right flank." I watched as Ward turned swiftly to the right, raising his rifle and aiming in one smooth motion.

A muffled groan as a round connected with a man I hadn't even known was there. His body slumped to the ground in a heap behind a tree. Ward continued to scan our surroundings. It was getting harder to see by the second, as the last remnants of sunlight sank further behind the horizon. "We're nearly there," Ward murmured.

Several agonizing minutes later, we moved out from under the cover of the treeline into the open field we had landed in. It was littered with the dark forms of Jumpers.

It took a moment for them to realize we were there. Between the lingering fog and the dusk of twilight, I figured we might have a chance sneaking past them unnoticed. Besides, it seemed they were busy rushing the men up ahead. But one of them stilled, off to our right, seeming to sense our presence. He was dressed in ripped brown fatigues. His feet were bare, and I could tell his appendages were elongated, his hands ending in curved talon-like claws. His back straightened, as he turned.

There were still NA men popping out of the woods into the open field here and there along the treeline behind us. Stragglers, like us. Most appeared to be either injured or helping another injured soldier. But this Jumper ignored them all. He seemed to be locked onto Ward and I. He crouched down as he began to move towards us, and I felt a gasp leave my throat involuntarily.

He must have been a man, once. But now he was something else entirely, his body ravaged by the disease to a much greater degree than the Jumpers I had encountered outside of Detroit. His eyes had changed significantly. They seemed to have shrunk and migrated somehow, so that they were further apart, nearly on the sides of his head. Now just small, dark orbs, rimmed with pale flesh.

The bottom half of his jaw had transformed completely; it gaped open, split up the middle, yawning pink on the inside. Its lower jaw ended in two appendages, of some type, which appeared to be able to move independently. They were lined with what appeared to be sharp, razor-like slivers of bone, or maybe cartilage. Perhaps they had once been his teeth. It was hard to tell.

"What the actual fuck?" I murmured to myself as we ran. The man's entire body had been transformed. He sported a rounded, sort of hunched back, along with his elongated limbs. Tufts of white; a fuzzy substance grew on his upper back and shoulders, long tendrils reaching upwards, reminding me of the image of the ant Topher had pulled up in the lab. It crouched down, as it ran, readying itself to spring forward.

The thing leapt on long, springy legs, and the distance it covered in one bound was incredible. Ward lifted his rifle, and a line of red exploded up the thing's chest. More of them were turning now, gazing over in our direction.

"Let's go!" Ward called back to me. Like that needed to be said.

Another Jumper ran at us out of nowhere, but Ward took it out at the last second, its head ballooning in a red mist just feet away. I heard a scrabbling sound behind me and turned to find another approaching from our 8 o'clock. This one was slightly different. It ran down on all fours, back limbs ridiculously elongated, legs bent at the knee so that they arched high above its rounded back. Its jaw wasn't split in two, but it sported a similar yawning maw filled with jagged teeth. That now familiar white substance dripping down in slippery strands. I raised my rifle, glancing behind me at the pods. We were so close now. Ward had gotten ahead of me. I saw him pause and turn back.

"Jesus, Kessler," his voice rang out over the officer's comms, "shoot the damn thing and let's go. What are you doing?" I scanned the ground up ahead near the pods, but didn't spy any fallen Jumpers in the near vicinity.

Behind the bowed-back Jumper, the one Ward had taken out began to stagger to its feet: just a bloody stump above its shoulders. *Jesus Christ.* I watched as a line of rounds ran up its chest before it could take more than a step forward.

I turned my back on the pods, keeping my eyes on the thing that ran after me now at a loping pace. "McCullough, Binson!" I barked into the comms. Thankfully, we'd had them added to the officer's comms. We didn't want the men getting wind of the details of what we were doing. "Get a sample tube ready."

"For fuck's sake!" Ward yelled back, drowning out their replies of acquiescence. "We don't have time for this. They've been coming in waves. We just hit the tail end of one. There will be more soon. We need to leave."

"It'll only take a minute," I snapped back. I glanced behind me again to see McCullough and Binson running out to meet me. I turned and sprayed the Jumper, pumping round after round into its body until it collapsed on the ground in a heap.

"That's a minute we don't have," Ward snapped back. "A minute in which more of my men could die."

"Tell your men to retreat, then. Get them on the pods. We'll be there as soon as we can. I'd appreciate it if you didn't take off without us... but that's up to you." I had told him nothing was going to stop me from gathering the samples we needed, and I meant it.

He let out a frustrated snarl. "You won't make it back to the pods without suppressing fire if another wave hits."

"Then provide us with suppressing fire," I yelled back, grounding out each syllable. McCullough and Binson had reached my side, handing me a sample tube. I removed the cap with shaking hands. "Gloves!" I shouted to McCullough. He pulled out a pair and handed them to me, while I handed him the test tube to hold. "Binson, glove up too, in case I need your help."

"Oh, interesting," I heard Ward's voice, low and guttural, in my ear. "So now you *do* want my protection. Do I have that right?"

"*Fuck you*, Ward." I hissed into the comms. My cheeks bloomed with heat as I snapped the second glove into place. Binson handed me a thin swab, and I took the test tube back from McCullough. I approached the Jumper, where it lay crumpled in a heap.

Its chest was practically split open, blood pooling on the ground beneath it, white strands still hanging from its open maw. "Binson, prepare a second test tube."

"God damn it," Ward muttered.

I decided to go for the strange white substance first. If we could grab a sample of that and a sample of blood, that would be a decent start.

"Here we go, boys," Ward's voice crackled back over the comms, "we've got another wave heading our way. Keep them off our right flank. Suppressing fire."

My hands shook as I knelt and used the end of the swab to scoop up some of the white material. The thing stank. Of rot, and damp earth, and something foul beneath it. I felt my gorge starting to rise, and I swallowed. The white substance didn't look as much like cobwebs up close. Wet, slippery strands stretched apart as I attempted to scoop some up, sliding right off the swab. I couldn't grab hold of them.

"Damn it, I need tweezers; something to grip it with," I barked in frustration. McCullough held out a pair of long, thin tweezers to me a moment later, and I took them gratefully, dropping the swab onto the ground. I managed to grab hold of a clump of the white strands, and I dropped them carefully into the tube, trying the best I could manage not to let the white substance touch my gloved hands.

"Captain," Binson murmured, "we need to get going."

I could hear the chaos, the pandemonium, ensuing behind us. Ward's voice, then Wren's, ringing out in my ears as they barked out orders, directing the men. Sounds of the swarm, over my shoulder. But I didn't turn my head to look. I had to stay focused. Just like flying, I needed to block out all the external noise and focus on what I had to do. I took a deep breath, steadying myself.

"We need these samples, Binson. That's why we're here."

I heard Binson sighing and felt him moving uneasily behind me. "Yeah, but they aren't going to make it back to the lab if we don't leave soon."

"We're about to be overrun, Captain," McCullough said. "I think it's time to go."

"We need a sample of blood–" I started.

"There's no time, Kessler. Move out. NOW." Ward yelled over the comms, the speaker buzzing in my ear. "That's a goddamn order. MOVE OUT!" It wasn't his words so much as the hint of fear I heard in his voice that caused me to comply.

I snapped the top onto the test tube and turned to find McCullough holding a plastic bag open. I dropped the tube inside, and he sealed it shut. I carefully peeled my gloves off, doing my best not to touch the outer surface, and dropped them onto the ground.

Captain Williams and his men might find them later, along with the swab, and realize we were up to more than a failed attempt to take out their munitions factory. But I couldn't worry about that right now.

My eyes widened as I saw a wave of Jumpers streaming out of the woods on the far flank. The last of Ward's men were clambering onto the pods. It was time to go.

We ran, sprinting for the pods. Ward waited at the door, the men crowded around the edge of each pod door, spraying the swarm with round after round as we climbed aboard. The pod doors were beginning to close, one by one. The glow beneath the neighboring pods told us they were preparing for take-off.

I was the last to jump aboard, and the pod door began to close immediately behind me. It was nearly shut when a loud thud emanated from the door. Then another.

A hand shot through the narrow opening to my left. Practically human, but oddly pale and sinewed. I jumped backwards, gasping, as it flailed wildly, claws swiping the air. It disappeared, just as the door slammed shut with a final shudder.

The walls of the pod were hammered, as Jumpers slammed against it. We were surrounded by thuds and clanging as they threw their bodies against the pod, over and over.

"Fuck me..." Binson murmured, eyes wide. The men were all silent, hushed.

All except for one of the soldiers, who cried out in pain. He looked like he had been seriously injured. He slumped to the floor of the pod, gasping for breath and letting out a moan. A fellow soldier crouched down beside him, holding onto him.

I tore my gaze away from them to find Ward watching me with narrowed eyes. He moved closer to me, until he was right in my face, his voice practically a whisper, "More of my men died today, because of you."

I swallowed, nostrils flaring and eyes going wide. My heart shuddered, skipping in my chest. "Because of me?" I said through gritted teeth. "I was doing what I was sent here to do. I was following orders."

Ward scoffed. "What part of your orders told you to abandon your squad? Huh?" He clenched his jaw, the muscle in the side ticking, and he lowered his voice, getting his volume back under control. "Wren said you just... took off. Up on the third floor. You left them. What were you doing?" He asked, with a cold, calculating look. "Where did you go?"

"What?" I frowned in confusion, my brows crinkling. "We were being shot at. We all scattered. I ran, so I wouldn't get hit. I tried to find cover, I–"

"You weren't told to run, to leave your squad." He held his arm out to the side, shaking his head incredulously.

"So... I should have just stood there and let them shoot me? Unless I was ordered to move?"

"Moving is one thing, finding cover is one thing, you ran off and left your team behind. I get you're a pilot, but things are different down here. On the ground, you run away from your unit; that's essentially desertion. I could technically have you declared AWOL."

"Oh come on, Ward," I scoffed, shaking my head in disbelief. "What the hell are you saying?"

"I'm saying, in the future, you stick with your unit. You stay with your commanding officer, which, for today's mission, was Wren. You do not leave and just take off without permission." He moved closer. I wanted to push him away. "I don't know where you went, or what you were up to, but I don't like it. And I will be *watching* you. *Captain.*"

I could see Wren staring at us, out of the corner of my eye. His expression clouded. My cheeks burned with rage and shame. They thought I'd run away? My mind whirred.

I had left the room, that was true. Searched for cover. But I hadn't been trying to run away. I was just trying not to get killed. I swallowed, thinking over what had happened after that. I'd spoken with the enemy. I Ielped one of their soldiers.

I wanted to tell them what I'd learned. It could be important intel. Information that could help us fight these things. But they would want to know where I got it. Would Ward report me to the Admiral? Try to claim I was some kind of... spy? My gut twisted at the thought. I knew he wanted me off his ship. And with my actions today, I'd practically handed him exactly what he needed.

I forced myself to breathe, taking a deep, steadying breath. "Look, in the air, they're called evasive maneuvers. I was trying to stay alive, take out the enemy. I didn't think I did anything wrong." Ward shook his head, snorted. "But I see what you're saying. I get it." I swallowed my pride and managed to murmur. "It won't happen again. You have my word."

Ward stared me down for a long moment. "Like I said. More of my men are dead, because of you. If you had stayed with the group, not gone off on your own on some solo mission, we wouldn't have wasted so much time searching for you. And if you had given up on gathering samples when I told you to, we wouldn't have needed to hunker down and ride out an additional wave of those things." His voice crumpled slightly. "This entire mission was a failure."

"I get it, Ward, okay?" My breath hitched in my chest. "I'm sorry. Is that what you want to hear? I'm sorry; I fucked up. I was just trying to do my job."

"'Sorry' doesn't bring back my men, Kessler." He murmured. "Next time, I expect you to follow orders, regardless of your personal agenda."

My hands clenched into fists at my sides, my nails digging into my palms so deeply that I was sure I was drawing blood. "My personal agenda?" I sneered up at him, his cold, dark eyes glued to mine. "You know what, Ward? It's not my fault the mission failed. It's not my fault that the goddamn factory is still standing. I had nothing to do with that. Okay?" He looked away from me, across the pod.

"You want to blame me for my own actions; that's fine. But I didn't cause your mission to fail. We were fucked from the moment they ambushed us in that factory. All those men that died; *that's* on you." Ward shook his head, chuckling, his lips splitting into a sick sort of grin.

His eyes found mine again, and they were so dark and fathomless, so full of pain and despair, that I instantly regretted what I'd just said, my stomach sinking.

The injured soldier cried out suddenly across the pod as we hit turbulence. The whole pod shifted and shook, as we were bucked and jostled inside. I grabbed onto one of the metal bars overhead, clinging to it, struggling to stay upright.

Ward did the same, one hand grasping onto a bar above, and the other onto a bar on the wall, over my head. He leaned over me, his forehead almost touching mine, as he looked down at the floor. My left hand landed on his chest as we were shaken back and forth. "Ward..." I murmured, reaching up, I cupped my hand over his cheek, and he flinched away. My hand hovered in the air, not quite touching him, as we swayed back and forth. "I'm sorry," I murmured. "I didn't mean–"

The turbulence calmed, and as the pod went still once more, he pulled away from me, turning and moving between the men, using the overhead bars to work his way over to the injured soldier. Ward knelt next to him, on his other side, grasping onto his arm, talking to him.

The man's eyes kept fluttering shut, then opening again. He was so pale. Too pale. He looked almost as young as the Southern boy I'd helped. I felt tears threatening to gather behind my eyes, and blinked rapidly, trying to keep them at bay.

She's not our enemy... just a person. Captain William's words drifted back to me as I closed my eyes, gripping onto the bars, head hanging down.

I wanted this to end. This nightmare, to end. I'd enlisted because I wanted to fly. Lying on my back, in the damp grass, staring up at those twinkling lights on the Air Force base high above, I'd seen the night sky as a place where I could finally be free.

Free from fear. Free from uncertainty, hatred, and death. All those horrible things that had plagued my hometown. Plagued the world, below. I wanted to leave it all behind. As though by taking to the air, I could somehow escape. Escape death.

But that was all I'd found, up here. The Northern Alliance space station didn't represent freedom. Or peace. It represented death. Suffering. And I wanted it to end. I wanted to bring it down. All of it. Starting with those things, down there. But not just them. The Northern Alliance, the Southern Coalition. The constant, never-ending war. I wanted to end it all. I wanted that, more than anything.

I never wanted to look into another man's eyes and see what I'd just seen in Captain Ward's; my own despair, reflected back to me. The death of hope.

10.

They carried the wounded soldier off first, taking him directly to Med Bay, as we all stood back respectfully, waiting for them to clear the area. I learned his name was Stowell.

Ward hung his head low, a defeated and deflated air to his posture. He paused as he passed by McCullough and Binson, and I watched as he muttered something to them before disappearing into the crowd.

I made my way over to them, my eyebrows raised. "Dinner's in about an hour," McCullough replied to my unspoken question. "Everything okay, Captain?" He inclined his head in the direction Ward had disappeared in. "What was he saying to you in there?" His brows were drawn with concern. Binson just looked pissed.

I shook my head. "Everything's fine. He was just being his typical self," I shrugged, "annoying." I sighed, surveying the hangar. "I'm going to drop the sample off at the lab, then hop in the shower. Why don't you two go get cleaned up, and we'll meet up at dinner."

They moved off in the direction of the First Lieutenant's quarters. It seemed Ward had managed to find space for them, after all.

I made quick work of heading down to the lab to drop off the sample to Lindsay and Topher. They jumped to their feet, eager to see what I'd brought them. I watched their faces fall, just a little, as I held up the single test tube in the plastic bag.

I mumbled some sort of explanation for why we didn't manage to get more, without going into too much detail. I told them maybe we would have an opportunity to head down for a reconnaissance mission somewhere more remote, where we could use our suits. What we really needed was access to just one or two of them at a time, not a whole horde.

Lindsay recovered from her disappointment quickly, or she was just good at hiding it. I asked if they wanted to join us for dinner, but they had already eaten, while we were down on the ground. I left them to their work, and made my way back to my private quarters to shower and change.

I stood under the hot water for longer than I should have, replaying Ward's words on the pod over and over in my mind, letting them really sink in. More men had died because of me.... because of *me*. I felt sick to my stomach standing there. I debated skipping dinner. But I didn't love the thought of sitting in my room alone either. I ultimately decided to dress and head to the Mess Hall.

The mess on board a Northern Alliance Carrier is probably one of the nicest parts of the whole craft. One whole wall of the Mess Hall on board *The Beagle* was taken up by a vast floor-to-ceiling window. In our current position, we had a breathtaking view of the Earth below and the surrounding stars.

Round wooden tables were scattered throughout the room, framed with a combination of benches and chairs. There was a large kitchen attached. On a night like this, a small team of men had likely stayed behind to prepare a meal for the Company upon their return. Much of the "cooking" that happens aboard a Carrier is done by machines, for ease and convenience, but the whole operation still requires human hands to come together fully.

They had music piped in through hidden speakers, and I entered the Mess Hall to find dinner already underway, the hall filled with music, conversation, and bathed in warm light from the globes hanging high above. I'd taken longer than I thought, between my visit down to the lab, and standing in the shower, scalding myself with hot water. McCullough and Binson had to be here somewhere, but I couldn't find them in the crowd. I saw Wren stand up, waving me over.

He was seated at what must be the officer's table, with several of the other First Lieutenants. I was starting to put faces to names now. I recognized Nathan, and the man sitting next to him, wearing glasses, although I didn't know his name. Powers was sitting on his other side.

I nodded to them as I approached, and they glanced at each other before sliding down on the bench to make room for me. I sighed internally. It seemed that word of blame being laid at my door, or at least of my solo escapade, had gotten around. Either that, or they had already been skeptical of me to begin with.

"Where's Ward?" I asked Wren in a clipped tone.

He inclined his head, gazing over my shoulder. I turned to scan the crowd and found Ward over at the bar. The Carriers are all equipped with a bar, kept fully stocked, albeit accessible only on non-duty days or after missions. A light on the wall above the bar would turn red whenever drink service was cut off. All the men knew what that glowing red light meant, casting the bar and faces below in an eerie, ominous glow. Boots on the ground. But for now, the light was mercifully off, and the taps were flowing. Somehow, getting a hold of alcohol was never a problem for the Northern Alliance Armed Forces.

Neither was it difficult for the men to obtain any manner of drugs, back on base. From legal, mainly weed, to illegal, things like Reversol, and the ever-popular Nitrous.

I'd never tried Reversol, myself. It was originally intended to treat early-onset dementia and was formulated to help reinforce the brain's neural synapses, strengthening the neural pathways responsible for memories. However, its unintended effects led to quite the opposite. Reversol created a temporary sort of brain fog, practically erasing memories, especially recent ones. It led to some pretty bizarre behaviors. People forgot who their friends and family were, what they did for a living, and even necessary everyday skills, like how to drive a car, for example.

Thankfully, the effects of Reversol were short-lived. Some people claimed they experienced a state of blissful ignorance, even euphoria, while on it. But there had been far too many accidents, because of the side effects, and I refused to touch it. Nitrous, on the other hand, I'd allowed myself to indulge in several times. It has very few negative side effects, and it leaves the user carefree and giddy to the point of hilarity. The only issue with Nitrous is too large of a dose will knock you out completely, putting you straight to sleep. Nitrous is also expensive and much harder to come by than alcohol, although I knew it could always be found back on base, for the right price.

Ward stood propped against the bar, a glass of dark liquid in his hands. I sighed, watching him. I supposed there were worse vices. "Straight to the hard stuff, this time." Wren shook his head as I glanced back at him. He held his hands up as the men chuckled. "I tried to get him a beer. He wasn't having it."

"Never a good sign," Nathan grimaced, taking a sip of beer himself. He had closely cropped dark hair and dark eyes to match. A full beard and mustache, but he kept it well trimmed.

His eyes were kind. He grinned at me, shaking his head, as he noticed me watching him. "We're in for an interesting evening."

"Oh god," I murmured, resting my chin in my hand. "What does that mean, exactly?"

"Could go one of two ways," the First Lieutenant beside him, wearing glasses, leaned in, holding up a finger. "Either he gets half shit-faced, gets up and sings in front of everyone, which... he isn't even very good, by the way."

I laughed, recalling that night at the bar back on base. The Lieutenant continued, "Then he'll continue to drink, until he's fully shit-faced, and we all go off on our merry way, laughing and singing–"

"Remember that time, after Raleigh," Powers said, grinning, and the men laughed and started talking all at once.

"Or," the Lieutenant went on, raising his voice, holding up a second finger, "or, he gets half-shitfaced, turns into a drunken, depressed, self destructive asshole–"

"Picks a fight." Wren chimed in.

"Tries to get into a fight," the Lieutenant said, at the same time, nodding, "then gets fully shit-faced, and we all go on our not so merry way." He paused, grinning at me. "Either way, we all wake up hungover tomorrow, wishing we were back at boot camp. Because that would be less painful."

"Fuck," I murmured, "you make neither those options sound enticing, I'm going to be honest." He laughed, a full-bellied laugh, the kind of laugh that was contagious. I found myself grinning back at him.

"Eh," he waved a hand at me, "you'll be fine; you just need a drink." A general chorus of agreement rose from around the table, while I shook my head and made noises of protest. Powers stood up, slamming down his empty glass with a thud on the pot-marked wooden table.

"I got ya, Reaper. Be right back."

"No," I turned, calling out to him, "really, Powers, I'm good." But he was already gone. "Jesus Christ…" I murmured, tilting my head back and staring up at the ceiling. "I said neither option sounded enticing. As in, I opt out. Not, 'get me a drink'."

"Oh, there's no opting out," the Lieutenant laughed again, "but nice try." He tipped his glass to me.

"Yeah, you get points for trying," one of the other men added, raising his glass in my direction, before taking a long sip. He stood and held his hand out to me. "First Lieutenant Stevens, Captain. It's an honor to meet you."

I nodded, lips tight, as I stood and reached across the table to shake his hand. I squirmed slightly at the attention. This was partially why I liked to keep my call sign to myself.

Stevens was tall and lanky, with a wide grin, his uniform slightly wrinkled. He wasn't deterred by my silence, grinning broadly at me. "It's a real honor, Captain." He repeated.

I nodded my acknowledgement and sighed to myself, staring out the window at the stars beyond.

"So, ah, how'd it go with the test tubes?" The Lieutenant wearing glasses asked, leaning forward again, voice lowered. "Did you get what you needed?"

I sighed more deeply. "Well, it was a start. Let's put it that way." I shook my head, thinking. "I don't want to put anyone at risk. What we need is a chance to just... swoop down, find one or two of them, gather the samples, and get out. There's no need to do this as part of a larger mission. Right?"

I held my hands out, glancing around the table for confirmation. Wren nodded slowly back to me. I had been speaking my thoughts out loud, but it made perfect sense. Why would we need to join a mission to gather samples in the first place? Especially if it meant I ended up getting blamed for the delays. I decided I would talk to Ward about it tomorrow. There was a more practical way to do this.

"Well, I mean," the Lieutenant sighed, drawing out the last few syllables, "that makes sense. To me, at least. But you know, good luck finding one or two of those things." He took another sip of beer before pushing his large, wire-rimmed glasses back up the bridge of his nose. He had a receding hairline and kept his hair buzzed short, as though he were trying to hide it. He looked too young for it.

I frowned at him. "What do you mean?" His eyebrows went up in response as Powers returned with our drinks, setting a beer down on the table in front of me. I shot him a quick grimace, but he just grinned lopsidedly back at me.

The Lieutenant continued, "I mean, good luck finding just one, like, wandering off on its own. They only travel in packs."

"What's this idiot blathering on about?" Powers asked, taking a sip of beer, wiping the foam off his lips with the back of his hand.

"Yeah, *I'm* the idiot." The Lieutenant pointed at himself, chuckling. "The stories I could tell about this one," he jerked a thumb at Powers, who punched him in the arm. "Ouch." He murmured, rubbing his arm. I grinned, watching them. "I'm First Lieutenant Caleb Molton, by the way." He held a hand out to me, and I reached across the table and shook it. "Also known as Moltonky." I snorted a little at the nickname, hiding it by taking a sip of beer. "And I've been stuck with this idiot next to me since boot camp."

"How unfortunate," I murmured, glancing at Powers. He chuckled, shaking his head, taking another sip of beer.

The officers laughed at that, and Wren slapped Powers on the back as he shook his head.

"Okay," Moltonky went on, "I like you already," he laughed again, "but to be fair, he's not a complete asshole. Unlike some of these guys." He glanced at the men around the table, raising his glass, "You know who you are," several chuckles, "although, we did just hand those Jumper's asses to them, didn't we? So, there's that," he shrugged.

"Cheers," Stevens murmured. And the men raised their glasses, clinking them together. I joined in, and we all took a sip.

"Back to what you were saying before," I leaned forward, catching Molton's eye again, as the men fell back into side conversations. "How do you know they only travel in packs?"

Molton nodded, setting down his glass. He leaned forward, voice hushed, in a conspiratorial fashion. "Well, after Houston– which was fucking brutal, by the way. Obviously, there was a lot of chatter back at base about what went down. It turns out there had been a couple of other units, in other companies, that had run into those things. And this has been happening all over the place. Like, I'm talking all over the goddamn South," he swept his hand, "it's not isolated to a specific area. And it sounds like it's always the same. It might start with just a handful of them, and those are the slow ones," he held up a finger, "they don't move as fast as the others that come later. But no one's ever seen just one of 'em, or two of 'em, from what I've gathered. There are always more, after those first few. And they tend to come in waves, like they did today."

I listened intently, nodding. This was important. I was feeling excited now. Who knows what else the men had learned, just by talking to each other. I took another sip of beer. My head was starting to buzz a little already. That's what I got for drinking on an empty stomach. "That's good to know." I nodded, keeping my voice pitched low. "Anything we can learn about them, anything at all, it's important. It all helps. We need to gather as much information as we can, so we can stop them."

"Stop them?" Moltonky sputtered, pausing with his beer halfway to his mouth. "Is that what we're trying to do?"

I frowned at him and watched as Wren shook his head, staring down at his beer. Nathan sighed, resting his chin in his hand.

"Last I checked, those fuckers were taking out the enemy." Molton shook his head. "I don't know about stopping them…" He held a hand over his chest. "I mean, I'm not saying that's what *I* think. They're taking us out, too. And who knows how long we have left until this thing spreads over the border? But you know… since when has Command given a shit about that? What's a few less soldiers in blue, if they're hitting the enemy where it hurts?"

I sat frozen, a frown on my face, letting his words sink in. Of course Command wanted them stopped; that was the whole point of the mission. Congress was demanding answers. But I wasn't about to tell them any of that. The Admiral had made it clear that the mission was highly classified. There was no way to prevent the men from seeing what was happening right in front of them, but I certainly couldn't go around advertising it. Or sharing information. I sat back, lifting my glass and taking another slow sip.

"Fuck Command," Stevens murmured. "Just wait until more of our sorry asses start turning into those things." An uncomfortable silence fell over the table. Wren threw Stevens what looked like a warning, sideways glance. Stevens quickly dropped his gaze.

I stilled, watching them. *More?* Wren caught my eyes flickering back and forth between them and busied himself with his drink.

"I hope one crawls up the Admiral's asshole." Powers muttered. I couldn't help but snort.

"I'm not volunteering for that," Nathan quipped. The men were laughing as Captain Ward made his way around the table, taking a seat that had been left open next to Wren.

"If you do turn into a Jumper, I don't think you're going to fucking care whose asshole you climb into. Much less that it's an asshole." Molton chuckled.

Ward shook his head. "They're clearly all mindless fucks. Walking around without a shred of themselves left. Just empty husks." The laughter around the table died away, replaced by an uncomfortable silence.

"At least they probably aren't afraid, anymore," Stevens murmured, staring down at the table.

"Wow," Powers murmured, "that got real dark, real fast."

"Captain," Nathan nodded towards Ward, "what number you on?"

Ward sighed, tilting his glass. "I'm not sure, Nathan. But thanks for asking." He nodded in his direction, giving him a wink and a grin, as he lifted his glass in a brief salute and took a sip.

"How's Stowell?" Powers asked.

Ward shook his head, eyes down at the table. "Not good. Last I heard." He fell silent for a moment. "I told them to keep me posted."

The table fell into a deeper silence. He'd been the one on our pod, with the stomach wound. I sighed, swirling the beer in my glass in a circle. I looked up to find Ward's eyes on me. But he looked away quickly, a frown on his face. My stomach twisted. We'd been having a decent time. The men needed this. Time to decompress, let off steam. I didn't want it ruined. I watched him for several seconds, flashing back to that moment on the pod, and how I'd felt the urge to comfort him. How I'd almost stroked his cheek. What was I thinking? He didn't need comfort from me. And I was sure he didn't want it. I'd almost embarrassed myself. In front of all those men, too. It was so unlike me. I'd just been rattled, after everything that had happened.

"Are we cool enough to sit with the cool kids?" I heard McCullough's voice over my shoulder, and turned and flashed him a brief smile, glad for the interruption. He grinned back at me, but his hazel eyes were heavy with concern.

He must have picked up on how shaken I was, earlier. I felt a stab of guilt at the thought. I was their Captain. I was supposed to stay calm. In control. Not let my emotions, fear, or otherwise, get to me. But I'd never been able to hide anything from him.

McCullough stared at the table in front of me, empty save for my beer, and frowned. "Didn't you get something to eat?"

I sighed, eyes sliding sideways. "Not yet." I wasn't sure I could, if I were being honest, but I wasn't about to say that out loud.

"You need to eat something," his frown deepened. "You shouldn't be drinking on an empty stomach." He was right. The beer was going straight to my bloodstream at this point. I could already feel it. I'd always been somewhat of a lightweight, which was embarrassing enough. I didn't want to advertise that to the men by getting drunk off half a beer.

"Oh, look at you, mother hen," Stevens crooned.

"Shut it, Stevens." Binson barked. But he was half grinning. "Do I need to kick your ass? Was that mission not enough?" He cracked his knuckles as he moved over and pulled a chair up to the table near Stevens.

Stevens just chuckled, shaking his head. "I'd destroy you, asshole."

"Sure you would." Binson laughed, and McCullough sighed. I hid my smile, watching them, glad they were getting along with the men.

McCullough cleared his throat. "I'm grabbing you a plate, if you won't get one yourself," he looked pointedly down at me.

"You need to eat, too." Wren turned to Captain Ward, frowning at his half-empty glass. "You'll regret it later if you don't."

"Jesus," Ward sighed, huffing out a breath. "I'll go grab us something. Calm down." He stood, leaving his glass behind. Was he offering to make me a plate, too? I stood as well, and he shot me a look. "I said I got it."

I climbed out of the bench. "No worries, I can get my own."

He rolled his eyes. "Oh, I'm sorry. I forgot, you're perfectly capable of getting your own food. How misguidedly sexist of me." He held a hand over his chest. The men chuckled. They were unaware of our earlier argument. Besides Wren, of course. He watched us under hooded eyes, a wary expression on his face.

"Very funny," I smirked at him. "It's not that, actually. I just want to make sure you don't poison my food."

"Ooh," a chorus of laughs and commentary rose from the table. McCullough sighed, crossing his arms. The look on his face reminded me so much of a disappointed parent that I couldn't help but grin.

But Ward seemed to find my comment amusing. He threw his head back and laughed. I could tell he was tipsy, at least. If not on his way to being half-shit faced. He shook a finger at me, smirking as he raised an eyebrow. "Good one. But I don't think I need to go to that level of effort to get you killed. I think you'll take care of that all on your own."

He watched me closely, waiting for my reaction. My cheeks flushed, and I turned abruptly and walked away from the table. "Oooh, burn." I heard one of the men exclaim.

Ward walked a step behind me, speeding up until he matched my pace. He didn't bother to look at me, keeping his eyes forward, the ghost of a smirk on his lips. I clenched my fists. He knew he'd gotten to me. And how was that? How did this man know exactly what to say, what to do, to push me over the edge?

I took a deep breath and forced my eyes forward. "The men were having a nice evening, you know. Before you joined us. It would be a shame to ruin it."

"Yeah?" We'd reached the kitchen, and Ward grabbed a plate, handing it out to me. "Well, I think Stowell's about to kick the bucket. So... you know. That'll probably ruin their evening, either way."

I glared at him, a sharp retort on my tongue. But I decided not to share it. I paused, considering the plate in his outstretched hand before reaching over and grabbing one myself from the stack.

Ward nodded. "Right. I forgot, you don't need my help. For anything. Ever." His eyes narrowed. "You know, because you're a one-woman show, or whatever." He studied me, a slow grin spreading over his features as I fought to keep my expression neutral.

He moved a step closer, his voice dropping lower. "I guess you're going to save us all, huh? All by yourself?" He was practically sneering at me now, his mouth curving in that wicked grin I despised.

My eyes narrowed, and I fought to halt the bloom of red spreading over my cheeks, as I fixed him with my iciest stare. The one I reserved for when my men had thoroughly and completely pissed me off.

"Oh, except for when you need me to sacrifice my men, to save your sorry ass." He moved another step closer to me. "Don't worry, next time I'll tell them to stand down, and let you get yourself killed. Gladly."

I took a deep, shuddering breath, eyes flickering back and forth over his features. He was still angry about the mission. That much was obvious. But his eyes... they held that same darkness I'd seen the first night we'd met.

I don't know what made me do it, but instead of escalating the argument, I moved closer to him, dropping my voice low. "I never said I didn't need your help, Ward. And no, I can't do this all on my own. I don't think that at all. If you're willing to help me, work with me, rather than against me, then I'll gladly accept your help."

He stilled, his eyes flickering back and forth over mine, before falling to my lips, as I spoke. My gut twisted as his expression darkened.

I ignored the fluttering in my core and continued, "I don't think I can save everyone; I'm not that naive. I just want to do what I can to make a difference. Even if it's just one tiny part that I play." I shrugged. "That's all any of us can do. And if enough of us are willing to do that, to try, then maybe we have a chance of winning, after all."

His eyes kept returning to my lips, as I spoke, but he pulled them away to meet my gaze, his chest heaving slightly. "There's no winning, Kessler, not anymore. It's too late for that." My heart sank at his words.

"Jordan," I said softly. His brows creased. "It's Jordan; my name." My heart thundered in my chest, recalling how he'd asked for my name, that first night we met. That night was very similar to this one. The scents of the bar, the music, the men's voices, the chatter and clatter in the Mess Hall, and the underlying buzz of fear. That fever pitch, of collective nerves, of men, on the edge of the abyss, unraveling. I felt myself leaning closer to him, involuntarily. His jaw clenched, that now familiar muscle ticking. He nodded, looking away, taking a deep breath.

"I'm going to call you Kessler, if it's all the same to you," he murmured, his expression cold, eyes hardened again. I swallowed, nodding, and turned away from him. I grabbed the first set of tongs I came to, throwing a clump of salad on my plate. Chicken. Selecting things at random, without paying any attention to what I was doing.

Why did I care? Why the fuck did I care what he did or didn't call me? I needed to pull it together. I was letting him get to me. Mess with my head. Why he wanted to do that was beyond me. But he was good at it. And a part of me hated him for it. I'd spent years wrapping myself in a thick layer of indifference. Never letting myself feel anything other than determination. Drive. Ambition, and pride. I didn't let any more dangerous emotions in, otherwise, I'd drown in them.

I was vaguely aware of him still standing in place, watching me, but I ignored him, grabbing silverware and a napkin, and moving to leave the room. As I did, a man in a private's uniform moved past me. He held his cap in his hands as he approached Ward, eyes heavy with grief. I sighed internally, watching out of the corner of my eyes as he murmured something to the captain.

Ward nodded, lips tight, and jaw clenching. He set the plate back down on the table and gripped the man's shoulder for a moment, murmuring something back to him.

I exited the kitchen and made my way back over to the table, back erect. I had a feeling Stowell hadn't made it. I tried not to picture his pinched, pale face. His cries of pain. Nope. Push it down. Push it aside. It was too painful to look any closer.

I set my plate down with a thud, a little too hard, and squeezed back onto the bench. The men beside me giving me space.

Moltonky watched me, eyebrows raised. "What'd you do with his body?" I looked up at him, brows creased. I thought he meant Stowell, for a moment, then I realized he was joking, as the others gathered around the table grinned, waiting for me to respond. "I mean, I can only assume you took care of Ward..." he shrugged, "prick deserved it." He downed the rest of his beer while the others laughed. I just shook my head, scoffing half-heartedly.

Ward returned a minute or two later, eyes downcast, as he sat down on the edge of the bench, his back to the table, head hanging down for a moment, then he turned and grabbed his glass, chugging the rest of it down. "Where's your goddamn food?" Wren asked.

"Stowell didn't make it." Ward replied simply, his tone clipped. He sat there, as the men hung their heads, silent.

Wren lifted his glass. "For Stowell." The others followed suit, repeating after him, and glasses clinked. Ward nodded. He sat staring out at space, at the Earth below, for a minute or two. I picked at my food, watching him.

"Had he been with you a long time?" I murmured.

Ward shook his head, chuckled slightly. "This was only his second mission." My stomach lurched at his words.

Then he stood, empty glass in hand. "I can't sit here. I'll be on the bridge." He turned and left abruptly.

Wren met my eyes with a dark expression. He just shook his head.

"Should we give him a minute?" Nathan asked, brushing a knuckle back and forth over his mustache, staring down at the table.

"Yeah," Moltonky nodded, "give him a bit. Then we'll go see if he wants company." I sighed, setting my fork down. I felt too sick to eat.

McCullough cleared his throat. "It's getting late anyway, we might head down to get some rest." I didn't respond, just stared back at him glumly. "You okay, Captain?" He asked quietly.

I nodded quickly. Maybe a little too quickly. "Yeah, I'm fine." I shrugged. "I might just go take a walk around for a bit. I dunno... I'll probably wander down to the lab. Check in on how it's going so far."

McCullough nodded, eyes on me, a solemn expression on his face. "Okay. We'll keep our comms on; just give us a shout if you need anything." I nodded to him gratefully and stood to leave. I felt suffocated suddenly, the noise and din of the Mess Hall overwhelming.

"Stop by the bridge later," Wren called out. I turned, unsure if he was speaking to me or someone else, but his intense blue eyes were locked on me. "If you're still up," he shrugged.

"We'll probably be up late. He has trouble sleeping sometimes. Doesn't like to be alone."

I blinked at him for a moment. "Do you really think that's a good idea?" I wasn't being sarcastic. I was truly curious. Why would he suggest I come sit up with them? With Ward? What good would that possibly do?

Wren smirked slightly, the corners of his lips curling up. He nodded, raising an eyebrow at me. "Yeah, actually. I do."

I swallowed, my throat suddenly thick, my cheeks growing warm. "Okay..." I said, clearing my throat, "I'll see how I feel later."

Wren just nodded, looking satisfied with my response, and went back to his drink. I turned and left, dropping my practically full plate off on the conveyor belt leading to the dish room as I went, with a stab of guilt. There were people down on Earth who didn't have enough to eat. I hated wasting food, but I knew it would only turn my stomach.

I fled the Mess Hall, taking random turns down the winding corridors of the station, which were mercifully empty for the moment. I needed to be alone. Needed space, and time to think. I decided to skip going to the lab. That had been more of an excuse, anyway. I wasn't hopeful that they could have possibly gleaned anything helpful this quickly. I knew most lab tests took several hours to run. Some might need to run overnight, or even over the course of a full day.

I ended up wandering the corridors aimlessly, nodding absentmindedly to any soldiers who passed me, throwing me a quick salute.

In the end, I headed back to my private quarters. I stood outside the door for a moment, debating turning back and heading to the bridge, but my stomach twisted and turned. I hadn't managed to eat much of anything at dinner, and the beer hadn't helped. Every time I thought of walking into the bridge, my stomach flipped over. I decided I would just have to disappoint Wren, and I ducked into my room.

I spent the remainder of the evening curled up on the couch, pulling up news reels. Anything and everything I could find on the Jumpers, and their spread. I was relieved to learn the disease hadn't managed to cross over the border yet. But there had been reports of sightings nearby, and there was talk of whether Congress should establish additional border control troops in anticipation.

Time was ticking. Meanwhile, I was here, messing around, failing to get the samples we needed, and following nonsensical orders. Why had Ward sent me into the factory in the first place? I was going to have to confront him tomorrow. Demand that we start doing things my way. Because we were running out of time. And I dreaded what the consequences might be.

11.

I woke up feeling oddly sore the next morning. It felt as though every muscle in my body was aching. Clearly, running at a crouch during the mission yesterday was something my body was far from used to. I touched the spot on my shoulder that the bullet had grazed gingerly. Thankfully, it was superficial, more of a scrape than anything else. But it still stung.

I groaned and forced myself out of bed and straight into a hot shower. I stood under the stream of scalding water until I started to feel more human again. I'd hardly had anything to drink the night before, but the combination of stress, alcohol, and lack of food, left me feeling less than stellar.

I got dressed in my officer's uniform and braided my hair into double braids, tucking them into a low bun, and pinning them in place.

By the time I made it down to the Mess Hall, I was relieved to find my appetite had returned, announced by my growling stomach.

I grabbed coffee first, then a full plate of bacon, eggs and toast. I found an open table over by the windows. I was pretty sure it was the same one we had sat at last night, and I started eating.

It wasn't too long before McCullough and Binson wandered over my way. McCullough glanced at my plate as he sat down, a forkful of food halfway to my mouth, and smiled.

"Glad to see your hunger strike has ended." He grinned as I scowled back at him.

"Thankfully, my appetite has returned this morning." I shrugged.

"Well, I can't say that's the case for everyone." He nodded over my shoulder, and I turned to see several of the Lieutenants had gathered at the table behind us. Most of them were nursing only a cup of coffee. Wren sat there with bloodshot eyes, sipping slowly from his mug. He saw me watching him and tipped his head towards me.

I turned back, a grin on my face. "Yeah, sure looks like it. I'm guessing they all had a bit too much to drink last night?"

"So, you didn't end up joining them?" Binson asked, stretching and yawning loudly.

I shook my head. "Nah, I didn't feel up to it; just went back to my room."

McCullough nodded. "That was probably for the best. We went back and played cards for a bit. Much calmer evening than they had, from what I've heard. Sounds like it was a wild night."

I sighed, running a hand over my hair and tucking the flyaways that had escaped back behind my ears. "Well, I'm glad I wasn't there then." I turned and surveyed the room. "I wonder when Ward will make an appearance. Sounds like I might be waiting for a bit."

McCullough scanned the room as well. "What do you need him for?"

I shrugged. "I want to talk to him about last night." I lowered my voice. "It made no sense that he forced us to head into the factory. I get he's the commanding officer, but that shouldn't get in the way of us doing our jobs. We need to focus on gathering the intel we need." I thought for a moment, swallowing a mouthful of coffee. I knew I could trust them; I just wasn't sure if I was ready to share what had happened in the factory.

Binson shook his head grimly. "Didn't make any sense to me, that's for sure."

"I have an idea. I'd like to propose a recon mission for tonight; just us." I paused, thinking. "I know using our flight suits near cities or high-value targets isn't viable." They nodded stoically. I'd filled them in about the EMP guns, neglecting to inform them that Ward had shot me with one. "But what if we have him set us down in the middle of nowhere, but close enough to a location that has had sightings reported recently? I think we could use our suits then. Swoop in and grab what we need, and get out quickly."

They were nodding, leaning in and listening intently. "Okay, I like the sound of that, but how are we going to find them?" Binson asked, frowning, "No one seems to know where they go, when they aren't attacking, that is. If we just choose a spot that's too remote, it seems like the odds wouldn't be in our favor of running across them."

I nodded, chewing my bottom lip. Then I sighed and leaned in closer, "I have a way we might be able to draw them to us."

McCullough and Binson frowned, looking at each other for a moment. "Okay..." McCullough started, trailing off. "What is it?"

"Good morning!" An oddly chipper voice called out over my shoulder. I jumped slightly, turning to see Ward standing there, a shit-eating grin on his face. "And what are we whispering about?" He moved over to the bench, taking a seat. He leaned forward, "I love secrets." He murmured.

I sighed loudly, sitting back and shooting the men a look. "Nothing, Ward," I muttered, taking a sip of coffee. "You're looking so... refreshed, this morning, Captain."

He shot me another grin. "And that surprises you? Hmm." He shrugged, taking a sip of coffee himself.

I couldn't help but grin a little, shaking my head. "Yeah, to be honest, it does."

"We heard you boys got up to some shenanigans last night..." McCullough grinned, "but apparently, you're no worse for wear."

Ward grinned more broadly, shaking his head. "Nope. I feel great this morning. And, good news, I received a message from Command: no boots on the ground tonight. We're ordered to hang steady and wait for our next assignment." He shrugged, "But I'm not anticipating they'll send anything our way for a bit. At least not for another day or so."

The men smiled, nodding, and tucking into their own plates of food. I noticed Ward wasn't eating again. Had he already eaten, or was he not feeling as well as he'd like us to believe? I had a hard time believing the man wasn't hungover. I'd seen him down at least two or three tumblers myself last night at dinner.

"Well, that's perfect, actually," I said, smiling over at him. "Because I'd like to speak with you about planning a recon mission for tonight. It would be just us," I nodded at McCullough and Binson. "No need to put any of your men at risk. They can enjoy the night off."

Ward's brow wrinkled slightly, and he frowned down into his mug. "What sort of thing do you have in mind?"

I leaned forward, explaining again my idea to use our flight suits, out in the middle of nowhere. "We can choose a location where we would be highly unlikely to encounter anyone with EMP guns, and if we stay away from any major cities, we can set down in our fighters and travel in our suits from there."

Ward's frown only deepened as I spoke. He nodded slowly, listening until I finished. "You want me to send you down, just the three of you, all by yourselves, to hopefully draw a horde of those things down on you?" He looked up at me, eyebrows raised. "Is this a recon, or a suicide mission, Kessler?"

I sighed loudly, tipping my head to the ceiling. I looked back at him, unable to hide my exasperation. "You don't want us joining you on your missions, because apparently, we only delay you, hold you up, and risk you losing more of your men. So... the solution is obvious; send us down on our own, we find a few of them, gather the samples we need, and get out. We'll be in and out quickly, no harm done, and no risk to your men. We'll have our suits. If we're in danger of being overrun, we'll just fly away." I shrugged.

"Sure, that sounds good, in theory. But there are a couple flaws to your plan. One, I don't know how you plan to find them on demand, and two, even if you do manage to do that, what makes you think you can locate just one or two of them? We've only ever seen them traveling in large groups. And three, just flying away sounds easy enough, but things can go wrong– go south, quickly. With only three of you, you'll have no backup, no cover fire. No one to watch your back while you're gathering samples," he shrugged, "you can't do that, and be shooting at the same time." He shook his head, cutting me off as I started to interject. "I don't like it. I don't like any of it. I think it makes the most sense for you to stick with joining us on our missions, gathering samples as the opportunity arises."

I frowned at him, struggling to keep my voice calm. "I understand your concerns, but I'm telling you, we can handle it. We can figure it out. If we are in any danger at all, we'll retreat immediately."

Ward shook his head. "No, I don't think so."

I stared at him for a moment. "What do you mean, no?" I said quietly. "It's not your call, Ward. I'm in charge of this mission." I pointed between myself and my men. "I'm the commanding officer, and I decide what we do. Not you."

Ward was smirking, shaking his head, as I spoke. "No, that's not entirely accurate. I'm the commanding officer aboard *The Beagle,* and you're aboard *The Beagle,* so I will determine *when* and *where* you and your men set down."

I grit my teeth, leaning towards him. "*I* am responsible for myself and my men. Not you. The Admiral made it clear–"

"The Admiral made it clear that *I* am the commanding officer on board." Ward glared at me; any hint of humor gone from his expression. "Do we really need to go over this again? Or should I call him and explain that you can't follow his orders? Maybe you need a reminder."

A deadly silence had fallen in the vicinity of our table as Ward's voice rose, floating over to where Wren and the other Lieutenants who had managed to make it to breakfast were sitting. I could sense them all watching us now, waiting to see how I would respond. I kept my breathing shallow and even. Not betraying a hint of what I was feeling externally.

"I understand the Admiral's orders," I said calmly, keeping my eyes on him. "What I don't understand, is why you and I seem to be at odds in carrying them out. I recall him giving you explicit instructions on the importance of the success of this mission. Maybe you're the one who needs a *reminder*." I watched him, one eyebrow raised, turning it back on him to respond.

Ward stilled, studying me closely. There was a long pause before he responded. "We'll move forward with the mission you've laid out." He began, his voice calm and even. "But you will not be executing this mission with just three men. I will be providing an armed contingent to accompany you, just as the Admiral suggested may be necessary." He swallowed, licked his lips, and picked up his coffee mug, then set it back down again. "Does that sound reasonable?" He asked.

I let out a breath, my chest deflating. I thought for a moment before nodding. That was likely the closest thing to a compromise I was going to get from him. "Yes," I said evenly, my voice cold and formal sounding to my own ears. "That sounds reasonable."

"Good." Ward snapped, his tone somewhat sharp. He stood abruptly. "Report to the bridge at 1400 hours. We'll map out the recon mission and execute tonight."

I nodded my agreement and watched as he stalked away, out of the Mess Hall entirely. McCullough and Binson sat back, sighing. Binson shook his head, grinning, as he downed his coffee. "Well, that was a nice little pissing contest. Thanks for the entertainment, Captain." He grinned at me over his mug.

"Do you think he left to go puke?" McCullough asked Binson, turning to him.

"Oh yeah," Binson nodded, smirking, "he was definitely leaving to go hurl. He looked a little green."

"I think you got to him, Captain." McCullough grinned over at me.

I shook my head, smirking a little in spite of myself. He had left his coffee behind, the mug almost full. "I don't think it was me that got to him. Maybe he wasn't feeling as chipper as he'd like everyone to believe."

Molton shook his head, migrating over to our table from the one beside us. "Yeah, he feels like shit."

"How're you feeling this morning, Moltonky?" McCullough asked, grinning at him and slapping him on the back as he took a seat.

Molton winced. "Oh, I'm feeling great; I ran six miles this morning." Binson sputtered into his mug, almost spitting out a mouthful of coffee. Wren made his way over to join us, followed by Nathan. "I'm just fucking with you. I think I'm dying." Molton sighed. "Somehow, we never learn..."

"Nope," Wren grimaced in agreement, shaking his head.

"Why does he do that?" I shook my head, my gaze on the doorway out of the Mess Hall. "Try to pretend like he's fine? Like nothing ever gets to him? It's such an obvious, fake act."

Wren shrugged, shaking his head. "Just how he is. He's always been like that. Back when we were just privates, we'd all be scared shitless, heading into battle. But he would always act like he wasn't afraid. He tried to make everyone else feel less afraid, too. And somehow, it seemed to work." He shrugged again. "I always felt better, knowing he was there, fighting next to me." Molton was nodding in agreement.

McCullough sniggered, watching me. "Are you being serious right now, Captain?" He glanced over at Binson, who shrugged and shook his head, smirking a little.

"What?" I frowned at them. "About what?"

"Like you don't do that? Try to hide how you're really feeling? When have you ever admitted you're scared, or worried about something?" He looked at me incredulously, and the other men at the table started to smile and chuckle, watching us.

"That's different," I frowned, shaking my head at him.

"How is that different?" He asked, laughing now. "It's exactly the same thing."

"No," I shook my head, shrugging. "If you're talking about flying, dog fighting, it's not the same."

"Oh come on, in what way?"

I shrugged again, leaning back. "Because..." I struggled to put what I felt into words, "that's not an act. I'm not feeling... afraid, when I climb into a fighter."

The men dissolved into a fit of laughter at that. "Ow," Moltonky groaned, a hand on his head. "Don't make me laugh right now."

"I'm being serious," I said, grinning. I shook my head. "I dunno, it's just different, somehow. Flying. Being on the ground, exposed, out in the open. Nothing to block a stray bullet from taking you out..." I trailed off, my grin disappearing at the looks on their faces. "It's different."

The men fell silent, eyes down on the table. "I don't envy you, what you do," I said, my voice dropping low. "I respect it. And I don't want to put anyone at risk." I sighed. "I'll go meet with Ward this afternoon. Come up with a plan that puts as few men as possible at risk but will hopefully still allow us to get what we need."

The men nodded, sipping their coffees and sitting quietly, staring off into space.

I met Wren's eyes, and he nodded solemnly at me. "Don't worry about it, Captain," Wren murmured. "We'll do whatever needs to be done to stop those things. It's only a matter of time before they take us all out. If this is our chance at stopping them, we're going to take it. You just tell us what you need, and we'll have your back. There isn't any man here who wouldn't do what needs to be done."

I nodded to him, tears springing unexpectedly to my eyes. "Thank you, Lieutenant." I managed to murmur.

I stood and excused myself, leaving them behind to enjoy the rest of the morning the best they could. I needed to get ready. Needed to have a firm plan in place on how we were going to execute this mission. I would work with Ward, find common ground, and do whatever was necessary to make this mission count. But first, I needed to get to the lab.

12.

The doors to the lab slid open with a whoosh, and a rush of stale air, scented with a hint of chemicals, hit me in the face.

The lights were once again dimmed, a pale glow overhead that wasn't strong enough to reach the corners of the vast space. I moved through it on silent footsteps, scanning back and forth. It wasn't long before I found Lindsay, eyes pressed tightly to a large microscope. She had to stand on a step stool to make herself tall enough to peer through the rubber sight.

"Linds," I murmured gently as I approached. I still managed to startle her. She jumped back, wobbly slightly on the stool.

"Jesus Jordan, you scared the shit out of me." She sighed, and her shoulders slumped, then she stepped down off the foot stool.

"Anything yet?" I asked, voice pitched low. I saw the lab techs working several tables away, glancing over at us. I knew it was probably too soon, but I was eager to hear if she'd been able to learn anything from the samples so far, meager as they were.

She sighed, rubbing the skin around her eyes, the indents of the microscope lens visible as red indent lines. "I spent the evening in the Biohazard Lab, preparing the samples." She nodded towards a door with a large biohazard symbol on it, over on the far-left wall. It was framed by a series of windows, allowing a view into the stark white space. "Until we figure out what this thing is and how it spreads, I'm taking every safety precaution I can." I nodded my understanding.

She sighed again, stretching her back, rotating her head on her shoulders as though she were working out the kinks. "I can say, preliminarily, that I am confident we're dealing with some sort of fungal infection, just like we suspected." She sighed, gazing back at the microscope. "I'm attempting to run some tests now, to get specifics, but I'm not sure we have enough raw material to work with at this point."

I nodded grimly, "I know...I'm sorry we didn't get more last night..." I trailed off, "But I have a plan. I'm hoping to meet with Ward shortly, get back down there, hopefully this evening." I paused. "There's no boots on the ground tonight, but I'm proposing a recon mission, just for the purposes of gathering what we need." Lindsay nodded at my words.

"Well, if he agrees, I could definitely use more samples of what you retrieved already; the white substance, plus blood and tissue, like we discussed." I nodded swiftly. "You should probably check in with Topher while you're here; he's rigged up something to patch into a video feed on the ground, and he wants to run some analysis on their movement patterns. The video feed should help us gather more information on their morphological changes as well."

Lindsay led me through the labyrinth of the lab back to where Topher sat ensconced at a small desk in a dark corner. He frowned at me as I explained what I had in mind.

"Okay…" he said slowly. "And how do you plan to draw them to you? You're going to just set down in the middle of nowhere and hope you stumble across some Jumpers?"

"Well," I took a deep breath, chest rising and falling once as I decided, "I learned something… some information that might be helpful."

An eyebrow went up, over the wire rim of his glasses, and Topher leaned back, crossing his arms over his chest, peering up at me. "Learned what?"

"A way to potentially… attract them. Draw them to us." I said slowly. I was reluctant to share how I'd learned the information exactly, but I didn't see much way around it. "We can use our comms. The transmissions: they're attracted to it, somehow. Especially the higher frequencies. I figured we could stay on the channel we used during the last mission, or maybe jump around a bit if that's not working. We might have to experiment, but we can at least start with the frequency we used for this last mission."

"Wait, what?" Lindsay hissed, glancing around, as though other people were hiding in the lab, listening in on our conversation. The lab techs were too far away to overhear us now. "You think they're attracted to comms transmissions? Electromagnetic radiation?" Her eyes went wide, and she sputtered slightly, "Wait, how do you know this?"

At the same time, from Topher, "How did you find out? Why didn't you tell us?"

I held my hands up as they spoke over each other, peppering me with questions. "Okay, okay," I said, "I ran into some... soldiers, last night." My voice dropped lower, instinctively. "Southern Coalition soldiers." Lindsay's eyes went wide. "They stumbled across me. I got cut off from the group. I was... helping one of them. He was injured."

Lindsay's eyebrows went up, her eyes flickering back and forth over mine. "Jordan..." She murmured.

"He was so young," I continued, "he wasn't a threat. I... anyway, they let me go. Their Captain. Escorted me safely out of the building." Her eyes grew wider in surprise. I just nodded. "Yeah." I shrugged. "They weren't the monsters I was expecting."

"And they told you this? That they're attracted to electromagnetic radiation?" Topher prompted.

I nodded, "Yes. Well, no, they didn't use that term." I corrected, frowning. "One of them was a radio operator. And one of the soldiers accidentally let it slip that we had drawn the

Jumpers down on our position by using our comms links. The radio operator said something about the high frequencies agitating them, drawing them in. He used some acronym, I think it started with a 'G'? But the lower frequencies... he made it sound like it was the opposite... that they didn't like them." I paused, thinking back. "I saw their radio, when we left, the dial was set to 750 MHz, and I asked how he was able to transmit, if the radio waves drew them. He told me then it was the low frequencies that were key."

"Jesus Christ," Topher leapt up, grabbing my arm. "We need to test this. Immediately. If we can draw them in with higher frequencies, keep them away with low frequencies; for fuck's sake, Captain." His eyes went wide. "We might be able to use this to control their behavior. We might be able to disrupt it entirely. Keep them where we want them."

Lindsay chimed in. "Ants are sensitive to electromagnetic radiation. Electricity... they often seem drawn to electrical boxes–" she paused for a moment, thinking, "occasionally they'll chew through wires, and they'll get electrocuted. When that happens, they release attack pheromones, drawing other ants to them, driving them to attack..." she trailed off again. "That may be how they're communicating...." She paced back and forth as she spoke. "So maybe the comms transmissions somehow disrupt their communication? Assuming this is some sort of combination between a fungal infection and a mutation with the host DNA of course, like we suspect, but how..." She stopped abruptly, moving over to the computer on the far wall. The screen lit up after a moment.

Topher watched her, his chin cupped in his hand, a thoughtful expression on his face. "Okay, so we test this theory out tonight, if you can," he said, "try drawing them in with higher frequencies on the comms link. We'll keep track of which frequencies you try. Cycling through, maybe every ten minutes or so? We don't know how far away they'll be as a starting point, though. I wonder how far away they can detect–"

Lindsay cut him off: "I don't think there's ever been any clear data on that, at least in terms of ants. But ants can detect the electromagnetic fields associated with the Earth, similar to some species of fish, migratory birds, and bats. That's how they're able to navigate. Scout ants use the Earth's electromagnetic field to guide them. They explore great distances from their nest to find food. They lay down a pheromone trail as they go to help them find their way back."

"Wait, scout ants?" I asked, frowning, turning to her. "What are they? Like they do recon? They go out ahead of the group?"

Lindsay nodded after a moment. "Yeah, usually to search for food sources. They'll scout ahead and signal the other ants to join them when they locate a food source."

I stared at her, taking in what she was saying. "Are they slower than other ants?"

Lindsay thought for a moment. "I wouldn't say they're slower, necessarily. They can move fast, but they just sort of wander around, searching for food."

I nodded, thinking. "But they wouldn't be the ones attacking, then? They'd be searching, signaling the others..." I thought back to Molton's comments about how the Jumpers start off with one or two, maybe a handful at a time, before the first wave hits. I thought of how the first Jumper I ever encountered seemed to be more idle, wandering around until he found... me. But he hadn't attacked me. He left that for the others, who came after.

"Right," Lindsay said, "they aren't soldier ants. Scout ants even look a bit different from soldier ants. The soldier ants are the ones that attack; fight to protect their nest. They are larger and have larger mandibles, typically." I frowned again, thinking of the split, mandible-like jaws that I had seen on some of the Jumpers. I shuddered involuntarily.

"I think we're getting somewhere," I murmured. "You should see the jaws on some of them. They're deformed, split in two, with these spiky things coming off of them. I'm not sure if they're shards of cartilage or bone, or teeth that somehow morphed, or what." I shook my head.

"Okay," Topher chimed back in. "We need images; we need the video feed. I'm going to get that set up for tonight. I'll get your helmet modified for you to wear, okay?" I turned back to him and nodded swiftly.

"We'll analyze their appearance, their movements. And we'll get the samples we need." Lindsay added. "I think this is making sense, the more we talk it through. If they're communicating via pheromones somehow... if they're sensitive to different frequencies, hopefully we can use all of that."

I nodded excitedly, then paused. "Wait, there's one more thing. He–Billy, the radio operator, he said something else, about the EMP shield over their building. He said he thought that helped, too. To keep them away."

Topher frowned, looking over at Lindsay, and she turned to him. Some brief message seemed to transmit between them. Once more, I felt that nagging feeling, like they'd discussed this already, without me. Or almost like... they knew something I didn't. I pushed the thought away. I was being paranoid now. They were just close, clearly. Had become close. If there was anyone on board this ship that I trusted, it was Lindsay. I knew she wouldn't keep things from me.

"That's good," Topher said, as they both turned back to me. "This is all super helpful information. This could be the difference in us figuring out how to stop them." He nodded at me solemnly. "And don't worry, Captain, we'll keep all of this to ourselves."

"We'll only tell the lab techs what they need to know to do their jobs," Lindsay added, then snorted a little. "Which, quite frankly, is very little. They're discrete, I'm sure we can trust them, but we'll tell them only what they need to know to run samples. Just to be safe." I nodded at her gratefully.

"Good." I thought for a moment, then breathed out a sigh. "Okay, so we'll do the video feed tonight. Get the samples. Now, all I have to do is work out the details with Ward." I bit my lower lip. "How soon can you have the video feed ready?" I asked, turning to Topher.

He shrugged nonchalantly. "Give me a half hour? Give or take. It shouldn't take long."

I nodded. "No issue there. I'm not meeting with Ward until 1400 hours. We'll figure out what time we're setting down from there." Topher nodded, and Lindsay moved over towards the far end of the lab, back towards the exit, clearly planning to walk me back. "Alright," I said, moving to follow her, "I'll see you later, before we leave." Topher held a hand up in a wave goodbye, and was already turning back towards the desk, to whatever he had been working on before I interrupted them.

13.

When I arrived at the bridge, right on time, I came to a halt halfway through the door. There was a flurry of activity inside the room.

Ward saw me standing in the doorway and waved me forward, a grim expression on his face. "Our plans are going to have to wait a few days." He said stiffly.

"What?" I asked incredulously.

He sighed, holding up a hand. "I know. It's beyond my control. Command is sending us back down."

"Already?" I frowned over at the topographical map rotating above the table.

Ward sighed. "We're heading to Colorado. Going to be camped out for a few days." He studied the map. "I doubt we'll see much action. We're there as a contingency only, just in case they route their men in that direction." He shook his head, shrugging at me. "It's not what Command is anticipating, but they want us on the ground as backup, just in case."

My frown deepened. "So, they're sending us down to go sit in the desert for a few days? Why can't they send a different Company?"

"It's not really the desert..." Ward started

"Have there been Jumpers sighted in the area?"

Ward shook his head slowly, eyes on the map. "No, no reports of activity in this area that we know of."

I moved closer to him, dropping my voice low. "Then why can't they send someone else?" I slapped my hands down on the edge of the table, peering closer at the map. "They're going to put me on this ship, then send us down to sit around a campfire in the middle of nowhere? How does that make any sense?"

Ward scoffed for a moment, then sneered at me. "I'm sorry, Captain, everything isn't about you. We're in the middle of a war. Obviously, they feel it's necessary. It's not for us to question orders; we don't know everything."

"Oh, please," I sneered back, waving my hand. "I'm not trying to make this about me. It's not. It's about those things taking out our men. It's about stopping this from spreading. We can't afford to waste several days sitting around twiddling our thumbs." I paused for a moment, looking up at him. "We just won't go with you. We'll stay here, back on the ship. I'll continue as planned with my men."

"Not an option. It's too dangerous, like we've already said."

"Then leave a unit or two behind to go with us," I argued, my face heating. Why did this feel so deliberate? So contrived? I convinced him to go along with my plan, and suddenly we're ordered to go camp out?

"Absolutely not," Ward chuckled, "I have my orders, I can't just decide to leave parts of the Company behind."

"Then we try to carry out the mission down there." I nodded at the map, "See if we can draw them in."

"There's been zero activity in the vicinity," Ward replied. "And either way, we're protecting resources to the north of our location. I'm not calling down Jumpers on us, bringing them closer. It's too risky."

"What resources?" I asked, one eyebrow raised.

"That's classified." Ward quipped back.

"Oh," I laughed, "of course it is." I crossed my arms over my chest. "I'm sure whatever it is, it's very valuable."

Ward's eyes narrowed as he stared back at me. After a moment, he turned away, moving over to the desk and grabbing a fistful of papers. He flipped through them, his back turned.

He was lying. My heart thumped in my chest. Lying about the point of the mission? Or lying about the whole thing? But why? Why would he do that? I struggled to imagine Ward inventing a whole mission like this on his own, but that nagging feeling of disbelief wasn't dissipating. And I couldn't ignore how convenient this all was.

Should I confront him? Now? In front of all the men bustling around the bridge? Accuse him of inventing orders from Command? I watched him as he pointedly ignored me, spreading the papers out on the desk. I stood there, deliberating, my eyes on his broad shoulders, the little hairs curling at the base of his neck. I felt a jolting stab of desire, heat coursing through my midsection. *Oh, for fuck's sake.*

"Fine." I snapped, sharper than I intended, my arms dropping to my side. I would let it go. For now. "But as soon as this is over, we're back to our original plan. We need those samples, Ward. And I'm going to get them. One way or another."

Ward glanced sideways at me, papers still spread out in front of him, a little smirk on his lips. "And I have no doubt you will."

I turned and left, stalking out of the bridge, that little fissure of doubt in my mind growing ever wider.

14.

It was a whole production, moving a Company of this size down to the ground for several days. I did my best to stay out of it, watching the scurry of activity with an aloof detachment. McCullough and Binson could tell I was pissed the moment they saw me. They pressed me for information, but I didn't say a word about my suspicions.

I asked McCullough to go fill Lindsay and Topher in on what was happening, and let them know that our mission would be delayed until our return. I was too angry, and I couldn't trust myself to be the one to tell them.

The men were in good spirits as we rode the pods down to the surface. A few nights on land, on a relatively low-risk assignment, sounded pretty good to them.

Molton was thrilled. He kept up a running stream of dialogue as we began to set up camp. I'd been assigned my own small tent, and made quick work of pitching it.

The plan was to camp out in a deep valley at the bottom of a ravine. We would have running patrols of men topside, keeping an eye out at all hours of the day and night, for any approaching hostiles. Ward set up a rotation schedule for each unit. That meant whenever a unit wasn't on patrol duty, their time was their own.

We landed in the early evening. The sun was already sinking low behind the distant mountains. I had to admit, as I took a break from the tent, standing with my hands on my hips, watching the pink and orange glow on the horizon, it was beautiful here.

We spent that evening huddled in circles around campfires, confident the light would be hidden from distant eyes by the cliff face towering over us.

Technically, we were on an active mission, so no drinking was allowed. But that hadn't stopped one of the men from smuggling a flask in his pack. The men handed it off surreptitiously, sipping discreetly, heads swiveling to watch for Ward, roving amongst the campfires. Although knowing him, I seriously doubted he would have an issue with it. But the men seemed to think otherwise.

They exchanged battle stories. I suspected mostly for my benefit, as I was sure they'd all heard them before. They had been together for most of them. But there was comfort in the retelling. The men laughed as Molton recounted some of the antics they'd gotten up to during boot camp.

I stared into the flames before me, watching them dance, casting shadows on the ring of men. I caught Wren watching me several times, from the other side of the fire. The flames flickering over his features, those otherworldly blue eyes fixed on mine. I tugged the collar of my leather jacket up higher around my neck, shielding it from the cool kiss of night air that caressed my skin whenever the wind gusted.

The wind at the base of the ravine was erratic, picking up speed like grains sliding through a funnel as it went barreling down the narrow valley. It resulted in a sort of dolorous whistling, like a mournful ghost was passing overhead, wailing its tales of ruin and destruction in some foreign tongue.

It only added to the tickling unease in the back of my mind. I was enjoying myself, I couldn't deny that. This was a welcome reprieve. But in the background, at the edge of my subconscious, an odd sensation, an unsettled feeling, nagged at me. The feeling that something was coming, something big, heading our way, wouldn't dissipate. Perhaps it was only the specter of war. Of an unwelcome future, rushing up to meet us, whether we liked it or not. Maybe it was the inaction. I'd always hated waiting. I wanted to be doing something. I *needed* to be doing something. I couldn't help but feel as though we were staring our own doom in the face as we sat here, huddling around the fire, drawing strength from the flames, and from each other. I only hoped that I would be ready when it came. Strong enough to meet it.

I sighed deeply and got to my feet. I could sense Wren's eyes still on me as I moved slowly away from the fire. I walked back towards our little clump of tents, Molton's, McCullough's, and Binson's beside mine.

The men had flung down packs, extra supplies, and sleeping bags in a huge pile beside the tents. I meandered over to it and flopped down, making a little nest for myself with the rolled sleeping bags. I lay back with my arms under my head and gazed up at the sky.

I was far enough away from the light of the campfire here that I could see the universe spread out above me, and those twinkling distant lights transported me immediately back to my childhood. I could practically smell the damp grass, the scent of hay, and impending rain. My long hair worn loose, spread out like a fan beneath me, the faint scent of that lavender shampoo Grandma used to buy. I felt an odd mix of emotions, lying there, gazing up at those same stars. So much had changed since those days. But not the stars.

Their sheer number was overwhelming and awe-inspiring. I remembered how I had dreamt as a child that someday soon we would travel amongst them. I pictured our space station, floating silently through space, on its way to explore other worlds.

Unfortunately, the never-ending war below had put significant strain on the system, causing delays in development, as all of our resources were poured into the war effort. But even prior to the war, all scientific progress had stuttered and come to a grinding halt. At least, in the US.

The political atmosphere had shifted in the early 20s, as the advent of fascism that ultimately led to the disbandment of the USA caused widespread lack of funding for important scientific studies, and social safety nets. The funding cuts affected plans to expand space travel. The US made advances in technology that got us as far as transporting troops just beyond Earth's atmosphere and back, before the program stalled.

The cuts affected the availability of healthcare and education. Thousands of people lost their jobs, flinging parts of the nation into poverty. Those were dark times, as the landscape of the United States changed, fracturing into two political parties with completely opposing beliefs.

There was widespread social upheaval, as they came after immigrants, blaming outsiders for all our problems. Women's rights and access to preventative healthcare were set back, decades of progress lost, in just a few short years, along with the rights of LGBTQA+. Anyone who was different, a minority, was in danger in those days.

Seemingly unable to resolve their differences, the actions of the leading political party becoming more and more erratic and destructive, several of the northern States attempted to declare independence. They had wanted to peacefully abstain, to create their own government, based on the Constitution, and remain true to it. They wanted to create a safe haven for minorities, women, where people would be free from persecution. Where we would never again live in fear. They sought to establish a beacon for science, art, music, and education. And most importantly, democracy. But what remained of the Federal government refused to let them go quietly.

What followed was several years of civil war, with multiple states fracturing, separating from the US to form a new Northern Alliance. The Southern region came together to form their own alliance under their fascist dictator, masquerading under a false pretense of democracy. And here we were today, still facing near-constant skirmishes on an almost daily basis.

I was grateful to have been born after the transition. Things had been fairly calm during my lifetime, all things considered. It was only in recent years that the battles had escalated, become larger, and occurred more and more frequently.

I thought back to the Admiral's words as I stared up at the stars. He had said we were close now, so close. But close to what? Taking over the South? Was that really what we wanted? What was our end game here? Ward was probably right; there could be no winner at this point. There was only pain, death, and suffering on both sides.

I would never understand why the alliances couldn't have separated peacefully. Why couldn't they just let us go? Let us live the way we wanted to?

I thought of the men I had met in the factory. They seemed so normal. Not evil, not monsters. Just people. Were there a lot of people like that in the South? Just normal people who didn't have an agenda? Didn't follow along with the political extremes? I sighed deeply. As things stood right now, I would likely never know the answer to that.

I was startled by a figure looming over me, out of my periphery. I jumped slightly, turning to see it was Ward. He slumped down on the pile of sleeping bags next to me, propping himself up on one elbow.

"What are you thinking about?" He asked, eyes flickering over my features in the dark.

I sighed, returning my gaze to the night sky. Where to even begin? I was quiet for a moment. "Just... lying here, looking up at the stars." Best to leave it at that. But my mouth kept going. "You know, I grew up on a farm. Out in the middle of nowhere. I used to think..." I paused for a second, a slow smile spreading across my face. I chuckled a little. "I used to think that I could fly."

He grinned back at me, face twisting in an odd expression. "Well, you turned out to be right, didn't you?"

I laughed again, my cheeks heating slightly now. "No, not like that. I mean, I used to think that I could actually fly. Like a bird. I dreamed about it all the time, when I was little." Ward's grin widened as he watched me.

"I'd sneak outside at night and run through the fields on my grandparents' farm." I spread my arms out over my head as I spoke. He was laughing now. "I'd go running through the fields, with my arms spread wide. I was convinced that if I could just run fast enough, I'd leap into the air and just... keep going. Take off. Fly away from everything. Leave it all behind." My smile faltered, and I dropped my arms down behind my head, my chest rising and falling, as I stared up at those stars. "But it never happened." I paused, swallowed. "So, I joined the Air Force. Figured I'd fly anyway. A different way." I shook my head. "I just wanted to be free. From all of it." I murmured, turning to him. "That was all I ever wanted. To truly be free."

He wasn't laughing anymore. His expression was serious, eyes flickering over my body, taking in the rapid rise and fall of my chest, surely noticing the trembling undertones in my voice. I blushed furiously, grateful it was dark, and lowered my arms, hugging them around my middle, suddenly feeling chilled, cold, out here away from the fire.

He was silent, watching me still, as I looked pointedly away from him, staring back up at the sky. I felt tears gathering behind my eyes and took deep breaths. Why was I so emotional tonight? And why did he have this effect on me? I didn't understand it.

Ward lay back, hands under his head, staring up at the sky now as well. We lay there in silence for a minute or so. "I grew up in a border town," he said softly. "Just a few blocks from a major crossing. There wasn't much traffic through there. What limited trade of goods that they'd agreed to, out of necessity." He paused for several seconds. "It was awful." He cleared his throat, and I turned my head sharply to look at him. "They were always having to search everything; streets would be locked down, cars in a gridlock. I used to walk past that fence," he snorted, "in my mind, it was as tall as a skyscraper. Rings of barbed wire at the top, to keep the enemy out." He shook his head. "But it never seemed tall enough."

I watched him closely as he spoke, his voice pitched low. "I was terrified. All the time. I pictured them flooding the fence. Climbing on top of one another, trampling each other, to get to the top. Knives and guns in their hands. They'd come for my mother. My sister. For me."

He sighed deeply, shifting his weight, moving his arms down, lacing his hands over his chest. "Sometimes raiding parties would drift our way. Camp out in the woods, somewhere on the other side. They'd always come at night. Sometimes they were just testing our defenses. But other times... they'd attack. I'd wake up to the sirens going off. My Dad used to sleep in his boots. He'd grab his gun, take off into the night—join the other men, to protect our neighborhood."

He smirked. "I had a hunting knife he gave me. I asked for a gun, but he wouldn't give me one, back then. Just that stupid knife. It was probably dull as heck. I'd sit at my window, waiting for them, that knife gripped so tightly in my fist." He held his hand open over his head, flexing the palm. "I'd have red marks. Indent lines, from the hilt, on my hand at school the next morning."

He dropped his hand back to his chest. "The first time I set boots on the ground, on the other side of that fence, I was sure I was going to die. I've never been so scared in my entire life." He smirked. "I thought I was tougher than them, by that point. I'd taken that fear I felt as a boy, that utter helplessness, and I'd turned it into something... cruel." He shook his head. "I never wanted to feel that way again. Never wanted to be afraid of those monsters, those demons, on the other side of the fence, just waiting for their chance to kill me. To take away everyone I loved." He paused, swallowing thickly. "I wanted them to be afraid of *me*. I wanted them to run when they saw me coming."

He laughed as I frowned over at him. "It sounds stupid now, saying it out loud. But I made a decision, at some point, walking down those streets, waiting for them to attack. Hiding under a blanket by the window at night, that useless knife in my hand. I decided that, as awful as they were, I would become worse. That was the only way to fight them and have any chance of winning. The only way to beat them. To protect my family." He shrugged.

"That doesn't sound stupid at all," I murmured. I watched him, in the dark, my heart wrenching at the thought. Just a little boy, terrified.

Ward just shook his head, chuckled again. "Imagine my shock when I finally set eyes on Southern soldiers, for the first time, and it turned out they were just men. Just people, like you and me. And they were scared, too."

I sighed, turning back to the sky above us. Ward continued, his voice dropping lower. "The first man I killed, he was terrified. Of me. And I thought that I'd feel good about that. Feel like I'd accomplished something. But all I felt was," his voice faltered a little, "... disgust. And..." he trailed off.

"I know," I murmured, turning to him. "I know how you felt." He didn't have to say it. And clearly, he couldn't. He just nodded, refusing to meet my eyes. His throat bobbed as he swallowed.

We lay there for a long time, in silence, watching the world continue to spin slowly around us. The stars shifted imperceptibly as the Earth continued its course. And nothing would stop that. The slow, inevitable march of time. Not our grief. Not our pain. Not our fear, or our hopes. As useless and fragile as the wind crying through the canyon, here and then gone, just as quickly.

15.

Things were different between us after that night. Something had shifted, in some subtle way. And while outwardly our behavior towards each other didn't change, everything felt different. And it made me nervous.

I had to stay focused on the mission. *My* mission. I couldn't risk becoming entangled in whatever this was, between us. Though my heart beat faster every time my mind drifted back to that night. How close we had been. How it felt lying next to him, just the two of us, alone under those stars.

We'd spent the next day idly. The men managed to set up some volleyball nets and held a sort of tournament. I refused to participate, but I enjoyed watching them periodically. Powers landed the winning match point. I watched, grinning, as the men lifted him on their shoulders, parading him around while he laughed.

I made a point that night to stay by the safety of the campfire, nestled in amongst the men. Ward joined our fire eventually, after he returned from monitoring the patrol. I caught him glancing over at me several times, but I kept my eyes downcast, on the flickering flames. I didn't trust myself to be around him, to be alone with him again.

The men got around to trading war stories once more. When the conversation stalled, Powers decided it would be a good time to force me to recount some of my missions. I tried to refuse, but he grinned at me from across the flames. "Come on, Reaper, we've been pretty patient; you can't keep quiet forever." He gave me a wink as I sighed and sat up a little straighter.

"Alright," I began, "I'll tell you about the time I got into a dog fight during what was supposed to be a training mission." The men quieted, leaning forward. I told them about my first dog fight, and from there, they asked about the Battle of Richmond, one of the battles the Reaper was most famous for. When I'd finally slaked their curiosity, Molton picked up from there, recounting a story about Ward from boot camp.

I sat listening, huddled next to McCullough, leaning against a fallen tree the men had dragged over. Wren slid off the tree to my left, and took a seat on the ground next to me. As he rested his weight against the trunk, it shifted slightly. "Sorry," he mumbled. "It was getting cold up there."

"No worries," I murmured back. I could feel his eyes on me as I started into the fire.

"Everything okay?" He asked a few seconds later.

I nodded, pulling my mind back to the present. "Yeah," I sighed, "I'm fine. Just anxious to get out of here. Get back to the ship. We're wasting time."

Wren nodded thoughtfully. "Yeah, I guess that's true. But, in the meantime, things are going well for us, overall. From what I hear, at least. There are rumors we're going to make a major push soon. They're saying we might actually have a chance to end this soon, once and for all."

I frowned at the fire. "That's all well and good, but what's the reason for that, Wren? Because if it's at all due to the Jumpers... then we're all fucked, anyway, aren't we?" I glanced up at him, heart heavy, hoping he'd somehow be able to convince me I was wrong. Wren only sighed heavily in response.

I shook my head, gaze returning to the fire. "I mean, so we take advantage of the situation, and succeed in taking them out at the knees, but what's left, afterwards? What's the state of the South after we win? And how far does this thing spread, in the meantime?" I sighed. "We can't take that risk. We can't afford to waste a second. Let the other companies focus on the campaign. Our focus needs to be on stopping this thing." I felt myself tense as the truth of my words fully hit home. "The entire company should be dedicated to this mission; we shouldn't be here right now, camping out in the middle of nowhere, doing nothing." My voice dropped lower. "This entire thing is bullshit."

Wren nodded, turning to me, as I turned and met his eyes. He was sitting closer than I had realized, our arms touching, his face inches away from mine. He had the ghost of a smile on his lips as his gaze roved over my features. When he spoke, his voice had taken on a different tone. Lower, husky. "I can see why they chose you, you know."

Something in his eyes shifted, the planes of his face thrown into shadows, in the flickering firelight. I felt sucked in by those outrageously blue eyes, always slightly unnerving, unsettling. My heart fluttered in my chest, picking up speed. Wren's gaze dropped to my lips, and my heart lodged in my throat. I stopped breathing.

We sat that way for what must have been seconds, but the moment seemed to stretch agonizingly, until the other voices around the campfire seemed faint, distant. Their conversation, interspersed with laughter, drifted to me as though from far away. I found I couldn't look away, as I watched the firelight dance over his features, almost as though I was being hypnotized.

Stevens slapped something onto Wren's chest: a flask the men had been passing around the circle. That was enough to break the spell, pulling his focus away from me. He turned and looked down, and I let out a rush of air, turning back to the fire momentarily, then turning to my right to start up a conversation with McCullough. Which was done easily enough. I made a point not to look directly at Wren for the remainder of the evening.

I was the first to go to bed that night, slipping away while everyone was distracted. Ward was correcting the details of a story that Molton had started recounting. Wren watched me go, but I pretended not to notice him.

I'd assumed we had one more night here, and some small, weaker part of me hoped that we did. I woke up the next morning and got dressed in my tent, as the first rays of sun streamed through the translucent walls. Part of me secretly hoped that Ward would catch me alone tonight, walking back to my tent. That he'd pull me into his arms, without saying a word. Kiss me. Drag me off somewhere, under the stars. My lips curled slightly. The things I would let that man do to me... I blushed just thinking about it, even as my mind flashed to Wren's eyes on mine, the night before, and my gut clenched, twisting in a stab of fire.

I rushed to get ready, managing to wipe the guilty expression off my face, wiping my thoughts clean, before I exited my tent, only to find Molton was starting to break down his tent beside me.

"What's going on?" I asked, frowning. "We're packing it in already?"

Molton glanced up, pushing his glasses back up the bridge of his nose, spotting me ducking out of my tent. "Yeah," he sighed heavily, "vacation's over, unfortunately." He shrugged, standing upright, placing his hands on his hips, taking in our surroundings. "I'm going to miss it here. This little canyon. It was nice while it lasted."

I smiled back, a little forlornly, eyes drifting to the mountains in the distance. "Yeah, it really was."

It took us nearly twice as long to pack everything up as it did to get settled in. But eventually, we loaded up the pods and stomped aboard ourselves.

The men were silent on the ride back up to the Carrier. I chewed my bottom lip, lost in thought, as we entered the hangar and disembarked. The metal floor of the hangar echoed dully below my feet as I strode reluctantly back to my quarters, surrounded by the too white walls of the Carrier once more.

Ward sent me a message, saying that we would reconvene tomorrow on planning our next mission to the ground, and would plan to execute it tomorrow evening. I was to meet him at 1300 the next day, on the bridge.

The location ended up being the thing we debated the longest, until Ward finally agreed to my suggestion to involve TODD. It took all of two seconds for the ship's AI to generate a list of locations that met all our criteria.

We were looking for somewhere in the middle of nowhere, where we would be unlikely to encounter the SC army, to reduce our chances of accidentally engaging the enemy. Especially considering we were going to be in our flight suits, we didn't want to risk running into any officers who might be carrying EMP guns. But we also needed a location where we would be likely to encounter Jumpers. And as Ward insisted on sending a unit down with us to provide cover fire if needed, we also needed the terrain nearby to accommodate a landing pod. My men and I would fly our fighters down to the surface and proceed in our flight suits from there.

Ward selected Wren's unit to accompany us without hesitation. Wren shot me a tight grin when I sighed and reluctantly agreed. I truly would have preferred it to be just the three of us, taking only McCullough and Binson, with the plan to retreat immediately, rather than bringing any of the men with us. But Ward would not budge on that point.

We were finally ready to head out. Topher had come down to the hangar with us, making sure the video feed in my helmet was working. He and Lindsay would have access to the comms link to communicate with me directly, along with the live video feed of the action on the ground.

Ward watched us with his arms folded, a slight frown on his face, as we tested out the live feed. If anything, he should be relieved that we were executing this mission. We stood a chance of obtaining all the samples Lindsay needed and the data Topher was looking for, in one swoop. This could mean a quicker resolution, which meant we would be off *The Beagle* faster and out of his hair.

I made a point of ignoring him as he stood there watching us ready for departure. I climbed into my fighter and flashed Topher a thumbs up as I finished my pre-flight check.

I felt my body relax, shoulders dropping, muscle tension easing, as I exited the hangar, McCullough and Binson not far behind me. I realized with a little jolt that it had been weeks now since I'd sat in a fighter. I enjoyed the brief flight down to the surface, soaking it all in, comforted by the familiarity of it all, muscle memory taking over as I effortlessly guided the fighter down to the target landing zone.

We sat in our fighters for several minutes. We'd agreed, at Ward's insistence, to wait for the pod to land before exiting. But the minutes ticked by, and as I peered through the rounded glass window, I felt a slight fissure of unease.

"Where the heck are they?" Binson muttered over the comms.

"Shh," I murmured back, "remember, comm silence until we're ready and in place." He didn't give a response, and I sat in the fighter, shifting my weight uneasily.

I kept an eye on the clock and made the decision that I'd allow them two more minutes before we exited the fighters. But it didn't come to that. I turned to see the pod descending, executing its rough landing onto the field.

The three of us began to exit our fighters simultaneously. I climbed out and stood on the wing momentarily, watching as the men poured out of the pod.

I engaged the boosters in my flight suit and lifted a few feet into the air, rising in a gentle arc before landing again on my feet near the pod, failing to suppress a grin. I was getting better at maneuvering more subtly in this thing. Given another week or so, it would become muscle memory, second nature. That's assuming I got any opportunities to practice.

I spied Wren standing off to the side, directing his men silently with hand signals only, as they fell into formation. I moved towards him, stopping mid-stride as Ward stepped out of the pod and moved over to one of the men, grabbing him by the arm and whispering something in his ear.

Wren caught me watching him, and the incredulous look on my face, and just shook his head at me in response. I made a beeline for him.

"What the hell is he doing down here?" I hissed at Wren, making sure my comm was switched off. That explained the delay in the pod's arrival, I thought grimly.

Wren just sighed and shook his head again. "He insisted. I tried to tell him."

I shook my head in disgust and turned abruptly to find McCullough and Binson. They stood waiting for me a few yards away, scanning the field and treeline behind us, heads swiveling in all directions. I marched over to them and gave them the signal to move out.

There was a hill near this location, and that was the determining factor in selecting this spot out of the list of possible locations TODD had generated. It was about a mile and a half from the landing zone, through a wooded area and a few fields. We moved silently through the trees. I was tempted to take to the air and fly over the woods, leaving Ward and his men in our dust, but I forced myself to weave calmly through the trees instead. The comms remained silent, as planned, the only break in the silence came from the shuffling of feet through the underbrush and the occasional stick snapping.

I checked to make sure my comms link was on and hoped the video feed was working. I'd check in with Topher and Lindsay once we reached the location.

Before long, the hill came into view up ahead. It wasn't barren, the slope dotted here and there with the occasional tree, but the cover here was sparse, and would allow us a good line of sight in all directions.

We made it to the top first and turned to see that more than half the group had split off, fanning out along the treeline below in a thin line, ready to provide cover fire. The rest of the men were heading up the hill to join us on the slopes. I sighed internally. Nothing like being babysat. They would be between us and the Jumpers.

I slid my rifle off my back and checked the safety. Odds are, I wouldn't need to fire a shot if this went as planned. The thought only irked me further. I was more than capable of handling this mission alone, with my men. In fact, we would have been able to move faster, taking to the skies without needing to worry about who we were leaving behind on the ground. I felt the urge to march over and tell Ward what an idiot he was, but I refrained.

I tapped my comms unit to unmute. "Come in, Topher, we're in position. How's that video feed looking? Over."

"Captain," his voice came through instantly. I pictured him sitting in the lab with a headset on, waiting for me, watching through my eyes. "It's like I'm right there with you." He murmured. "Lindsay's here too."

"Good," I whispered back. "You're going to call out the next comms channel in advance, and I'll have the men switch over to that frequency. I'll remain on this channel to keep our lines of communication open." We'd already discussed all of this in detail, but reiterating it was reassuring. We'd direct the unit to switch frequencies every ten minutes or so, until we drew Jumpers down on our location.

"Affirmative," Topher murmured back. A second's pause. "First frequency: 3.6 GHz."

A long press on my helmet switched me over to the general comms link. "Switch over to 3.6 GHz, gentlemen. And let it rip."

A few chuckles before they were cut off as the men switched their comms over to the new channel. I lifted my finger off the helmet and was back on with Topher. "Nine minutes and counting until the next switch," he murmured in my ear.

I watched the men around us on the hill. I could hear those closer to us, their voices drifting over naturally, carried on the light wind that blew as we stood exposed on the peak. I was unable to feel it anywhere but my face; I'd left the shield up for now, opting for fresh air versus the stale recycled air inside the suit. I could see the men all talking at once, calling out God knows what over the comms. I should probably be glad I couldn't hear them. I grinned at McCullough, and he shook his head, laughing back at me.

We waited, moving in idle circles, eyes on the treeline below, waiting for that first Jumper to appear, but nothing happened. Eventually, I heard Topher's voice buzz suddenly in my ear. "Next frequency: 6 GHz." I long pressed on the general comms and switched over to a cacophony of voices. Someone was singing loudly in an operatic style voice. I stifled a grin. "Next channel: 6 GHz," I called out, straining to be heard over the din. I repeated the channel twice more as the men quieted and switched over.

Another five minutes went by on the new channel. I was growing bored of watching the treeline, triggered by leaves rustling and branches swaying idly in the wind. "I'm not sure this approach is making sense now, Topher," I murmured. "We were on 3.6 GHz at the factory when we supposedly drew them down on us. If that were true, you'd think it would work a second time. Maybe there just aren't any in the vicinity?"

Topher sighed, "Or they're too far away. Like I said, we can't account for distance, that, and the time it might take for them to travel to you once they detect you're in the area. Maybe the first frequency band triggered them, but it could take half an hour for them to reach you–" he cut off for a moment, and I could hear Lindsay's voice faintly in the background. "Yeah, I know," Topher murmured. "Yeah, for sure." He cleared his throat, "Lindsay is saying we have no idea what their range is, regardless. They might only be able to detect activity from a certain distance away. I mean, it is what it is, we just have to wait and see what happens."

I sighed, nodding in agreement. "Yeah. There could be none around here for a hundred miles for all we know... but we did plug in the data we had on recent encounters." At least, Ward said he gave TODD access to that data when he generated target locations. I frowned slightly. I had assumed he actually did that, but he had been over at the computer terminal while I sat across the bridge from him. Could I be sure he'd actually done what I'd asked? I shook my head slightly to clear it. I had no reason to think he'd do something like that. Trying to undermine my authority and keeping me on a short leash was one thing, but directly attempting to sabotage the mission was another entirely.

I scanned the hill below, trying to pick him out from the crowd, but I had no idea where he'd ended up. He must be hidden somewhere amongst the trees.

I paced uneasily back and forth, making the rounds, walking the peak in a loop over and over until I guessed I was probably making Topher and Lindsay dizzy.

It took about twenty-five minutes. Twenty-five minutes until the first Jumper staggered out of the treeline below. A dark figure against the grass, shuffling oddly, its movements erratic and somewhat jerky.

Binson clapped a hand on my shoulder, pointing, nearly making me jump. "There, Captain," he was too excited to notice I'd already spotted it. To the north of our location, thankfully. The pod and our fighters lay to the south. It would be ideal if they approached from the north.

I switched over to the general comms and heard the excited chatter of the men. Those on the hill were already falling into shooting stance, rifles trained on the lone figure shambling below us. "Hold your fire. I repeat, hold your fire." I watched the thing that had once been a man as it approached the base of the hill. "Let's draw him in, as close as possible, before we take him down."

"This is Topher speaking, Captain." he must have switched over to the general comm frequency since I obviously couldn't hear him back on the original channel at the moment. "We recommend shooting at its feet or something first. Try to spook it a little before taking it out. We'd like to rule out that this isn't just a random straggler."

I swallowed, nodding at his words. That made sense. As much as I wanted to avoid calling a horde down on us, we needed to test our theory. We needed to be sure the comms had attracted them, and capturing the Jumper's behavior on camera would give us information on how they were potentially communicating. "You heard him, folks," I called out over the comms, pointing at the soldiers closest to the Jumper. "Aim for the ground at his feet, on my signal."

I waited. The tension thick in the air, as the Jumper scuttered ever closer. The men on the hill had fallen back instinctively, moving to the sides, creating a clear swath of ground for him as he moved closer. I watched, with an odd little fissure of surprise, tilting my head to the side. "Wait, can he not see us?" I murmured to Topher. I had forgotten I was still on the general comms, realizing too late that the men were all listening in. Oh well, they'd get an earful today. We could brief them afterward on keeping quiet about what they'd learned.

"Captain?" Topher asked, the confusion evident in his voice.

"Look at him. He doesn't seem to notice the men over to the sides. He's not heading towards them. But he should be able to see them easily, right? I mean... are they... could they be blind?"

I watched as the Jumper stilled, pausing for a moment. He turned to his right, head swiveling over in my direction, before changing his trajectory, moving up the hill towards the peak, to where I stood.

"Did you see that?" I murmured into the comms. I realized we had all fallen silent. The men were still, waiting for my signal and watching the Jumper. The comms had gone silent. Other than me, no one else was talking. "It was like he heard me just now and changed directions. The comms have quieted otherwise. I don't know if he can see any of us..." I thought for a moment. "Binson, wave your arms around; something to get his attention."

Binson stood over to my left, the Jumper's right, about ten feet away. He followed orders, waving his arms over his head. "Nothing, Captain." He said over the comms. "I think you might be right, it didn't even flinch."

But it did then, at his words. We watched as it stilled again, head swiveling in Binson's direction. A long white string stretched from its cheek, just below its left eye, down to its shoulder. The string stretched further and detached as the thing turned, swinging down towards the ground, before stretching and finally separating into two; a clump falling onto the grass.

"Disgusting motherfuckers." Binson murmured.

"Try staying quiet for a moment, but this time, jump up and down." Binson gave me a look back at that one, and I snorted slightly. "I'm not fucking with you, I'm trying to see if it responds to movement."

Binson sighed and began to jump up and down. Sure enough, the thing swiveled back in his direction, taking several shuffling steps closer, hunching down, lower towards the ground as it went.

"Captain, this is Lindsay," her voice came in over the comms, with a muffled sort of quality at first, then a jostling, as Topher must be handing over the headset to her. "Switch back to the other comm frequency for a moment."

I turned to Binson, "Binson, draw him around the side of the hill. He's moving slowly enough. Let's keep him alive for now. Everyone else stays silent. But you talk to him, keep him locked on you, okay?" I watched as the thing paused, shifting back and forth, unsure who to follow now that he could hear me talking as well. "Never mind, I'll do it. I'm going to switch over to the other frequency for now." It made more sense since I was going to be the one talking.

I switched over quickly, "Back on Linds," I murmured. "What's up?"

"Okay, so ants have varying degrees of vision, depending on what kind of ant you're dealing with. Some have what is likely blurry vision, compared to vertebrates, while some are completely blind. Those are mainly the subterranean types; they don't spend much time above ground. Bulldog ants have good vision as far as ants go; they can detect the size and shape of moving targets from a meter or so away. There are even some types of ants that can see ultraviolet light. It really is all over the place. But with the responses to movement, they may not be responding visually, depending on the distance. They might be responding to the vibrations traveling through the ground. Once we have more samples, if we can extract DNA, assuming ant DNA is what we're dealing with, we can hopefully determine a lot more from there. But certainly, based on what we're observing right now, it appears, subjectively, as though he doesn't see you. I would guess he may be responding to the comms transmissions and vibrations."

"I agree," I said, watching him stalk steadily closer to me. His eyes were pitch black. Narrow and wide set, as though they had migrated to the side of his head. His nose was all but gone, and his mouth had grown larger, both at the sides and vertically, stretching impossibly wide, full of jagged teeth, filthy, discolored, and elongated. "It sure feels like he's hearing us, versus seeing us."

I moved over closer towards some men on the hill below, holding a hand out to them to indicate they should stay still, hold their position. I continued to talk to Lindsay. "Look, it's like he doesn't even notice them standing there," I watched as the thing stalking me passed by the men, tracking it with wide eyes, their rifles trained on it, as we moved past them.

"It does seem that way," Lindsay murmured back. "Maybe try shooting at its feet?" She suggested. "Since we're suspecting they may communicate via pheromones, we want to startle it somehow. Trigger an attack response and the release of attack pheromones to see if it draws others to it.

"You got it," I murmured, switching back over to the general comms frequency. "This is Captain Kessler, commencing fire to startle the Jumper, over."

I lifted my rifle and aimed at the ground a foot or so away from the Jumper's feet. A line of dark earth appeared as the rounds ripped into the ground, kicking up dirt. The Jumper jerked back in response, issuing a low hissing sound as it recoiled. I waited a few seconds, and realized it seemed to have lost track of me momentarily, as the comms had fallen silent once more. "I'm right here, you ugly bastard," I murmured into the comms. A few men sniggered. "Come and get me you piece of shit." I moved a few steps closer, firing again near its feet.

It reacted differently this time. The rounds kicking up dirt once more, black holes punching into the ground. As the last round flew, it shrank back onto its hind legs, crouching low, and it sprang at me, flinging its body forward, arms ending in claws like long bony talons, spread wide.

I gasped and fell a step or two back, stumbling. It landed on my legs, its head level with my groin, as we fell back in a heap. A cacophony rang out in my ear over the comms. I heard Ward's voice calling out to Wren, but I couldn't process what anyone was saying, as a bubble of panic burst open in my chest. At least I had my suit on; it would offer some protection. The thing was scrambling just as I was. My rifle had been knocked out of my hands and lay off to the side, over my head. I reached for it, twisting my body to the right.

The thing scrambled forward, gaining purchase as its thick talons scraped into the ground, it slid up, over my body, moving closer to my face. "Your face shield, Jordan, close your helmet!" I heard Lindsay's voice standing out, as she cried out in my ear. *Fuck.* Thick strands of white, slimy threads dripped from its gaping black maw. I managed to slam my right hand against the side of my helmet, the shield sliding down over my face just in time as it lunged forward, white strands of pus-like strings slapping against the glass with a wet thud. Its teeth scraped the shield, as I stared into its mouth and down its pulsing throat. I felt its body jerk on top of mine as the crack of a rifle rang out.

The rounds must have hit it in the side of the chest. It slid to the side, taking the bulk of its weight off of me, enough so that I was able to push off the ground with both feet, scrambling back as I went for my rifle, grabbing it and sliding out from underneath the thing at the same time.

Wren stood several yards away, his rifle still trained on the Jumper as he stalked forward, his chest heaving.

"Thanks," I muttered, breathlessly. He nodded wordlessly to me before refocusing on the Jumper.

It writhed on the ground, blood leaking and spurting from the holes in its chest. I watched as I scrambled to my feet, heart still racing, peering through the white slime that coated my face shield.

"Are you okay?" Lindsay asked. The thing on the ground stared up at me, black eyes swiveling, as it struggled to draw in each breath. I felt a brief stab of pity. It hardly looked human anymore. It was easy to forget that this had been a person, once. A person that someone presumably cared about. Loved, even. I gritted my teeth and nodded, turning away from its suffering.

"Yeah," I managed. "I'm okay." I lifted a finger and pointed to my face shield. "I got some of the samples you wanted."

Lindsay snorted in my ear, and I grinned a little. "Binson, McCullough," I called out, "Come help me with this." I turned back to the Jumper, fading fast on the ground below. The light was starting to fail now, settling into dusk. "Let's get everything we need from this one."

Binson and McCullough rushed over and began prepping sample kits, collecting the white material from my face shield, and using a spare set of gloves to carefully wipe the rest of it off. It left a film on one side of the shield, but at least I could see better than I could before. "We'll have to sanitize your suit when you get back," Lindsay said wryly.

We'd been working at gathering samples for a minute or two when I heard a commotion start up on the comms link. I heard Ward's voice ring out, "We've got Jumpers, to the west.

Incoming." He cleared his throat. "These aren't stragglers, either. Looks like this might be the start of a wave. Get into position, everyone. Fire at will."

We picked up our pace as much as possible, moving quickly to collect samples under Lindsay's direction, ignoring the spattering of rifle fire and commands called out over the comms the best we could as we worked.

I ended up being very grateful for Lindsay's voice in my ear. Not just because she'd possibly saved my life by warning me to close my face shield, but also because gathering the samples was more difficult than I thought it would be. I didn't think of myself as squeamish by any means, but my gut twisted slightly as the thick flesh parted below the scalpel in my hand. We drained blood into syringes and filled the sample kits as fast as we could. Lindsay stopped me briefly and asked me to hold up the hand of the Jumper, for her to get a closer look at the talons.

"Do you have anything with you that you could use to cut it off?" She asked, her voice hesitant. I stared at the scalpel in my hand.

"No way this thing is going to do it." I sighed. "Normally, I carry a knife strapped to my leg, but I took it off because of the suit." I glanced up at Binson and McCullough, and they shook their heads.

"Stand back," Binson said a moment later. I tucked the scalpel away carefully and got to my feet, moving a few paces back.

Binson peppered the arm with his rifle until the hand hung loose. He grabbed it in his gloved hands and twisted it, one foot on the thing's arm to hold it down, bone cracked and splintered under his boot as he stomped down repeatedly.

I looked away in disgust and surveyed the hill below us. I tapped over to the officer's channel and murmured, "Ward, we're about done here. Thanks for the cover fire." I added, somewhat reluctantly. Although I hated to admit it; he had been right. I had vastly underestimated the amount of time it would take for us to gather all the samples. There would have been no way we could have accomplished this on our own.

"Good," came his gruff reply. "We'll begin the retreat. And you're welcome, Captain." I could hear the grin in his voice. I shook my head, watching as Binson dropped the severed hand into a large plastic bag McCullough held out for him.

"Hang on," I interjected, "just a second. I want to test out one more thing." I paused, thinking rapidly. I hadn't told him anything yet about the radio frequencies. I'd sort of implied testing different frequencies to draw them in was Lindsay's and Topher's idea and left it at that. I hadn't shared the theory that there were also certain frequencies they didn't like, that might deter them. "I want the men to switch to a lower frequency on the comms. We'd like to test a theory that the low frequencies might deter them."

Silence on the other end of the officer comms. I watched the chaos unfolding below us as I waited for his response. A soldier narrowly avoided being taken out by a Jumper as it leapt towards him, abnormally long legs bowed beneath it as it readied to spring. It reminded me more of a grasshopper than an ant.

"Another theory? Hmm?" Ward murmured back to me, his voice purring in that key that made my core throb. "And what are all these theories based on, exactly, Captain?"

I sighed, my heart thumping a little in my chest. "I'm not a scientist, Ward. I'm just trying to gather the data they need." My response came out terser than I intended.

"Fine," Ward said coolly, those seductive undertones disappearing, "What are we switching to?"

"750 MHz," I snapped back at him.

"750 MHz..." his voice trailed off. "Do our comms even go that low?" I frowned for a moment. I wasn't sure, now that he'd asked the question.

"I'm not sure, actually," I admitted, "I've never tried it before. But I assume they must, right?"

"I'll give it a shot first," he replied. I waited while he presumably jumped off the channel and attempted to tune down to the right band. I sighed again, holding up one finger to McCullough as he waved to get my attention, arms held out wide, he pointed down to the pack at his feet. A large, insulated backpack, bright orange, with a biohazard label on the front, sat open on the ground. He mimed zipping it shut, and I nodded my head, giving him the thumbs up. He was still on the general comms channel.

"Okay," Ward was back, mumbling in my ear. "I was—" his voice cut off abruptly, and rifle fire rang out through the comms link. "I was able to switch down to 750; a lot of static on that band." He was slightly out of breath.

It was time to get out of here. "Okay, let's tell the men to switch over on the general comms and get loud. We'll see if it elicits any sort of reaction from them. Then I think we should get the heck out of here."

"Agreed," he murmured, "Hopping over. Over."

I switched back to the general comms and listened as he directed the men to 750, before making the switch myself. I had to tap rapidly against my helmet, watching as the blue glowing numbers that appeared in the corner of my suit's visual projection scrolled down to 750 MHz.

Ward had been right; this band was full of static. Just a constant sort of background hum. Topher's voice rang out in my ear. "Try to keep an eye on the Jumpers closest to you, see if there's any visible reaction to the new frequency." I surveyed my surroundings, mindful again that they were watching through my eyes.

I located a small knot of Jumpers further down the hill and began to move closer. They'd engaged with two of the men. They fought them off with rifle fire. One of the soliders was holding a bayonet, stabbing the Jumper that managed to evade the spray of bullets right in the chest as it lunged at him. I could see the men's mouths moving as they called out over the comms. Some were singing loudly. Someone was reciting the opening passage of the NA constitution. I watched as one man scrambled backwards as he shot at a headless Jumper, sprinting erratically towards him.

"Jesus," Topher murmured in my ear.

"Yeah," I replied stoically.

"I'd heard they could continue moving without their heads for a while. Hearing it is one thing, but seeing it..." He trailed off. I wanted to tell him to ask Lindsay if ants could live without their heads, but figured I'd better wait until I saw her in person. We had to be careful about what we said over the general comms.

I watched with wide eyes as the Jumpers slowly began to react. It was subtle, at first. I noticed one of them was twitching slightly, shying away from the men closest to it. I scanned the hill, seeing similar responses in the other Jumpers. It was almost as though they were in pain.

"Holy shit," I heard Topher murmur in my ear. Then a moment later, "What?" I waited, assuming he was listening to Lindsay. "Okay, Linds says have them shift a little, up to 900 MHz."

I frowned for a moment, then shrugged. "Okay, you got it." I cleared my throat. "Ward, can we shift to 900 MHz, from 750. Repeat, shift to 900 MHz."

"You heard her." Ward's voice called out over the comms as the men quieted. "Switch over to 900 MHz general comms. Over."

We moved to 900 MHz, and I watched in awe as the Jumpers visibly recoiled. They weren't retreating, but they were affected. They continued to attack, but their movements were sluggish, uncoordinated, almost as though they were uncomfortable moving closer to us.

"Yes," Topher murmured, "Linds says she thinks maybe broadcasting in this range is disrupting their communication with each other." Topher paused, his voice growing more excited as he spoke, "Maybe the lower frequencies are messing with their signaling via pheromones?" He paused again, and I was half listening, half watching the surrounding sight of the men pointing and laughing. High-fiving each other as they took out the skittish Jumpers.

"What about an EMP? A blast?" I heard him ask. "Centered around 900 MHz? But what frequency is the electromagnetic radiation of the Earth's magnetic field?" They were having a whole side conversation now that I couldn't follow, but I felt a little jolt at the mention of an EMP blast. *The EMP guns.* Could an EMP gun work on the Jumpers? Had anyone ever tried that? Why would they? Why on earth would anyone think to shoot a Jumper with an EMP gun?

I turned, scanning the treeline below for Ward. I wanted to run over to ask if he had his EMP gun with him, although I couldn't imagine why he would have brought it. The gun I'd taken from the factory was back in my quarters on the ship. I'd shoved it in a drawer in the little kitchen area.

"*Jesus Christ*!" I heard a familiar voice ring out over the comms, with an undertone of urgency I'd never heard from him before. *Wren*. "We've got hostiles, incoming from the south."

That was when all hell broke loose. Our moment of celebration was over. The Jumpers weren't in retreat, but they were continuing to shirk away from us. Chaos rang out over the comms. The sky was growing darker by the second, as a deepening twilight began to fall around us.

"Goddamn it. How did they find us?" Binson asked incredulously.

"They must have seen us land from a distance," Ward replied sharply. "Or maybe we triggered some sort of monitoring system on the way down. Who knows. Either way, we need to get out of here. Now. We don't have enough men for this."

My heart leapt into my throat at his words, and I listened with a growing sense of dread as he ordered the retreat. He directed half of the men to maintain cover fire on the far side of the hill and had the men retreat in waves.

McCullough and Binson approached me. "Captain, we should go," McCullough murmured, grabbing onto my arm. He carried the orange backpack in one hand. I reached out and grabbed it, slinging it over my shoulders awkwardly in the flight suit.

"We can't just–" I started, but Ward cut me off instantly.

"Get the hell out of here, Kessler; get back to your fighters."

"We're not going to just leave you–"

"The most important thing is getting those samples out of here and back to the ship. Get going."

I sighed internally, knowing he was right. I wasted another few seconds deliberating. "Okay, let's get moving," I murmured to the men, and we engaged our boosters, taking to the sky. I watched for as long as I could, turning backwards as we flew. Men in NA uniforms continued to stream down the hill, running as fast as they could away from the enemy camped out in the trees. The NA men took turns dropping to one knee and firing on the soldiers to cover their retreat.

We swiftly left them behind, and I faced forward, keeping an eye on how close I came to the treetops below. I felt a sharp pang of guilt mixed with fear. To my right, a glow of pink bloomed on the horizon as the sun made its descent below the edge of the world.

16.

We'd been flying for several minutes when I spied something moving in the field below. It was a small figure in a vast space. So small, I felt with an instant certainty that it must be a child. I slowed, dropping behind McCullough and Binson, as I swooped lower, trying to get a closer look.

I maintained control of my descent until I maneuvered to an upright position, dropping down low over the field in the direction of the small figure wandering through the dusk alone.

My breath caught in my throat as I drifted closer. It was a girl. A little girl in a pink dress. Long brown hair tied back in a half ponytail, with a little bow. I slowed to a halt, hovering about ten feet off the ground, still at a distance away. I didn't want to frighten her. She must be lost. Wandering out here alone.

"I have something here, hang on," I called out into the comms. "It's a little girl. It looks like she's lost." Her head swiveled in my direction.

I watched with a stifled curse on my tongue as she turned, dropping into a low crouch. Her dark, beady eyes were wide set, having migrated to the sides of her face. Her lips were non-existent, her open maw rimmed with pale flesh, stretched taut around jagged teeth. Scrambling, her legs bowed, she skittered in my direction, before lunging towards me.

"*Fuck!*" I cried out, shooting upwards as I watched in horror, her head passing beneath my feet, her too wide jaw open in a feral snarl.

"Shit," Topher murmured in my ear. I had forgotten he was still there.

"Captain? What the hell happened?" I heard McCullough's voice ring out. I turned and scanned the air around me as I rose, glancing back at the small figure in the pink dress as she shrank in the distance.

McCullough was nowhere in sight. Neither was Binson. The sky surrounding me was empty. My little detour felt like it had only taken seconds. How had they gotten that far ahead of me?

Granted, it was getting dark, and I strained my eyes, peering up ahead, before remembering to switch my view to night mode. I turned in a slow 360 circle, scanning for them, as I continued to search just above the treetops. Had we been flying higher than I realized? Maybe they were up above me somewhere?

"Where are you guys?" I called out, shooting upwards as I continued to scan the area. My eyes locked on an object in my periphery. There they were. I let out a sigh of relief. Two figures in flight suits approached from my right. I must have gotten turned around somehow, drifted farther out of our flight path than I'd realized.

"Sorry about that," I murmured, waving to them. "I must have gotten turned around. I saw a little girl down in that field. She was turning into one of them. A Jumper." I swallowed thickly.

"Jesus, that's awful," Binson murmured back. "Where are you, though, Captain? I can't see you. I thought you were right behind me."

"What do you mean you can't see me?" I said slowly, eyes locked on the two figures zooming closer. "You're headed right for me."

"What?" Binson asked, his voice incredulous.

Fuck. I had just a few seconds' warning before they slammed into me. I gave the suit full steam and attempted to shoot upwards. But they seemed to anticipate it somehow. The lead figure moved upwards simultaneously, crashing into me heavily. I gasped for breath, the wind knocked out of my lungs by the impact.

"Captain!" I heard McCullough's voice calling out to me, as though from a distance, as I grappled with the man who'd crashed into me. We went in a headlong spin, shooting ever higher, before I felt my feet snag on something. A tree? I frowned down in confusion, realizing it was the second man, clinging to my legs now, leaving behind a trail of white exhaust from his boosters. One seemed to be sputtering, puffing out clouds of white as we spun and twirled.

He'd knocked us off course enough that we ended up shooting in the other direction as we straightened out. We were heading for the ground now, trees below us growing larger, their branches stretching up to meet us. "For fuck's sake, you're going to kill us all!" I screamed into the man's face in front of me, his dark eyes boring into mine, were cold and calculating.

They were Southern Coalition. They had to be. They didn't have their own flight suits, as far as I knew, and these looked like NA issue. Probably stolen. Taken off dead men.

They seemed to be able to communicate with each other. They had me locked in their embrace, unable to move. I stopped struggling, killing the jets on my suit as the ground flew up to meet us, allowing them to control our descent.

They managed to lead us down to the earth in a somewhat coordinated landing. We still crashed, but it could have been a lot worse. We landed in a heap, hitting the ground once, then rising again, before crashing down a second time, sliding to a halt.

Think. I told myself. *Think.* I needed to get to my rifle, but it was strapped onto my back, the orange biohazard backpack slung on top of it. I attempted to lift my arm to reach for my rifle, but the men tightened their hold that had gone slack momentarily when we landed. One of them held my arms as the other reached behind my back. *Goddamn it.*

"Where is she? What happened?" I heard Binson calling out as I tried to maintain my calm, fighting the panic blooming in my gut, rising in my chest.

"She's been taken down by two men in flight suits," Topher called out in my ear. "They must be SC. They've crash-landed in a field, I think they have her pinned down."

I fought and twisted with all my strength, turning and pressing my back to the ground, trying to prevent them from removing the orange backpack as it pressed into my spine.

I realized with a start that they didn't seem to be armed. No rifles slung over their backs. The suits. They had the small blaster built into the suit. But, so did I.

I lifted my right arm and aimed at the man holding my legs. He ducked at the last second, and the round skimmed his shoulder. His grip loosened, and I kicked wildly at him until I was free. I scrambled to my side, onto my stomach and then on all fours until I could make it to my feet.

I sprinted for the treeline as I felt a tug on the backpack, jerking me back. We ran into the trees, the man tugging backwards, trying to pull me off my feet. He managed it eventually, and I fell back, legs flying out from under me.

"Location?" Was that Ward's voice, calling out?

"I can't see them anywhere nearby in the fields below us. We must have overshot them."

"How did she get that far behind us?" Binson responded.

"She made it to the treeline. They're in the woods now." Topher murmured.

"She could be anywhere," McCullough responded.

"She has the samples," Topher moaned.

"My fucking rifle is pinned down under the backpack." I managed to gasp while struggling. "I can't get a hold of it."

"Coordinates, Topher!" It was Ward, I realized with a jolt. "Can't you track her flight suit? Get me her fucking coordinates." He growled into the comms.

"Hang on," Topher called out. I kicked at the man who held me down, my boot connecting with the underside of his jaw. He let out a garbled cry and fell back. I got to my feet again and ran, just as the other man came after me, feet pounding into the ground, twigs and branches snapping.

I ran as fast as I could, sneaking a hand back to grip my rifle as I went. I looked down and confirmed the strap was still around my chest. But it was completely pinned down by the backpack, now a bright orange target on my back in the shadows beneath the trees. I kicked myself internally. If I had my knife with me, I could try to cut the strap and pull the rifle loose. The scalpel was in the sample bag, secured safely in its own sealed plastic bag.

A shot whined past my ear, and I flinched, ducking to the left, crouching below a low hanging branch, I changed my direction. That had been a lucky reminder not to run in a straight goddamn line. I wasn't sure the blaster in the flight suits could penetrate the suit itself. I was probably fairly protected. But I didn't want to assume that and be wrong. If it were the case, that also meant it was unlikely I could do much damage to them either, unless I could get a clear headshot.

I listened as Topher called out my coordinates. "She's moving fast, heading north at the moment."

A long pause. Ward's voice sounded through the static hum. "Plugging in the coordinates now. She's headed back this way, I'll intercept her." Rifle fire rang out in the background. "Wren, continue to lead the retreat. Don't stop. Keep up the return fire."

"We're attempting to locate her now," McCullough chimed in, his voice broken up by static.

More rounds whizzing past my head, I ducked and wove through the trees, changing directions as randomly as I could. I could risk slinging the backpack off, attempt to hold onto it, while removing my rifle. But it was bulky, and the odds of me doing all of that while running and avoiding getting shot seemed pretty slim. I couldn't risk them taking the sample bag. Clearly it had caught their attention. I had to make sure it could be recovered. I needed to keep it away from them for as long as possible.

I continued forward, wracked with indecision. I slung my right arm back and let off a volley of shots blindly. It was enough to stop the rounds whizzing past my head for a moment or two.

We continued in that way for another minute or so. They'd shoot at me, and I would fire back randomly, praying a stray bullet would happen to hit one of them.

I glanced up at the sky above me as I ran. I could attempt to take off again, shoot up into the sky, and hope I could outfly them. I was supposed to be The Crimson Reaper for Christ's sake– I should be able to outmaneuver them. And in a fighter, I had no doubt I could. But the suit was still new to me, and who knew how many flight hours they'd logged in their stolen gear.

The trees grew too thick here, regardless, branches intertwined over our heads, blotting out what little fading daylight was left. I couldn't risk trying to take to the air here. But I could wait for a break in the trees, a clearing, and take my chances then.

"Fuck!" I heard McCullough call out. "She's somewhere dead ahead, coordinates are north of our location, but we've hit the woods again."

"We won't be able to land in this shit." Binson murmured.

"I'm watching for a clearing," I panted at them, trying to keep my voice down. "If I get an opportunity to take to the air again, I will."

"We're setting down Captain, we'll follow you on foot. Hang on."

"We should stay in the air, fly ahead and look for a clearing." Binson called out. "Topher, anything on the map? Can you try to direct her to a clearing?"

"I'm on it," Topher murmured over the static hum peppered with rifle fire.

"We're at the pod now," Wren chimed in. "We'll hold them off as long as possible."

"No," Ward shouted. "Get the men out of here. Go. That's an order." He snapped.

"How the fuck are you going to get back? Even if you do find her?" Wren asked, exasperated. "Move out, let's go!" He called out.

"We'll figure it out." Ward snapped back. "There're still the fighters. Topher, updated coordinates, stat."

There was a brief pause of only static, then Topher called out the coordinates.

"Got it." Ward was gasping now. "I'm nearly there."

I could hear the stomping of their feet close behind me now. They were gaining on me. I swung my arm back and shot again, arm bent at the elbow, I swung it back and forth in a line behind me, strafing, rounds fanning out. One of them must have hit home, I heard a shout behind me, and the footsteps paused.

Unfortunately, they took a page out of my book, a line of rounds started to my right, bullets whining ever closer. *Fuck.* I lunged forward, throwing myself at the ground as the bullets flew over my head.

I attempted to tuck and roll, but my momentum only carried me so far, until the bulky backpack wedged itself between me and the ground, stopping me from rolling further.

I was screwed. One of them ran towards me, arm outstretched, aimed at my face. I glanced back and hit the gas on my blasters. I shot backwards, narrowly avoiding the rounds he peppered into the ground where my body had been. I swerved back and forth, dodging the surrounding trees. A large tree loomed to my left, and I killed the blasters abruptly as I swerved to avoid it.

But I had been a fraction of a second too slow to react, and my shoulder slammed solidly into the trunk. I let out a startled cry at the hot flood of pain that shot through my shoulder, up my neck and down my back. I slid to a stop, several feet away, dirt flying up into my mouth. I shrugged my good shoulder down and managed to shuck the strap of the backpack off. Getting to my knees quickly, I slid first my injured shoulder, then my arm, weak and tingling, out of the backpack. I reached up, rotating my right shoulder, with a brief burst of thankfulness that I'd injured the left, rather than the right. I gripped my rifle, and swung it up over my head, shrugging out of the strap with another gasp of pain.

I moved backwards, leaving the pack on the ground, and taking cover behind a tree, I knelt down on one knee, lifting my left arm as high as I could, I set the end of the rifle on my forearm, holding it steady for a moment, aiming back in the direction of the SC soldier, forcing my left hand to curl, to grip the rifle, as I scanned the trees for him.

He came sprinting towards me, arm raised in front of him. I aimed, holding my breath for a moment, and hit him square in the chest.

He jerked backwards, and I moved closer, dropping to one knee again, shooting over and over, round after round into his chest and head, his body twitching. I stopped, breathing heavily, staring down at his body.

"Kessler, it's me," Ward called out in my ear. I stilled and turned to see a figure moving at a crouch towards me in the shadows.

I stood upright, watching him move closer, until he was right in front of me, dark eyes wide. He slid a hand behind my neck, pulling me to him, peering at me.

"Are you okay?" He asked. I swallowed, staring up at him, his chest rising and falling rapidly, as he gasped for breath, and nodded. I couldn't help but feel a little thrill of electricity run through me, as he leaned forward, nearly resting his forehead on mine.

He pulled away abruptly a second later. "Any left?" He asked, his gaze dropping to the body on the ground at my feet, his hand still on my neck.

"One more," I murmured back, "I think I hit him earlier, but I doubt it took him out."

Ward nodded, scanning the trees ahead. He looked back at me, his chest still heaving. He must have sprinted all the way here. My eyes widened. "The backpack!"

I turned and scanned the ground. Ward's hand falling away from me, hit my left shoulder on the way down. I cried out in pain, moving forward, towards where I'd dropped the backpack, searching for any sign of orange amongst the shadows.

"You're hurt?" Ward asked.

I ignored him, eyes combing the forest floor. "I dropped the backpack, back this way." I ran further ahead, Ward trailing behind me, as I searched the ground frantically. "It's not here," I turned back to him, eyes wide. "It should be right around here."

"Fuck," he murmured, eying the surrounding woods. "The other one must have grabbed it."

"We're heading your way," McCullough rasped out, breathing heavily. "We'll keep our eyes out for him."

"Slow down," Binson rapped out. "We're making too much noise."

Bullets whizzed past my head, and Ward and I ducked instinctively, turning towards the sound of voices and movement in the forest behind us.

"We need to go—now," Ward yelled, and we turned and ran.

We ran south, heading back towards the field beyond the woods. We could hear soldiers calling out behind us, shooting blindly now in our direction.

I spotted movement to my right, low, beneath the trees, and opened my mouth to call out to Ward. "There— he's off this way," I turned and headed towards the direction the shadowed figure had disappeared in. Crouching low, I struggled to grip my rifle in my left hand, my shoulder sending sharp waves of pain radiating down my back and chest.

I never saw it coming. The Jumper sprang at me out of nowhere, and for a moment I was confused, still certain it was the man in the flight suit. Then it was on me. It slammed into my chest, knocking me onto my back, slamming my injured shoulder into the ground as I screamed in agony. My rifle fell out of my grip. I writhed in pain, as the Jumper loomed over me, odd skittering sounds issuing from its ragged split jaw, moving like pincers, snapping over my face. *I'd left my face shield open again*, I realized in a stab of panic, like a freaking idiot. I tensed, eyeing those slimy white strands as they swung above me, ready to fall into my open mouth.

The Jumper lurched sideways as Ward slammed into it, his momentum carrying them both several feet away, where they crashed to the ground, rolling in a heap of limbs.

No. He didn't have a face shield, only his helmet. I felt a sick wave of dread washing through my gut, my stomach clenching, I struggled to rise onto my right elbow, teeth gritted against a wave of nausea and pain.

I managed to struggle to my feet, crying out something incoherent in Ward's direction. I came to my senses and scanned the ground for my rifle. Staggering over to it, I raised it, but I could barely lift my left arm, still half numb from the pain of the impact. I forced my arm up in an arc and gripped the gun, attempting to hold it steady.

I watched, tears of pain streaming down my cheeks, blinking rapidly, as Ward managed to rise up, straddled over the Jumper. He stabbed in a downward motion, his bayonet held in both hands, plunging it into the Jumper's chest over and over.

Eventually it lay still. Ward lowered his arms, dropping the bayonet, and turning to look for me, chest heaving, as I stood there, trembling, still attempting to steady the rifle on the prone figure beneath him.

"You okay?" He managed, between gasping breaths.

I nodded, still breathing heavily myself. "You?"

"Yeah," he murmured, getting to his feet.

We took off in silence, scanning the dark woods for any sign of movement.

Several minutes later, we ran into McCullough and Binson. We heard them before we saw them; shots ringing out up ahead, voices crying out over the comms.

We staggered to a halt, and I couldn't help but grin. Binson stooped over a dark form on the ground, rising to his feet with the orange backpack in his hands. McCullough waved to us as we approached.

"Good job," I panted.

"Now, let's get the hell out of here." Ward muttered.

17.

We flew back to the fighters. McCullough managed to carry Ward somehow. And Binson carried the orange sample bag, and my rifle, although I was reluctant to part with it. My shoulder was killing me. I was worried that I'd managed to dislocate it, or worse. Now that some of the adrenaline had started to wear off, it felt like it was on fire.

I felt a flood of relief wash over me when I spied the gleaming hulls of the fighters in the moonlight below us. Ward climbed into the back of my fighter, in the navigator's seat.

I pulled on the pilot's headset and pointed for him to grab the set hanging next to his seat.

"Well," he said a moment later, through the headset, "at least I'll be able to brag that I flew with The Crimson Reaper. How many men can say that?" And although I was in a massive amount of pain, I managed to turn and roll my eyes as I shot a smirk at him.

I paused, as I settled in, scanning the cockpit, running through a quick pre-flight check. "Thank you," I said quietly, "for coming to find me. You didn't have to do that."

He was silent for a moment. "We needed to recover those samples." He said, his voice strangely cool now.

I snorted a little, then nodded to myself. "Of course." I murmured back. Because up until now, he'd displayed nothing but concern as far as gathering samples went. I bit back a sharp retort, shaking my head, and focused on getting us airborne.

Despite my shoulder screaming in agony as I manipulated the controls, I enjoyed the flight back to the Carrier as much as possible. Although I doubt you could say the same for Ward. I may have taken a few unnecessary turns. Made a few slightly frivolous maneuvers. Nothing a seasoned fighter pilot, or navigator, couldn't handle.

I glanced back at him, as we touched down in the hangar, and he shot me a grim smile that was more like a grimace. He looked slightly green around the gills. I suppressed a grin.

"Well, I certainly hope that was worth the bragging rights," I crooned to him, and with a suggestive wink, I pulled the headset off, as he stared back at me, and climbed out of the fighter. Making my way across the wing, I jumped down, landing on my feet. I grit my teeth, suppressing the urge to cry out at the jolt of pain that shot up my back and shoulder and through my neck.

I looked over to see Lindsay and Topher running towards me across the hangar.

Lindsay moved as though to hug me, and I shrank back. "Ah," I murmured, "watch the shoulder. I think I may have dislocated it."

Lindsay frowned at me. "Sorry! Yeah, we could tell you were injured. Well, I'm glad you're back in one piece, for the most part. And thank you, for getting the samples, and retrieving them."

I nodded grimly. "Hopefully we got enough this time."

Lindsay grinned slightly, nodding back. "There will certainly be enough for a good start. I think we'll be in great shape." She paused for a moment, thinking. "The only thing better would be a full specimen."

I groaned at the thought of attempting that.

Lindsay grinned, somewhat sheepishly, and nodded. "I know... but that would allow me to fully study their morphology, internal organs, catalog any changes..." she trailed off, at the expression on my face. "But what you got today is great." She glanced over at Topher. "Come on, I'll walk you down to sick bay."

"I got it," Topher said, nodding to her. "It's good to see you back, Captain," he grinned over at me. "I have to say, that chase scene through the woods made for one hell of a ride."

I snorted a little and grinned back. "Thanks," I muttered. "And thanks for helping them get me out."

He nodded again, his expression solemn, before turning to Linsday. "Go on, we all know you're dying to get back to the lab."

I grinned at her, and nodded, and she beamed back. "Okay, I'll come find you later." She turned and jogged out of the hangar.

"McCullough and Binson took the samples straight there," Topher said, watching after her. "I told them I'd meet up with you and get you to Med Bay." He nodded in Lindsay's direction. "She just wanted to make sure you made it back safely."

"Yeah," I shrugged, forgetting for a second that I couldn't. I instantly regretted it. I nodded back towards the fighter behind us, at Ward climbing out gingerly. "I may have taken a little detour. I wanted the captain to get the full experience of flying in a fighter." I smiled wickedly at Topher, and he grinned back, shaking his head.

"Well, we got a little taste of it back here, for a few seconds, at least. I decided to stop watching at that point." I laughed out loud. "Come on, let's get you to Med Bay."

Fixing my shoulder, while unpleasant, was at least a fairly quick process. The doctor insisted on securing it in place with a bandage afterwards, wrapping it tightly in layers of white gauze, although I tried to insist it wasn't necessary.

Topher stayed with me, whispering in my ear every time he deemed the Med Bay staff to be at a safe distance away. "So,

Linds and I were chatting while you were heading back, we think that an EMP blast may have an affect on the Jumpers. Given what they told you about the EMP shields," he shrugged, "plus what we observed today, it seems promising. We know ants use the earth's magnetic field to find their way; it's how they navigate. We theorize that an EMP blast might disrupt their ability to navigate. Not only that, but research has shown that electromagnetic energy in the range of 900 MHz, resulted in ants being unable to follow a trail, and locate attack pheromones. Granted–" he paused for a moment.

We waited until the nurse moved farther away, placing a chart on the counter by the doctor. Topher continued, his voice dropping lower. "These are old studies we're talking about, and we have no idea if this will actually work. But it's worth a try. Especially after seeing how they reacted to the different GSM frequency bands today."

I nodded, following the gist of what he was saying. I still had no idea what GSM meant. He took my nodding as encouragement to continue. "Now we just need to figure out a logistical way of testing out the theory."

"What about an EMP gun?" I murmured excitedly to him. "It was the first thing I thought of when I heard you and Lindsay talking over the comms. I have no clue what... frequency they operate on, but do you think it could be possible?"

Topher's eyebrows went up as I spoke. "Like the anti-flight suit guns the South uses?" He tilted his head to the side, nodding, staring off into the distance as his eyes flickered back and forth. So apparently everyone knew about those guns, except for me. "I'm sure the energy of an EMP gun isn't likely to be centered around the right frequency band, and I'm not sure if it would be strong enough...." he trailed off, "but, what if we were to modify an EMP gun, and center the energy around 900 MHz? I think we would stand a chance at least of disrupting their communication, both via detection and release of pheromones, and their ability to navigate. The colonies they tested that specific energy band on ended up disbanding completely. They just..." he trailed off, "fell apart."

I took a deep breath, nodding to myself as he spoke. "What about the taser effect the guns have now? Do you think that would happen to them? When I was shot with an EMP gun, I couldn't move at all, for nearly a full minute. The sensation and ability to move started to come back very slowly. Even once I was able to move again, I was weak, uncoordinated. I could barely stand. Those side effects would be extremely helpful."

Topher frowned at me. "Wait, when were you shot by an EMP gun?"

I shot him a look. "Ward. Don't ask."

Topher raised an eyebrow, then ran a hand over his beard. "Well, it would be nice if it could weaken them enough that they could be taken out more easily, that's for sure. Hopefully it would have a similar effect, but we won't know until we test it out."

"Okay," I said slowly, "and you think you can do this? Modify an EMP gun?"

Topher grinned at me. "I won't give up until I can."

"Okay," I nodded, "let's do it."

"First things first; I need you to get me an EMP gun," he whispered.

I grinned back at him. "I already have that covered."

18.

Topher escorted me back to my private quarters, and I handed off the EMP gun to him. He took off abruptly, practically running back to the lab.

All I wanted to do was take a shower. I paused, though, my eyes on a flashing icon in the corner of the large screen on the wall.

"TODD," I murmured, "Can you pull up that message for me?" I waited for a second as the message loaded. Was it from the Admiral? Did he want an update on my progress? At least now I had something preliminary I could share with him.

"Message from *Captain Ward*: Come see me on the bridge, immediately, when you get this."

I sighed, shoulders slumping forward. I stared longingly at the door to the bathroom and turned and left the room.

I walked into the bridge with my head held high. If he was planning on scolding me for my little flight maneuvers, I was going to be ticked off. I was filthy and sweaty from the sprint through the woods, and I certainly wasn't in the mood.

I was a little surprised to find Ward alone. He sat in front of the desk, rather than the battle table. The lights on the bridge were dimmed low.

"I got your message," I said bluntly. "Do you need something?"

Ward sat with his fingers interlaced, his chin resting on his hands. He seemed to be thinking before he spoke. "Yeah, I do. I need you to tell me where you got that idea from."

"What idea?" I asked, frowning.

"That idea about 750 MHz, or 900... affecting the Jumpers. Where did that come from?"

My frown deepened. "I told you... I came up with that plan with Lindsay and Topher–"

Ward shook his head. "I know. I know you guys planned everything together. But where did you get that idea from?"

"What makes you think it was my idea?" I asked, folding my arms across my chest. "Maybe that information was part of my briefing." I shrugged awkwardly, forgetting my shoulder was tied down. "Maybe the Admiral told me." He opened his mouth to respond, but I cut him off. "And why does it matter, anyway? It worked. That's all you need to know."

Ward raised an eyebrow and sat back in his chair. "I guess that's true. I guess it's probably not relevant." He cleared his throat, glancing away from me. "Then again, I guess it might be relevant to me to know *when* you knew."

"*When* I knew?" I mimicked his emphasis as I parroted his words back to him.

He nodded at me slowly. "Yeah, I'm a little curious *when* you knew that certain comms frequencies draw them in."

I wasn't getting where he was going with this; my eyes flickered back and forth over his features as he waited for me to respond.

"For example, did you know when we set down at the factory? When I directed everyone to our company's general comms channel. Did it occur to you then, that using the comms on that channel might draw the Jumpers down on us?" He stood, striding over to me. "Because if you did, if the Admiral had already told you that, as part of your briefing, a little heads up might have been nice." He moved closer, until he was only a foot or so away from me. "You know, before it got my men killed."

I glared at him. So, we were back on this again. "Of course I didn't know then." I spat at him. "Is that what you think of me? You think that I would be that careless? Or that deliberately–"

"No," he spat back, "I don't, actually. That's why I'm asking. Because I can't imagine that you would do that if you knew. I don't want to think that you would take that risk, just so you could have a chance to gather the samples you needed.

But let's be clear, Kessler, you've said, on more than one occasion, that you will do whatever it takes, whatever is necessary, to get the samples needed to solve this thing. So don't act shocked that the thought crossed my mind."

I stared back at him, my heart thundering in my chest. My lips parted, stretching in a slow smile. "You want to know when I found out about it, Ward?" I watched him closely, a slightly odd expression on his face now, as though my smile unsettled him. "It was in that goddamn factory that *you* sent me into for no reason."

I knew I should stop, should shut the fuck up, but my mouth kept running anyway. "I ran into some enemy soldiers in that factory. An injured soldier, and a radio operator, trying and failing, to save his life. I placed a tourniquet for him, and showed them how to stop the bleeding."

Ward swallowed, his throat bobbing, as he took in what I was saying. "Their captain stumbled upon us, and he decided to spare me. *They* are the ones who told me all about the comms frequencies. They said we stirred up the Jumpers by using our comms, and that we needed to avoid the frequency band we were on. They said the lower G…" I trailed off, "G… something, frequencies were safe, that they didn't like them. They said transmitting at those frequencies kept the Jumpers away." That and the EMP shield… but I decided to leave that part out, for now. He didn't need to know everything.

"You talked to them? You..." Ward studied my face, a hand reaching forward, just for a split second. But he stopped himself, taking a step back, he ran his hands through his hair, and turned away from me.

"Damn it, Kessler..." he turned back to face me. "Do you have any idea what could have happened? And what do you think Command would do if they knew about this? Do you have any clue what the–"

"What? You think that counts as fraternizing with the enemy?" I shook my head and scoffed a little. "You'd call that treason? Really?" I put my hands on my hips. "Well, now you know. Now you can run back to the Admiral and tell him what I did." Ward just shook his head. "I didn't meet up with them on purpose, Ward. And I'm not a fucking spy. It was an accident. But I'm glad it happened; otherwise, we might never have found out what we needed to know. Certainly not this fast. Not on our own."

He continued to stare at me, an incredulous expression on his face. "So, that's why you lied to me. When I asked you where you went? You thought I'd accuse you of being a spy? That I would tell the Admiral about it?"

I stared back at him. "Yeah, that's the gist of it."

He had the audacity to look offended as he stood there, shaking his head, staring back at me. His lips curved, with that sick little twisted grin that always made my stomach clench.

"Nothing you have said or done since you found out I was being assigned to this ship has made me think otherwise," I said, my voice low, "you expect me to trust you, after how you've acted towards me?"

Ward laughed, shaking his head. He put a hand over his forehead, fingers pressing on his temples on either side. "For fuck's sake, Kessler." He murmured. Eventually, he let his hand drop. "You have to stop."

"Stop what?" I asked, snapping at him.

"Stop... stop running off like that! At the factory–and again today. You managed to separate yourself from McCullough and Binson. You put yourself at risk, put the mission at risk, more people could have died–"

"I didn't run off; I told them I saw something." I swallowed. "I saw a child, Ward." I leaned forward, tears threatened to build behind my eyes, at the thought of her little face, her features still babyish, still half human. "A little girl, turning into one of them. She has a family somewhere, parents..." my voice broke off.

Ward sighed. "I get it, Kessler. But you need to think strategically when you're down there, on the ground, you can't just... go off on your own because you see a kid, or you're looking for cover. You can't just break protocols, do whatever pops into your head."

I snorted. "Oh, okay. Good to know that's what you think of me."

"I didn't mean it that way," Ward sighed, "What I'm trying to say is, if you keep taking unnecessary risks, at some point, it's going to get you killed."

"Maybe," I said, shrugging. "Or maybe it'll be what saves us. Maybe, me doing 'whatever pops into my head', will be the difference between us beating this thing, or getting wiped out by it." I shrugged again. "You're right, in a way. I do follow my instincts. That's how I fly, too, if you care to know. That's how I've managed to keep myself alive, up here," I spread my arms out.

He just shook his head, folding his arms across his chest, as I continued. "Sometimes I break protocols. Sometimes, I even take *unnecessary* risks." I walked over to him. "And don't try to tell me you don't do the same thing."

He sneered back at me, as I leaned closer. "You have a reputation, you know." I pointed at him, my finger poking into his chest. "You're famous for risking your life. Running out into battle, in front of your men. Acting like you're invincible. Like you don't care if you get shot. Like you're not afraid of getting killed."

Ward grimaced, rolling his eyes slightly, he looked away from me. "They say you have nine lives, and you've already used eight of them. I've heard stories about you... and I didn't believe they were true, at the time, but now I do."

He met my eyes again, and smirked. "You've come after me, twice now. You ran through enemy lines, through a forest full of Jumpers." His eyes narrowed, and I sensed him still. "And why is that, Ward? Is it because you have a death wish? Or is there some other reason?"

His eyes flickered back and forth over mine, his gaze dropping to my lips briefly as I spoke. Those last few words I uttered were merely a whisper. I waited for him to respond, hardly daring to breathe.

And he just glared back at me. His eyes were so full of something, close to pain, but maybe even closer to hatred, that my breath caught in my throat.

"I told you," he managed to grind out, through his clenched jaw, "I wanted to make sure we recovered the samples."

That was an answer, but it wasn't the truth. And it certainly didn't explain why he came back for me at the factory. That time, his excuse had been that he was just following orders.

"Oh, of course," I murmured back to him. "I know how much those *samples* mean to you. How important they are to you." His gaze darkened further somehow, which I wouldn't have thought possible a moment ago.

Several seconds ticked by before he spoke. "I think you should go," he said slowly. "I shouldn't have asked you to come here."

I nodded, licking my lips, watching as his eyes tracked my tongue. "I think I will," I said simply. And I turned and left the bridge, without looking back.

19.

We spent most of the following day idly. The men rested, recovering from the last mission, building up strength for the next. I felt lazy, and chose to skip the gym that afternoon.

I was glad I did when we got the call at around 1500 hours. Boots on the ground again, tonight. The lack of time to prepare made me feel slightly uneasy. While I had no prior experience in the combat branch before this mission, I had the impression that the amount of time between missions was shrinking, along with the lead time to prepare.

None of that felt very reassuring. It made me curious whether it was because we were gaining momentum in the fight against the South, or if it was for the opposite reason. Maybe things weren't going well. Maybe it was a sign that Command was scrambling... becoming desperate.

I joined the other officers on the bridge, without waiting for an invitation. The men were already deep in conversation, pointing to the floating terrain map, marking coordinates.

I stood off to the side, with my arms crossed, watching them, trying to gather what the situation was. Wren's gaze kept drifting my way, then back over in Ward's direction. But Ward either didn't realize I was there, or he was ignoring me purposefully.

When he finally acknowledged my presence, maybe ten minutes later, I was pretty sure I had gathered the gist of the mission.

"Kessler," he said, nodding to me briefly, a quick duck of his chin, "I assume you'll remain behind for this one." He went on quickly, before I could get a word in. "Since the last mission was a success, and I'm sure the lab team hasn't had time to process everything yet."

My lips stretched into a tight line. Ah, so that's why he hadn't bothered to include me. I cleared my throat. "I can see why you would think that, Captain," I said smoothly, "but there's one more thing my team needs, and I'm planning on retrieving it tonight."

Ward cocked an eyebrow at me. "Oh?" He straightened, "And what's that?"

I smiled sweetly as heads turned in my direction. "A body."

Ward sighed, frowning a little. "A body." He repeated slowly.

I nodded, still smiling. "Yes. A full specimen."

His frown deepened as the men murmured to each other. I ignored the general chatter and continued. "My team requires a full specimen, to study the morphology of the disease."

"Is that even safe?" Someone muttered. I turned, but wasn't able to identify who had spoken.

"We'll be taking proper precautions. Full biohazard protocols." I murmured.

"Just how are you going to–" Ward started, and I could hear the edge in his voice, but I cut him off swiftly.

"You let my team worry about that," I said sharply. This was nonnegotiable. I was done playing games. This thing was affecting children now. At least one child, for certain. And that was one too many. Every day we wasted, every hour, put more people at risk. Every delay meant more people would suffer. I was done with the delays.

"Kessler, is this really necessary?" Ward sighed, setting down a stack of papers on the table, causing the 3D map to glitch and shudder momentarily.

"Yes," I snapped, my voice a little too sharp. "It is necessary." I swallowed, pausing, forcing myself to stay calm. "Every day, every hour, that we delay in getting my team what they need to figure this thing out, means more people get exposed. More people get killed. More people suffer."

Someone sniggered, "More Southerners."

My eyes flashed in anger, and my blood ran hot as I surveyed the room. "More *people*," I said firmly. "They are *people*." I paused. "This is affecting children now. And I won't be the reason for children dying. Not to mention, our own men." I watched them, gauging their reactions to my words. "I assume you still remember what happened in Houston?"

The room went still, icy cold, at my words. I grimaced satisfactorily. "Unless you want a repeat of that; and that could happen tonight, or tomorrow, or next week..." I trailed off, walking slowly over to the side of the room, towards the desk. "Who knows when the next Houston will take place..." I shrugged, turning back to face them. "I suggest you let me do what I need to, and keep your opinions to yourselves."

My eyes landed on Ward, on those few syllables, and I stared him down, waiting for him to respond, my expression daring him to disagree.

He looked away, eventually, down at the map below, shoulders sinking as he let out a deep breath. He was silent for a brief pause, then he spoke, without glancing my way. "We leave at 1700 hours. Prepare your team."

"What's the mission objective?" I asked him stiffly.

Ward looked up at me, his gaze calculating. "We have our orders." He cleared his throat, "Our target is located on a corner downtown in a small village." He waved his hand, and the 3D image shifted, zooming in on a building on a street corner. "That's all you need to know." He said, his tone sharp. "You worry about your mission, and I'll worry about mine."

I felt my jaw clench. If that's how he wanted to play this, then fine. Why did it matter? I met Wren's gaze briefly, his eyes full of some unreadable emotion, as I nodded once. Then I turned and left the bridge.

We rode a pod down. It felt oddly empty, with just the three of us on board, but I had insisted we needed our own pod to ourselves, at least for the return journey. Ward had assigned one to us to ride down as well.

I had paused, just before boarding, and scanned the busy hangar for Ward. My gaze fell on Wren, directing men into pods. I held up one finger to McCullough and jogged over to Wren. He paused as he saw me approach, one eyebrow raised. "Everything okay, Captain?"

"Yeah," I nodded, "what's the officer's comm frequency for tonight?"

Wren sighed, his eyes darting away from mine before he spoke. I thought for a moment he was going to refuse to tell me. This was getting ridiculous. I was already preparing my retort when he spoke. "We're going with 750 MHz; sticking with the low frequencies. To be safe."

I frowned slightly and bit back the retort on my tongue. It made sense. Ward wouldn't want to risk drawing Jumpers down on his men. Better to deter them, if possible. But of course, it meant the odds of my mission for the evening being successful were now that much lower. I nodded back, one quick jerk of my chin, before turning away.

"Jordan, wait!" I paused mid-stride, turning back as Wren jogged over to me. "Just... stick close tonight, okay?" He swallowed, taking in my expression. "I know you can handle yourself; it's not that. I just..." he trailed off again, looking uncomfortable.

I nodded briskly. "I'll be careful, Wren," I said evenly.

"Okay." He sighed, "See you down there." I gave him a grim smile back and rejoined McCullough and Binson.

I had also spoken with Lindsay, at length, about how to safely transport a body aboard *The Beagle*, and in the end, she had accompanied me to the pod, leaving her lab techs behind to continue their work, as she and Topher set up an area in the pod for us to store the body.

We were in our flight suits, as they would provide us with the most protection. I just prayed we wouldn't encounter anyone with an EMP gun down below. I was fairly certain Ward, or at least Wren, didn't hate me enough to neglect to tell me if wearing the flight suits in this village was a bad idea. But then again, I wasn't one hundred percent sure, given the current state of things.

Topher and Lindsay planned to meet us in the hangar afterward to spray us down with a chemical cocktail designed to neutralize any organic matter. They would also plan to decontaminate the pod itself.

The landing was even rougher than usual, likely in part due to the pod being too light. The weight was thrown off, and there wasn't the usual buffer of bodies packed in beside us. I nearly went flying across the pod and clung to the metal rails overhead for dear life as we finally slid to a stop.

Binson chuckled a little. "Whew, what a landing."

"No kidding," McCullough muttered. "Who knew it would be even worse in an empty pod. Jesus."

I let out a deep exhale, tapping my helmet and lowering the face shield. I watched as they did the same.

"Okay, remember, we're doing our own thing this time. Stick close, and we'll break off as we need to."

Binson and McCullough exchanged a glance. "Is Ward going to be okay with that?" McCullough asked cautiously.

My eyes narrowed at his name. "Leave that to me to worry about." I adjusted my rifle strap, then checked the chamber again for the 3rd time. "He's shown little interest or concern so far for what we're planning." I added, "I don't expect that to change now. Let's just get out there and see what the situation is. Hopefully, we can get what we need quickly and get back to the pods. We can wait here for the rest of them to be ready to leave, if we're done first." I shrugged. "That or we can let him know over the comms that we're heading back in. It might be good to offload the body without an audience anyway."

McCullough remained silent. But Binson murmured. "Sounds like a plan to me."

I nodded, my head bobbing inside the suit. "Let's get going then."

They followed me down the ramp, out into the open field we'd landed in. I spied the treeline to the north of our position, allowing myself a moment to get my bearings. The trees in the distance, and especially the ferns growing beneath them, reminded me of the swamplands in Florida, although I knew we were far from there.

We'd set down somewhere in South Carolina, near the coast. Ward's men were tasked with taking out some sort of target from what I had been able to gather, although I had no idea what could possibly be of any importance to the Northern Alliance in such a small, isolated village.

My vague plan at this point was to trail behind the men, follow them into the village, and wait for the activity to hopefully draw Jumpers down on us. I had no clue whether there were any in the vicinity, but I figured it was worth trying, regardless. Our alternative for the evening was to sit idly on *The Beagle*, twiddling our thumbs, and I'd never handled downtime very well.

We moved slowly through the stretch of woods that separated our landing zone from the village. The ferns grew thick beneath the trees here; between the underbrush and fallen dead trees and branches, it was difficult to traverse the terrain at anything faster than a slow crawl. We picked up speed as we exited the woods, and suddenly the village lay before us, across a field full of tall grass and wildflowers.

The men moved swiftly and silently through the field, eventually entering the village down a dark street. The town was eerily silent and still, with a rural feeling to it that reminded me of back home. There were only a handful of streetlights dotted sporadically throughout the downtown area, flooding pockets with golden light. There was a large park, a sort of commons, in the center of the village. We moved at a semi-crouch along the storefronts, down the first street, sticking to the shadows.

I watched as the units directly in front of us paused, the soldiers falling to one knee, one after the other, fists raised. The three of us stopped as well, dropping down to one knee instinctively.

"Have we already reached the target?" Binson murmured over the comms link I'd set up for just the three of us to use.

"Our odds sure don't look great at the moment, Captain," McCullough murmured, taking in our surroundings.

I nodded my agreement in the dark as I sighed. "I know. Sure seems pretty quiet. I doubt we'll run into any Jumpers out here, but you never know."

Binson shifted behind me, and I turned to see him lifting his feet gingerly, one after the other, examining the ground below. "What the hell?" He murmured.

I turned to face him and tilted forward, somewhat awkwardly, in the suit, to examine the sidewalk below us. I lifted my right foot and set it back down, feeling it slide slightly as it made contact with the sidewalk below. I hit the flashlight on my suit, switching it to the lowest setting, and shone it on the sidewalk below.

Something sparkled and winked, reflecting the light back up to us. It took me a moment to process what I was seeing. The sidewalk below was littered with tiny pieces of glass. I turned to the building at our backs and studied the darkened storefront beside us. A black pit yawned open, the center of the window was missing, framed by jagged shards of glass that still clung to the edges.

I spun, shining the flashlight towards the last storefront we'd passed, to find the glass in the window frame to our rear was still intact. I breathed a little easier at the sight.

"Glass," McCullough murmured. "Someone broke the window."

"Someone, or *something*," Binson murmured back. We pivoted, left and right, glancing up and down the silent street.

"It is a little odd, isn't it, that there's no one out and about? It's not that late," McCullough muttered.

"What day is it?" Binson murmured back, "Friday?"

I paused, thinking for a moment. I wasn't sure. It was easy to lose track of time, of which day it was, on board the Carrier. The days all ran together.

"Shouldn't people be out shopping..." I stared across the street at what looked like a pub. A sign hung out front, with three interlocking golden rings. I couldn't read it from here; the name of the pub was written in fancy scrolling script.

"That looks like a bar," I murmured back. The lights were off.

"Did they find out somehow that we were coming?" McCullough mused.

Binson hissed in my ear, "Something's not right, Captain."

The first round fired managed to hit one of the remaining slivers of glass hanging in the window frame above our heads. It shattered instantly and fell on us, glass shards tinkling down on our helmets like rain.

I flinched, crouching lower and raising my rifle, as the men began to scatter. The surge of soldiers moved forward. They were heading for the alleyway up ahead. "Move out," I called to Binson and McCullough. "Follow them, find cover."

We ran, joining the others down the first alley we came to. The alley was shrouded in darkness and was mercifully empty. No enemy soldiers waited for us in the shadows, only controlled chaos, as the men moved as swiftly as possible through the narrow space.

We followed the units in front of us, around to the back of the storefronts, and found ourselves exiting onto another street, lined with more shops on one side, and a residential neighborhood on the other. Rolling hills were visible, rising above the roofs, covered in more of the primitive looking forest.

"Target is two blocks to the west, and three to the south. Continue to push forward," Nathan's voice rang out up ahead, calm and steady. On our other side, Stevens directed his unit to stay behind to lay down fire on the hostiles to our rear.

I raised my face shield and turned to my men, pointing to my now open helmet. They reached up and raised theirs. "Let's stay here," I murmured to them, once their shields were raised. I nodded to the woods behind the rows of homes across the street. "Maybe we'll have an opportunity to run across some Jumpers. I like our chances here rather than moving deeper into town."

"Sounds good, Captain," Binson replied easily, turning to keep an eye on the woods. McCullough simply nodded his agreement.

We hunkered down in place, and we waited. And waited. The sound of gunfire in the streets behind us grew steadily louder. Eventually, I felt the world around us shudder, shifting, with a loud boom. Heavy artillery of some type. We eyed each other nervously.

"Hope that was us," Binson muttered. I let out a slow stream of air through my nose, nodding solemnly, my eyes fixed on the dark yards and the gaps between houses across the street. The lights remained off. No one seemed to stir behind the blank facades. Had the civilians been evacuated? Or were they all hiding? I pictured them; families, with small children, crouching, huddling together in their basements. The children whimpered in fear. My gut clenched, and I gripped my rifle harder.

I tapped the side of my helmet, cycling back to the officer's comms. I was just listening in for any updates, I told myself. I waited in silence, my mind spinning. Where was Ward? Wren? The officer's comm frequency was completely silent, and I felt my pulse pick up, swallowing a lump in my throat. Maybe they'd switched frequencies for some reason? What was taking them so long, though? It felt as though they had been gone for ages.

"Ward?" I muttered into the comms. "Come in, over." Nothing. I waited, my pulse ticking in my throat. I could feel my heart thumping in my chest, hammering away against the suit.

"Wren? Are you there? This is Kessler. Come in, over." I didn't attempt to hide the urgency in my voice.

But Wren didn't respond. Nor did any of the other First Lieutenants.

I turned and gazed up the street, in the direction Ward had led the bulk of his men in as they pushed closer to the target. It felt as though we'd been waiting here for well over an hour now. Too long. Far too long, given what I'd managed to overhear about their plans before departure. What if something had gone wrong?

I felt the first flutters of panic in my chest, as though my heart was suddenly working too hard. The blood in my veins felt as though it was too thick, or my blood vessels too narrow. There was a resistance there. A squeezing. And I found myself breathing heavily. A tingling began in my hands and fingers. I was starting to feel that old, familiar feeling of a mission having suddenly gone horribly, terribly wrong.

"Something's wrong," I said abruptly, turning back to McCullough and Binson. "The officer's comm has gone silent. I think we need to move. We need to go after them."

"Hang on," McCullough held up a hand, "maybe they just switched frequencies."

I shook my head, and my helmet shifted back and forth at a slight lag to my movement. "No," I murmured back, already turning and starting to move down the street in the direction the men had gone. "Something's not right."

"Okay," Binson sputtered, "and what the hell are the three of us going to do about it?" I spun back in his direction, to see he was stalking after me, his arms held out at his sides. "Captain, we should turn back if you think something's gone wrong. We should return to the pods, head back to the Carrier–"

I cut him off, "I'm not leaving them behind. Let's go see what's happened, see if we can find them–"

McCullough cut me off this time. "We don't even know where their target was exactly, Captain. How are we supposed to find them? They could be anywhere."

"Nathan said the target was two blocks to the west and three blocks south," I replied sharply. "It's a building on the corner," I recalled that much at least had been shared in the briefing. "We head in that direction and attempt to locate them. Maybe they're pinned down somewhere."

As I spoke, I felt the first raindrop falling, landing on my cheek. Binson must have felt the same thing. He held his hand out, up to the sky, as though feeling for raindrops, for only a second, before realizing he was wearing his flight suit, and wouldn't be able to feel anything. He shook his head, rolling his eyes at himself.

The world shook again, with another resounding crash. But this time it wasn't artillery fire. We ducked instinctively, and I watched McCullough peer up at the sky and followed suit. Dark storm clouds were rolling overhead. Just thunder.

"Damn it," McCullough muttered, "just what we need."

"Come on," Binson sighed, turning to head up the street in the direction the men had disappeared in. "Let's get going. The sooner we get out of here, the better."

McCullough gave me a long look, but I just met his gaze steadily. He shook his head resignedly and followed Binson.

We'd made it maybe a block and a half before the deluge began. A heavy, driving rain, falling in sheets, to the booming of not-so-distant thunder. I raised my face shield, as McCullough and Binson did the same up ahead. Rain rendered the shields next to useless, given the flight suits weren't equipped with any means of clearing droplets. Even a light shower could cause visibility to be poor. A massive oversight, in my opinion. I couldn't imagine trying to fly in one during any sort of inclement weather.

The storm covered up the cacophony of battle to the point it was disorienting. The remote pepper of rifle fire seemed sporadic and became harder to localize. I kept thinking it was just around the corner, or down the next alley, but the streets surrounding us remained empty and silent.

My unease only grew as we encountered no one, traversing the now-slick sidewalks. Binson and McCullough stopped more than once to argue, slowing us down. When they stopped a third time, debating which block the target was located on, I growled through the comms at them to get their asses moving, and we continued forward, sticking to the deep shadows under awnings.

Just as we reached the opening into a dark alleyway, a volley of shots rang out to our left. We paused, attempting to peer down the alley, and caught a glimpse of movement at the far end. Their uniforms looked dark, possibly blue, or black. "Friendlies," Binson murmured, "finally."

We had made it about halfway down the alley, when a man darted out from a doorway to my left. A civilian, I realized, with a jolt of surprise. He was dressed in a dark sweater, brown hair worn long, almost to his shoulders, his dark eyes went wide as they met mine. I watched him take in my features, eyes flickering over my face, before dropping down to my chest. I brought my rifle up in his direction, just as his gaze flickered behind me. I flinched and began to turn, but it was already too late. The rain must have helped to hide the sound of footfalls. I felt a crushing blow to the back of my head, just as the lights went out.

My eyes opened what felt like seconds later, although I had no way of gauging how much time had actually passed. I found myself in what felt like a small space. Maybe a bedroom. The room was dark; nearly pitch-black at first, until my eyes began to adjust. I could see a dim source of light; the sky, through a window in the wall to my right, high above my head, a grey rectangle against the black wall. The window was open, and the sound of falling rain drifted into the room, along with the scent of wet earth.

I groaned as I moved onto one elbow, a shooting pain running from the base of my skull to the crown of my head, like a bolt of lightning, that left my skin tight and tingling in its wake.

I was able to move to a seated position and was relieved to find that I did not appear to feel dizzy. My head was killing me, but I was able to move, sit, and hopefully, stand. And fight.

I looked down, sensing something was wrong, and realized with a stab of unease that I was no longer wearing my flight suit. They must have removed it when I was unconscious. I scanned the rest of my body, shivering now, in only the thin tank top and leggings I had donned under the suit. At least the rest of my clothing didn't seem to have been disturbed, and I felt no other aches or pains.

I scanned the room quickly, searching for any sign of my rifle, realizing with dismay that, naturally, they had taken that too. I hadn't brought my knife with me.

I got gingerly, slowly, to my feet, my head throbbing with another shooting pain in protest, and moved over to the door. Locked. Of course. I moved over to the far wall, grabbed a chair that was sitting there, and carried it over below the single window, setting it down as quietly as I could.

Standing perched on the chair, I peered down into the street below, squinting, scanning the shadows lining the storefronts across the street through narrowed eyes. Nothing. No movement, no soldiers, friendly or otherwise. I was pretty sure I was facing the other side of the street now, in the direction we had been heading down the alleyway. My ears strained for a moment, listening for gunfire. I heard nothing over the driving rain and distant thunder.

My eyes went wide, and I raised my right hand to my ear. My comms unit. They hadn't thought to search for it; it was still in my ear, partially hidden by the hair that had come loose in my helmet. I tapped it, with trembling fingers, switching quickly over to the comms link I set up for just the three of us.

"McCullough, Binson, come in, over." A moment of silence, with only the low hum of static, accompanied by the pounding of my own pulse inside my head.

Then McCullough's voice came through, crackling in and out. "Jesus, Captain. Where are you?"

I breathed out a gasp of relief. "I'm in the building," I managed, keeping my voice low. "In that same alleyway, through the first door. At least I think so. Unless they've moved me somewhere else." I swallowed thickly, taking in a deep, gulping breath of fresh air through the narrow window. "A man, a civilian, distracted me while someone knocked me out. They've taken my flight suit, and my rifle..." I paused, glancing around the room, then back at the street. "I'm looking through a window now, I think it's the same building still, overlooking the street that was to our left."

"Got it," McCullough said roughly, his voice thick with anger. "Hold tight. We ran into armed civilians, probably the same group. After that, we stumbled onto Wren's unit. We'll double back. We're coming to get you."

"Okay," I murmured, letting my head tip forward, I rested my forehead against the upper windowpane. The cold glass was soothing against my temples.

"Describe what you can see, through the window, Captain." I heard Binson chime in now. "What floor do you think you're on?"

I proceeded to describe my location, as best as I could tell, within the building, using the view from my window. The men stayed quiet for the most part, although I could hear them muttering from time to time to each other, or maybe to Wren. I realized remotely that they may be trying to keep me talking, to help me stay calm.

When the door behind me slammed open, bouncing off the wall and nearly closing again, I thought for a brief moment that it was them. My heart leapt into my throat as three men in civilian clothes stepped into the room.

The first one was the tallest. The man in the alleyway with shoulder length brown hair. He sneered at me for a moment before closing the distance between us, dragging me by the arm roughly off the chair. My body weight brought me crashing to the floor, and his grip on my arm tightened, causing a sharp shooting pain to run through my arm and shoulder as they bore my weight.

I scrambled to get my feet beneath me, managing not to cry out by biting down on my lip.

He started to pull me towards the door. "Who were you talking to?" He sneered, turning and bending down to get in my face. His breath stank. I turned my face away, grimacing.

"I wasn't talking to anyone," I said loudly, "where are you taking me?" I wanted them to know I was being moved to another room. I scrambled for purchase on the wooden floorboards, my stocking feet slipping forward. If I could slow them down, even by a few seconds, that might be the difference in them reaching me in time.

We played tug of war with my arm for a second or two, and as I managed to lean back, I let him gain the upper hand for a moment. I relaxed my legs, allowing the momentum to pull me forward. I swung on my arm, as it screamed in pain, bringing my legs up, I managed to slam my right foot into his nose.

I heard and felt the blow land with a sickening crunch, as he cried out in pain, his grip on my arm relaxing instantly. I pulled back, shaking my arm to relax it as it throbbed with pins and needles.

"*Fucking cunt,*" the man ground out, both hands over his face, as blood dripped down onto the scuffed floorboards below.

I rotated my shoulder, trying to get the sensation back, as the next one came at me. I crouched, lowering my center of gravity, both fists up, waiting for him. He paused in his approach, seeing me drop easily into a fighting stance.

I didn't wait for him to make the first move. Using that split-second pause to my advantage, I shot forward, landing a blow to his eye with my right fist, then a quick second jab with my left.

I heard chatter on the comms now, in the background, as the man staggered back for a moment, one hand lifted gingerly to his eye. He managed to open it and was turning on me when their voices grew louder, more excited, but coming through as raspy whispers. I prayed they had entered the right building.

The third man lunged past the second, just as he was recovering, his raised fist moving towards me. His fist connected with my jaw as I attempted to lean back to avoid the blow. But I was a fraction of a second too slow, and my head snapped to the side from the impact, throbbing in a blinding, searing pain. I felt a wave of nausea sweep over me as that shooting pain ran up the base of my skull once more. I swallowed thickly, worried for a moment that I was about to puke.

The third man lunged for me, grabbing me around the waist. He took me down, roughly, to the floor. I managed to keep my neck strained and just avoided slamming the back of my head, my weight coming down on my shoulders and upper back instead.

I was filled with a blind sort of panic then, crushed by his weight on top of me. He struggled to his knees, pushing me back down as I attempted to rise. I fought him, but he grabbed me by both wrists, pressing my hands to the floor over my head.

I brought my knee up, attempting to slam it into his groin, but he collapsed down on top of me, his thigh between mine, pinning me in place. He was more than twice my size and strong. I managed to lift my arms up, an inch or so at a time, before he slammed them back down again. I lay my head back against the floor, chest rising and falling rapidly, and I struggled to take several deep breaths, allowing my muscles to go slack.

There was a shifting, as his weight lifted off my thigh, only to be replaced by rough hands gripping my legs, yanking down on my leggings. I kicked out, my foot connecting somewhere in the other man's torso. He let out a muffled yelp. "Hold her down for fuck's sake," he yelled at the man pinning me down. "Stupid bitch," he muttered, "we'll teach you what happens to stuck-up Yankee cunts like you who are stupid enough to cross over the border."

I felt an icy shot of real fear sluice down my spine at his words, and fought against the rising panic. They would make it. They would make it in time. The little voice in the back of my head murmured, whispering to me. *And what if they don't?*

There had to be something... something I could do to stop them. Gain the upper hand. Anything. My mind spun in circles, eyes flickering wildly over the ceiling. I strained my neck, searching the bare room around me, as though I would find some sort of weapon.

I studied the man on top of me frantically, eyes on his waist. Was he carrying a weapon? Maybe a handgun, or a knife, tucked into his belt? I felt my leggings start to slide down, as they tugged on the right side, and in a desperate attempt to break loose of his hold on my arms, I let my head drop back again, then brought it forward, slamming my forehead against his without warning, with a sickening, bone-jolting impact that left my vision momentarily black, and my ears ringing.

His grip slackened, but I barely registered it, as I writhed back and forth in pain beneath him, his moaning in my ear blocking the first peppered shots that rang out from the doorway.

Chaos erupted in the room. Shots rang out. Men cried out in pain and rage. I felt the man's weight lift off me, and I managed to roll to my side, pushing at the floor, my feet sliding, I scrambled back, towards the far wall.

It was over in seconds. I felt a hand on my arm, and I jerked away, pressing myself against the wall, turning and squinting up at the figure that loomed over me.

He shrank back, one hand still reaching out to me, hovering in the air beneath a set of piercing blue eyes. *Wren*.

I took a deep, gasping breath, and the air exited my lungs in a strangled sob. Wren stared down at me, his eyes sweeping up and down my body. I reached down, struggling to pull my leggings back up over my hips. I watched as his gaze hardened in an expression I had never seen on his face before.

He stood and turned away from me. I flinched back against the wall, squeezing my eyes shut, as a volley of shots rang out, too loud in the small space. I sat there for several seconds, trembling, keeping my eyes squeezed shut.

I heard a series of wet-sounding slaps. Flesh connecting on flesh, followed by grunting. The floor vibrated beneath me with the force of repeated impacts. I felt movement and turned to see McCullough at my side, crouching low in front of me. His eyes were fixed across the room. Several men crowded around a slumped figure. The man with shoulder-length brown hair, now tousled, scraggly, slick, and matted in places with blood. His head hung forward, both arms held up in the air. He was slung between two men, who held him upright, as Wren pummeled him with his fists, over and over. I flinched involuntarily at each blow.

"Stop," McCullough called out, his gaze on me. "Stop it," he yelled, getting to his feet. He moved over and grabbed Wren's arm, holding him back. Wren pulled away, attempting to shove him off.

"I'm going to *fucking* kill him. Slowly." I heard him growl.

I let out a shuddering breath as McCullough murmured something in Wren's ear. Binson moved swiftly to my side as I attempted to rise to my feet. I grasped onto his arms to steady myself.

"Take it easy, Captain," he murmured.

"I'm okay," I said, a little too sharply back. I lifted a hand to the back of my head. "I was knocked out for a bit. Unconscious. My head hurts, but otherwise, I'm fine."

His eyes swept over my features, and he nodded briskly. "Okay. Let's get you out of here."

We moved a step towards the door, then paused, as the men dragged the brown-haired man, now unconscious from the looks of it, out the door, and somewhere off down the hall.

Wren stood there, chest heaving, watching them go. He turned to us as we moved forward, his jaw tight, his eyes lit with a sickening inner malice that made my stomach clench. I felt something shift in the back of my mind, despite the crushing weight of exhaustion that swept over me, now that the fear and adrenaline were wearing off. An odd, remote, almost clinical sense of curiosity at the depth of stark anger displayed on his features.

We stood there, completely still, other than our chests rising and falling, and his gaze swept over me once more, lingering on my jaw. It ached, sore from that last blow.

When his eyes met mine again, I uttered the first thought that came to my mind. "Don't tell Ward."

Wren's jaw tightened further, as though he were biting down on his own teeth. His gaze hardened, brows furrowing slightly.

"What?" He scoffed slightly, as though he hadn't processed what I'd just said.

I cleared my throat, and Binson's grip on my arm tightened slightly as I swayed. "I said, don't tell Ward what happened." I swallowed thickly. "It won't do any good."

Wren didn't move. He continued to stare at me, eyes narrowed, before turning to Binson. "Get her out of here," was his only response. He turned and left the room, turning left and heading down the hall.

McCullough, Binson, and I shuffled out the door behind him, turning right, moving down the hallway, and a set of narrow stairs. I didn't breathe easily until we were back outside, out of the dark alleyway, and on the main street once more. Lifting my face to the sky, I gulped down the cool night air and relished the feeling of the raindrops falling down on my upturned face.

20.

I allowed Binson and McCullough to take turns supporting me during the walk back to the pods, and they held me, propped up between them, as we rode the pod back to the Carrier. The constant rattling and vibrating of the pod made my head throb in waves of agony.

I saw they'd managed to recover my flight suit from the building. It lay on the floor of the pod in a heap, bouncing and jostling. There was no visible damage from what I could see. But my chest burned with rage as I stared down at it. What had happened to the man with the brown hair after Wren had his men drag him from the room? I felt sick to my stomach, and I wasn't sure I wanted to know.

I'd managed to avoid running into Ward on the way back to the pods, and when I stepped off the pod, I found Lindsay and Topher were still waiting for us in the hangar. With everything that had happened, I had forgotten to call ahead and let them know the mission had been unsuccessful.

Lindsay took one look at me and ordered the men to march me straight to Med Bay.

I sat on the exam table while doctors and nurses fluttered around me. They shone a bright flashlight in my eyes, for longer than seemed necessary. I watched as the wounded were carried in and tended to. Too many wounded. I felt my stomach lurch at each new injury and wondered again what the hell had happened down there.

I told them I was fine. Told them to stop wasting time on me, and help the others. But they insisted on scanning my brain with some sort of odd helmet connected to dozens of wires, before they finally declared I seemed to have miraculously managed not to get a concussion, from what they could tell. I was ordered to return the following morning for a checkup and warned that I should call immediately if I experienced any nausea, vomiting, or odd visual symptoms. I nodded in agreement, downing the pills they gave me with a gulp of water.

I was also told I must eat something after taking the medication. McCullough and Binson escorted me straight to the Mess Hall from there, while Lindsay returned to the lab. Topher had already retreated there before I even left for Med Bay, after having mumbled some sort of platitude to me awkwardly under his breath.

"Ask TODD to call me on the lab extension," Lindsay said, gripping my arm as she turned to leave us on the way to the Mess Hall. "Any time tonight, Jordan. I don't care how late it is. If you need anything. I'm serious." She held my gaze for several seconds until I nodded my agreement. I hadn't told her what happened, but she seemed to sense it had been something serious enough to rattle me.

The Mess Hall was thankfully quiet. McCullough and Binson seemed reluctant to let me out of their sight. They led me over to the officer's table and had me take a seat and rest, while they brought me a full plate of food. McCullough reminded me sternly that the doctors said I had to eat something. I nodded and sighed, picking up my fork to placate him.

I just wanted to be alone. And he seemed to sense that. He drifted over to the bar after I took a bite or two, satisfied that I would follow orders. He and Binson posted up at the bar, gulping some sort of dark liquid in short tumblers. They murmured together, their eyes straying to me repeatedly.

I had no idea whether Wren had informed Ward yet of what had happened. But it was pretty clear he hadn't told Molton.

He staggered into view, coming around to the other side of the officer's table. "Mind if I join you, Captain?" He asked cheerfully, taking a seat before I had a chance to respond.

I sighed internally and leaned back, taking a sip of my water. Molton frowned over at my glass.

"Need a drink?" He asked, smiling at me, his voice thick.

I shook my head, wincing slightly. I had forgotten I needed to keep my head as still as possible. But thankfully, the meds were starting to kick in, and the pain came as more of a throbbing versus a stabbing. "Can't," I said, attempting to keep my voice light. "I suffered a minor head injury on the mission. No alcohol. Doctor's orders."

Molton grimaced and shook his head. "Ah, I'm sorry to hear that, Captain. Glad you're okay."

I nodded, keeping my lips pressed shut in a tight line.

"Well, we lost a lot of good men today." My stomach sank at his words. He shook his head, his voice suddenly gruff. "And as a result, Ward is getting properly shitfaced. And I'm already well on my way to being drunk, personally." He peered through the wall of windows, out into space.

"I can see that," I replied, a small smile twisting my lips as he grinned in response. I quickly wiped it away, my mind flashing intrusively back to my hands, pinned down, over my head. The feeling of that man's weight against my body, the crushing panic.

Molton let out his signature barking laugh, and the sound eased the panic rising in my chest slightly. I looked up to find his gaze fixed on me. His eyes were bright and sharp behind his wire-rimmed glasses.

"You know, my family's from the South. Originally." He said quietly, his gaze fixed intensely on mine. I felt my eyebrows rise involuntarily. He just nodded. "So's Wren's."

I looked down at my drink, frowning slightly. Wren's family, from the South? I thought Ward had mentioned something about him being from California.

"There's a lot of folks down there who are ass backward. They don't know what century they're living in, much less what year." Molton sighed deeply, his gaze falling to the beer in his hand. "But, there're a lot of good folks, too. Regular people, like you and me. They work hard. They keep their heads down. Family's everything to them. That's all they have, really. That and their land. What the government hasn't taken from them. My family were farmers, way back when. They used to own their own land, acres and acres of it. Going back generations. But at some point, the government tanked the economy. Remember learning about how they put all those tariffs in place? Before everything went to shit?"

I nodded wordlessly, my focus fixed on him, taking in every word. I watched as he sighed again, taking a sip of his beer, before setting the glass down heavily on the wooden table.

"He conned people. Regular, hardworking people, into thinking he cared about them. Thinking he was going to make their lives better. Instead, he destroyed the economy, took away all the systems in place that helped farmers, like my grandparents, all the subsidies and loans. It got so bad, they couldn't afford to keep the land anymore. Had to sell it off to the highest bidder. And you know who that was?" He paused, watching me over the rim of his glass, as he lifted it once more.

I shook my head, unsure of the answer, although I had an inkling. "One of his cronies. The idiot who ran that sham department of efficiency. One of his companies set up a website, allowing farmers a way to take out additional loans on their land, so they could keep it. But the result was, the rich landlords swooped in, bought up all the farmland, and ended up owning it, while the hard-working folks had to work themselves half to death, just to make ends meet, in the hopes that they could somehow one day afford to buy their own land back." He shook his head, chuckling. "It was a scam. The whole thing was a scam. That idiot was no better than a traveling snake oil salesman. And they voted for him, for a second term. Put him *back* into power. Gave him control of everything."

Molton sighed again, gazing back out at the stars. "They gave up, eventually. Left. With basically nothing but the clothes on their backs. They managed to find people, friends of friends of theirs, to help smuggle them across the border, to the north. They moved up the coast to Maine. And we've been there ever since."

He fell silent for a moment, staring out the window. "I have a girlfriend, you know. Back home. She's a teacher."

"Really?" I said, taking another bite of food. "What does she teach?" I asked between swallows.

"Elementary, at the moment. But her passion is history," he said, turning back to me, with a faint look of pride on his face. He reached into the pocket of his shirt and pulled out a creased photograph, handing it over to me.

I took it and gazed down at the young woman in the photo. Long, auburn hair that fell in soft curls. Green eyes, and pale skin, her cheeks peppered with freckles. She was grinning up at the camera. Molton sat beside her in the photo. Rocky sand and the ocean, just visible over their shoulders. "She's beautiful," I said, a smile on my lips. I felt my eyes sting slightly, gazing down at them. "You look so happy together."

"We were," he said, his voice soft. "That was a great day." I nodded briskly and handed the photo back to him.

He held it in one hand, his beer in the other, and stared down at it wistfully. "You know, Shannon, she knows nearly everything about what happened. What led to the downfall of the United States. She knows more than most. She's spent hours interviewing the elderly folks in town, back home. Visits them on Sundays. She brings them muffins She wants to write a book about it." He grinned. "She learned not to ask them to talk about any of it. She just... she has a way about her. And people end up opening up. Telling her everything they went through." I'd stopped chewing, gaze fixed on him.

"She'd tell you that both sides used propaganda before the war. She'd tell you it was worse, in the South, sure. But both

285

sides... there were a lot of similarities. And she says maybe... maybe they never stopped."

I swallowed thickly, then reached for my glass of water, gulping it down, the ice tinkling the only sound in the quiet Mess Hall.

"If she were here right now, she'd ask, 'Who benefits from our division?'" He paused, tucking the photo back into his pocket. "Who benefits from our hatred of one another? From our fear?" His voice dropped low, and he leaned forward. "It's only ever been the people who have the real power, not them. And they know it. That's why they put systems in place. To keep us down. Keep us marginalized. Especially in the South, Captain. But here, too." He shook his head, pointing at the table. "Don't kid yourself about that."

I felt myself trembling slightly, suddenly weak with exhaustion. "But it's the people; it's us. We're the ones who have the real power. We always have. We just need to realize it. Need to come together." He shook his head, "Those poor bastards, down South, they have no education system to speak of. It's a joke. Every aspect of their lives is controlled by what's left of a dying oligarchy, clinging to power. And the people are the ones suffering, while the rich get richer. Many of them are religious fundamentalists, and they use that. They use that to control them. Keep them in check. And yes," he waved his hand. "There are those who are racist, sexist, all of that..."

My gaze dropped to my plate, my stomach churning slightly, as I flashed back again to what had nearly happened to me only just this evening. "But that's true, even in the North." Molton insisted, his voice dropping low. "There are bad people everywhere. Bad seeds. But here's the thing: the majority, the vast majority of people, are good. And they want to do good. They don't want this war any more than we do. It's their brothers, their husbands, out there, dying. Just like we are. And most of them are just like you and me. And they'd give anything for a chance at freedom. A chance at a good life. That's all any of us want, really."

I nodded down at my plate as he spoke, tears stinging behind my eyes. I took a deep, shuddering breath. I knew he was right. Although it was hard to feel that way at the moment. Most people were good. I thought of Billy. The young soldier I'd helped. Captain Williams and his men. They were people, I reminded myself. People. Not monsters. Not all of them.

"Anyway," Molton sighed, taking another sip of his beer. "I tend to get a little philosophical when I drink."

I looked up at him, with a grin, and nodded thoughtfully. "That's one of the more pleasant possible side effects, I'd say."

His grin widened at my words, and he got to his feet, tipping his empty glass towards me. "Well, I only came here to get another beer. And I think I'll grab one more, which should be my last, and head back to the bridge." He paused, gazing at me thoughtfully, "You should come join us, Captain. I think it would be good." He began to make his way back over to the bar. "For everyone," he added. I just nodded, as though I were considering it.

He waved a hand at me in farewell and joined McCullough and Binson at the bar to grab another beer.

I finished my dinner in solitude, and I did feel slightly better afterward. Although my head still throbbed, it was a dull, more distant pain, and my jaw was sore when I moved it too far to the side, but it was subdued at least, for now.

McCullough and Binson stopped me as I rose to take my dishes to the drop-off. I told them I would be fine to head back to my room alone, insisting I didn't need an escort. They agreed, reluctantly, and went back to their drinks.

I had planned on just returning to my room, but I felt too restless to sit still, and I wasn't sure I wanted to be alone.

Without any real plan, I ended up wandering the corridors of the Carrier. I stopped whenever I reached a bank of windows to stare out at the vastness of space. The stars, always a comforting sight to me back home, were truly breathtaking up here. The swirls and clouds of distant arms of the galaxy we rotated in, appearing in vibrant colors. No matter how many times I saw them, they were still astonishing.

I wrapped my arms around myself, hugging them to my chest, as I turned and continued down the corridor. I was so lost in thought, I had paid no attention to where I was going. I'd managed to wander back towards the bridge somehow.

I stopped in front of the set of double doors, a thin blue glow surrounding the frame. I bit my lip, staring at the door, unsure of whether I should enter.

I moved to turn, to head back to my room, and go to sleep. I was tired. But the doors slid open silently, startling me, and Powers peeked out into the corridor. He grinned when he saw me standing there. "Reaper!" He inclined his head to me. "You're just in time to join the fun." *Oh god.* I sighed internally.

"Actually," I said, "I'm really tired, I was just thinking I might head back–"

He cut me off, his voice pitched low. "You might want to come in, after all, Captain. It's all over the news." I frowned at him in confusion.

"What's all over the news?" I said slowly. But my feet were already moving forward, not waiting for a response, I moved into the bridge, eyes sweeping the room, and locking onto the large screen on the right wall.

The sound was muted, apparently, or just turned down so low I couldn't hear it. But a reporter sat at a desk in a newsroom, the red ribbon of text below running swiftly across the screen read *'Bizarre illness continues to spread throughout the South; now threatening to spill into the Northern Territories.'*

"Oh god..." I heard myself mutter. I turned to Powers with wide eyes, and he just nodded, holding up his glass to me in a silent, macabre cheers. Molton stood off to the side, watching us.

"Yeah," he said, shaking his head, "shit's about to get real."

I groaned audibly and turned back to gape at the screen. Captions, in large white text, flashed above the headlines. I watched the reporter's mouth moving for a second and turned my attention to the captions. '...we move next to our field reporter, Jim Davies, down at the border, bringing us the latest news on the spread of this terrible, terrible disease. Jim–'

"Look what the cat dragged in," I heard Ward call out from across the room, and I turned to the table to see heads swiveling in my direction. Ward stood there, glass a quarter full of dark liquid. He swirled it slowly, glaring at me, before downing it and setting the glass down on the table with a thunk. "Perfect," he said. "You finally decided to show up."

I glanced over at Wren warily. He looked away. Down at the floor, not meeting my gaze. "I hope you enjoyed your little disappearing act this evening," Ward said archly. I felt some of the tension in my body ease at his words. He clearly had no clue what had happened. Either that or he was truly the world's biggest asshole. "You're just in time." He nodded at the screen before us. "Breaking news. This thing is finally reaching the border." He snorted. "Big surprise."

I turned my attention back to the screen, not wanting to miss what they were saying. "Can we turn the volume up? Unmute? I can't hear–" I started.

"I can't hear it–" Ward chuckled, "I mean, I can't listen to it. Can't stand it." He waved a hand at the screen dismissively. "Not right now." He turned to me. "These fucking morons. What did they think would happen?" He scoffed, shaking his head, hands splayed out. "I can't..." he trailed off, laughing. "I can't..." he started laughing again and turned away from me. "Let me get you a drink, Captain."

I crossed my arms, glaring after him. He was clearly wasted. I turned to look over at Moltonky. "Is this shit-faced, or only half-shit faced?" He opened his mouth to respond, and I added. "Please tell me this is fully shit-faced."

Molton just shook his head, sighed, and downed the rest of his drink.

"I'm fine," Ward called out over his shoulder.

"I'm not drinking tonight," I called back. He moved to a counter next to the screen, where a coffee dispenser took up most of the space. He pulled open a cabinet and removed a glass bottle of dark liquid.

"Fine, then I'll drink it myself," he retorted.

"No," I called out to him, moving over to join him at the counter. I put my hand over his on the bottle. "I think that's enough, Captain," I murmured to him, my voice pitched low. I didn't want to embarrass him in front of his men, but he clearly had had enough. Why weren't they stopping him?

Ward's gaze slid from my hand on his, up my arm, to my face. I watched his eyes linger on my hair, traveling up its lengths. I'd taken my hair down from the braid I'd had it in for the mission. The tight braids had only made my headache worse. It hung loose around my shoulders now, falling in odd bends and kinks, after having been coiled tightly all day. I knew it was a mess, but I was too drained to care.

He gave me a smirk and shook his head. "No, I don't think it is," he said softly. "I still can't feel anything, so... time for another one." He moved to grab the stopper with his other hand, and I pulled on the bottle, tipping it away from him.

"What the hell is that supposed to mean?" I asked, glaring at him. "So, all this alcohol is supposed to make you feel something? Is that it?"

He just smirked at me again, then laughed, as though I had said something funny. He nodded at me. "You should probably go, Captain. You should go to bed."

My eyebrows went up. "Oh really? I should go to bed?" I scoffed, unable to keep from laughing at that. "Um, I hate to break it to you, Ward, but you are clearly the one who needs to go to bed. You've had enough, and I think you could use some sleep."

"No," he shook his head, shooting me that wicked smile of his. The one that always made my gut twist. "That's not what I need at all."

"Okay," I said, pulling the glass bottle from his hand and setting it firmly on the counter, as far away from him as I could. I turned away, hiding my flushed cheeks. "You are wasted. Wren!" I called out, leaning past Ward, to try to find Wren over at the table.

"Yeah!" He called out to me. I watched him get up and jog over to us. "What's up?" He asked. He looked exhausted himself. Dark circles rimmed his blue eyes, which appeared duller somehow, missing their typical brightness.

"I think he needs help. We should get him into bed." Ward snorted, looked like he was about to say something, then fell into helpless laughter. I clamped my mouth shut, cheeks starting to burn. I looked back at Wren. "Seriously, Wren. He's had enough."

Wren sighed deeply, ran a hand through his mussed blonde curls, and shook his head at me. "I know, trust me, but..."

"I have a better idea. Why don't you hit me, Captain?" Ward quipped.

"What?" I turned back to him, brows furrowed in confusion.

"You heard me." He grinned at me. "Why don't you fucking hit me? Hmm?" He shrugged, his expression becoming serious. "You've wanted to, haven't you?" His voice dropped low. "Be honest, how many times have you wanted to hit me? Hmm?" He raised an eyebrow at me. "I bet you'd love to just sock me right in the face." He shrugged. "Go ahead."

I shook my head, letting out a huff of air. "I am not going to hit you, Ward," I said firmly. It didn't matter that part of him was right. Spot on, actually. It would probably feel extremely satisfying to punch him in the face. But I was having no part of... whatever this was.

Ward shrugged. "What a shame. Your loss." He turned to Wren. "How about you, MacMillan; take your best shot."

Wren sighed deeply, turning to Ward, shoulders slightly slumped. "I don't wanna hit you, Grant, okay? Don't do this."

I had the distinct impression this had happened before. I recalled Moltonky joking at dinner the other night about Ward trying to get someone to fight him. Apparently, that wasn't facetiousness.

Ward shook his head. "Just hit me. Come on." He moved over towards Wren, squaring up against him. Wren shook his head.

"I said I don't want to. I'm not doing it; not this time." The other men were getting to their feet, starting to head over to us.

"Come on, man, just get it over with. Don't be a fucking pussy." Ward murmured, grinning.

"I'm not a pussy," Wren pointed at him. "And fuck you, okay? You're not going to goad me into hitting you. I've told you–"

"Fine. That's okay," Ward shrugged, like it was no big deal, moving a step back, turning towards the approaching men. "Let's do something else then, huh?" He thought for a moment. "Hey, did I ever tell you guys about the time we got leave, out in California? Back in Wren's hometown." Ward glanced back at Wren, grinning wickedly.

"Damn it, Grant, shut up." Wren shook his head, his eyes half glazed in anger. I realized he was pretty far gone himself. *Goddamn it.* I had been counting on him to try to keep Ward in check, but it looked like that wasn't going to be happening.

"You should've seen this girl, he–"

Molton put a hand on Wren's shoulder. "He's just baiting you, man, don't–"

But Wren shrugged him off, moving closer to Ward. "I said, shut the fuck up; I'm serious." The atmosphere in the room hushed a little. For the second time today, my gut twisted as I watched Wren. I'd never seen him angry before today. He was normally always so calm and collected.

"Come on, Ward, let's call it a night, head back down." Nathan called out.

Stevens stepped forward, both hands raised. "Man, just let it go, alright? It's okay. No one blames you, you've gotta stop doing this to yourself."

I cringed inwardly at his words. Was that why he did this? Because he blamed himself? Wren had said he beat himself up after Houston. Maybe he hadn't just meant that figuratively. This was what he did? Look for someone to kick his ass, after a loss?

Ward ignored him, eyes fixed on Wren. "I remember that picture of her, you used to have back at boot camp. The one where she's—"

That was apparently enough. Wren pitched forward and took a swing at Ward's face, his fist connecting with a solid thud. Chaos ensued as he battered him, landing several blows. Ward pushed him, both hands on his chest, and ducked, avoiding another blow. He spun back to face him, laughing, as Wren recovered and sprang forward, grabbing him around the middle and tackling him to the ground.

Ward landed on his back, with Wren on top of him. He pounded him again with his fist. Ward was still laughing, turning and spitting a mouthful of blood onto the floor.

"Stop it!" I heard myself yell. I turned to find Molton. He stood there with his arms crossed, shaking his head, watching them. "Molton," I called over to him, gesturing at them, "stop them, do something!" He sighed, uncrossing his arms, lowering them to his sides, still shaking his head. I turned back to the men on the ground. Ward's face was a bloody mess; he was going to have black eyes tomorrow, possibly a broken nose. *Goddamn it.*

They paused for a second. The men were all calling out, either egging them on or yelling at them to stop. I couldn't hear anything, but I watched as Wren leaned forward and said something to Ward. Whatever it was, it pissed him off, because he started fighting back for the first time. He took a swing at Wren's face, knocking him sideways and managing to push him to the floor. They were locked together now, each getting a blow in whenever they could; the fight erupting into pure chaos.

I tore my eyes away from them and turned back to find Molton, who stood there, still just shaking his head. Nathan and Powers stood next to him. My heart racing, I moved over to them, grabbing Nathan's arm.

"Nathan, please! Do something!" I turned to Powers, exasperated. "Powers!" They studied me for a second, then Nathan sighed and turned to Powers. He nodded briskly, and they moved forward, shoving their way between the men. They grabbed hold of Wren, each taking an arm, and attempted to drag him backwards, off Ward.

Several of the others joined in to help them, and together they managed to drag them apart. Ward lay splayed on his back, arms out over his head, chest heaving. Wren looked spent as well, slumping down to lie on the ground, chest rising and falling rapidly. He'd taken a few blows, but he looked relatively unscathed compared to Ward. *Fucking idiots.* I shook my head. My eyes caught on the screen to the right. The news was still on, detailing the spread of the Jumpers over our borders. That's what we should be focused on. Not this bullshit.

I moved forward, stepping gingerly over limbs, making my way between the men until I reached Ward. I knelt down beside him, and his eyes swiveled over to me.

I shook my head, studying his face. "Really?" I said, eyebrows raised. "What the hell is wrong with you? Huh?" He laughed weakly, another dribble of blood releasing, trailing down his chin, onto his neck.

"I don't know." He murmured. "If you figure it out, you let me know, 'kay Jordan?"

I froze, his words breaking through the red haze of my anger. *Jordan.* He'd used my first name. I shook myself, pushing away the little thrill that went through me. So he'd used my first name. So what? It meant nothing. He was wasted. He was a drunken, self-destructive idiot. And an asshole, when sober. I gritted my teeth and slid a hand under his shoulder. "Come on," I muttered, "let's get you up, you need to go to Med Bay."

"No," he murmured, shaking his head. "No, I don't. I'm fine."

"You are anything but fine." I retorted quickly. "But I can't do anything about that right now. Let's go get your face fixed at least."

Ward chuckled darkly, seeming to find that amusing. I attempted to push him up to a seated position and looked up to find several of the men moving over to help me.

Wren had made his way back over to us and moved to the other side of Ward as he stood. He managed to stay on his feet, although he swayed back and forth, unsteady for a moment. The men helped him cross the room, leading him over to the table, where he plopped heavily into a chair.

Wren shook his head, a grim, somewhat contrite expression on his face. "There's nothing to be done about it, once he's like that. When he's determined to fight someone, he'll find a way." He swallowed, "He would've just ordered one of us to do it, eventually." I nodded, but my expression conveyed my annoyance.

"Then you should refuse," I said, my tone clipped. "Refuse to hit him, next time. He needs help," I said, crossing my arms over my chest. "It's not healthy, not..." I shook my head, trailing off.

"No, it's not." Wren agreed, watching the men over at the table. "But this is war." He turned back to me. "He carries the responsibility for all of us on his shoulders now. And he was just as bad before, when it was just our unit. Now that it's the whole company..." he shook his head. "Don't get me wrong, I think he's a great captain. But... I'm not sure he can handle it. It's too much pressure..." Wren shrugged. "If this is what he needs to do, to get through it... then yeah, we'll hit him, if we have to. If it helps."

I sighed deeply, forcing myself to relax. I guess it made sense, in a twisted sort of way. I felt deflated suddenly, exhausted. I moved a step closer to Wren, dropping my voice low. "You didn't tell him, did you?" I couldn't be sure, but my gut was telling me Ward didn't know.

Wren shook his head slowly, a dark look coming into his eyes. "Not yet," he replied gruffly. "He knows something happened, but no details." I frowned at him. Wren shook his head at my expression. "There's nothing to be done about that. He knew you were... delayed. The other units were holed up on the edge of town. They had to wait for us while we went back to find you." I winced slightly at his words. So, somehow, I'd managed to be a burden. To delay the mission, yet again. How many men were injured or killed while they came back to save me? My gut roiled, and I turned away, facing the wall of black before us, the stars suddenly blurry, while I got myself back under control.

"I was able to distract him from asking any further questions, for now." Wren continued. "But I imagine he'll be asking for more details, for an explanation, once he's sober." He looked back at me, and seemed to sense my inner turmoil, as he looked suddenly uncomfortable, and unsure what to say next. He took a step towards me, his brows creased, and I cleared my throat, looking away again.

"Great," I said, in a clipped tone. "Keep him in the dark. If he demands answers, tell him to ask me what happened. I'll figure something out."

"Why?" Wren had frozen in place, and I could feel his eyes on me. "Why is it so important to you that he doesn't find out?"

"Because," I snorted, "what do you think he'll do with that information? Hmm? It's already hard enough as it is to get him to agree to what I need to get this mission completed." My voice lowered to a hiss, "Do you think it will be any easier once he hears what almost happened?" I felt myself teetering on the edge of exhaustion now, suddenly overwhelmed by a panicky, trembling sort of anxiety. Today had been too much. I could feel my control slipping.

Wren's jaw was tight, and I watched as his hands clenched into fists at his sides. He looked like he wanted to hit someone, again. I felt a stab of coiled heat travel through my gut as I recalled his expression in that dark room, just before he lost his temper. "Just keep it to yourself, okay? I'm asking you to do this, for me."

His eyes met mine again, as cold as ice. But then his features relaxed, and he nodded, once. The slightest of movements. But it was good enough.

I nodded back, releasing a rush of air, and turned to eye the reporter on the screen again. She had a guest with her now. A man I recognized, with a little jolt of surprise. Evans. He was a well-known reporter, covering mostly politics, but he'd visited the Air Force before. Come by a few times, actually. He'd interviewed me after one of our larger battles. One of the skirmishes that had made The Crimson Reaper famous. I'd insisted on remaining anonymous, going only by my call sign, and refused any pictures. He'd promised me he wouldn't betray my trust. And he hadn't.

Evans was gesturing wildly as he spoke, intent on relaying some important message. I tore my gaze away from the screen. I could always pull up the clip later, back in my room, and find out what he was saying. I returned my focus to Ward, where he sat with a group of men around the battle table.

"We need to get him down to Med Bay," I said to Wren.

He nodded solemnly. "Why don't you take him?" He suggested running a hand through his hair, looking tired and defeated.

"Fine," I said bluntly. It had been a long day. I was done being civil at this point.

Wren sighed, taking in my body language. "I'll take him, if you want. But I think it'd be good if you did. You calm him down."

My eyebrows went up, and I couldn't help but laugh. "I calm him down?" I asked incredulously. "You have got to be kidding me." I shook my head as Wren grinned. "God, I'd hate to see what he's like when he's not calm then." I rolled my eyes. "Good lord, let's get this over with."

I made my way over to the table and held a hand out to Ward. He just stared at my open palm, then up at me. "What d'ya want, Kessler? A high five? I don't know... what..." he shrugged, trailing off, laughing to his men, gesturing at my hand like it was ridiculous.

"Come on," I said, sighing, "I'm taking you to Med Bay." He opened his mouth to protest. "You're going, and I don't want to hear a goddamn word about it. Do I make myself clear?" I gave him an icy stare as I slipped into the tone I used with my own men. "Let's go. Get your ass up."

He groaned, and I grabbed onto his arm, pulling him to his feet, as Molton, standing behind him, pushed against his back. I heard one of the men mutter, "Is he coming back, or?"

"Nope," I called over my shoulder. "Call it a night, gentlemen." I heard muttered commentary; a few of the men laughed, and someone called out, "Good night," in a suggestive, sing-song voice. I chose to ignore them.

Ward raised a hand over his head in a lazy motion, waving to the men as we exited the bridge.

21.

Ward remained silent as we made our way slowly down to Med Bay. Unfortunately, it was quite a distance away. As far from the bridge as you could get, on the other end of the large Carrier, it was positioned on the lower level, near the hangar, for obvious reasons.

I elected to stay silent as well, seeing no point in attempting to speak or reason with him in his current state. That was a conversation better left for the morning, for when he was sober. Or better yet, hungover. I grinned slightly at the thought, and Ward caught me smiling and fixed his gaze on me.

"Glad to see that my pain amuses you," he muttered. He ran a hand through his hair, pushing it off his forehead. He must have hit a bruise, because he winced slightly.

"God, Ward," I murmured, rolling my eyes. "I don't find anything about this amusing." I shook my head, staring out the window as we moved past it. "Just the opposite, in fact."

"What's the opposite of amusing?" Ward asked thoughtfully, head cocked to the side, as he squinted a little. "I don't quite know, at the moment." He chuckled slightly, shrugging.

"I find it upsetting, that's what it means," I snapped at him. "Why would you think this would be funny to me?" I shook my head. "I don't think you forcing your men to beat your face to a bloody pulp is in any way amusing."

Ward sighed deeply. "Here we go," he muttered.

"Here we go?" I whirled on him, eyes going wide. "Oh, okay, fine then. You know what, I don't care. Do whatever you want, in your free time. As long as you get off my back, I don't give a shit what you do." Ward nodded as I spoke, but his lips twisted in a way that implied he didn't believe me.

"I don't care," I said again, turning away from him and marching down the hallway with my arms crossed.

"Sure you don't, that's why you were begging Nathan to stop us," he quipped. I stopped walking, staring at his back as he continued down the hall past me, my mouth gaping open. I didn't think he'd had any awareness of what was going on in the room at the time, given the circumstances, but apparently he didn't miss much, even when wasted.

I debated leaving him there. Surely he could find his way to the Med Bay on his own. But he was also drunk, and I didn't fully trust him to actually make his way down there. *And why did I care?* I asked myself with a stab of frustration. So what if he didn't go to Med Bay; let him ruin his stupid face. What the hell did I care? It had nothing to do with me. My gut twisted in anger and frustration. Because I did.

That was the only obvious explanation. Because he was right, I did care. And the thought filled me with fury, mixed with dread. I couldn't care about him. Couldn't. I wouldn't let myself. I forced myself to move forward, to stay calm. I would see him safely down to Med Bay and leave. That was what I would do for anyone else, it made no difference who he was. That was human decency.

I kept my lips pressed firmly together as I continued down the hall, several steps behind him now. I told myself to just stop talking, it wasn't worth engaging with him. I managed to stay quiet for a while. But it didn't last very long. I have a hard time letting things go.

"I'm only here right now because Wren asked me to bring you down to Med Bay. I'm doing him a favor." I said, through gritted teeth.

"Oh, okay, got it," Ward nodded, "so it's *Wren* you actually care about. Noted." He shrugged nonchalantly, but his jaw was clenched tight, that muscle ticking away.

I smirked, and he glared over at me. "Now who cares?" I murmured; eyes locked on his. I couldn't help myself.

Ward came to a halt, moving closer to me, swiftly closing the few steps between us across the corridor. His dark eyes smoldered. "Personally, I don't give a shit who you care about, Kessler. But as the commanding officer aboard this ship, I would be remiss if I didn't remind you that fraternizing with a subordinate is not only frowned upon, but grounds for immediate dismissal." He ground out the next few words. "So, if I were you, I would maintain a distance from First Lieutenant MacMillan." He shrugged. "But like you just said, I don't give a shit what you do."

My whole body tensed, shoulders raising to my ears involuntarily. *This fucking asshole.* "You're a real piece of work, you know that?" I hissed at him. "How is it you manage to twist everything I say, and somehow turn it against me? And why are you doing it, exactly? Hmm? Do you just enjoy watching me squirm, or is there another reason?"

Something behind Ward's eyes shifted at that last question. I'd struck a nerve, apparently. I felt my gut twist, and it wasn't just because he was so close to me.

"Just one of my many talents, I guess," Ward shrugged, affecting that fake nonchalance that I hated so much.

"Does anyone actually buy into that?" I demanded.

"Buy into what?" he asked, one eyebrow raised.

"That air of fake nonchalance," I said calmly. "That bullshit act, where you go around, pretending you don't give a shit. That you don't take anything seriously, that nothing bothers you. Do your men actually believe it? Because I sure don't."

"It's not an act," He ground out, but I was already shaking my head, grinning at him.

"No, don't try to deny it. It absolutely is an act. You do care. You care a lot." I moved closer to him. "You care so much, you need to drink yourself half to death and force your own men to beat your face in, just to feel something. Just to feel physical pain, because that pain hurts less than the other kind. So don't bullshit me, Ward."

He took a step back, but I followed. I stabbed him in the chest with my finger. "Do you think I don't remember the night we met?" I asked, eyebrows raised. "Don't try to tell me you don't feel anything. Because I know you do. You feel everything. All at once," I couldn't stop myself, as the words came tumbling out, my voice cracking slightly, "and it's too much for you. You can't handle it. You're afraid it will crush you."

His gaze finally broke away from mine, and his eyes dropped to his feet. His chest was heaving slightly. And I felt nothing but a grim sense of satisfaction, watching him. I'd finally gotten to him. But my own chest was rising and falling, and I could feel my heart hammering away. *Who had I been talking about, really?* I shook my head, pushing the thought away.

"Look, Ward," I swallowed, "I don't know what happened, what caused you to want me off your ship in the first place. And I don't know why you keep working against me. But I'm asking you again for your help." His eyes rose to mine, chest still rising and falling rapidly. "I've tried asking you before, and you've blown me off. So, I'm only going to ask you one more time. Help me, Ward, don't work against me."

"I'm not," he protested.

"Yes, you are," I said, keeping my voice calm, tone neutral. "What was that bullshit mission in Colorado? Hmm? Did they really send us down there to camp out for two days? Or was that just a convenient excuse to delay gathering samples?" He looked away, suddenly unable to meet my eyes. Confirmation enough.

"And that first mission," I continued, "you were upset with me because I delayed your retreat and caused you to lose more men. But you're the one who ordered me to stay with my unit; to keep moving forward."

I studied his features as he stared out the window, his profile framed by the cold, distant stars. My voice dropped lower. "Why did you send me into that factory in the first place? Away from where the Jumpers were? If you had just let me hang back, like I asked, then I could have gathered the samples right away. I would have been done before your men ever left the building. Why did you do that, Ward? I haven't been able to figure that out. I would love to hear an explanation."

He was watching me closely now, eyes narrowed. But he offered no response. "I'll tell you why I think you did it. I think you did it because you were trying to make me look bad. Trying to get me to fuck up. Because if I fuck up badly enough, you can go back to the Admiral and get him to kick me off your ship. What I don't know, is why." Ward remained still, silent.

"And tonight, you deliberately left me out of planning the mission. You didn't even invite me to the briefing, I don't–"

"Don't get me started about tonight," Ward practically growled at me.

I clenched my fists at my side, willing myself to stay calm. "They're talking about these things crossing over the border tonight, Ward. This mission is our chance, our only hope of stopping those things–"

He shook his head in frustration, fists clenched. "Hope?" He scoffed. "There is no hope." He moved a step away from me, turning and pacing up the corridor.

"So what, you're just going to give up?" I asked, exasperation leaking into my voice. "Where is the man I met in that bar? Huh? Because he wouldn't just give up. *He* would fight back. He would continue to fight until he couldn't any longer. He wouldn't just give in to–"

"He's *tired*." Ward snapped, spinning back around, right in my face. I jumped back slightly. "He's tired," he repeated, his voice quieter, "of watching his friends die. Tired of sending them to their deaths." All the anger went out of his body, and he shook his head at me. "He just wants this to end."

I moved closer to him, slid my hand over his cheek. I was careful not to touch the bruises already forming around his eye.

"That's what I want, too." I murmured softly to him. "So help me end it."

I looked up into his eyes, his gaze sliding down to my lips briefly, then back to my eyes again. He didn't seem to be breathing, he was so perfectly still. Then he took a deep breath, his chest expanding. "That's what I'm trying to do," he murmured quietly. He shook his head slightly, his stubble rough against my palm, as he shifted under my hand. "And I can't let you get in my way of protecting my men. I'll do anything—anything I have to, to protect them. That's all I care about. Can you understand that?"

I stared back at him, my brows crinkling in confusion. "What do you mean? How would I do that?"

He just shook his head again, swallowing, his gaze dropping away from mine. Then he reached up, gently took hold of my hand, and lifted it away. He met my gaze one last time, his eyes filled with nothing but pain. Then he dropped my hand and turned and walked away.

I stood there for a long time, after he left, staring after him, down the empty corridor.

22.

When Ward had sobered up the next morning, he came to find me, to demand answers. But I was in no mood to give them.

I'd wandered down to Engineering with two coffees in my hand. I set the extra coffee on Curtis' desk as I walked past, and he thanked me with a grunt and a wink. He didn't seem to be in the mood to talk today, which was more than fine with me.

I wound my way through the engine room, and finding a spare desk and swivel chair open in a remote corner of the massive space, I took a seat. There was a small window on the opposite wall. How kind of them to give the engineers at least a tiny glimpse of the outside world.

I sat there glumly, letting the grind and hum of the machines that kept the ship running drown out my connection to the world outside my head. When I heard footsteps behind me, I jumped.

Ward frowned down at me, then dragged a chair over to the desk and made himself at home.

"What are you doing down here?" he asked, raising his voice to be heard over the cacophony around us.

I shrugged, staring sullenly down at my coffee. "I brought Curtis a coffee."

Ward continued to frown. "What? He has a coffee maker down here..." he trailed off with a hint of incredulity in his voice.

I shrugged again. "He doesn't like the coffee down here; it's not the same as the coffee from the Mess Hall."

Ward just stared at me for a moment, the hint of a smile on his lips, before he shook his head and leaned back in his chair, studying me. "You know, I've been assigned to this ship for years, and I've never had Curtis so much as say good morning to me. Not even since I was promoted to Captain."

I snorted, his words eliciting a little smirk from me for a second, before I wiped my features clean.

Ward sighed heavily and leaned forward again, elbows resting on the table. "Where were you yesterday, Kessler?" he asked, his voice barely audible. "Because yet again, I found my mission delayed, waiting on you, while more of my men were put at risk." He gritted his teeth. "And please don't tell me–"

I cut him off before he could continue. "It's none of your business, Ward," I said coldly. "You made it abundantly clear that we were to keep our separate missions to ourselves.

You didn't bother to fill me in on what your team was doing last night; don't concern yourself with mine."

Ward grimaced, leaning closer. "I thought you might say that. But here's the thing, your team showed up with Wren's unit, and rumor has it, they had no clue where you were." His eyes bore into mine, and I squirmed uncomfortably under his gaze.

"We got separated. It was an accident." I said icily. "Due to circumstances beyond my control," I added, as he opened his mouth to retort.

"Really?" he asked, pursing his lips together, with a thoughtful expression, as though he was tasting my words, like a mouthful of wine. "Circumstances beyond your control..." he repeated. "Care to elaborate?"

My cheeks flushed as I thought of how to even begin to put into words what had almost happened to me last night. My head still throbbed this morning, and I knew I had probably delayed my mandatory health check with the docs in Med Bay for longer than was prudent already.

I shook my head, ignoring the shift in his expression as he watched me. I knew he could tell that I was flustered. "No." I snapped at him. "I don't."

Ward let out a sigh, hand over his chin, he sat with his elbow propped on the tabletop, pausing, as though he were considering his next tactic.

"I asked Wren for your officer's comm frequency," I said, watching him closely. "And he gave it to me. But when I jumped on to check on your status, there was only dead air. I tried repeatedly to hail one of you over the comms, and nothing. Because of that, I went back to look for you." I swallowed thickly. "I thought something had happened. I..." I paused, my cheeks flushing, as I realized what I was saying. That was all true. If they had responded over the comms, I never would have gone looking for them in the first place.

I leaned forward, sneering at him. "So, before you go off again about how I once again put more of your men at risk, why don't you take a look in the goddamn mirror."

His expression had turned dark as I spoke, but I paused only long enough to come up for air before continuing my tirade. "Because at least I made an effort to coordinate with your team. You didn't do shit to include me, or my men, in your plans last night. In fact, I suspect you had Wren give me the wrong frequency, deliberately, so I would be SOL." My cheeks burned hot now, and I got to my feet, leaning over him. "And if that's true, then *fuck you*, Ward. Fuck both of you. I really hope you're proud of yourself."

I couldn't help the tears that had sprang to my eyes, or the way my voice betrayed the depth of my emotion, and he stared up at me with a look of horror on his face. "I am sick to death of your interference, your delay tactics, and your... your constant undermining of my mission. Because it nearly got *me*

315

killed, this time. So don't you dare lay any more deaths at my feet. I'm the one trying to save lives. Why don't you wake the fuck up?"

Ward rose to his feet. "*Jesus Christ*," he murmured. "Jordan, what happened last night?"

I could only shake my head. "Ask your right-hand man. I'm done talking to both of you." I turned away briefly before turning back. "You know, you say you'll do anything to save your men, yet you won't do the one thing that can actually help save them. Save all of us. Not just your men, but their families, their loved ones back home, too."

"What's that?" Ward asked, his chest heaving.

"Be honest, Ward," I said simply, shaking my head at him. "With yourself. And with me."

I turned and left him alone, staring after me.

Ward was notably distant, cold, towards me in the following days. He kept a distance away from me physically, too, finding some excuse to leave whenever I approached. I kept running over our last few conversations in my mind, my cheeks burning in shame whenever I recalled the way I'd acted and what I'd said.

I'd always been able to control my emotions; keep them hidden, below the surface. Strangled, before they could breathe freely, and grow. I had always viewed it as a strength. But my control had seemingly become fragile over the past few weeks. I had slipped. I'd never meant to reveal my suspicions to him, much less goad him into asking Wren what had happened to me. I ran our conversation from our walk to Med Bay, through my mind more than once as well, trying to recall his exact words. I didn't understand what he meant. Why would I come between him protecting his men?

Anything that had happened had been an accident. I'd never done anything deliberate to hurt his men, or put them at risk. And I thought deep down he knew that. But maybe he didn't. Maybe he didn't trust me. The thought that he still somehow believed that of me, after everything that had happened, hurt more than I cared to admit. And I couldn't shake the feeling that he wasn't being honest. Not just with himself, but with me.

I decided I was fine with the cold distance. The barrier he was putting up between us. If he wanted it that way, that was more than fine with me. I'd let him get too close already; let him affect me too much. I wouldn't make that mistake again. If he wanted to continue to hate me, blame me, for the deaths of more of his men, then so be it. It was better than the alternative. I hoped Wren would blow him off and direct him back to me when he asked about what happened that night. I knew if he found out, he would use it as an excuse to try to prevent me from joining future missions.

I stalked through the Carrier, in a foul mood, giving Ward the cold shoulder back for a day or two while we waited for orders. And I had managed to avoid interacting much with any of the officers, spending as much time as I could alone, when I was suddenly called to the bridge.

Wren found me, sitting on the edge of the pool, shoes and socks discarded in a pile. I sat swinging my legs back and forth, enjoying the resistance of the water, and staring idly out the window at the far reaches of space in the distance.

I asked him why Ward was calling for me, and he shook his head, sighed, and ran a hand through his loose curls. "Some reporter's shown up," he muttered.

"Reporter?" I frowned, "On a Carrier?" That was nearly unheard of. Members of the press were given clearance to attend events, pinning ceremonies, and things of that nature. But to have a reporter show up randomly on a Carrier seemed bizarrely out of the norm.

"Yeah," Wren nodded, "he has clearance, all his credentials. I got the impression he was sent directly by Congress. Sounds like they're demanding an update on your research mission."

"But it's supposed to be highly classified. The Admiral was explicit, on a need-to-know basis–"

"He's got a letter from the Admiral. Seal and all. I didn't get to read it, but I'm sure Ward will hand that over immediately to you before you speak to him."

I sighed deeply, a hollowness forming in my gut at his words. Well, if that were the case, I would give him the information I was allowed to. Although I had precious little to share.

I toweled off my legs and feet and followed Wren to the bridge. My mouth twitched in a grin as I took in the gangly silhouette of Ernie Evans, standing beside Ward at the large window across the room. He wore his dark hair slicked back; not one hair out of place. He gave me a broad grin as he turned, his brown eyes seeming to sparkle somehow.

"I hear it's *Captain* Kessler now," he strode over to me, hand extended to shake mine. But he jerked to a stop abruptly and gave me a wobbly salute first. I nodded back and moved to shake his hand. "Congratulations, Captain."

I couldn't help but grin back at him. "It's so good to see you again, Evans," I replied. Ward was staring down at the floor, arms crossed, rather than looking at us, but I saw his eyebrows raise at my words.

"When I learned you were the one in charge of this mission, I pulled every string I could to get approval to come aboard. I'd like to speak to you about your progress." He held a hand up, "I understand it's *top secret*," he put the words in air quotes, "details aren't necessary. This is just a general interview. Congress is pushing for answers, and the people deserve to know that efforts are being made to learn the truth about this affliction." His expression had flipped quickly from congenial to icy, and I felt a little fissure of doubt growing in my gut at his words.

I turned to look at Ward and found him holding a creased piece of paper out for me with one hand. I could see the Admiral's seal from here. I moved over to him and took it wordlessly, my eyes flickering back and forth over the lines of text. The signature at the bottom sure looked authentic.

"From the Admiral himself," Evans said, his tone clipped. "He was gracious enough to concede to the interview. By order of Congress." My back was still to Evans as I raised my eyes to Ward's. He gave me a long, dark look. I cleared my throat.

"Well then, let's get to it, I suppose," I turned back to Evans. "Where should we sit?"

Evans looked around the room and gestured to the large battle table with one hand. I began to move towards it, as he pulled out a chair on my side of the table, and stepped back, offering me the seat. Ward had moved around to the other side of the table, and I caught the subtle eye roll as he pulled out a chair for himself.

"Thank you," I murmured, as Evans pulled out a chair at the head of the table, directly next to me, and took a seat.

He turned to Ward. "I'm sorry, Captain Ward, Congress was very specific in their request. I'm to be granted an interview with Captain Kessler, and Captain Kessler, alone."

I was careful to keep my expression bland, fighting the urge to smirk, as Ward stared openly at Evans for a long, uncomfortable moment, before turning to me. "You okay?" He asked.

I blinked several times at him. Was he serious? What was he going to do if I said no? Put a stop to the interview? Defy Congress and the Admiral? I realized my mouth was gaping slightly and closed it before nodding briskly. "Absolutely." I turned to Evans. "He doesn't bite."

"Not hard, at least," Evans said, throwing me a wink.

Ward's glare was sharp enough to cut glass as he got to his feet and moved towards the door of the bridge. "You have fifteen minutes." He called over his shoulder.

"There was no time limitation–" Evans began.

"That's how long you have before I kick you off of *my* bridge," Ward growled, before disappearing through the doors.

Evans waited until the doors slid shut again before turning back to me. "Is he always that pleasant?" he asked with a grin.

I snorted a little, "Pretty much. I think you caught him on a good day." He sighed, shaking his head.

"Well, since it seems our time is limited, let's not waste any sugar coating, Captain," Evans turned to me. "I know you can't divulge details on your findings thus far, but please, tell me you've found *something*. Because the people of the Northern Alliance," he paused, "make that the people of the Southern Coalition, as well, deserve some answers. This is the greatest threat we've faced collectively since the last pandemic. And I hate to say it, but my intrepid reporter senses are tingling. In fact, they're doing more than tingling. They're on high alert, Captain. Defcon..." he faltered, "... eleven. Whatever that means. Whatever the highest level is... that's what they're on. This thing is big. And it's about to get bigger." He flipped open the notebook he'd been gripping in his hands, clicking his pen. "I've already been briefed on the general purpose of your mission, but if you could describe it again for me; in your own words."

I'd felt myself straightening, my spine now ramrod straight as I listened to his rant. Well, it seemed the press were taking this seriously, at least. And so was Congress. I gave him a brief description of the purpose of my mission. And he proceeded to ask me questions. I answered as smoothly as I could, pausing only when I felt I might verge into dangerous territory. I avoided any details on the samples gathered thus far, who was working on them, how many people were assigned, and things of that nature.

Evans took notes as I spoke, nodding almost continuously at my words. He interrupted me occasionally to ask a clarifying question.

When he seemed to be finished, he sighed deeply, leaning back in his chair. "Do you have anything so far... that makes you hopeful there will be a way to stop these things?" I smiled knowingly at him.

"That information is classified, at this time, but I can only say that I certainly do have hope. We all should have hope that we can beat this."

"Ah," Evans murmured, watching me closely, "they say hope is the only thing stronger than fear. Do you believe that's true, Captain?"

I frowned, not sure where he was going with this. Was this an interview or a philosophical debate? I took a deep breath, staring out the window at the stars winking back at me. "When I was a little girl," I began slowly, "I used to dream of flying." I grinned and chuckled a little. "I used to really believe that I could. Like a bird, you know? Not in a fighter. But I grew up, at some point, and realized that wasn't physically possible."

"Alas, we're all bound by the laws of physics." Evans nodded.

"But what I was really dreaming of all along... wasn't flying. It was freedom." I met his eyes again, as he stilled, pen held in the air over his notebook, "I dreamed of freedom from... everything, down there." I nodded down at the floor. "I dreamed of peace. Even though I suppose I hardly know the meaning of the word." I met his gaze, unblinking. "So yes, Evans, I would say I believe in hope. That it can be stronger than fear." I shrugged. "How else can you explain all this?" I held my arms out, indicating the ship around us. "How else can you explain men and women, my fellow soldiers, flinging themselves at the enemy? Running headlong towards death? If hope weren't stronger than fear, then none of that... none of this, would be possible."

He watched me, solemnly, before bending forward and writing something in his notebook. He set his pen down gently off to the side and spun the notebook around to face me.

I frowned slightly, leaning forward to read the line he'd scrawled, in neat print, at the bottom of the page: '*Can you be confident this conversation isn't being recorded right now?*'

I felt my blood run cold as I stared down at the words on the crisp, white page. And I raised my eyes slowly to his. I paused for only a few seconds before shaking my head no.

He nodded grimly, leaning back in his chair. We studied each other for a moment before I cleared my throat. "Evans, have you ever had a full tour of a Carrier before?"

Evans stared at me for a moment, then a slow grin broke out over his face. "No, actually, I haven't, Captain. I've heard the Mess Hall is always quite a sight."

I nodded in agreement. "It's worth seeing, for sure. Why don't we walk down there? I wouldn't mind a coffee. We might even bring one down to Curtis, in Engineering, I always bring him a cup. The engine room is quite a sight as well. You wouldn't believe the amount of horsepower a ship like *The Beagle* runs on."

Evans grinned more broadly, snapped his notebook shut, and got to his feet. "Lead the way, Captain."

I was true to my word. I led him down to the Mess Hall, and we chatted about innocuous things the whole way there. We marveled at the view out the wall of glass, and Evans stopped to chat with a few of the men. He asked a bunch of questions about life on the Carrier and told the men he would include the information in an upcoming article.

We grabbed coffee, and I prepared an extra cup for Curtis, and we headed all the way down to Engineering.

Curtis was just about as glad to see me as always and was happier to see the still steaming mug of coffee in my hand. He waved to us dismissively when I asked if I could show Evans around, and he displayed zero interest in who Evans was or why he was here.

As we made our way to the main engine room, I warned Evans about the noise level. "It's going to be louder than you think," I said, one eyebrow raised. "Should we ask for earmuffs?" Evans shook his head.

"I think we'll be fine," he replied with a wink, taking another sip of his coffee.

I showed him into the main engine room, and pointed out the various components, like Curtis had for me during a previous visit. We stood there for a few seconds, listening to the hum of the engines, the floor vibrating beneath our feet. "Why don't we find somewhere to sit?" I asked, just as Evans turned to me, about to speak. "I think there are a few tables on the far side of the room."

Luckily, I remembered correctly, and there was no one in sight. We took a seat on the bench at the table, Evans sliding to a stop just a foot or so away from me. He leaned forward, setting his notebook and pen down, along with his coffee. "I'm going to be honest with you, Captain, and I hope you'll be honest with me." He began. "There are rumors, that this thing isn't... naturally occurring. Rumors that it was... created. Manufactured, by someone. A bioweapon. To put it plainly."

My eyebrows went up. "The South?" I asked.

He smirked. Shook his head. "The South couldn't do something like this." He shrugged, "Not unless it were some... freak accident. And even then... they'd have to be doing real science for something like that to have the opportunity to occur." He looked away, down at his pen. "No, Captain, not the South. Their education system is broken. In their schools, they teach their children how to be good little fascist citizens. Not biology."

He watched me carefully, waiting. My gut twisted violently at the implication of his words. "Russia then? China? Or Japan?" I blurted out, as I ran through the list of possibilities in my mind. Both Russia and China would have the scientific acumen needed. Although it would make little sense for Russia to have been the ones to release something like this. At least not in the South. Why would they attack their own ally like that?

Evans inclined his head for a moment, as though he were considering. "All possibilities... sure." He shrugged, clearing his throat. "But there's someone a lot closer to home that would have the capability, and the motivation." He looked pointedly at me. I felt my stomach clench.

"No," I murmured. "It's not possible." My eyes darted to his notebook. "This part of the interview is off the record, by the way." I said leaning forward, my tone sharp.

"That goes without saying, Captain." Evans leaned forward, closer to me, and I strained to hear him over the engine noise. "I never reveal my sources; you know that better than anyone." He laughed, "I'm not asking you this on the record, as part of this official interview. I'm not asking you this as a Captain, in the NA Air Force. I'm not even asking you this as a citizen of the Northern Alliance. I am asking you this, as a person. A human being. As a person, who believes in hope. Believes in freedom. In peace." He paused, his gaze intent on mine, "Do you have any reason to believe, over the course of your investigation, that this disease could be man-made?"

I stared back at him, keeping my gaze steady, unblinking, despite my heart racing. "No." I said firmly, and while his expression hardly changed, I sensed something subtle shifting in his posture, and felt instantly that I had let him down. "No," I continued, "I have encountered nothing that would prove, or disprove that, either way."

He licked his lips, then nodded slowly. Leaning back, his posture relaxing. "Thank you, Captain. For being honest with me." He nodded again, seemingly to himself. "This thing is going to continue to spread, you know. Reports indicate it's targeted mostly men, so far, SC soldiers, the vast majority of the victims have been SC soldiers..." his voice trailed off. "But it's going to come for women, for children... as it continues to spread. It's already happening. There are isolated accounts."

I sat very still, taking in every word the best I could over the constant drone of the engine room. *Victims.* He was the first person I'd ever heard use that term in regards to the Jumpers. How easy it was for everyone to forget they hadn't always been monsters.

He paused again, his gaze becoming distant. "You know, there's more than one type of courage, Captain." He looked back at me. "I could write a book about your courage, as a fighter pilot. But I'd like this next article I write, to be different. I'd like to write about a different sort of courage. The courage it takes to speak out, when those in power want you silenced. The type of courage it takes to care enough about the suffering of others, of people, innocent people, to give them a voice, when they can't speak for themselves. The courage it takes to tell the truth. No matter how terrible, and inconvenient it might be."

"What are you saying, Evans?" I leaned forward, "are you truly telling me that you think *we* did this? You think we purposefully created this... this thing? Then deliberately infected people in the South? That's the sort of evil twisted shit they would do to *us*. Not the other way around. What proof do you have?"

Evans snorted, shaking his head. "Cui bono, Captain? Who benefits?" he shrugged, "look around. The Northern Alliance has made more progress against the South in the last three weeks than we have in years. This is crippling them, taking them out at the knees. Now sure, let's say you're right. Say they somehow developed this, maybe with the help of Russian scientists, right? Then they... what? Accidentally release it? Some sort of breach or lab accident, and it spreads." Evans shrugged again. "Sure, I guess that's possible. Some sort of freak accident. And it's possible we released it by accident, too. But either way, who benefits now? Clearly only us."

I shook my head, opening my mouth to retort but finding myself at a loss for words.

He continued, "I mean, we benefit... for now. Like I said, it's only a matter of time until it spreads completely across the border. Spreads into towns, major cities. This thing won't stop until it takes us all down." He leaned forward, his voice intense, his dark eyes boring into mine. "They want you to believe it's us versus them; they always have. Because it furthers their agenda, keeps the masses in check. Gives us an enemy to fight. But in reality, Captain, it's never been about that. It's never been us versus them; this has always been about power. Who's in power, and who wants to keep it that way."

I was angry now, my fists clenched tightly. I forced my hands to relax, pressing them down on the table between us. "*We* are the bastion of democracy, Evans. Not them. We are the only thing preventing the spread of fascism. Of suffering. Of hatred. Bigotry, misogyny–"

Evans waved his hand. "I'm not denying any of that. But who is spreading fascism, bigotry? It's not the people, Captain. It's not their fault. They are ignorant. They are misinformed. They are purposefully marginalized and suppressed and fed only the information their leaders allow. They are caught in the middle, and just like always, history repeats itself, and *they* are the ones who will suffer. The ones who will pay for the actions of their leaders as they fight to hang on to every shred of power they have."

I swallowed, considering his words. "That may very well be true, in the South. But Congress is different; they are not dictators, they're not–"

"Of course they're not," he waved his hand in the air, swatting away my retort like a fly. "But they are still the one percent, Kessler. They are wealthy... they have the kind of wealth that you and I can only dream about. They have power. And don't kid yourself, they want to keep it that way." He leaned forward again, conspiratorially. "Now, Congress called for this investigation, and they're the ones that granted me permission to travel here, and throughout the base, conducting interviews. They want this story told. There is a contingent of them that I'd trust with my own life. And I believe most of them are motivated by more altruistic reasons... but at the end of the day, power is power, Captain." He sighed, leaning back, his smile grim. "Look... I don't want the South to win." He shook his head. "I'm gay, Captain." He shrugged, snorted. "Do you know what would happen to me, in a society like the one in the deep South?"

I grimaced, swallowing hard and nodded. "Of course I do."

"Do you think I want them to win? Do you think I don't live in fear of that happening? Of waking up to hear that they've breached our borders; that they've taken over our territory?" He laughed darkly, "Why do you think I've dedicated my entire life to journalism? To uphold free speech, the protection of the truth; facts. To stop the spread of lies, propaganda, and misinformation? I want us to win, more than anything, Captain." He leaned forward, slamming the tip of his finger into the tabletop. "But not like this. Not like this." His voice dropped lower, and I leaned forward. "If we do this, if we let the people in power who are doing this get away with it, we are just as bad as them. The South. We are no different than them. And that means they win. That means *they* win. No matter what happens, if we stoop to their level, then they've already won."

My jaw tightened. I nodded once, letting out a rush of air, my thoughts racing. So, he didn't suspect Congress, specifically. Then who? My eyes glazed over, then I focused back on him. "I don't know anything." I said slowly, choosing my words carefully. "I'm sorry to disappoint you."

Evans stared at me, as I leaned back, my heart nearly in my throat. He reached down into his pocket, pulled out a crisp white card, and slid it across the table to me.

I sensed movement and lifted my gaze to find Ward strolling towards us, eyes narrowed, glued on me. So, he'd managed to find us.

I picked up the card, scanning the printed text. '*Ernie Evans, Field Correspondent, The Associated Press*' followed by a series of numbers.

Evans cleared his throat. "That's my personal comms link. You call me, and I'll answer. Any time of the day or night. You have my word."

I met Evan's gaze once more, my stomach flipping. He still thought I knew more than I did. Thought I didn't want to tell him the truth. Not yet, at least. Or maybe, he thought I was too afraid. That I was being silenced. My gut roiled, and I felt a faint wave of nausea pass through me. Silenced by who? I hid my inner turmoil beneath a mask of nonchalance and nodded once. One brisk ducking of my chin, which seemed to satisfy him, as his expression became lighter somehow.

"I bet you will." Ward quipped as he stood over us, a wicked sort of smirk on his lips. I flicked my eyes up to him. He stood there, arms crossed over his chest, I shot him a dark warning glare.

Evans only chuckled, eyes darting back and forth between us, then he shook his head. "Captain Kessler was kind enough to give me a quick tour. We stopped by the Mess Hall, as well. I spoke with some of your men. It's all very impressive, Captain Ward." Evans stood, he slapped his notebook shut, and nodded once to me. "It's been a pleasure, as always, Captain Kessler. I hope our paths cross again."

I stood and nodded back to him, giving him a small smile, and reaching a hand out for his. He shook my hand, grip tight, and nodded once more to me.

"Time's up," Ward grinned at him. "Let me escort you to the hangar. We can certainly stop to see anything else you might like to see, on the way there."

Evans nodded, and they moved across the engine room together. Ward didn't look back at me, but Evans did. He shot me one last serious glance before disappearing around a corner. I sat there for a long time after they left. My coffee growing cold, forgotten on the table before me.

23.

The lull in action was starting to wear on all of us. We had been expecting new orders to put boots on the ground at any time, but Command seemed to have gone radio silent. The only orders that came through stated explicitly that no bodies were to be recovered and brought back aboard the Carriers. Indefinitely. The news spread throughout *The Beagle,* and the disturbing mandate only added to the level of tension on board, which was already at a fever pitch. The men spent that afternoon and evening attempting to relax, treating it as an off-duty day until we heard otherwise. But we heard nothing further from command.

The same thing happened the following day. And the day after. And the mood aboard *The Beagle* continued to grow more and more tense, as the days of idleness dragged on and blended together. The calm before the storm, as we all waited to see what fate held in store for us.

I spent most of the afternoon on the third day, as I had spent the previous two. Down in the gym, lifting as heavy as I could, while Binson and McCullough took turns spotting me. McCullough watched me warily as I started another set. I knew I was overdoing it, without being told. I could already feel I was going to be sore tomorrow. But I kept going. I couldn't seem to stop. There was something about the pain, the burning ache in my muscles as I pushed them to their limit, that had a calming, soothing effect on me. I felt restless. On edge. And this was one of the few ways I knew to purge my body of that nervous energy.

McCullough kept his thoughts to himself and let me run myself into the ground, until I collapsed onto the mat, chest heaving, and stomach churning. I hoped I wasn't about to puke. I'd done it before; pushed myself too hard in workouts, to the point that I threw up.

"I think that's enough, Captain." McCullough's voice rang out from where he sat on a bench across the gym. "We could get orders any second. You'll be exhausted if we end up shipping out tonight. You'll only put yourself and the rest of us at risk if you keep going."

"I'm done, McCullough," I grunted, still panting heavily. "Don't worry about it."

"Good," he snapped at me, his tone somewhat sharp. "We should go get cleaned up. Get ready for dinner."

I sighed deeply, still trying to slow my breathing, and nodded. "I'll meet you there." McCullough nodded and left the gym, taking Binson with him.

I took my time showering and changing for dinner. I threw my hair into a high, messy bun, while it was still damp, not caring what I looked like. I was in a rotten mood, and didn't foresee that changing anytime soon.

I moved slowly through the corridors until I found my way to the Mess Hall, nodding absentmindedly to the groups of soldiers I passed exiting.

Molton took one look at me as I approached the officer's table, and he got up and left. He returned a moment or so later, placing a drink down in front of me. A tall glass, full of clear liquid that looked like water, packed with ice, with green leaves floating in it. I took one look at it and smirked, grinning, despite myself. He sat down across from me, pushing his glasses back into place, and grinning back at me.

"Molton, what the heck is this?" I asked, poking at the leaves with the thin straw sticking out of the glass. I leaned forward, a crisp, minty smell making my nose wrinkle.

He laughed, in that contagious way of his, and nodded at the drink. "That there's the only cure I know for whatever's eating you." He nodded encouragingly as I took hold of the glass and took a sip, gingerly. It was different, that was for sure. But I had to admit, it wasn't bad.

He grinned as I nodded my approval. "Okay, okay..." I trailed off, grinning back. "Thanks. I hope it helps." I sighed deeply, feeling my shoulders slumping forward. I resisted the urge to scan the room. It didn't matter if he was here or not; he wouldn't speak to me, and I didn't want to talk to him.

Molton nodded, his expression serious. "I hope so too, Captain," he added. The others joined us shortly. McCullough and Binson wandered in, Stevens in tow, pulling Powers along beside him, in a headlock. They were laughing hysterically, Nathan not far behind, grinning at their backs.

I sipped my drink slowly. I could tell it was strong. And whether it would do me more harm than good remained to be seen. But for now, it seemed to be helping. I managed to choke some food down, too. My appetite wasn't great lately. I'd had to force myself to eat more often than not. But I'd spent the past three days punishing my body in the gym, and I needed to eat, not only to recoup those calories, but to give my body what it needed to build muscle. After all, that was supposed to be the whole point.

I didn't attend much to the conversation, listening in here and there, too stuck inside my head to participate in any meaningful way.

Ward showed up, eventually. A glass of dark liquid in his hand, once again. He had a plate of food with him at least, this time. I watched him eating and wondered if he felt the way I did. If he had to force myself to eat. He didn't seem to find the meal appetizing, either way. He spent most of the meal pushing his food around on his plate, a dark, closed-off expression on his face.

"Well," Molton said, during a lull in conversation, "we're a cheerful bunch tonight, aren't we?" He sighed loudly.

Wren shook his head. "It's never easy, sitting and waiting. Waiting on orders..." he trailed off.

"Waiting to find out when we get to go back down. Try not to die. Again." Stevens murmured.

The group fell silent again, staring down at the table, out into space, anywhere but at each other.

"I have something that might help," Wren said lightly, and heads turned in his direction as he pulled a device from a pocket somewhere. It took me a moment to recognize what it was.

"Yes..." Powers hissed. "I'm in!" He raised a hand in the air, and the men laughed. I watched as Wren handed the odd-looking contraption over to Powers. "You won't tell on us, right boss?" He grinned, winking over at Ward. Ward snorted and waved a hand dismissively, taking another sip of his drink.

Powers shrugged, then covered his mouth and nose with the clear rubber mask. He hit the button on the canister, releasing a puff of Nitrous, and breathed deeply. He repeated the motion once more. I watched as his eyes fluttered closed. He lowered the mask and handed it off to the next man, low chuckles and whistles around the table as he leaned forward, grinning, and began drumming on the table, buzzing his lips together in a jaunty sort of tune. The men laughed, and I felt the atmosphere around the table begin to improve significantly.

Even Nathan took a hit, albeit brief. When it came to my turn, I hesitated for a few seconds, looked at my drink, then shrugged. "Fuck it," I said, and the group let out several whoops and cheers. Mixing a strong drink like this with Nitrous probably wasn't the smartest idea, but I was frankly beyond caring at this point. I caught a glimpse of Wren, frowning over at me, as I fit the mask over my mouth and nose and took two deep breaths. More than that, and I risked overdoing it.

I stared out into the distance as I sat there, waiting for the effects to kick in. I knew from experience it usually took a few minutes for me to feel anything. I tore my eyes away from the stars in the distance, framing the Earth below, to find Ward watching me. His eyes were full of that same pain, that same sorrow, they'd held the last time we'd spoken in any meaningful way, in the hallway on the way to Med Bay.

His face was still slightly bruised, sporting faint crescents of purple and yellow hues under his eyes. He looked so damaged, so broken, at that moment, that my heart thawed, just a little, as I stared back at him. He held my gaze. Held it too long.

It felt as though the world around us just... kept going, while we sat there, frozen in time, in a moment that stretched, but didn't break. Didn't end. And suddenly I couldn't breathe. Couldn't take it. I stood abruptly.

McCullough frowned up at me, and I felt Wren's eyes on me. Watching us, his gaze darting back and forth between Ward and I.

"You okay, Captain?" McCullough asked. I just shook my head. I suddenly wasn't sure I could speak. Not without bursting into tears. I gritted my teeth. I hated weakness of any kind. This had to stop. I reached down and grabbed my drink, taking a sip, stalling for time, as I swung my legs over the bench, one at a time, until I stood with my back to the table.

"I'm going to go," I murmured, and I left.

I made my way back to my room. I tried to settle down, find something to do, but that restlessness I'd managed to ease in the gym returned once more, and I felt almost jittery. I paced up and down, feeling trapped in the small space. I wanted to go somewhere else. Somewhere where I wouldn't have to talk to anyone. See anyone.

I could feel the pleasant effects of the Nitrous finally starting to kick in, at last. I grabbed my bathing suit and made my way down to the pool, drink still in hand, grinning. I had a feeling it would be empty this time of day, and I was right. Not a soul in sight.

I changed in the locker room and grabbed a towel, throwing it on a chair, and stepped down the short set of stairs into the hot tub, sighing gratefully as I sank into the water, up to my chin. I faced the large window beside the hot tub, staring out at the stars, thinking.

I sipped my drink idly and sat in that hot tub for what felt like an hour, maybe two. The Nitrous had taken full effect at this point. I was blessedly relaxed and happy, to the point of delirium. I moved my hands back and forth in the water, and pictured myself passing out, sliding beneath the surface, lying there unconscious, drowning. I snorted in laughter, finding that idea hilarious. I couldn't stop laughing for several minutes. I realized remotely that it was probably a really stupid idea to be in here alone, drunk, and high on Nitrous at the same time. But I didn't care. My drink was nearly gone when he found me there.

I looked over to see him watching me, standing uncertainly a few feet away from the hot tub. I cleared my throat, sitting up a little, wiping the sweat dripping down my face away from my eyes. I could feel the little hairs on my neck, framing my face, curling against my skin in the steam that rose from the water in clouds.

"You cooked yet?" Wren asked, grinning at me. But there was some hint of sadness in his eyes that made my stomach clench.

"What is it?" I asked, "What's wrong?"

He shook his head, moving closer to me, crouching down at the edge of the hot tub. "Nothing. Nothing's wrong." He paused. "We just didn't know where you were, that's all. McCullough went and checked your room, after a bit, to make sure you were okay." He shrugged. "They were worried about you. You seemed... upset. At dinner." Wren shrugged again.

"*They* were worried about me? But not you? Huh?" I asked him archly, tilting my head sideways. I wanted to ask if Ward was worried. But I didn't.

Wren scoffed a little, looking down at his feet. "Course I was," was all he said. I watched him, my head still buzzing from the Nitrous and whatever was in that tall drink, only ice and mint leaves now. Wren swallowed, his throat bobbing. Was he nervous? I wondered why.

"The light went on," he murmured a moment later. "Drink service cut off for the night." He shrugged, "You know what that means." I did know what that meant.

"Boots on the ground," I murmured. "Tomorrow?"

"Yeah," Wren murmured back. He cleared his throat. "Ward's expecting a briefing, could be any time now. Or maybe they'll wait until morning. I'm sure he'll want to talk to all of us afterwards." He glanced at the tall, empty glass sitting beside me. "You good?"

If he was asking if I was sober, sober enough to join them for a briefing, the answer to that was definitely no. I chuckled a little, picturing myself stumbling onto the bridge, falling all over. Wouldn't that be something? That would be a first for me. I shook my head, giggling, and Wren just shook his head, grinning back at me.

I slid through the water, moving over to a higher bench, and pulled my arms, heavy and sluggish, out of the hot water, resting my elbows on the deck behind me. Wren watched me, eyes changing, becoming heavy and darker, slightly glazed over. With desire, I realized with a start. Lust. He wanted me. And I couldn't help but feel a little thrill run through me. An answering throbbing in my core at the look in his eyes. At least someone did.

"Why don't you join me?" I heard myself ask, in a low, husky voice.

Wren's eyes widened, just as likely at my tone as at my words, and he seemed to snap out of whatever spell he'd been under momentarily. He swallowed and ran a hand through his curls, pushing them off his forehead. "I can't do that, Jordan," he murmured, shaking his head.

"Why not?" I asked, pushing him. It was probably for the best, I thought. But I was in an odd, reckless sort of mood. Too far gone to care.

"Because." He said, shaking his head again, his voice low and rough, "he'd kill me."

We stared at each other for several seconds, anger building in my chest. "No, he wouldn't, actually," I shook my head, glaring at him now. "He doesn't give a shit. Trust me, he made that very clear."

Wren smirked, scoffing a little, and he looked away from me, out the window, into the void. "You're joking, right?"

he said, his eyes returning to mine. "You can't possibly believe that."

"Oh, I do," I assured him. "He practically gave us his blessing."

"Then he's bluffing," Wren said, eyes narrowing. He looked angry himself now. "That's bullshit." I just shrugged. "Is that why you've been upset?" he asked. I just looked away from him, tight-lipped. "Good lord." He murmured, running a hand over his face. "You do realize he tried to save you, twice. Right?" I frowned over at him, and he continued. "He ran through a... a field of Jumpers, through enemy lines, into the woods, back at that factory, to find you, and bring you back."

I shook my head, scoffing, "That was–"

But he cut me off, "Now granted, he does crazy shit like that, on a fairly regular basis. Bastard seems to have nine lives, but that's neither here nor there. He risked his life, to save you. To go after you. And he did it again, that night at the hill."

"I didn't ask him to," I snapped, eyes blazing, heart in my throat.

"You didn't have to," Wren snapped back.

I fell silent at that. And we stared each other down for a long moment, both slightly out of breath.

"He'd kill me. He'd never forgive me. Never." Wren shook his head. "And you're sitting here, thinking he doesn't care?" He licked his lips, standing, and shaking his head, looking back at me. "Maybe you're not as smart as I thought you were."

He shrugged. "I'll send you a message if he wants to meet with us." Wren turned and walked away, across the deck. "Try to sober up, before then." He called over his shoulder, and then he was gone.

24.

I didn't get a message from Wren, over the comms that night, which was probably for the best. I spent the rest of the night sulking in the hot tub.

I eventually managed to drag my weak, limp limbs out of the water, feeling thoroughly cooked and exhausted, the restless, nervous energy finally drained from my body. I dragged myself back to my room, managed to drink some water, and passed out.

Thankfully, while I'd had enough to drink the night before to make me buzzed, and apparently, enough Nitrous to make a fool of myself, it hadn't been enough to make me sick. I woke up the next morning with a headache, grateful it wasn't worse. I had managed to sleep in, for the first time in a long time. Long enough that I had missed breakfast. I downed some painkillers, drank some coffee, grabbed a snack from my little kitchen, and got a slow start to the morning, enjoying the lazy solitude.

I was still lounging when I got the comms message around 1100. I was to report to the bridge at 1200 hours. Not much of a warning, but I was glad in a way. At least I wouldn't have much longer to wait to find out what the next mission would be.

I got dressed in my officer's uniform and braided my hair, still frizzy and unruly from hours spent in the heat last night, into one thick braid.

I walked as confidently as possible into the bridge as the double doors slid open for me, steeling myself to meet Wren's eyes without flinching. It wasn't as though what I'd done was awful. Besides, he'd been the one to start it, looking at me that way. But I was still feeling a mild sting of embarrassment, and a roiling mix of emotions at what he'd had to say.

I entered the bridge to find the men scattered all over the room. Some sitting, some standing. All silent. Faces drawn. Eyes downcast. I froze immediately.

Wren had no trouble meeting my eyes. He stood, leaning back against the command center, hands in his pockets. But when our eyes met, he just shook his head, face pale and tight.

"What happened?" I asked, eyes wide, as I surveyed the room. "Where's Ward?" I snapped next, realizing he was oddly absent.

Molton sighed, pushed his glasses up his nose, and flopped down onto the bank of low couches in front of the blank screen.

Wren cleared his throat, "He had to excuse himself from the room for a moment. He'll be back shortly."

I stood frozen, processing that. What had happened then? Clearly, some sort of bad news had been received. And why were they all gathered here so early? It certainly seemed like they'd been here for a while, and I wasn't late. I was sure I hadn't messed up; the comm message TODD relayed had said 1200 hours.

The doors slid open behind me, as Ward's heavy boots pounding against the floor echoed through the silent bridge. I turned to him, but he barely looked in my direction, stalking past me, over to the table.

"TODD, pull up the map of the landing zone," he called out as he went. The 3D map sprang into existence immediately, and the lights in the room dimmed, the only glow coming from the slowly rotating map itself, and the faint glow of millions of stars through the wall of windows.

I swallowed, moving closer to the table, taking in the terrain. A field, surrounded by tree-covered hills, with mountains in the distance. The landing zone was clearly indicated, but there was nothing to hint at the location from what I could tell. The men moved slowly, gathering over near the table.

Ward cleared his throat, and his voice came out with an odd raspiness. "We'll set down at 1500 hours, outside Atlanta."

My eyes widened as his words sank in, and I scanned his features as he spoke. Atlanta was a major city. A cultural center for the South. In terms of targets, it ranked second only to DC.

Ward's face was drenched in lines of alternating light and shadow. I attempted to read his expression, his body language, but could glean nothing. Other than his voice being off, he might be talking about any other mission. But this wasn't any other mission. If D Company was targeting Atlanta, it could only be as part of a major push. Anything less would be a suicide mission. I swallowed thickly, my throat suddenly dry. Were we really at that point? Ready to try to take Atlanta? It didn't feel like it somehow.

"We're going to have a hike in, boys. They're directing us to set down far enough away that we don't risk triggering their systems. They don't want us to show up as even a blip on their radar. They've sent over clothes for us, weapons."

"What?" I asked, brow furrowed. "Are we taking Atlanta? Why do we need different weapons?"

Ward paused, took a deep breath. "We're going in as civilians." He said, eyes flickering in my direction, but not quite looking at me. "And you're not going."

"What?" I asked, my voice ringing sharply in the dim space.

"Like I said, we're going in as civilians. Posing as a group of raiders, just traveling through town. There's no way we can bring you with us."

"For what purpose?" I asked, frowning, hands gripped on the back of the chair in front of me so hard that I might snap it in half.

Ward cleared his throat again, voice rough, "Our target is the airport. We need to permanently take out the EMP shield over the airfield. Another advance team has already gone in ahead of us and taken out the tech that generates the EMP shield over the city. Our orders are to assist in taking over the airfield by bringing down the shield in any way possible. Intel will have hackers working on it 24/7 as well, but they've made a change to their algorithms." Ward shrugged, "They aren't hopeful they can bring it down in time. They're sending us in to manually take it out. This will be a smaller team, but our full company will be waiting on the outskirts of the city, hunkered down in the woods."

I shook my head, "So, why am I not going, exactly?" I frowned down at the map.

Ward sighed again, staring down at the floor, arms propped on the edge of the table. "Because you're a woman," he said, meeting my eyes, "and no," he held up his hand, stopping me as I opened my mouth to retort, "it's not because I'm a sexist pig, it's because they are." He inclined his head at the table. "Atlanta is one of their largest cities. Outside of DC, there isn't a more dangerous place for a woman in combat uniform to set down–"

I cut him off, "You just said we'd be dressed as civilians. How would anyone know I'm a woman in combat?" I had wanted to keep my voice calm and even, but it was already rising.

"Do you think they'll take more kindly to a female raider? Carrying a gun? It will make no difference to them who you're traveling with or why. Down there, it's illegal. They won't stand for it."

"You're not leaving me behind," I demanded, arms crossed over my chest. "If the rest of the company is camping out, hiding out in the mountains, then why can't I stay back with them?" I raised an eyebrow, "Is hiding in the woods too dangerous for me, too?"

Ward sighed. "The rest of the company will be hiding out in the woods while we enter the airport. Once the shields are taken out, they'll join us as part of the main assault. Ultimately, we plan to take control of the city."

My eyes went wide. "How can we possibly be ready for that? That will be a massive undertaking."

Ward nodded, eyes dropping to the ground. The men moved restlessly at my words. "From what Intelligence has been able to gather, since we brought the shield over the city down, Jumper activity has spread quickly." He swallowed. "Rumor has it that it's pure chaos down there. The SC is camped out in a sector of the city. Here," he zoomed in on the city map.

"Breaching it will be... challenging. But taking the rest of the city should be mostly a matter of taking out the Jumpers. We'll also have to deal with any patrols roving through at random... any armed civilians or raiders... but most of them are hopefully bunkered down wherever they can find shelter." He met my eyes again. "I'm not risking bringing you down there, into that," his voice dropped so low that I could barely hear him, eyes cold, and voice dangerously soft.

"I'm willing to take the risk," I said, spitting the words at him. "I knew the risks when I enlisted. What do you think happens to me if I need to eject from my rig when I'm behind enemy lines? Huh? You think this will be the first time I'm putting myself in a risky situation? For fuck's sake Ward, I'm a goddamn fighter pilot."

Ward stood up and moved over to me, leading me away from the table with a light touch on my arm. The men seemed to take the hint and began murmuring amongst themselves. Ward led me all the way over to the counter against the far wall before turning to face me.

"You are staying here, and that's final." He snapped, his chest heaving slightly.

"You can't be serious." I shook my head in disbelief, "You can't leave me behind, it's not..."

"It's not what? Not fair?" He chuckled, "Well, get over it." He shook his head. "Do you know what they'll do to you down there, once they realize you're a woman?"

I frowned, shaking my head as Ward continued. "I've been in major cities like Atlanta before. Things were bad enough then, I can only imagine what it's like now. You may understand the risks of an emergency landing, but that would be a worst-case scenario, Kessler; not the fucking plan."

He sighed, his voice dropping low again. "Look, we aren't bringing you with us. There is no reason to. No benefit. We may be down there for several days anyway; you wouldn't be able to quickly transport a specimen back. Besides, I can't afford any distractions or resources spent on making sure your team is safe. It's just not worth it– and I won't risk it."

I studied him, eyes narrowed. Did he know? Did he know what almost happened back in South Carolina? It felt like he knew. My gaze flickered to the table, searching for Wren. I found him, watching us, but he dropped his eyes instantly from mine and proceeded to stare down at the map. *Goddamn it.* I forced myself to unclench my fists. Well, if he did know, it was my fault. I'd told him to ask Wren what happened. I couldn't blame Wren if he'd folded under Ward's interrogation.

I stood there with my jaw clenched, fighting to keep my voice calm, as I focused back on Ward. "I have just as much of a right to be there as any man here-"

"That is not what this is about." He glared at me. "They don't give a shit what rights you have. They will make an example out of you."

I had fought too hard for this. Fought too hard to be here. I had earned an equal spot with my blood, sweat, and tears. But it still wasn't enough, I realized, with a sinking feeling. It would never be enough. Not until the sort of misogyny that ran rampant in the South was stamped out for good. And I doubted that day would ever come. How many countless generations of women had fought against oppression? When would it end? I'd practically killed myself in boot camp. Pushed my body well beyond its limits, in an attempt to keep up. To be perceived as one of them. And in reality, I couldn't just be as good. I had to be better. Better, just to earn an equal spot. But in the end, it didn't matter, did it?

I knew it wasn't Ward's fault, but the thought of being treated as weaker, less than, simply because I was female and a target, made my stomach churn.

Still, part of me knew he had a point. There was no added benefit to my joining them, and only the possibility of increased risk. Not just to myself, but to the men around me as well. But it felt like a defeat. It felt like accepting, or giving in, to their ideology. Their need to control us.

Even worse than all of that, the thought of them, down there, without me... suffering, wounded. Dying. While I sat here, doing nothing... I couldn't take it. Couldn't stand it.

"Then I'll hide that I'm female," I insisted.

Ward snorted and gestured to my long braid. "Yeah, that'll work."

I pulled my knife out of the sheath on my right thigh in one smooth motion, lifting it to my braid, grasped in my other hand, "Then I'll cut it off," I said, moving to press the blade down.

"No!" He held his hand out, and I felt the entire room go still as I froze in shock at the tone of his voice.

We stared at each other, neither moving a muscle, my heart pounding in my chest. I lowered the knife slowly and saw the tension in his stance ease, almost imperceptibly.

"That will never work," he murmured, eyes sliding down my chest. I felt my cheeks flush. My fatigues, especially when wearing a combat vest, hid a lot, but certainly not everything. And flight suits would be out of the question in Atlanta.

"You are staying here," he said firmly. "That's an order." He moved closer to me, his voice dangerously soft, "And don't you even think about trying to sneak onto a pod. If I find out you're down there, I will hunt you down myself, and I will have you court-martialed. Do you understand me?"

I stared at him, and he stared back, unblinking. I was filled with a dull, muted rage. My chest heaved, and I could feel my eyes wanting to fill with tears. I slid the knife back into its sheath without breaking eye contact.

"Fine." I spat at him.

"Fine, what?" He asked, moving swiftly until he was inches away from me, his voice a threatening growl.

I swallowed dryly, hesitating as long as I dared. "Fine, Captain," I murmured. And I poured every ounce of hate I felt for him into my eyes as I glared at him. And he glared right back, dark eyes burning.

He moved a step back, retreating over to the table. I took a deep breath, trying to calm my breathing, my body still trembling with pent-up rage.

"McCullough and Binson will accompany you then," I spoke softly, "I trust you can manage to assist them with whatever support they require, to gather the remaining samples we need."

Ward nodded, jaw clenched tight. "I understand the importance of gathering samples, Kessler. That's not what this is about."

I continued to glare at him. Not bothering to respond. He was forced to look away first, turning back to the table to continue the briefing. My cheeks burned with shame and anger as I turned away and left the room.

25.

I stood off to the side in the hangar, watching as the men made their final preparations to leave. McCullough and Binson hung back at my side until I nodded towards the pods and urged them to get going.

McCullough looked back at me twice. He shook his head slowly as he entered the pod. I knew he felt sorry for me, that I was being left behind. My gut twisted in shame as I watched them go. The thought of sending my men down there without me made me sick to my stomach.

I stood there, staring at my feet, trying to calm down, reminding myself that it wasn't my choice. I didn't have a say in the matter.

"Hey," a pair of boots came to a stop a foot or so away from mine, and I raised my eyes to find Ward hovering over me, leaning closer, his voice dropping low. "I'm sorry." He said roughly. "I know you're upset. But trust me, it's for the best."

I glared back at him, lips in a thin, tight line, as I clenched my jaw, biting down on the quick retort that sprang to my mind.

He eyed me back warily for a moment, his expression shifting into something close to anger. "You can hate me all you want," he snapped, his tone clipped. "I can take it." I continued to stare back at him silently. He shook his head after a moment, looking away from me, over at the men boarding the pods. "Right. Then I'll see you in a bit. This will probably take a few days."

He turned back to find me still glaring at him, arms crossed tightly over my chest. I felt like I was holding myself down, holding myself together– a spring wound tightly, that was about to break.

He shook his head at me, eyes narrowing. "Aren't you even going to say goodbye?"

I snorted slightly, looking away, my eyes landing on Wren, halfway between us and the pods. He stood there, watching Ward and me. I shot him an icy glare before looking away. I was certain now he'd told Ward what had happened, and while I knew I was partially to blame, I couldn't help but feel hurt and angry that he'd betrayed my trust.

I felt myself shrug. Shoulders lifting and falling again in a brief spasm. My throat was tight, and my chest ached. I gripped my arms tighter, overcome by a sudden wave of grief, mixing with that tide of anger and shame that was already threatening to swallow me whole. What if they didn't come back?

Ward made some sort of noise, halfway between a choking sound and a laugh, and his voice was full of contempt as he moved closer to me, whispering. "I forgot; you don't do goodbyes on the eve of battle, do you, Captain?" I forced myself to meet his gaze, my stomach flipping at his words.

His eyes were dark and full of a sort of wild hunger I hadn't seen since that first night we met. My breath caught in my throat as he reached up with one hand, his knuckles grazing my skin in a brief caress, just beneath my chin.

I was slow to react, raising my chin in response, my eyes fluttering closed for a split second. And then he was gone. He'd turned and stalked away, back towards the pods. I stood there for a moment, watching him, my heart pounding in my chest, unsure now if he'd ever actually touched me, or if I'd imagined it somehow.

Wren stood there, waiting for him. He began to turn to follow Ward as he moved past, his eyes lingering on me. He nodded to me once, in his own sort of goodbye.

My throat burned, and my eyes started to fill with tears at the simple gesture. I nodded back, trying to keep my expression clear, blinking rapidly.

A brief spasm of emotion crossed over Wren's face as he turned his back on me and followed Ward onto the closest pod.

I watched as the pods exited the hangar, one by one, chest heaving, wiping my eyes as I fought to keep the tears at bay, and lost, thankful the men inside could no longer see me.

I stood there for a long time after they left. The hangar door remained open, and I stayed there amidst the howling wind, the air becoming colder by the second, until I was shivering. Until my whole body was shaking. Until I was so cold, I couldn't take it any longer.

I slammed my fist against the red button on the wall as I exited the hangar, retreating to the solitude of *The Beagle*.

I knew it could be anywhere from hours to several days before they might return. I did my best to keep busy, feeling the anger and shame at being left behind bubbling up whenever I got bored.

But it was no easy task. Not with the ship silent, nearly empty. I invented little tasks— organizing and taking inventory of supplies down in the lab. We weren't due to take inventory, but it was a task I could take on for Lindsay while she worked on more important things. And it gave me something to do.

I spoke to TODD like he was a real person. Which let's be honest, I'd fallen into the habit of doing anyway, but it became even more routine, and more of a comfort given the isolation I was feeling.

Hours stretched into days, stretched into nearly a week. Five days. Five days, and nothing. Not a peep or a squawk on the comms. I scanned the planet below for military activity.

Watching the various types of radar and sensors lighting up green and then red, all centered on Atlanta far below.

I stared at the glow of the city, idly. As though watching the activity would somehow tell me where they were amongst all that chaos. My gut clenched whenever a plume of light furled into the sky on the 3D map, indicating an explosion. Had they taken over the airfield yet? Were our bombers going in? I sat there for hours, sprawled sideways, legs over the armrests of the chair, my mind spinning, *1984* lying open, forgotten, in my lap.

I pictured them down there and made up countless fake scenarios in my head, imagining what they might be encountering. What kind of horrors. I flipped on the comms link and spent a ridiculous amount of time scanning random frequencies, hoping to somehow stumble on the right band, desperate for any update. But I heard nothing but static. I knew that on larger joint missions like this one, Command preferred to employ automatic frequency hopping. With the massive range of comms frequencies available, the odds of me stumbling on the right one the company was using at any given moment were pretty slim.

I stared glumly at the 3D map of Atlanta as I listened, the headset pressed over my ears, the buzz of static driving me half mad. I had never felt so useless, so ineffectual, and stuck in my entire life. Not since adolescence, stuck back on the farm. Waiting for life to start.

I forced myself to try to use the time meaningfully, the best I could. I exercised. I ran miles at a time on the treadmill. I lifted weights, pushing myself further than I probably should have, especially with no one there to spot me. Every afternoon, I found myself wandering into the gym, pushing myself until I was sore, sweaty, and exhausted. On the fifth day, I lay there on the mat, drenched in sweat, close to vomiting. I'd promised myself I wouldn't do this again. Wouldn't push myself too far. So much for that.

I lay there, chest heaving, and told myself that this would be the night. This would be the night they would return. How they would be loud and boisterous, and annoying. How I would wish for the peace and quiet of the nearly empty ship.

But I couldn't deny the seed of doubt growing in the pit of my stomach. What if they just... didn't come back? What if something so catastrophic happened that none of them returned? I tried to picture it. Molton and Nathan. Powers. McCullough, Binson. I thought of Wren. Thought of *him*, never returning.

I just managed to make it to the trash can in time; wave after wave of revulsion roiled through my stomach, heaving until I collapsed back on the mat, my entire body shaking and weak.

So, I told myself it would be tonight. And once my body had stopped throbbing, and my stomach had calmed, I rose to my feet and dragged myself to go shower.

I surveyed my gear and selected a tank top I had never tried on before, pulling it on over my little black bra. It was low-cut, with a plunging V-neckline that revealed far too much cleavage for decency. I pulled the towel off my hair as I walked into the bathroom. The mirror was covered in condensation. I swiped a hand over it in annoyance, ran a comb through my hair, and used the towel to scrunch some of the water out.

I left it down, in damp, loose waves, to air dry. I surveyed my reflection. It was the most feminine I'd allowed myself to look in months. I almost thought better of it. I should probably change. And twisting my hair into a bun would take two seconds. But it took forever to dry that way. I didn't want to go to sleep in a few hours with it still wet. Besides, I argued, there was no one here to see me, anyway.

I pictured the men coming back then, pictured him seeing me, with my hair down. My stomach twisted, a flash of fire sweeping through my core, as I remembered how he had cried out when I'd been about to cut it off.

I smirked at my reflection and turned abruptly and left the room, flicking the lights off as I went. So be it if they came back tonight.

While I felt like I was all alone on the vast ship, that wasn't entirely accurate. There was still Curtis and his crew down in Engineering. But he was so old. Ancient, really. And he hardly spoke more than two words at a time. His crew were an odd, awkward bunch. They almost never came above deck. I'd ducked down to visit Curtis twice already during the course of the week, bringing him a cup of strong coffee, with cream, just how he liked it. It gave me something to do. But I elected not to visit him tonight.

There was the medical team, of course, but they were on standby, down in the Med Bay. With their own adjacent quarters and kitchen, they had no reason to leave, and rarely were seen elsewhere on the Carrier. My small team was tucked away in the lab, too. I'd spent several hours there each day, the first few days. I'd even convinced Lindsay and Topher to play cards with me for a bit one night.

We'd shared a few drinks, and Lindsay had taught us how to play a game I'd never heard of before, called euchre. We'd laughed about our old instructors, and they'd swapped rumors about the people they knew in Intelligence. I'd recognized a few of the names at least. But I'd spent so much time there, I ended up feeling like I was getting in their way. Like I was hovering over them. I didn't want to slow them down or make them think I was trying to rush them on the results. It wasn't that. I was just bored.

I wasn't sure Lindsay was sleeping, as it was. I'd caught her twice in the past few days, once sitting in a chair, once, inexplicably, on a stool, head down on the metal table below, fast asleep. She'd startled awake quickly on both occasions as I approached. The second time had been just this morning.

"Linds," I'd sighed, "are you sleeping here?" I shook my head, "I mean, are you spending the night in the lab? That's not healthy. You should go back to your quarters; get some real sleep."

Lindsay shook her head. "I'm fine, Jordan. Don't worry about me." She grimaced, wiping her hair off her forehead and pulling it back into a loose bun. "I've pulled plenty of all-nighters before. I know what I'm doing."

I sighed, plopping down into a chair across from her. "I know you do…" I trailed off. "But look, we're all under a lot of pressure right now. Just don't forget to take care of yourself."

She nodded briskly, pulling herself to her feet as she gripped the table in front of her. "There's something I need to show you," she said, waving to me to follow her.

I stood quickly and followed her deeper into the lab, winding between the tables. She stopped at one of the tables pushed against a wall, a large microscope off to one side, a bank of computer terminals, and a massive machine with blinking green lights. A screen on the wall to the right lit up as she tapped on a keyboard.

"These findings are preliminary, and I'm running everything again to confirm. But Jordan– you're not going to believe this." She inclined her head towards the screen as I turned back to her.

An image appeared now, a diagram, with row after row of different colored lines, some bands of color glowing more brightly than others. "What is it?" I murmured, studying the image carefully. I knew just enough to guess that I was looking at a microarray.

Lindsay cleared her throat. "These are the results of the DNA analysis I've been conducting. The results are... interesting, to say the least." She paused for a moment, then continued, her voice dropping even lower. "We were correct in assuming what we're dealing with is a fungal infection. It's a variant of the Zombie-Ant fungus. I'm positive about that." The images on the screen flickered and were replaced by another similar set of alternating color bands. "There are also certain genes, sequences, that can be traced back to ant DNA. One species, in particular, I think, although narrowing that down further might be challenging. But that's not the most interesting part."

I stared up at the screen as I took in what she was saying. "There is this one section of genes that repeats over and over, and it shows up in multiple samples. I couldn't find a match in any of the ant DNA samples I ran a comparison against." She paused for a moment, typing something rapidly on the keyboard. "It took me a long time to realize I was searching in the wrong place. I needed to broaden my search, and it took several days before I got a hit."

A new image appeared on the screen, a string of what looked like gibberish to me, alternating sequences of letters and a string of numbers at the top of the screen. "What you're looking at now is a section of DNA from another species entirely." Lindsay nodded at the screen, a hint of pride in her voice. "This is *Ceuthophilus pallidus,* from the *Raphidophoridae* family, order *Orthoptera*." I turned to stare at her, eyebrows raised. "Commonly known as the Camel Cricket. Or sometimes referred to as the Spider Cricket." She grinned at me.

I shook my head slowly. "So, you're saying this thing has ant DNA, and Camel Cricket DNA... mixed with fungal DNA..." I trailed off.

"That's exactly what I'm saying," Lindsay continued, "And here's an interesting little fact about Camel Crickets," she typed something on the keyboard, and a new image flashed on the screen. I assumed what I was looking at was a Camel Cricket. I'd never seen one before. There was something grotesque about it.

It had a high, rounded body, almost as though it were stooped over, or curled in on itself. It was segmented, its carapace covered in rounded segments down the length of its back, almost like an insect version of an armadillo. Its rear legs were long, rising high above its back. It had two additional sets of legs that didn't arch quite as high. Its overall, hunched appearance, and all those legs... it reminded me of an elongated, bloated spider. I shivered slightly, staring up at it.

Lindsay chuckled. "I know, right? It's a disgusting little thing, isn't it? And get this, the Camel Cricket has a unique adaptation, as far as I'm aware. When they are startled, their only defense mechanism is reflexive. They really are completely harmless, despite their appearance. When they're triggered, they reflexively jump *towards* their attacker. It's an attempt to startle their enemy; scare them away. And they do this instinctively. Rather than running away, attempting to escape, they end up jumping towards you, flinging themselves at their enemy, repeatedly. Oftentimes, ending in their demise, as there is little they can do to fight back against a threat."

I pulled my gaze away from the images flashing on the screen; a video of a Camel Cricket jumping towards the person filming, as they screamed in terror at the tiny insect flinging itself towards them, slamming into the camera.

I stared over at Lindsay, and she grinned grimly back at me. "Remind you of anything?"

"So..." I replied slowly, "they don't even mean to attack you? They just jump at you because they're scared?"

She nodded grimly at me. "That's right." She sighed, crossing her arms and leaning back in the chair. "There's a significant amount of Camel Cricket DNA, although I obviously am extrapolating; we can't make blanket assumptions as far as the Jumpers go. Who knows what they're motivated by, what they're thinking or feeling? We don't know what's going on in there, on a cognitive level. But... it's an intriguing correlation with their behavior, isn't it?"

I let out a deep breath, nodding in agreement. "It definitely is." I watched as she switched back to the DNA sequences, her eyes flickering over the images rotating on the screen above. We fell silent for a moment or so.

"So, Lindsay," I said slowly, my mind falling back on the interview with Evans. "What do you think, at this point?" I nodded to the screen as she turned to look at me. "Knowing what you know now..." I trailed off for a moment, uncertain how to frame the question. "What are the odds that something like this occurred naturally?" I dropped my voice to a whisper as I spoke, watching as she leaned forward. "Do you think it's possible this thing could be natural?"

Lindsay stared back at me solemnly, falling silent. I watched as she returned her attention to the screen above us, scrolling through image after image. She bit down on her lip, eyes glued on the screen. And I felt my stomach sink.

"Jordan," she sighed, after a long pause, "what I'm seeing right now, in front of me, is the DNA from three different, distinct species, not just from different families, but from different orders, entirely... all spliced together." She sighed again, running a hand over her mouth, her chin, before letting it fall back to the table. "I'm trying to imagine a scenario where that occurs naturally... and I can't come up with one."

We stared at each other before I finally nodded. "And, you're sure?" I asked, my voice sounding tired to my own ears.

She hesitated only for a second before nodding. "I'm sure."

I swallowed, staring back at the screen. "Okay then," I said quietly. "Who knows? Besides us?" I stared up at those glowing bands of color on the screen, my vision swimming slightly.

Lindsay sighed. "Only Topher." She murmured quietly. "I think I've managed to shield my lab techs from ever accessing the full data at once. They have no clue what we're dealing with, as far as I can say." I nodded my approval.

"Good," I murmured, turning back to her. "Let's keep it that way, okay?" I said lightly. "Until we know what we're dealing with... let's keep this on lock."

Lindsay nodded solemnly back to me. I knew that went without saying. But still. My stomach, already roiling all morning, was doing somersaults now.

I had thanked her then and went off to search for Topher.

I had found him further back, in a far corner of the lab. He was standing over a workbench, littered with tools and scraps of paper, looping handwriting scrawled all over, parts of the writing with lines crossed through, arrows, and notes off to the side.

He was typing furiously on his laptop, pausing and turning to me, his hair sticking up at odd angles, as though he'd been running his hands through it, or perhaps even pulling it out.

"Hey," I murmured cautiously. "How's it going back here?" He sighed deeply, continuing to type. I cleared my throat. "I just spoke with Lindsay; she updated me on the genetic results so far."

Topher's hands paused; fingers curled in mid-air over the keyboard. "Yeah," he muttered, turning to me and pushing away from the table. "Holy shit; right?" He sighed again, running a hand through his hair, he reached back up a second time, and attempted to flatten it, combing through it roughly with his fingers. "Someone in an underground lab somewhere fucked up, big time." He shrugged. "Either that, or we got sick of shooting at those assholes and decided to send them a little present." He shrugged again. "But you know, what's a little fungal infection, between enemies?"

I sighed deeply, placing my hands on my hips. "For fuck's sake Topher, will you keep your voice down?"

He frowned at me. "Isn't the crew all down on the ground right now?" He sighed at the look I shot at him and leaned back in his chair, arms crossing over his chest. "Sorry," he mumbled. "You don't need to worry, Captain, I'm not going to go spouting off about this, okay?"

I nodded grimly. "I know that," I said gently, "but a little discretion would be good." I bit my lip, pausing, before continuing. "So, you assume this was us?" I asked gingerly, not sure I wanted to hear his answer.

He stared at me for a moment. "Don't you?" He asked, incredulously. "Who else would it be?"

I shook my head, sighing loudly. "I dunno, Russia? Japan? Maybe China?" I said, shrugging. "Don't you think it could have been someone else?"

Topher frowned slightly, head bouncing side to side as he considered my words. "Sure, it absolutely *could* have been. The fact that it actually worked as well as it did makes me think of Japan, or China, more so than Russia. But ultimately," he shrugged, "I'm a big fan of Occam's razor, Captain." I stared back at him. "The simplest, most elegant explanation is usually the closest to the truth."

He glanced over at his laptop screen, his face thrown into shadows in the dim lab. "We stand to gain the most from this thing taking them out, and we have. I'd put my money on this originating with us. And even if we didn't create it, it still seems likely we're the ones that released it."

I swallowed thickly, watching him. "So, what do we do now, then?" I asked, throwing my arms out at my sides. "You're telling me you think we did this, ourselves, and then they created this task force, sent us out to solve this thing, all the while, knowing exactly what it is, and where it came from?" He frowned over at me. "Do you think that means they already know how to stop it?"

Topher swallowed, his throat bobbing. Then he stood abruptly and moved away from me, across the lab. "Come on," he called over his shoulder.

I followed him to the far wall, to another grouping of terminals. He sat down in the chair, spinning around once, then pushing off and zooming back and forth between keyboards, monitors lighting up as he went. "All I can tell you is there's been a hell of a lot of chatter lately, in all sectors. I monitor certain..." he trailed off for a moment, "channels, let's say, on a regular basis." He grinned over at me, "And so do my friends. I can tell you right now that people are scared. A lot of people. High up. Officials. Members of Congress."

"How can you know that?" I asked, watching him with wide eyes.

"There's little I can't access, Captain." He shrugged, his back to me. "And people aren't as careful as they should be. They don't think anyone is watching." He chortled slightly. "Rumor has it, this thing has the brass up top, and Congress itself, scared shitless." He spun back around to face me. "So, my answer would be no, I don't think they have any clue how to stop it. I think they created a monster they didn't fully understand, and they let it out of the box, so to speak, without considering the wider implications."

I stilled, taking in his words. "Which are?" I asked, my heart pounding in my chest now.

"Well," Topher shrugged, "I mean, I've been running simulations, in my downtime; we all have." I swallowed thickly. I assumed by 'we', he meant his hacker friends. Topher turned back to a keyboard, a few taps of his fingers pulling up a map of the continent down below us.

"This is right now," he said, "as close of a model as we can generate based on the data we have access to." He slammed down on a key, "And this is two weeks from now." I watched as the little dots, and in some cases, circles, of red, began to glow and expand outward, their diameters swelling. My breath caught a little in my throat as he spoke again. "And a month from now..." The red spread, circles growing larger until they overlapped. Dots and more circles were popping up across the border now, until both halves of the continent were covered in a swath of red; only tiny gaps of black remained here and there.

"Jesus Christ..." I murmured, staring at the screen until my vision glazed, eyes unfocusing. I blinked rapidly, staring at the location of my hometown.

"You have to understand, Captain, we're still in the early stages of this thing. Without anything to check it, it's going to continue to spread rapidly, as the number of infected grows, the new infections spawned begin to take off, growing exponentially, until this thing takes over. This has the potential to wipe us all off the map, indefinitely."

I swallowed thickly, turning my gaze back to him. "We need to call the Admiral. Alert command. Congress. They need to do something..."

I trailed off as he shook his head. "They already know, Captain. They're already starting to scramble. It's sinking in. They've fucked us. They've fucked us all. Big time." He sighed, crossing his arms over his chest, as he stared at the map. "All we can do now is come up with a way to slow down the spread. Fight them off, take them out. Try to contain this thing the best we can."

I nodded, watching him. "The EMP gun," I murmured. "Have you made any progress?" Topher grimaced slightly at my words, and I felt my stomach sink.

"I'm getting somewhere with it. I'm stuck on this one part, my calculations..." he trailed off for a moment. "I know you said we need to keep this on lockdown," he paused. "But I have people, a network of people," I frowned, and he held up his hands, "a *small* network of people, that I trust, implicitly." He stood up, moving closer to me. "I don't need to say what this is for; I don't need to tell them anything, beyond what they need to know to help me brainstorm, okay?" He frowned, placing his hands on my shoulders, eyes level with mine, he met my gaze head-on. "Captain, I can't stress enough to you how vital, how important it is, that this works." I swallowed again, nodding. "We need this to work. It's our only hope right now for a weapon we can use against them."

I hesitated only for a few seconds. "Do it," I said, my voice sounding oddly hollow. "Do whatever you have to." He nodded, his hands dropping to his sides, relief smoothing over his features. "Call me as soon as you have something."

He nodded again. "I will." He thought for a moment. "But what are we going to do after that? Say I'm successful, modifying the gun, and we test it out, and it works. That's one gun," he shook his head. "We're going to need a heck of a lot more... a whole army's worth." He shrugged. "What do we do then? What's our next move?"

I thought for a moment. "I go to the Admiral; tell him we have a weapon that's effective against them. We tell him everything you just told me; the simulations, everything." I waved a hand, "We don't have to mention anything else about what we suspect. We give them the technology; we tell them we need to mass produce it."

Topher nodded, smirking slightly. "Sure, and that all makes sense, but you have to remember, the EMP guns come from the South. Right? I mean, they don't have flight suits themselves. They've never issued them, at least. If they do have the technology somewhere, they aren't using it. They came up with these guns, somehow, to use against *our* flight suits, and Command has never seen a need to develop similar technology ourselves." He trailed off for a moment, "I suspect the South didn't develop the technology without help, but that's neither here nor there. The point is, we don't produce EMP guns. How are we going to get these into mass production, that quickly?"

He glanced back at the map. "I mean, I'd estimate we have two weeks, maybe three, at most, before this thing reaches the point of no return." He chuckled slightly. "I don't know about you, but I have next to zero confidence that they can pull something like that off in time to make a difference."

I stared at him, my gaze flickering from him to the map, and then back again. I finally nodded my understanding. "Well, we'll have to worry about that when the time comes," I added slowly. "I may have a potential solution..." My voice trailed off.

Topher watched me, his expression careful. Then he turned and started off towards the far side of the lab again. Pausing and doubling back to the terminal to click a button, the map on the wall disappeared, and the screen went dark. "Right." He called back to me. "I'm getting back to work."

I was left alone, staring at my dim reflection on the screen before me. I stayed there for a long time, thinking.

26.

I had made my way slowly to the bridge from there, with only the sound of my own footsteps echoing in the empty corridor, to keep me company.

I sat at the desk in the bridge, my chin resting in my hands. Eventually, I grabbed the comms headset and switched on the comms radio, taking shallow breaths as I moved the dial, turning it down to 750 MHz. I listened to the hum of static for a moment. Then I hit the transmit button.

I held my breath for a second, then murmured, "Billy, do you read me? Over." I waited, listening to the static crackle and hiss over the line, picturing my voice, ringing out hollowly in that dimly lit room. I pictured Billy, seated at the radio, drenched in that golden pool of light from the lone desk lamp. Would he know it was me? Would he answer back?

I tried again. "Billy, this is Captain Kessler. Do you copy? Over. I need to speak to you; it's urgent." I winced slightly. Not just at the tone of my voice, but the risk of using my name. All I could do was pray no one else was listening in on this channel.

I heard nothing but the continuous crackle and hiss of static, and I sat there for several seconds, head hanging low. I clicked the transmit button, one last time. "Billy, I need your help..." I paused, my voice trailing off. "I... I have no one else to go to. Please. Please answer."

I waited, tears springing behind my eyes. I had been feeling so emotional all week. Things felt like they were coming to a tipping point. Not just with Ward and I, but with the battle raging below me; the war itself. The Jumpers. I was still struggling to process everything I'd learned in the lab today. My brain railed against it, trying to put the pieces together in a different order. Trying to recreate reality into a scenario where we weren't the ones responsible for all this carnage, and where there wasn't so much riding on this. On the outcomes of my own actions. This couldn't possibly be real. I couldn't really be sitting here, in this chair, waiting for a man I hardly knew, a man from the South, to respond to my desperate plea, because I had nowhere else to turn. No one else I could reach out to for help. No one else I could trust.

I heard the static swell slightly, seeming to grow louder. "Captain Kessler?" I heard a voice, faint and garbled, as though it was coming from far away. And it was, I thought, gripping the microphone tighter, I leaned forward in the chair. "That really you?" A pause for a second, "You got Billy here. Over."

"Billy," I spoke back into the mic, raising my voice, trying to speak as clearly as possible. "It's really me. I hear you. And I... I can't tell you how glad I am to hear your voice." I paused for a second, trying to choose my words carefully. "Billy, I need your help. And I think... I think, maybe you need mine." I paused again. "Everything you told me was true. About the comms link, the different frequencies." I paused again. "We tested it. Over." I waited breathlessly for him to respond. I didn't want to divulge too much, too quickly. I needed to be careful. Move cautiously.

"Well..." Billy's voice came in again over the comms, louder and clearer this time, as though he had moved his mouth closer to the microphone. He drew out that one word in a drawl. "No shit, Captain. Pardon my French." He chuckled slightly. "But we told ya so." He laughed again. "I'm surprised to hear you woke folks up there needed us to tell you that. Aren't y'all supposed to be smart?"

I grinned widely, letting out a low chuckle as his words and teasing tone flooded me with relief. I shook my head, grinning, as I responded, my voice thick with humor, "I guess that's a little ironic, isn't it? Over."

Billy responded immediately this time. "I'd certainly say so, Captain. But tell me, what is all this about needing my help?

I mean, I owe you one and all, if it's come down to that. But I can't begin to imagine how I can help you."

I nodded, swallowed, and took a deep breath. "Tell me, Billy, are you all still sitting on a stockpile of EMP guns?" I squeezed my eyes shut, as I hung my head, gripping the microphone tighter. "Cause I really hope the answer is yes, for all our sakes. They might just be the key to fixing this whole thing. The Jumpers." I thought for a moment, framing my next words. "They're going to wipe us out, Billy. All of us. If we don't stop them. I've just seen simulations of the spread of this thing over the next few weeks. And it's bad."

There was a pause, and Billy chimed in. "Well, I'm surprised to hear you say that, Captain, I must admit. We didn't think this thing was hitting the North yet. Not as hard as it's been hitting us." He paused. "If anyone needs help, I figure it's us. This thing is starting to spread to civilians, Captain. Women, and children... it..." His voice faltered, broke off. "People are dying, Captain." He chuckled, "I mean, they're not all dying; not the ones that turn. That's worse than dying. It's inhumane. It's... horrible. We're just people, Captain, like you and yours. And these poor folks down here, they're innocent. They don't deserve this." He paused again. "But I know you know this already. You know we're the same. I saw it in your eyes that day. When you looked at Nolan, and decided to help him."

I swallowed, holding back the tears threatening to spill, for what felt like the tenth time today. "I do know that, Billy. I do." I managed to respond. "And I think... I think I may have a way to stop this. My team and I. And it involves those EMP guns. We're working on a solution. And we still need to test it out." I added briskly, "But, if we're right, those guns may be our only hope of stopping this thing." I stopped, figuring I'd divulged enough for now. "Over."

There was a long silence. I sat there with my eyes squeezed shut, listening to the ebb and flow of the static. "Well now," Billy's voice came back over the comms link, drifting to me on waves of energy, from that backwater swamp down in Florida. "An EMP gun... against the Jumpers..." he trailed off. "I reckon you might be onto something there, Captain." I felt a small wave of relief flood through me, forcing myself to relax my death grip on the microphone. "Captain Williams is away, at the moment. But I'm expecting him back, in not too long. How's about we set up a time to connect again? Say, in 72 hours? I think he needs to hear what you have to say. Over."

I nodded as I listened to his words. "Yes," I said immediately. "Yes... 72 hours. I'll do whatever I can to arrange that, Billy." I glanced up at the clock, noting the time. "If you can get me Captain Williams in 72 hours, I'll do whatever I can to be here, to speak with him. Over."

"Good," Billy murmured. "That sounds good. Same channel, same time. Three days from now. Over."

"You got it. Over." I murmured back. I felt slightly better now that there was a plan forming. I just needed Topher to finish that gun, then convince Ward to let me test it out. My stomach spasmed at the thought of him.

Billy spoke up again as I sat there, lost in thought. "We found your... trash... you left behind," he murmured. "Figured you've been studying those things. Huh? I bet Captain Williams will be very interested to hear what you have to say. Very interested. Over."

"Yes, Billy." I said, "And I'm very interested to speak with him, as well." I paused for a moment. "Thank you. Thank you for listening. For answering me. I can't tell you how much it means, and how much depends on this. Over." I could hear the note of desperation in my voice as I spoke. And I felt a shiver run down my spine, as I thought of that map; those red circles swelling, until they swallowed us all.

"I'm here, Captain." Billy's voice rang back, the speaker rattling slightly. "And I'll be here. We'll be in touch."

"Thank you," I murmured, and I placed the microphone back. I sat there for several minutes afterwards, listening to the hum of the static, eyes fixed nervously on the black screen on the wall in front of me. The one the Admiral would appear on whenever he briefed Ward. As though he were there, watching me from the other side, listening.

27.

Later that evening, I busied myself in the Mess, preparing dinner for one, asking TODD to play some music for me to try to drown out the quiet.

I had my back to the door, and the music was blasting. Otherwise, I would have had at least some inkling. But as it happened, I didn't realize they were back until I turned around and was startled by them crowding into the Mess Hall. I nearly jumped out of my skin, catching the plate in my hands as it almost tipped onto the floor.

Captain Ward stood there in front of the men. A wave of relief flooded through me as I fumbled with the plate, a lump forming suddenly in my throat that made it difficult to swallow.

Ward just stood there, watching me. He was filthy. Covered nearly head to toe in what appeared to be mostly mud, mixed with blood.

He stared at me, the whites of his eyes contrasting with the mud, an odd, unreadable expression on his face. I froze completely as he stared me down, his eyes practically burning.

Then he waved a hand forward. "Let's get something to eat, boys." They moved in a grumbling, mumbling horde, shuffling past us and into the kitchen. And soon enough, the sound of utensils and clanging filled the room.

He closed the distance between us, and a few of the men drifted out of the crowd to follow him over towards the tables. I spied Wren as he gave me a solemn nod, and my heart leapt a little, a flood of relief filling me.

Ward stopped a few feet away, still looking me up and down. "What are you doing?" he growled after a moment, his low, gravelly voice practically reverberating through my chest. I swallowed down my nervousness. A group of men still stood, seemingly frozen behind him. They had a lost look to them, and they were all similarly filthy. *What the hell happened down there?* Clearly, they'd been through hell and back.

"Making dinner," I cleared my throat and moved to set the plate down on the closest table. "I would have made more if I knew you'd be coming back tonight."

"I tried to send a message through the comms this afternoon," he grumbled, "did you not get it?"

I shook my head, frowning. "No, I didn't." I paused for a moment. "I wasn't in the command center all afternoon, so I must have missed it. But I thought I told TODD to forward any incoming comms."

"What were you doing then?" he eyed me up and down, suspiciously, like I was going to say I'd been roller skating, or belly dancing, or some other ridiculous activity.

"I was exercising... showering..." His glare deepened, and his gaze swept up and down my still slightly damp hair. "I'm sorry..." I murmured, confused. "You were gone for five days. Did you expect me to sit in the command center the entire time, waiting for you?"

Ward just stood there, staring at me, a bleak expression on his face now. He suddenly looked tired. Exhausted, even. He walked over to the other side of the table and sat down heavily. My plate of food sat there, still hot. I bit my bottom lip for a second, staring down at the plate, and then slid it over to him, placing the fork and napkin beside it.

He looked up at me, eyes wide, with genuine surprise. "Here," I said simply, "go ahead and eat. You look famished."

He continued to stare at me for a moment, then down at the food. Then he shook his head no, and attempted to push the plate back over to my side of the table. I held out a hand to block it and slid it gently back, taking a seat across from him.

He studied me wearily for a few seconds, then he sighed deeply, picked up the fork, and started eating. "Thank you." He murmured between bites. "We haven't had a real meal in two days. Closer to three." I felt my eyebrows rise.

"What on earth happened down there?" I asked him, voice low. He didn't look at me. Just shook his head.

"You don't want to know." He murmured gruffly.

"No," I said firmly, "I do, actually."

He looked up at me from under raised eyebrows as he continued to eat. "Okay," he nodded slowly. "But I think you should change first."

I let out a huff of air, turning my head to the side. Then snorted in disgust. You have got to be kidding me. What the hell was wrong with this man?

"You have to be joking right now." I stared at him.

"No," he muttered, shaking his head, refusing to look at me again. "I'm not," he shrugged, "I think it would be for the best."

"Well, I'm sorry to hear that," I hissed back at him. "Sorry if my outfit isn't to your liking."

He chuckled a little, still shoveling food into his mouth. "I didn't say that."

"Good lord," I muttered, a wave of warmth creeping over my cheeks. "You know what, why don't you come find me when you have something that isn't rude or nonsensical to say." I sighed, pausing halfway as I moved to stand. "Are McCullough and Binson okay?" I hadn't seen them in the mass of hungry men, but that didn't mean they weren't there. Ward nodded, and I felt my stomach unclench slightly. "Did they manage to get the samples Lindsay asked for?"

The men had started to join us now, taking seats further down the bench from us, giving us some space. Powers caught my eye, winking at me, a cheeky grin on his face, his eyes sliding down to my cleavage. *Goddamn it.* I realized soon enough that most of the men nearby were side-eyeing me. Some were just more subtle about it than others. They'd only ever seen me in uniform, and they'd just spent five days down in the shit. Add to that, most of them probably hadn't seen, much less been with, a woman in weeks, perhaps months. What had I expected?

I stood, pressing my hands down on the table, cheeks flaming.

Captain Ward finally looked up at me as I stood over the table, his eyes sliding up my body to meet my gaze. He cleared his throat. "I think so. I gave them the support I could, given the circumstances."

"Care to share what those circumstances were? Or am I not allowed to hear about it? Given I'm too fragile and female." My voice came out sharper than I'd intended. He'd clearly been through hell, and I knew I should give him some space. But I had been waiting for five days. And the suspense had been killing me.

"We can talk later," he said wearily.

"Fine," I responded in a clipped tone. Then I turned and left the room as quickly as possible, while still looking dignified.

I could hear the volume rise in the room behind me as soon as I exited into the corridor. The men were whooping and laughing, all talking at once. I heard catcalling, and someone whistled loudly.

"Shut the *fuck* up!" Captain Ward called over the din and roar, and there was instant silence. My cheeks burned as I rushed back to my quarters.

28.

Several hours later, I pulled my leather jacket out and slung it on over the tank top. The scent of the creased, soft leather reminded me of home. A worn American flag patch was stitched onto each shoulder with gold thread; the corner of the flags sported 50 tiny yellow stars, one for each state, from back when the states were still unified. The jacket was an antique, and I'd been offered a significant sum of money for it several times. But I could never bear to part with it.

I refused to change tonight, but I was also getting cold. I had been warm enough in the tank top after the steaming hot shower, but the ship tended to run on the cooler side, and now I had goosebumps on my arms. Still, I wasn't going to give him the satisfaction of knowing I'd changed my shirt because of him.

When I figured they'd had enough time to eat, shower, and get settled in for the evening, I left my quarters, heading down to the command center.

Sure enough, I found Ward there. But he was alone, sitting in the dark. When I first entered the bridge, I thought it was empty for a moment. The overhead lights were off, and as my eyes adjusted, I realized Ward sat there with his chin in his hand, elbow propped on the desk. It looked like he was pulling up old comms logs. *Strange.*

He looked up at me as I entered, and his eyes narrowed to slits. This was off to a good start.

Pulling up a stool, I joined him at the desk. "What's that?" I asked, trying to keep my tone casual.

He quickly swiped over as I spoke, and the projection went dark. "Nothing." He murmured. "Look, I did the best I could to help with the samples, like I said. McCullough and Binson took them straight to the lab as soon as we arrived. Is there really anything we need to discuss tonight?" His brows creased as he looked over at me. He seemed to study my features, eyes flickering back and forth over my face and landing again on my hair. I wore it down still, basically dry now, it fell in loose, soft waves over my shoulders. It had grown so long, the ends trailed below my bra.

He looked away. "I'm... tired." His shoulders slumped a little as he cleared his throat. "It was rough down there."

"No kidding," I said. I let him sit with the silence for a moment or two. My heart twisted at the dull expression in his eyes, rimmed by dark circles. I wasn't sure I wanted to know what it had been like down there, after all. Maybe he was right.

I sighed, watching him. "Do you want to talk about it?" I asked gently.

He seemed to consider for a moment. "Honestly, no. Not really." He shook his head and ran a hand through his brown hair, tousling it further. *God, why did he have to be so fucking hot?* I couldn't stand it. Couldn't stand being around him. I grimaced a little and saw an answering flash of confusion pass over his features, before remembering to fix my face.

There was no point denying it anymore. Pretending it was something other than what it was. Sure, he pissed me off; drove me half mad. But that was only partially because of his behavior. He also drove me mad because I was slightly crazy about him. And I had only been lying to myself, trying to pretend otherwise. The way I'd felt while he was gone, while I waited in agony to learn whether he lived or died, had been enough to finally force me to admit how I felt.

I realized he was watching me intently, and I suddenly wasn't sure if I'd missed something he'd said. I shrugged nonchalantly. "No, I guess not. But you all looked..." I trailed off for a moment. "Terrible. It looked like whatever happened down there was awful. I thought maybe you'd want to talk about it." I shrugged, feeling my cheeks starting to color slightly as the words came out.

I felt silly now, but it was true. They looked like they'd been through the wringer. Him especially. His eyes had a dark, haunted look to them even now as he watched me. He may be, well... him. But he was still a human being. It was the right thing to do, to ask if he wanted to talk about it, make sure he was okay.

He sighed deeply, chest swelling and collapsing as he took a long breath in and out. He put his head in his hands, massaging his temple on the right side for a minute. "Ward, are you okay?" I asked, frowning at him.

He nodded. "Yeah, I'm fine," he said gruffly. "Just a headache. I get them sometimes." I nodded, frown deepening. No wonder he was sitting here, alone, in the dark. He probably had a migraine. I decided I should go, give him some space.

"You're right. It wasn't good." He said simply. "We got into some shit. Repeatedly. I.." he trailed off. "We've barely slept. We slept in abandoned buildings, in between skirmishes, grabbing a few hours of sleep in shifts, whenever we could. But it was so..." he trailed off again. "There were–" he seemed to choke, on the next word. And I felt a sudden, irrational urge to go to him, but I forced myself to stay where I was.

"I'm glad you weren't there," he said thickly, raising his brown eyes, glazed over with anguish, to look at me. "I know you're still upset with me, but it would have been the icing on the cake." He shook his head. I remained silent. He waved a hand, "Anyway, the city was hell. And outside the city, it was just as bad... between the terrain, and the fucking *wildlife*. We came close to a goddamn blood bath. We're lucky any of us made it out alive."

I stared back at him as he fell silent. There weren't many details there, but at least he had opened up somewhat to me. At least he hadn't refused to talk about it completely. "God," I murmured. "How many?" I hadn't even thought to ask earlier.

He just shook his head, eyes falling to where his hands lay folded on the desk.

I bit my bottom lip, heart sinking. "How many?"

He stared at his hands. "Seventy," he said, his voice thick with unspoken emotion, as he struggled to maintain his composure, jaw clenched tight, his throat bobbing. My heart leapt into my throat, and I suddenly felt like I was going to be sick again. "We'll see what the final number ends up being... there were a few wounded brought back..."

I swallowed back my tears. "I'm so sorry, Grant," I managed to murmur. I caught myself a few seconds later. I had never called him by his first name before. But he seemed not to have noticed. He didn't react, at least. He continued to stare down at the desk, the muscle in his jaw ticking.

"The First Lieutenants..." I started, trailing off. "Nathan, Molton... did they all make it?" I didn't breathe as I waited for him to answer.

"Not all." He murmured. "Nathan and Molton made it. Stevens, we lost." He shook his head, "Johnson didn't make it either." My gut clenched tight at his words, as I pictured Stevens laughing and joking with the other men.

I reached over and put my hand on his, without thinking. Then I cringed inwardly, unsure how he would react, flashing back to how he had removed my hand from his cheek, the last time I tried to touch him.

But he didn't move a muscle. He didn't grasp my hand back, but he didn't push mine away.

After a moment, I cleared my throat, which seemed to break the spell. His hands shifted under mine, and I pulled back instantly. He sat up straighter, turning away from me towards the giant window across from us, staring out into the vastness of space, the curve of the planet below us. It always felt surreal to me, sitting here, looking out at that view. It couldn't be found anywhere else, outside of the Northern Alliance fleet.

I studied Ward's profile. He looked... angry, now. His jaw was tight, his posture tense. He seemed to be refusing to look at me. He'd shown me one brief flicker of emotion. Well, an emotion other than anger. And apparently, he was already regretting it.

"I'm sorry," I said quietly. "I understand if you don't want to talk about it. Do you... do you want me to go?"

He didn't respond immediately. But then he nodded briskly, folding his arms over his chest, still refusing to look at me.

I felt myself start to chafe, my ire starting to rise, the unshed tears that had been threatening behind my eyes already,

ready to spill without warning. What was his problem? I mean really... was it so awful to talk to me? To treat me as an equal?

"Did I..." I trailed off, not knowing how to ask what I really wanted to ask. "Did I upset you, somehow? I didn't mean to..." I trailed off again.

He snorted, then chuckled slightly. "You didn't mean to what?" He eyed me up and down, a skeptical expression on his face.

My cheeks colored slightly, and I cleared my throat, refusing to look away from him. "I didn't mean to upset you. If there's something I said–" He cut me off abruptly.

"It's not anything you said, Kessler." he shook his head, chuckling again.

"Okay..." I said slowly, trying to read between his words. "So, it's something I did, then?" I asked, one eyebrow raised.

"You could say that." He glared at me now, eyes heavy with anger again. There was the Captain I was used to. I guess our little moment was over, as short-lived as it was.

"Do you want to go ahead and tell me what I did to upset you? Like an adult? Or do you prefer to keep playing games like a child?" I tried to keep my tone reasonable, but the emotion leaked out, and I snapped at him. I almost instantly regretted it. I'd pushed him many times before. But that might have been a step too far. His eyes narrowed dangerously.

"I'm the one playing games? Why don't you change back into your uniform? And put your hair up," he said quietly.

"Are you kidding me?" I said slowly, my cheeks starting to flush.

He stood and walked a few paces away, his back to me. I got up as well, moving around the table.

"What was this supposed to be? Hmm?" He turned suddenly and moved closer to me. His features were drawn in anger, but his voice held a hint of something else. Was it frustration? Desperation... or pain?

"Is this supposed to be some sort of a... a punishment?" He snorted, "For leaving you behind?"

I glared back at him, hands on my hips, heart pounding in my chest. I raised an eyebrow at him coolly. "And was it?"

"Was it what?" His chest was heaving slightly now, like he was out of breath.

"A punishment."

He just stared back at me, seemingly speechless, for once. "You should go back to your quarters." He said, his voice nearly a whisper, his eyes roving over me.

"No," I glared at him, raising my chin defiantly. "I have just as much of a right to–"

"Just... stop..." he trailed off, shaking his head, his hand at his right temple again, pressing. "Just... stop."

"No, I don't think I will," I said, moving closer to him. "You don't get to control me, actually, like a puppet. Not what

I wear, or how I do my hair... and not what I say. And like I was saying, I have just as much of a right to–"

He closed the distance between us so quickly that I stopped mid-sentence as he reached up and pressed his thumb over my mouth.

His touch was gentle enough, but my breath caught in surprise, and my cheeks burned at the imposition.

"I'm only going to say this once," he growled, "You need to go. Stop talking, and get out of my sight." His voice was pitched low, menacingly soft. I was filled with a tide of rage burning through my core. He was so close, leaning over me, his thumb rough and calloused on my lips. He stood still like that, unmoving, for several seconds, then his fingers curled under my chin, gently, almost a caress. I still wasn't breathing. We stared into each other's eyes for a heartbeat, then two, frozen in place.

I don't know what made me do it, but a jolt of anger and defiance, mixed with desire, shot through me, and without thinking, I parted my lips and slid my tongue over the tip of his thumb, pulling it into my mouth.

It was like I'd sent a shockwave through him. He hesitated only for a split second before plunging his thumb deeper into my mouth, his eyes darkening with hunger and desire. I licked it, sucking on it, and he grabbed my hip with his other hand and pulled me roughly to him. Pulling his thumb out of my mouth, he gripped my chin, pulling my mouth to his.

He kissed me urgently, his arm wrapping around me. I could feel him, already hard against my thigh, and I pressed against him as he kissed me, sliding until his length was positioned over the tightness, the throbbing between my thighs. I rubbed against him, and he let out a guttural moan. He slid a hand up to my chest. I hated this man. Hated him. But I wanted him, ached for him, and his touch felt like heaven. Like a drug that I never wanted to stop consuming. A craving that I knew I would cave to over and over again.

He pulled back, his lips leaving mine. "*Fuck, Kessler,*" he murmured. Then he turned and walked away from me, moving across the bridge, running both hands through his hair. He stared out the window, hands on his hips, with his back to me. I could tell from here that he was breathing heavily.

"Get out. Leave. Now."

"Ward–," I began, but he cut me off.

"That's an order." He snapped, turning his head to the side.

I took a deep breath, cheeks burning with shame and desire; I turned and stalked out of the bridge.

29.

Back in my quarters, I paced back and forth, combing a hand through my hair as I walked, gently tugging through the knots. I couldn't seem to stop moving. Couldn't slow down my racing pulse or my thoughts. I kept feeling his hands on me, his lips on mine. His tongue in my mouth, his hand sliding up to my chest. The way he'd practically moaned my name. *Fuck.*

What had I done? What was I thinking? We'd crossed a line we couldn't go back over. I had crossed a line. Me.

I was wracked with shock. Guilt. Shame. My cheeks burned again, and I felt tears threatening to pool in my eyes. Blinking rapidly, I moved to my bed, perched on the edge. Mostly, I was angry. Angry at myself for being so goddamn stupid. So goddamn weak.

I'd let my lust for him take over, control me. And despite my shame, I still couldn't get over the unrelenting burning. I wanted him. Wanted more.

If I had thought kissing him, touching him, would help, would make it go away, I'd been so wrong. It only left me aching for him. Left me craving him. I'd had a taste, and it wasn't enough. Not even close.

And he had pushed me away, ordered me to leave. My cheeks burned hot. How would I ever face him again? How would I look him in the eyes tomorrow? I grabbed my pillow and threw it against the wall, letting out a guttural scream. It was the only thing in here I could throw safely without risking breaking something. I stood and resumed my pacing.

I lay in bed, spent. What felt like hours later. I had paced and ranted at myself until I was physically exhausted. I had already pushed myself hard in my workout that afternoon. I crawled into bed, praying that it would help me drift off to sleep.

But I had no such luck. I had changed out of the stupid tank top, shoving it in the bottom of my bag, out of sight. I donned my loose PJs, a long-sleeve top and baggy drawstring pants and slid between the sheets.

I didn't have a clock anywhere nearby, and although I knew I could ask TODD for the time, I didn't want to talk to anyone right now. Not even him.

I had no clue what time it was, but I knew it was late, and I would pay for this tomorrow. But sleep wouldn't come. I lay there, tossing and turning, twisting back and forth. I couldn't get comfortable. And I couldn't ignore the aching, burning, throbbing between my thighs any longer. I knew I wouldn't be able to sleep until I eased it. Found a release. But I couldn't bring myself to do it. It wasn't what I wanted.

I gave in, eventually, eyes half closed; I had been on the brink of falling asleep, right on the edge. But my brain was replaying those brief moments with him, and I kept jerking back to consciousness. I lay on my side, half asleep, and slid a hand down to my clit, massaging it through my pajama pants. Moving faster and faster in small circles. I tried. I really did. But it wasn't working. It wasn't enough. I felt nothing but frustration. I lay there, panting. Furious with myself.

I heard a faint knocking on the door to my quarters. I sat up immediately, head turning towards the door. "TODD," I said, voice thick with exhaustion. "Show me the door." The screen on the wall flashed to life, with a bird's eye view of the corridor just outside my room. My mouth dropped open slightly.

Ward leaned outside the door to my quarters, one hand propped against the wall. He was staring down at the floor. What on Earth was he doing here, in the middle of the night? I sighed deeply and murmured, "TODD, turn the screen off." The screen went dark instantly, plunging the room into darkness again.

I stood and moved slowly over to the doorway. I paused in a momentary panic, looking down at my PJ top. Should I change? I wasn't wearing a bra, and the shirt was pretty thin.

The last thing I wanted was to embarrass myself even further. But this was taking too long. I didn't know what he wanted. For all I knew, this was some sort of emergency.

Steeling myself, I pressed my palm on the panel, and the door slid open. I crossed my arms over my chest at the last second, providing myself with some sort of coverage.

Captain Ward stood there, propped against the wall still. He'd been looking down at the floor as the door slid open. He raised his eyes to meet mine, and I knew I didn't need to worry about what I was, or wasn't, wearing.

His eyes were dark with hunger as he stared into mine. He didn't move, didn't say a word. We stood there, frozen for a moment.

"Ward? Did you want something?" I said, slowly.

He cleared his throat, eyes dropping to the floor for a moment, then back up to mine. He looked slightly flushed. Was he blushing?

"Yes." He said, through clenched teeth. He seemed to be deliberating over his next words. I stood there with my arms crossed, waiting. He cleared his throat again. "Can I come in?"

I raised an eyebrow at him, a slight curve to my lips. "What?"

"I said, can I come in?" he repeated, a faintly embarrassed expression on his face now.

I suppressed a grin, watching him squirm, his discomfort obvious now. He looked away from me, glancing up and down the corridor, as though he was nervous someone might see him.

"Can you come in... what?" I asked, my eyebrows raised.

He stared back at me, an incredulous expression on his face. He grinned, shaking his head a little, as he stared back down at his feet for a second. "Can I come in, *please.*" He said, drawing out the last word in that low growling tone that made my knees weak, his eyes locked on mine, his expression suddenly serious again.

I took a step backward, my arms falling to my sides. And he straightened, still watching me intensely. I turned my back on him, my cheeks flushed, and moved further into the room.

I heard the door slide shut behind me, but I kept my back turned, waiting a beat longer, suddenly nervous. I finally turned to face him, and he closed the distance between us. He lifted a hand and cupped my chin, eyes roving over mine. Then he tilted my chin up slightly and pressed his lips over mine.

He was gentler, this time. His kiss not as urgent, as rough, as it had been earlier. But he kissed me deliberately, deeply, pulling me into his arms. I felt a flood of relief course through me, and felt myself relaxing into his arms, some of the tension leaving my body. *He wanted me.*

And soon enough, I could feel just how much he wanted me. His hand migrated to my lower back, he pulled me closer to him, and I could feel the hard length of him pressing against me. I practically moaned with relief. I wanted him naked. Inside me. His skin against mine. He grabbed the bottom of my shirt next, and I lifted my arms over my head as he pulled it off.

He took my breast in his hand, massaging it for a moment as he continued to kiss me. But then he leaned back, staring down at me. "*Fuck me*," he murmured, bending down and taking my nipple in his mouth. I let out a breathy moan as he sucked on me, teasing me with his tongue.

He pushed me backward toward the bed until the mattress hit the back of my legs. I sat down, moving backward, expecting him to join me. But he stared down at me, that dark look in his eyes again. Then he gave me a sort of cocky grin as he got down on his knees. He peeled my pants off, taking my panties with them in one smooth motion.

I tried to sit up, but he placed a hand on my stomach and pressed me gently back down, as he moved my knee to the side with his shoulder, sliding closer to me. *Oh god.*

He gave me a wicked grin, like he was reading my mind, and before I could start to murmur a protest, his mouth was on me. Tongue licking, sucking on my clit. I fell back on the bed, every ounce of willpower, of protest, leaving my body in an instant.

I arched my back, eyes closed, making god knows what kind of noises. I writhed against him, riding his tongue, his mouth, the pressure building, and building. "Oh god," I murmured, "Ward..." my cheeks flushed, burning with heat and desire. I could hardly take it anymore.

He stopped abruptly just as I was about to explode. He pulled his clothes off and joined me on the bed, climbing over me, his skin against my stomach, against my chest, like warm silk. He kissed my neck, licking and teasing me with his tongue as he grabbed himself and nudged into me. Gentle and slow at first, until I opened fully for him, and he began to pump harder, taking me.

I gripped his back, pressing up against him with my hips, back arched so he could seat fully, deeply, inside of me. He never stopped kissing my neck, my shoulder, driving me crazy with his tongue. He'd been silent the whole time. But as I started to move with him, in time with his thrusts, he let out a quiet moan, his mouth hovering just over my ear. The feeling of his breath, the sound, sent shivers down my spine as I bucked harder beneath him.

He started to lose his composure then. His control. He rode me harder, and I exploded with pleasure, revelling in each thrust inside of me. I didn't know what this meant for us. For the mission. And at that moment, I didn't care.

He paused, eventually pulling gently out of me, and I let out a little sigh at the absence of him. He lay down on his side, next to me, panting, gasping for breath for a moment. Then he guided my hips sideways, and I could feel his head against me, nudging back inside of me.

He eased back in and wrapped his arms around me, cupping my breasts in both hands, his lips on my neck again, on my back. He caressed me, and I could feel him starting to lose control again. His thrusts became harder, faster, his panting breath rapid against my ear.

He paused again, forcing himself to slow down. And I felt him slide partially out of me. One hand sliding down to my clit, he massaged me, gently at first, in slow, light circles, his lips on my neck, my shoulder, my back. Kissing me, the pressure of his teeth on my neck sending shivers down my spine. I felt my body break out in goosebumps as I rocked my hips.

I moaned, unable to stop the sound escaping from my lips. He thrust slowly into me, his fingers still moving against me. And I moaned again, much louder this time. I could feel his grin against the side of my face.

"Yes," he murmured.

"Yes, Captain," I murmured back, without thinking, and I felt him freeze a little; go still, just for a moment. But then he resumed his slow circles, sliding himself halfway out of me again.

"I'm sorry, Jordan." He murmured against my cheek, "I'm sorry. I tried. I really did." My eyes fluttered open at his words. "You have no idea how hard I tried."

"Tried what?" I murmured back, my mind a fuzzy haze. I had no clue what he was talking about.

"To stay away from you." I frowned a little in confusion. But his fingers were making their slow, winding circles against me, and I couldn't stay focused for long. "I tried from the beginning." My frown deepened, and I thought back to that day in the Admiral's office. Was that why he'd asked them to send someone else? Asked them to pick a different ship? I thought of how he had asked to speak with the Admiral in private. What would he have said?

His lips brushed my cheek, sliding over my ear. And I let out a shuddering gasp, my hips bucking. "When that didn't work, I tried to keep it strictly professional. Keep you at arm's length. I knew I couldn't let myself get close to you. Couldn't let my guard down." He swallowed, pushing deeper into me, letting out a breathy groan. "But I can't take it anymore. I can't."

I felt my heart quicken; my cheeks flushed hotter at his words. "You were so fucking beautiful tonight. When we got back, and I saw you standing there, with your hair down, I knew you'd done it on purpose. To hurt me. To torture me." He pushed deeper inside me, pumping harder, as his fingers moved faster, in tighter spirals. His other hand twisted my hair, grabbing a fist full, tugging, pulling my head back. I arched my back further, letting my head fall against his shoulder. "And that shirt you wore. *Fuck*." He chuckled darkly, and I moaned again, and he moved faster, the sound exciting him.

"Did you really not get the comm I sent?" He asked breathlessly, his voice held an edge of amusement.

"No," I gasped, "I really didn't, I swear." I thought for a moment. "But you're right, I did it on purpose," I admitted, grinning a little. "I thought... hoped, you might be back tonight. Knew there was a chance, at least, that you would see me like that." I swallowed, my throat bobbing. "And I didn't care. I wanted you to."

He pumped harder at my words, fingers moving quicker now as the pleasure and pressure built inside of me. "Yeah?" He chuckled, "I suspected as much."

I turned my head towards him, and he claimed me with his mouth, kissing me deeply as he plunged into me, over and over, fingers caressing me in a steady rhythm.

I turned away from him, panting, and let out a little laugh. "If I'd known that was all it took, I would have done it sooner."

"Oh really?" He asked, slipping into his old routine of fake nonchalance. But I could hear the undertone of excitement in his voice.

I pressed my hips back into him as he thrust harder into me, his fingers pausing. "Of course I would have." My cheeks flushed, but I continued. "I've been going crazy for you for weeks." He let out a low groan at my words, and I kept going. "Hating you at the same time." He groaned again, louder now, thrusting faster, his fingers resuming their teasing.

He moaned, "Goddamn it, Kessler, you have no idea... You drive me fucking insane."

My eyes widened. I knew, obviously, at this point, that he wanted me, and hadn't I sensed all along that there was something else there, underneath his anger and coldness? But he had been so... awful at times. I was a little surprised at his admission.

He left a trail of kisses along my cheek and down my neck. His lips hovered over my ear, and he kissed me, nipping my earlobe, sending shivers of pleasure down my back. He pressed a hand down on my hip, holding me in place as he thrust deeper into me. "Wanting you, and wanting to keep you safe, has been a constant goddamn distraction."

I arched my back as he thrust harder into me, one hand sliding up my stomach to cup my breast. He slid his other hand higher until he held both cupped in his hands, pumping into me as he held them. I let my head fall back against his shoulder. "I've been crazy about you from the first night we met."

I couldn't help but smile a little at his words, but I was having difficulty staying focused as his rhythm inside me picked up.

He slowed, then slid halfway out of me again, his hand sliding back to my core, fingers finding that spot again. He moved in small, rapid circles, simultaneously moving his hand up and down. My core bursting with pleasure, pressure, and heat, I arched against him, my hips bucking back and forth involuntarily, in time with his hand. "I know this is wrong. I know I shouldn't be here. And I'm sorry." His voice dropped to a whisper, "But I just couldn't stay away any longer."

My eyes fluttered shut, as my back arched farther and farther, his fingers the center of my universe for now. Every stroke brought an unending pleasure that I never wanted to stop. "I'm just not strong enough," He murmured against my ear.

But my mind had shrunk to that spot that burned and ached and throbbed, and I felt the pressure build until I couldn't take it any longer. I exploded in a climax that rocked through me, wave after pulsing wave, moaning and panting against him. He didn't wait long before nudging back into me. His cock felt even harder, thicker than it had before, stretching me even wider. And this time, he let himself truly lose control.

He took me, roughly, until he found his own release. And it was everything I had wanted. Everything and more. He lay there panting, completely spent, his weight half on me, half on the mattress. He eased out of me, eventually, and I moaned a little. He got up, a minute later, and went into the bathroom. I lay there panting, wet and throbbing. Feeling fully satisfied.

He came back, bumping into the table in the dark. He lay down heavily on the mattress, and I got up, heading into the bathroom myself.

I avoided my own gaze in the mirror. I should feel more shame than I did, I argued. But I couldn't bring myself to, at that moment. I'd wanted him since that first night we met, at the bar. I'd tried to deny it, how many times? Because it wasn't just that I wanted him, either. Physically. I wanted *him*.

I thought back over his words to me, that night. How they'd manage to rock me. How I'd felt something dark and angry, come loose, wake up. Shift, inside of me. I wanted to live. *Really* live. Like he did. I felt that same burning. That same all-consuming need. Like my need to fly. A need to soar. To feel everything. Experience every moment. To live truly, with no regrets.

I raised my eyes and met my gaze in the mirror, finally, taking in the dark circles beneath my brown eyes. My black hair cascaded around me, a tangled, tousled mess. My lips were plump-looking, bruised. Red marks on my neck, from where he'd bitten me. I hoped those would be gone by tomorrow. I sighed deeply and turned away, flicking the lights off as I went.

I joined him, back in bed, and startled him awake. He bolted upright, calling out something incoherent, clearly not aware of where he was, his voice fuzzy with sleep and thick with fear. I could tell he thought he was back in Atlanta. I reached out to him, placing a hand gently on his arm. "Ward, it's okay. It's just me. You're on *The Beagle.*"

How he'd managed to fall asleep that fast was beyond me. But I remembered he was probably still exhausted from Atlanta. He'd said he hadn't slept well in five days. And he may have already been up all night, unable to sleep, just like I was. Burning. For me.

Ward calmed, his chest still heaving slightly, and he climbed off the bed, stumbling to his feet, he began searching in the dark on the floor for his clothes. He pulled them on, while I lay back, propped up on my elbows, watching him, unable to see his face clearly in the dark.

I reached down and pulled the comforter up over my chest, feeling suddenly self-conscious. "Are you leaving?" I asked, in a small voice.

Ward sighed, not looking in my direction. "Yes. I can't stay the night here. We can't have the men seeing us in the morning."

My cheeks flushed at the thought. "Yeah..." I murmured. "I get that. But do you have to leave immediately? Right now?"

He sighed. "I shouldn't have come here in the first place, Kessler." He ran a hand through his hair, staring down at his feet in the dark. "I'm sorry. This is my fault. I should have stayed away." He shrugged, his voice dropping almost to a whisper.

My cheeks burned in the dark. "What are you saying?" My voice faltered, "Are you saying this was a mistake?" The volume of my voice rose involuntarily. I felt a panicking sense of dread and shame filling me at his words. And a quick flash of anger at myself, that I cared so much.

He was quiet for a long time. "No, I'm not saying that. But... I'm technically your commanding officer, I should never–"

"Ward," I scoffed. "Come on, I don't give a shit about that. You can't be serious. You didn't take advantage of me in any way."

Ward just shook his head at my words. "I just..." he trailed off, finally looking over in my direction. "I'm sorry, Jordan. Really, I am. I just– I have to go."

I shook my head, looking away, staring at the wall as the sound of his boots echoed across the floor and out into the corridor beyond.

30.

I woke up the following morning to the odd certainty that the Carrier was moving fast. I could feel it in the hum of the beast that was *The Beagle,* and sensed immediately, before opening my eyes, that we were traveling at a rapid pace.

I got dressed as quickly as I could and stumbled out into the corridor, watching as men rushed in all directions past me. I made my way towards the Mess Hall, stopping a soldier who looked vaguely familiar in the hallway outside the entrance. It took me a few seconds, but then I recognized him as the private who'd escorted me to my room when I'd first arrived.

"What's happening?" I demanded, holding a hand out to stop his forward motion.

He stared back at me, eyes wide, for a moment, before managing to sputter out. "We've been ordered back to base, Captain, immediately." He leaned closer, his voice dropping low. "I heard they're ordering all Carriers to be inspected and sanitized. Health checks, for all of us, too." He licked his lips, looking around us in the corridor, as though he might find someone hiding there in plain sight, listening in on our conversation. "People are saying someone got infected. Maybe on another Carrier." I stared at him, my mouth gaped open. "You know, turned into a *Jumper*."

I swallowed thickly, snapping my mouth shut and blocking the expletive that I'd been about to release. "Thank you, Private," I murmured. "Carry on," I nodded to him, as he snapped into a salute, suddenly remembering who he was talking to, at the use of his title.

He scrambled away down the corridor, and I stalked into the Mess Hall, eyes peeled for Ward, or Wren, or one of the other First Lieutenants. But our regular table, over by the wall of windows, was empty, and the men were nowhere in sight. I stopped long enough to grab a coffee and turned and made my way towards the bridge.

I didn't love the idea of running into Ward this early in the morning. My stomach roiled slightly at the thought, but I swallowed my feelings down, and I let my feet carry me to the bridge, nonetheless. I needed to know what was happening.

The doors to the bridge slid open with a whoosh of air, and I stepped inside to find about five different conversations going on at once. Nearly all the First Lieutenants appeared to be gathered, and most of them seemed to be arguing, or at least, debating, loudly.

The volume of the conversations died down slightly, heads turning as I entered the room, then picked up again immediately. Ward was seated at the battle table, across from the door, arms crossed over his chest. He met my eyes briefly, his expression heavy and solemn, before dropping his gaze back to the table. My stomach tightened as I watched him for a moment. A dull throbbing in my core that set off a wave of anger. My body betraying me yet again, as I struggled not to flash back to last night. To the feeling of his skin against mine. His lips on me.

I hoped my cheeks weren't flushed, as I kept my expression blank. I moved closer to the knot of men over by the couches, approaching Wren, who stood there with Nathan and Molton, huddled together, voices pitched low.

"I heard we're heading back to base." I said, forcing my way into their little group.

Wren nodded to me; his expression grim. "The entire fleet has been ordered back. Full inspection and sanitization of the ship, mandatory health checks." He shrugged, slipping his hands into his pockets, as I sipped my coffee. I had a pounding headache. The lack of sleep and emotions after last night were getting to me.

"Speculation and rumors are running rampant." Nathan added.

"Understandable." I murmured back, over the rim of my mug.

"We're fucked." Molton said, shaking his head, his eyes wide behind his wireframes. "That's it. We're all fucked. Once it spreads on board, on Carriers..."

"Come on man," Wren murmured back, shaking his head.

"What's to stop it spreading back on base? Is bringing all of us back together in one place really a good idea?" Molton asked, shrugging.

"The ship is going to be sanitized." Nathan murmured.

"Sanitized my ass." Molton quipped back. "You can't sanitize germs that are already inside people," he chuckled, looking around the room.

"Orders came down too for all personnel to wear face shields at all times, or gas masks if we have them. On the ground, I mean." Nathan said, turning to me.

"Too little, too late," Molton quipped, "who knows how many of us already infected." He glanced at each of us, eyes narrowed. "Carriers." He uttered it like a curse word.

I couldn't help but laugh. Wren and Nathan started chuckling as well. I sighed deeply, as the laughter died down. "Well, there's no test for it, as far as I know." Any trace of a smile disappeared from their lips as I spoke. "And we still don't know all that much about how it spreads. I have no clue what the incubation period is..." my voice trailed off, as I too glanced around the room. "I guess you're right, who's to say whether any of us have been infected."

"I don't know what good health checks will do." Molton said glumly.

I frowned, thinking for a moment. "I could go check in with the lab team; see if they have any insights. Maybe there are warning signs..." My voice trailed off again as I contemplated the idea. I was sure Lindsay would have shared any details like that with me already.

I avoided looking over at Ward, as we stood there, chatting, wasting time as we waited to arrive back at base. None of us seemed to be able to tolerate waiting in silence. We kept the conversation going, moving over to sit on the ring of couches in front of the floor to ceiling screen.

Someone turned on the news, a few minutes later. Aerial footage, over Atlanta, as a reporter voiced over, explaining the efforts made so far to eradicate the city of the Jumper presence that had quickly taken over, in the few days after the shield went down.

The men fell noticeably quiet, as the city swung into view, the drone flying low over the buildings and eerily empty streets. For the most part, at least. I spotted NA tanks, trucks, and SUVs roving through the streets as the reporter continued to speak, sharing the latest news of the spread of the contagion at our borders. Another voice chimed in, and they began to debate where the first breach would occur.

"We're going to hear from Ernie Evans, of the AP, later today; he has an update for us on the progress of the investigation, ordered by Congress, as they attempt to determine the nature of this disease, and how it is spreading." The female reporter announced.

"And more importantly, how to stop it." Her male counterpart added.

"Although, you know Craig, some are saying that Congress is not doing enough to put a stop to this."

They flashed back to the studio, a woman in a dark suit, leaning back in her chair, turning pages of notes as she spoke, one eyebrow raised.

"Yeah, Captain," Molton muttered, pulling my focus away from the screen. "Why don't you get off your ass and go solve this thing." He waved a hand at the TV, his accent becoming exaggerated. "Can't you fix this?"

I snorted, a grin breaking out over my features, faltering, as I turned to see Ward making his way over to us, his eyes meeting mine. I just shook my head at Molton, then returned my gaze to the screen. "I'm trying," I murmured. "I'm trying."

Ward moved around the far couch and took a seat. I didn't look at him. I kept my gaze fixed on the two reporters, although I was no longer taking in a word they said.

"How much longer?" Wren asked a moment later, turning to Ward.

Ward sighed, running his hands through his hair. "About ten minutes, give or take a few." He shrugged, crossing his arms over his chest. The men nodded, turning back to the screen. Ward stared over at me, as though he were trying to relay some message, some sort of apology, with just his eyes. My throat burned, and I looked away from him, keeping my expression blank.

I wouldn't give him the satisfaction of seeing any sort of reaction from me. I sat back, sipping my coffee, my eyes on the news, until we finally saw the base in the distance, through the bank of windows to our left.

Home sweet home, at least for a while, I thought. The familiar sight of the NA base triggering that same swell of emotion; pride, mixed with apprehension, that I always felt when I saw it again after a long absence.

We broke apart, then, scattering back to our quarters to grab our belongings. Molton called out to me to meet up tonight, at the dive bar down on the lower level. The one where I'd first met Ward. I was careful to avoid Ward's gaze as I nodded vaguely. Maybe I would meet up with them. Maybe I wouldn't.

Wren watched me, his expression careful, as I turned to leave, as though he could sense something was off, but wasn't sure what was wrong.

I felt nothing but relief as I gathered my things and went to join the men to disembark *The Beagle*. I was looking forward to some time away from the ship. Away from the men aboard.

The only real downside to all of this was the apprehension over whether I might end up having to call

Captain Williams from somewhere back on base. If we weren't back on board *The Beagle* within 72 hours, I would need to come up with a plan, and a location on base that I felt was secure and safe enough to call him from.

I elected to stop down at the lab before leaving, on the off chance that Lindsay and Topher hadn't left already. My luck held, at least partially. I found Lindsay quickly after entering the vast space. The overhead lights were all at full strength for once, and the brightness of the lab was jarring.

Lindsay was shutting off a computer terminal when I entered, and she waved to me wearily. "I'm glad I caught you," I said by way of a greeting. "You heard about the mandatory health checks?" She nodded grimly.

"Yeah, they warned us about sanitizing the ship," Lindsay sighed, looking around the neatly organized lab. "I made sure any sensitive biological material is locked up safely in the Biohazard lab. We should be ready to go." She shook her head. "I don't know how effective any of this will be."

I sighed at her words. "That's what I was hoping to ask you about. I know you're still in the process of running tests, but have you learned anything about how exactly it spreads? It's a fungus, right? So, how does it spread from person to person? Spores or something?"

Lindsay sighed again, folding her arms over her chest, she leaned back against the table behind her. "So, it's hard to say for sure, but my theory would be that there are two different transmission routes. Transmission is likely essentially direct to begin with. So, by that I mean, from a Jumper to an uninfected person, say a soldier, who comes in direct contact with the Jumper on the ground. We know that odd white substance is fungal material, and it's responsible for transmission, not in the form of spores, but in mycelium or hyphae."

She took in my blank expression and clarified. "So, hyphae are the thread-like strands in the fungus, and they make up a web, or a network, called mycelium. Traditionally, say in a forest environment, the hyphae grow and spread out, forming a weblike network, known as the mycelium, and that web is thought to have the capacity to communicate via electrical impulses," she grinned, "which is insane to think about. It reminds me almost of nerve cells in the brain, spreading out in a network, transmitting electrical impulses... it's possible this network of mycelium spreads throughout the forest, in a sort of underground web."

"Crap," I murmured, my eyes growing wide.

"Yeah," Lindsay nodded, "crazy, right? So, anyway, the infection, I'm sure, can spread by the direct transmission route; what we refer to as contact transmission. A soldier comes in direct contact with the white fungal material, and if he or she takes in enough of that material, typically via the nasal or oral route, and survives the encounter, they bring that infection back with them."

"Then what happens?" I asked urgently. "How long do you think it takes before the infection starts to take effect? What's the incubation period like?"

Lindsay frowned again, looking at the floor. "Jordan... the Admiral called last night. Contacted the lab directly, I... I was going to tell you, but it was super late." Lindsay shook her head. "He was asking similar questions. I told him what I'll tell you; the incubation period for fungal infections in general can range anywhere from a few days to several weeks, or even months, just depending on the exact type and nature of the infection."

Lindsay shrugged. "We simply don't have enough data to say definitively at this point. But the men on the ground are being put at risk. Every single one should be wearing protective gear. I was quite blunt with him, and I don't think he appreciated it," Lindsay frowned again, "but truthfully, and this is just conjecture, I suspect the Admiral is holding back information. I suspect that there have already been multiple cases of Northern Alliance personnel contracting the disease. And I think they've covered it up; kept it under wraps. It only makes sense, given the number of troops who have been in direct contact with Jumpers."

I flashed back to an early moment, when someone had mentioned something about men changing into Jumpers. I had thought they were joking around at the time. But I recalled the warning look Wren had shot the man who'd spoken. Had

424

something happened aboard *The Beagle*? Maybe before we arrived? I racked my brain, trying to recall when the conversation had taken place and who had been there.

Lindsay shook her head, sighing. "I told him we can't do our jobs effectively without full disclosure. But I don't think he agreed."

"Well, good for you, Linds, for standing up to him at least. That's not easily done." I sighed.

"No," she snorted, "he's intimidating as fuck," she shrugged, "but it needed to be said."

I bit my lip, thinking. "Maybe I'll ask to speak with him, while we're back on base. I haven't heard from him at all."

I found that slightly odd. That I had zero contact from the Admiral, but he had called Lindsay directly. Although I left that part unsaid. I guessed it made sense in a way; what could I possibly tell him that Lindsay couldn't?

"I would say from the models Topher and his pals have been running on the side, we can hypothesize at least, that the incubation period is likely on the shorter side; probably more like days than weeks. Otherwise, we think the spread, the rate of transmission, would be slower. But again, without full data, which I'm sure we don't have, we're left somewhat in the dark."

"What's the other route?" I asked, changing the subject abruptly. "You mentioned there were likely two routes of transmission, the direct route, and what's the other one?"

Lindsay's expression shifted, darkened. She looked down at the floor for a moment, then back up at me. "The other route would be indirect... more specifically, airborne. Spores." She nodded at me. "In general, fungal spores are known to have the ability to travel long distances. They are super lightweight, and they can ride the currents in the air. Carried by the wind, they have been documented to travel hundreds, or even thousands, of kilometers. Depending on the air currents, weather patterns," she waved a hand, "it's complicated, but it's certainly possible for spores to spread vast distances, before triggering a new infection elsewhere."

My eyes went wide as she spoke. "Detroit," I murmured. "Where my team first encountered Jumpers. There was an isolated pocket of them in the woods, outside Detroit. We assumed the men who were infected had traveled there somehow, maybe by air. Maybe a band of raiders who had access to an aircraft," I frowned, "but we never found evidence of one in the vicinity. You don't think that's how they got all the way up there, do you?"

Lindsay shrugged again. "I mean, it's a possibility, but I'm guessing we'd be seeing a lot more cases by now. I'd expect them to be popping up all over the place if this thing were traveling that far via airborne transmission." Lindsay looked down at the floor again for a moment. "But in terms of local transmission..." she trailed off. "I think it's safe to assume that anyone in the vicinity of someone infected is at risk for breathing in spores. I can't say at what point an infected person starts releasing spores, though. We'd need to do a lot more, detailed and difficult research to know the answer to that."

I shook my head, my heart pounding harder in my chest. "So, any of the men, any of us, that have been near them, fought them... even if we didn't come in direct contact, it's possible we could be infected, already, and not know it?"

Lindsay's eyes were full of something more than sorrow, closer to pity, and I felt my chest cave in slightly at her expression. "Yes, it's very possible, Jordan. Especially anyone in direct contact, but anyone who has spent time near them..." she trailed off, glancing around the lab, "even any of us who have worked with the samples." She swallowed thickly. "I've tried to be extra cautious, knowing fungal spores might be in play, but..."

She shook her head at me as she met my eyes again, my expression, one of pity, now mirrored her own. "I did most of the work with the raw samples myself; I tried to keep Isla and James, my techs, out of it. I don't trust them to be as mindful." She shrugged. "I sent them off already. Sent them both a comm this morning to head straight to be checked. Isla had a headache last night, anyway. I made her go to bed early." Lindsay chuckled darkly, "Although, I would guess the health checks are next to useless. I tried asking the Admiral what they were screening for exactly; what criteria they were using– he told me that information was classified." She snorted again, shaking her head. Her voice dropped to nearly a whisper; her expression clouded. "I don't know what on earth it is we're doing, Jordan." I sighed deeply, staring down at the floor myself now.

Lindsay continued, "My best advice would be to use not face shields, but fully enclosed helmets. Suits, ideally airtight, with a filter, are even better. If you can wear your flight suit, any time you're going to be on the ground, or potentially encountering them, that would be best." She paused, "I told the Admiral all of this... that face shields aren't enough." She shook her head, her expression clouding over again. "But it sounds like the order came down this morning for face shields to be used, going forward."

I felt my hands clenching into fists. "It's not an easy solution..." I said after a moment. "We have gas masks, but I doubt there are enough for everyone on board. Flight suits might be best, but they would make the men vulnerable to EMP guns. Still, he can't just ignore this. Something has to be done."

Lindsay shook her head. "Regardless, I'm sure they don't have enough flight suits for everyone. Think of what that would cost..."

I shook my head, sighing. She was right. That, and the time it would take to properly train everyone, were certainly barriers. "I'm going to ask to speak with the Admiral," I said briskly. "When I get back. Tonight. Now." I amended.

Lindsay only nodded absentmindedly. "Good luck, Jordan. Maybe you'll have better luck than I did."

31.

The health checks ended up feeling like just as much of a formality as Lindsay had implied they would be. A process that took forever and felt entirely useless.

After what felt like hours of waiting in line, I moved to the front of the queue. A woman in navy blue scrubs finally faced me. She was wearing an N95 mask, with a rounded plastic face shield hanging from a headband. She checked my eyes with a bright flashlight. Presumably, they looked human enough, because she nodded in a satisfied sort of way. She took my temperature with a forehead scanner and drew a small vial of blood from my right arm. That last part at least seemed somewhat promising. Although I questioned how long it would take to process the thousands of samples that were being collected today, with every single Carrier ship in the fleet called back to base.

In the end, the actual health check took less than five minutes, and I was cleared to enter the base.

I marched straight to the Command station, located on the second ring, and announced myself to a bored-looking pair of soldiers who stood guard outside the main entrance to the Command wing.

They showed no visible reaction to my demand to meet with the Admiral immediately. Nor did they blink when I stated my name and rank and added that I was the commanding officer in charge of a top-secret mission and had urgent information to share.

One of them finally moved, a moment later, walking off down the corridor away from me, murmuring into his comms unit. He returned after a brief pause, in which he presumably listened to a response, and informed me that the Admiral was unavailable at the moment, but my message had been relayed to him, and he would contact me at his earliest convenience.

I gaped at him open-mouthed for several seconds, before turning abruptly and marching off down the corridor.

I discovered, with a modicum of relief, that my private quarters had not yet been moved, although the paperwork for my promotion had already come in. I was glad for it, as I held my palm over the screen next to my familiar unit and entered with a sigh.

I threw my things on the bed and sat for a moment before getting up, and making the rounds. I greeted my men with as much enthusiasm as I could muster, given the current state of things. Naturally, after we caught up on what they'd been up to, I was peppered with questions, to which I could only shake my head and shrug, keeping my lips sealed tight. They eventually got the message, and after giving me shit about how "important" I was, they let it go reluctantly. McCullough and Binson made their way over to me when the men had found other things to occupy their attention. I greeted them with a curt nod.

"I need to speak with you later. Alone." I muttered. They shot each other a grim expression and nodded in response.

"What do we do now?" Binson asked, eyebrows raised. "Mess Hall?"

I considered this and shrugged, then nodded in agreement. It was already late afternoon now; we might as well get an early dinner in before the Mess Hall became overcrowded. I had missed lunch, while standing in line.

We made our way there and found that what felt like half the base at least had the same idea. The lines for food took ages, and we took in the line at the bars and shook our heads at each other.

"We're meeting up with the crew from *The Beagle* later, at this bar down on the lower ring, anyway," Binson leaned in and murmured to me. "You should come with us. Nothing else to do besides drink tonight, is there?"

32.

I spent some time in my quarters after we ate, attempting to read and get some downtime in. But I was too restless, unable to focus on my book, and too distracted to do anything else. I remembered I still technically had to write up reports for Command on the last two missions. The Admiral hadn't bothered to reach out and ask for any updates, I reminded myself, grumbling. But it would be worthwhile to have everything documented in writing. I logged into my secure drive from the small terminal in my quarters and tried to keep my mind focused on recounting the details from our last few missions.

I was startled by a knock on my door sometime later and asked the ship's AI system to show me a view of the corridor. Binson and McCullough stood there waiting for me. I checked my watch and sighed, forcing myself to log off and join them. Thankfully, I had thought to change earlier. I'd swapped my uniform for civilian clothes, choosing a simple knit sweater and jeans, my hair half up in a clip.

They grinned at me as the door slid open. "Ah, ready, Captain?" Binson offered me his arm, and I took it, shaking my head. "Are you already drunk somehow, Lieutenant?"

Binson laughed, "I may have run into some of the guys, passing a flask or two around." I shook my head again, grinning back at McCullough, trailing behind us.

"Oh, this is going to be a fun night," I said, "I can feel it."

The familiar scents and sounds of the bar hit me as we waltzed through the doors. It was crowded. Far more crowded than it had been the last time I was here. There was a live band, as usual, although my favorite drummer was noticeably absent.

The men from *The Beagle* were already posted up in the far corner, in the same booth I had been sitting in when Ward first approached me. I sighed internally, steeling myself, and my face was as void of any emotion as possible as we approached the table.

"HEY-OH!" The men called out in a general chorus, greeting us though it had been weeks, rather than hours, since we had last been together. "There they are!" Molton was already handing Binson a beer, seemingly conjured out of nowhere.

Ward was nowhere in sight. And I felt an odd little trickle of disappointment as I surveyed the crowd around the table. We hung out for a few minutes, and I stood there awkwardly, in no mood for small talk, attempting to keep the sour look that had settled over my features at bay the best I could.

Someone pressed a drink into my hand, and I glanced down at the green leaves sticking out of the rim and found myself grinning instantly. I turned to see Molton hovering over my shoulder.

"Thought you could use one," he murmured to me, grinning around the rim of his glass.

"Thanks, Moltonky," I shook my head, and took a sip. "It's been a long day."

He nodded. "That it has." He responded simply. I was tempted to confide in him; tell him what Lindsay had told me earlier, and how I had requested to speak with the Admiral and been turned away. I hadn't received any messages yet over the comms link. How long would he make me wait? Was he avoiding speaking with me on purpose?

Molton's eyebrows rose as he glanced over my shoulder, and felt a hand on my elbow. I turned to find Ward, standing there. "Care for a dance?" He asked, a somewhat chagrined expression on his face.

My heart skipped a beat, but I shrugged nonchalantly, keeping my expression purposefully neutral. A non-committal response. Ward took the glass out of my hand and set it down on the edge of the table. Keeping hold of my hand, he led me out to the middle of the dance floor.

I expected some jeering from the men, or a few catcalls, at minimum, as he took me in his arms, but they remained silent, glancing pointedly away from us.

I found their lack of reaction even more abrasive. "What did you tell them?" I asked him archly, peering up at him. Ward frowned, glancing over at the men.

"Tell them? Nothing." He shook his head. "I'm not a complete asshole, Kessler."

I sighed, looking away. I held myself stiffly. "You could've fooled me," I muttered under my breath.

He pulled me closer to him, and I felt my heart thumping in my chest, as I couldn't help but soften against him. "I'm sorry, Jordan," he murmured, close to my ear. "I didn't mean to upset you. I just– it's complicated."

"Is it?" I asked, a note of sarcasm in my voice. "I would have thought it should be simple enough. Either you care about me, or you don't. Doesn't sound all that complicated to me."

Ward sighed audibly, and I shrugged. "But you let me know when you figure it out, I guess."

"Jordan," he murmured, "of course I care about you. In fact, if you recall, I was the one who–"

But he was cut off abruptly, as some sort of commotion exploded on the periphery of the room. A fight, breaking out, I realized, with a stab of annoyance. A common enough occurrence. Men scrambling, fists flying; I knew they kept at least two large, beefy men, on standby at all hours of the night, hovering near the entrances on either side of the bar, waiting to toss unruly patrons out on their asses.

But something was off, I realized with a small pang of unease. There was an urgency to the cacophony, an edge of fear to the voices crying out. Someone screamed. And the band stopped playing, as one by one, the musicians turned, their notes trailing off into a dissonant chord as they stopped dead still, watching the knot of people pushing and jostling as they moved across the bar.

I heard a low skittering hissing sound, and the next thing I knew, a man was bounding out of the knot of soldiers, knocking them to the floor, as he pitched himself forward. People were screaming in earnest now, crying out and scrambling away.

I felt my heart actually pause, stuttering, before lodging in my throat. It was Powers. Hot tears prickled behind my eyes as I stared down at him.

Powers' eyes were like two dark holes in his head. Pitch black pupils filling the orbs, not a speck of white in sight. He appeared possessed, practically demonic, as he emitted a low growl that shifted into a wet, choking cough. He clutched at his chest, at his throat, as he staggered forward. I realized with a jolt that he was heading straight towards us. Ward and I still stood frozen, out in the middle of the floor. Powers lurched forward, spewing a steaming mass of white bile onto the dance floor.

I stared down at the all too familiar strands swirling in the spreading pool of liquid. "*No, no–*" I moaned.

My voice seemed to break Ward out of his stasis. He turned, wrapping his arms around me, and half pushed, half dragged me across the room, as I strained weakly against him.

Ward called out to the men, "Help me," and their response lagged, as they stared behind us, some of them open-mouthed, watching Powers in horror.

Chaos erupted truly a moment later, a press of bodies, as people ran in all directions, leaving a hole in the middle of the room, as Powers staggered back and forth, his breathing clearly labored.

Ward kept one arm wrapped around me as we watched. My whole body was trembling. I felt like I might be sick. We were pushed and jostled, and I felt a stab of dismay at the timing. None of us were armed, as at least some of us surely would have been back on the Carrier. We'd donned our civilian clothes. I hadn't even thought to bring my knife. How stupid of me, I realized, now that it was too late.

But what would I have done, I wondered, if I'd had it on me. Stab him? Cut his throat? It was *Powers*. Maybe he was still technically human. Other than his eyes, he *looked* human, at least.

"Pin him down!" I heard someone call out. Nathan moved forward, as Ward pressed me backwards. I found myself in Molton's arms. He nodded at Ward grimly.

"No, Ward," I pitched forward, grabbing his arm, attempting to pull him back, but he slipped out of my grasp. Molton gripped me firmly, one arm around me still, as he held me back.

"Captain, I think we should hang back," I could barely hear him over the din of the crowd and the pounding of my own heartbeat echoing in my ears.

I watched as the bartender, trapped behind the bar, eyed Powers warily, moving over to a red phone on the wall. He lifted it to his ear and punched a button. His lips moved as he gestured wildly at the lone figure in the center of the room, now down on all fours, taking deep, gasping breaths.

I willed them to wait. Wait until help arrived. But Nathan and Ward had recruited several others to join them, Wren included, I realized with a fissure of unease. They moved cautiously, in a slowly closing circle around Powers.

As their circle closed in, he moved into a crouch, balancing on his back legs, still a normal length for now, as though he were readying to pounce.

He let out a low snarl, his head shifting to the right. I watched as he locked onto the bartender, who continued to speak into the phone.

One of the men rushed forward, and the others followed suit seconds later. Powers lunged forward, but they managed to subdue him almost immediately, grasping onto his flailing limbs and pinning him down to the ground in a crush of bodies. They avoided his head, as he bucked and growled, letting out a low keening sound of frustration. He managed to lift himself up in the air momentarily, and there was a general gasp from the crowd watching, but with their combined efforts, he was subdued once more, and a general cheer went up around the edges of the bar where the crowd was gathered.

An alarm was blaring now. Red flashing lights bathed the entrance to the corridor. A voice floated to us through the open door.

"Return to your quarters, repeat, return to your quarters. Full lockdown procedures are in effect. Full lockdown procedures are in effect. Five minutes and counting."

What the hell did that mean? I frowned over at the men on the ground. The crowd around us seemed unsure of what to do, as though they were unclear whether the orders applied to them. But then people began to trickle out the doorway, with backward glances towards the men on the ground.

I jumped at the feel of Molton's hand on my arm. "Come on, Captain, I think we should head back to our quarters."

I shook my head. "I'm not leaving them," I said through gritted teeth, unable to hold back several tears that managed to leak out, trickling down my cheeks.

Molton just stared wearily back at me. "Look, I know we don't know exactly how this thing spreads, but... you're sort of... important, Captain. I think we should get you out of here, not risk any further exposure. Okay?"

I sighed, my chest deflating in a rush at his words as I continued to watch the men pinning Powers to the ground. *What about them?*

"I'll stay here, in case they need backup," Molton murmured. I nodded weakly, suddenly feeling numb, as I turned my back on them and left them behind.

I followed the crowd, a tide flowing up, out of the lower ring, until we reached a branching corridor with a door at the end of a hall. Breaking off from the mass of bodies, I headed down the narrow corridor. I had a vague recollection of there being an access door to a maintenance stairwell somewhere around here.

I poked my head through the door to find I had been correct. The alarm was deadened slightly in here, no speakers blaring from the walls. The stairwell was lit with what looked like emergency lighting only, a soft warm glow at my feet on each landing. I knew it would take me forever to march up all these stairs. Sighing deeply, I began my ascent, wiping the tears I couldn't seem to stop as I went.

I was about halfway there when I got a message on my comms. My heart jumped at the ping of the notification bell in my ear. I long-pressed until the message began to play. "Captain Kessler," the Admiral's voice, a low, pleasant rumble. "I'm sorry I missed you earlier. I have pressing matters to attend to and may not be available to meet with you for a few days. I will send you another message to arrange a time, as soon as possible. Thank you for your patience." I frowned as I quickly climbed the last few flights, picking up my pace.

I finally made it to my quarters, my chest heaving, my throat burning. I paced my room, unable to calm down, a restlessness overtaking me. So, the Admiral had time to send me a voice message, but couldn't take two minutes to speak with me? Possibly for several days. My chest filled with a bubbling wave of anxiety. I wanted to vomit. First Powers, now this.

Something felt off. I needed to *do* something. This thing was on the verge of growing wildly out of control. People turning on base... *One person*. I reminded myself, trying to stay calm. But my heart was racing, and the emergency alarm was still blaring out in the corridor, setting my nerves further on edge.

What would they do to him? To Powers? Would they kill him? Quarantine him somewhere until he fully turned? I flashed back to Colorado, his lip-sided grin, in the flickering firelight, forcing me to tell the men all about the battles that had made The Crimson Reaper famous... how he was always making us laugh, always cracking a joke, when things got too serious. I clamped my hand over my mouth, as I bent forward, wracked by silent sobs.

What would happen to him? And what about the rest of the men, holding him down back in that grimy bar? Would they have to enter quarantine? I felt like I was on the verge of a breakdown, my entire body trembling involuntarily.

I paced back and forth for some time, attempting to calm myself down, recounting everything that had happened over the past few weeks, methodically. I realized I was mumbling out loud to myself, and was tempted to jot down notes, but I didn't want to risk writing down information that was sensitive to the mission.

I marched over to the small docking station set into the wall and pulled up the comms menu. I pulled the crisp white card out of my bag and dialed the number.

It rang several times before Ernie Evans picked up. "Captain, it's good to hear from you." I could hear the grin in his voice.

"How did you know it was me?" I asked, clearing my throat, attempting to keep my tone light, as my voice came out sounding hoarse and strained.

He chuckled slightly. "An unknown number, calling with an NA area code? I took a wild guess." A brief pause. "Besides, I was hoping I would hear from you."

I sighed and nodded to myself. "Well, you got my attention."

He chuckled again. "Good. And what do you have for me?"

I shook my head grimly. This was it. My last chance to change my mind. But I sighed, and pressing my fingers against my temples, trying to ignore that distant blare, heralding our doom, I chose to continue. "I've got information on the projected spread of this thing. And it's bad. We're talking two to three weeks."

"Until it spills over the border?" Evan's voice was rapt now. "We thought it would be sooner than that."

I snorted lightly. "Until it takes over. Until it's so widespread, there are more infected than there are uninfected." I paused briefly. "Until it's too late." Dead silence on the other end of the channel. "You can run that story. An anonymous source. And go ahead and throw in that someone turned, on the Northern Alliance Air Force Base." Silence again for a moment.

"Captain, this is..." Evans let out a low whistle. "This is going to stir people up. This is huge, this is... I need more details, I need..."

"I can't give you detailed information," I sighed, thinking of Topher. "Not without putting my own contacts at risk." I thought for a moment. "And I want things stirred up. I want people to protest outside Congress. I want them in the streets. People are not taking this seriously enough. And we'll all pay for that mistake. I think we're on the verge of a solution. A weapon, we might be able to use against these things, but it's going to take a helluva lot of pressure and urgency to get this done. I think it's going to take people working together, across the border. And I'll be honest, Evans, at this point, none of that seems very feasible to me." Silence again for several seconds.

"Captain," Evans paused briefly. "Do you spend much time on social media?"

I snorted loudly. "God no. I avoid it like the plague. Why?"

"Well, I can understand that. But it's useful, you know. While a lot of things in the public media are locked down, under control, especially in the South, there are... areas on the web that are harder to control. And there are ways of getting around their filters and blocks. I've managed to connect with a... a movement, of sorts. Let's call them... the Northern Light. There is a... growing collective consciousness, people who have their eyes wide open. A network of people who see things as they are, who want a better future. People, even in the South, who want to put an end to all of this. Not just the war itself, but the lies. The propaganda. They want the truth. They want freedom. Democracy." I swallowed thickly. "If you need assistance... contacts, across the border. I can connect you with the right people."

"How?" I murmured, my heart was pounding now. If my personal comms unit was being monitored, I was well and truly fucked, at this point. "How is that even possible? How do you communicate with them?"

Evans cleared his throat. "Like I said, there are ways around their attempts to control our activity. We are very careful. And every day, the movement is growing, picking up momentum. We've been using coded messages. Codes to mark our social media posts and interactions. Innocuous, everyday things that they'd never suspect have another meaning. Their filters will catch any obvious buzzwords, and get our posts taken down. We change them up every so often. I can communicate securely when needed. And I have a list of contacts, including fellow reporters, in the South, that will get the truth out there, if you have something to say."

I swallowed again, thinking. "Well, I appreciate this, Evans. We plan on testing our weapon. When I have the outcome in hand, if I can't get the traction I'm hoping for..." I bit my lip, thinking, "You'll be hearing from me again."

"I'll be on standby, Captain. Anything you need, you let me know."

"Thank you," I murmured, sighing.

"Goodnight, Captain. Stay safe." He sounded very far away, just then. I hung up the comms and went to lie down on my bed.

Staring at the ceiling, I couldn't stop seeing Powers' face. His lop-sided, goofy smile, that single dimple. I worried about Ward. About Wren. Molton. Were they still in the bar? What were the odds that they had all been exposed? I pictured invisible spores, like tiny round balls, with spikes sticking out, floating through the air around them, in that dingy bar. How long did they have? How long did any of us have?

33.

I felt only the slightest pang of guilt when the news hit. We were back aboard *The Beagle* by then. I had been woken during the night multiple times by the sirens going off. In all my years in the Air Force, I had never heard those alarms go off outside of a drill. I lost count after four, in the muddled haze of sleep. Each time the alarm went off, I had to talk myself down. Convincing myself it wasn't one of our men. Telling myself they were all fine.

I woke the next morning feeling like I hadn't slept at all, with a pillow lying on my head; my feeble attempt to block out the racket in my sleep.

All companies were ordered to return to their Carriers first thing in the morning. Our evacuation to the Carriers had been what could only be described as semi-chaotic. I had never seen anything like it. The men still maintained a facade of order and discipline, but it was a thin veneer, and the surge of panic underneath it was palpable.

We stood now, gathered once more on the bridge, in small groups of twos and threes, the men muttering amongst each other, as we waited for Ward to speak. My initial flood of relief at seeing all the men there—well, besides Powers, of course, left me feeling drained and exhausted in its wake.

We hadn't received any orders, but we'd all gathered on the bridge naturally. The need to hear what was next from our leader was apparently unanimous amongst the officers.

Rumors were flying. The estimate of how many times the alarms rang out during the night ranged from four or five up to eight. Someone had claimed they heard that an entire unit had turned during the night. From F company. The men speculated that they were putting them down, like rabid dogs.

"What else can they do?" Molton muttered, as we overheard that little snippet of speculation from the men huddled together at our backs. I only sighed in response, my stomach twisting as I thought of Powers.

Ward stood, hunched over the battle table, pulling up records and scrolling through logs. I had the distinct impression that he was just stalling. Wren stood at his side, whispering intermittently in his ear, while Ward just nodded.

"Turn it up," someone said. I turned towards the screen, gazing at the red ticker that ran across the bottom of the screen.

"TODD, turn it up four," Molton called out.

After a delay, TODD's voice rang out. "Turning up, four." Molton massaged his temple as TODD spoke, and I grinned weakly.

The reporter's voice, now clearly audible, carried to us on a wave of silence as the men hushed and turned towards the screen as one. "Next, we bring you an exclusive report; we are the first to break this story, and trust me, you won't want to miss this. We now go live to Ernie Evans, with the Associated Press."

The screen split in two, and Ernie's familiar face stared down at us. His expression was grim, and there were dark circles beneath his eyes that hadn't been there when I had last seen him.

"Gwen, that's absolutely right, we have urgent, breaking news for you this morning. I personally, through one of my direct contacts at the Northern Alliance, whose identity will remain anonymous, have the grim duty of sharing with you, reports of multiple soldiers turning on board the NA Base itself." Evans paused, looking straight into the camera, as hushed whispers broke out in the room. I ignored them as he continued. "The situation has become dire, Gwen. We are additionally receiving intelligence that the previous trajectory of the spread of this thing, may have underestimated the speed at which we are approaching a point of no return."

"A point of no return?" Gwen repeated, brows furrowed. "Wait, wait, back up a second, we need to know more about the situation on the Northern Alliance Base. As you know, Ernie, the NA is the only thing standing between not only us, and this terrible affliction, but also between the people, and our enemies to the South." She raised an eyebrow. "I mean, we need to clarify what this means for Northern Alliance families. What is the potential impact of this? If this thing is spreading amongst the ranks, how long before our national security is compromised? Our borders?"

Evans nodded throughout her speech, and he opened his mouth to respond, but she cut him off, not quite done with her fear-mongering. "And lastly, just what on earth do you mean when you say, *"the point of no return"*?" She paused, her expression stern. "Those are very loaded words. So, let's break this down and clarify what exactly it is we are saying here."

Evans nodded once more, and after a brief delay, he adjusted the comms unit in his ear and replied, "Gwen, I'll be as clear as I possibly can, and I'd like to address the second part of your question first. What I mean by the point of no return. By that I mean, when we reach a point, in the spread of this disease, at which we have widespread infections across the Northern Alliance. This timeframe is much shorter than we were initially led to believe. Now, whether this timeframe has shifted, because of new data, new information, that has been collected in the study of this thing, or whether that initial information we were given was inaccurate, I certainly can't say. But, I can share that according to anonymous sources, we are looking at two to three weeks before this spreads out of control. Before it's so widespread that our odds of coming back from this are extremely slim and growing slimmer by the day."

Gwen just stared back at Evans, frozen, for several seconds. I had to chuckle grimly to myself at the expression on her face.

Footsteps approached, and I turned to see Ward had joined us, coming to a stop beside me with his hands in his pockets, staring up at the screen with his brows furrowed.

He didn't look at me, keeping his eyes fixed on the screen, as the men exploded, all talking at once. "That's it. We're all fucked." Molton threw his hands up, shaking his head, turning to Nathan.

I glanced back at Ward, and he still refused to look at me, but he leaned sideways and murmured, "Hmm, an anonymous source, who knew about men turning on base last night, and had data on the trajectory of the outbreak..." Ward shook his head. "I wonder who could have called him..."

His voice trailed off as he turned to peer down at me, and I looked away pointedly, staring back up at the screen, keeping my expression neutral.

"Regardless of who it was, it seems like we're running out of time, Ward." I turned back to him a moment later, his eyes still on me. "I'm going to check in with Topher and urge him to have our prototype ready to test out as soon as possible." I squared up to him, staring him down, as my voice dropped low, "And the second he says it's ready, my men and I are down on the surface. No delays. Understood?" My tone was icy, but Ward seemed unfazed. He only smirked back at me.

"You just let me know when it's ready, Captain." He replied glibly, "And I'll escort you personally." His smirk morphed into a wicked grin. "You call me, anytime, day or night, and I'll answer."

My cheeks flushed, despite my best efforts, as I nodded sharply and turned away from him. I strode away and out of the bridge, but I could still hear him laughing behind me, his voice echoing in my ears as I stormed down the corridor to the lab.

34.

I was halfway there when Lindsay reached me. Her expression was frantic, eyes wide.

"Jordan!" She called out from down the corridor, jogging towards me.

"What happened?" I asked sharply, picking up speed. We met in front of an alcove leading into a small seating area under a bay window, the space lined with leather couches. Lindsay grabbed my hand and pulled me into the alcove. A private passing by gave us an odd look, before snapping his attention forward and continuing on his way.

"What happened?" I repeated, my voice pitched lower.

"It's Isla, one of my lab techs," Lindsay managed. "I'm worried something's happened to her." I frowned as she led me further into the alcove, pulling me down onto the far couch, as she glanced back at the corridor, now empty. "I can't find her. And it seems she never went in for her health check."

"How do you know that?" I asked, brows furrowed.

"I had Topher pull up their database," Lindsay shook her head, as I opened my mouth to retort. "I know; he says there's little to no chance they'll ever realize he accessed it. But Jordan, there's no record of her."

I shook my head again, sighing, as I gazed out the window, my eyes drawn to the expanse that yawned endlessly beside us. "How is that even possible?" I said slowly, "The way they had the health checks set up... I don't see how she could have managed to get onto the base without going through the checkpoint. That was the whole point, right? They weren't letting anyone on board without getting checked out. A heck of a lot of good that did." I added glumly.

Lindsay sighed. "I know. We said the same thing. But she's not here either. She's not in the lab; she's not in her quarters. We checked with the staff down in Med Bay, and she never went there." Lindsay held out her hands and shrugged, "I mean, obviously we haven't combed the entire ship yet, with just the three of us, but Topher and I and our other tech, James, we've searched everywhere we can think of that she might have gone, and nothing."

"Okay," I said, staring down at the floor of the ship, thinking. "It's definitely odd, but she must be here somewhere, still aboard the ship. You said she had a headache the night before, right? Maybe she wasn't feeling well and just slept through the next morning. Didn't think she needed to bother reporting to base? I don't know."

"But they sanitized the ship, remember?" Lindsay was frowning at me, "when we were all back on base, they came through and sprayed the shit out of everything, with chemicals. So, where was she when that was going down?"

I shook my head again. "Okay, you're right, I forgot about that. But just because she wasn't in the system as having the health check done, doesn't mean she never went on base. Maybe she told them she wasn't feeling well at the checkpoint, and they sent her straight to the Med Bay on base? That would make sense, right?"

Lindsay let out a deep sigh, nodding. "Yeah, okay. That's a possibility."

I nodded in agreement, "I'm sure there's some simple explanation like that." I shrugged. "It would have been nice for either Isla or someone else to send us a comms message and let us know what was going on."

"Yeah," Lindsay nodded again. "I can try calling over there and see if she's been admitted in the meantime."

I nodded in agreement, feeling my pulse returning to normal. "Has Topher made any progress? I'd really like to get down on the surface to test it out as soon as possible." I chewed my bottom lip. "Tonight would be ideal."

Lindsay nodded, glancing back at the corridor. "He's close. I'm hopeful he'll have it ready in the next day or so."

"Good," I murmured back. "Ask him to call for me as soon as he's ready. I'll arrange for us to head down right away. I don't think we can afford to waste any more time."

We parted ways, both feeling only moderately better. I had planned on heading straight to Topher to check in, but knowing that most of the morning had probably been wasted already as they searched for Isla, I elected to leave him be for now, not wanting to hold him up further.

I sent a message to Binson and McCullough to meet me at the pool instead. I arrived there first and waited by the hot tub, staring out the window, lost in thought.

They strode in a few moments later. If they thought the location was odd, they didn't mention it. I filled them in on the events of the past twenty-four hours, including the Admiral blowing me off. I left out the part about me being Evans' anonymous informant.

We agreed we would be as prepared as possible for departure to the surface to test out the modified EMP gun. My plan was to take one or more of the small troop Carriers down to the surface. I detested the pods and would rather take our fighters, but I knew there was little to no chance that Ward would allow us to travel to the surface without a unit or two, and I knew now that we may need them, especially if the EMP gun didn't work.

The troop Carriers could fit possibly a half unit each, and they would be faster than the pods. Hopefully, Ward would agree to that plan.

I left them and headed back to the bridge from there. As much as I was reluctant to speak with Ward at the moment, I wanted everything planned out in advance, so we could depart as swiftly as possible when Topher gave us the go-ahead.

But he wasn't on the bridge or in the Mess Hall. I moved through the corridors, irritated now, stopping to ask the men here and there if anyone knew where he was. But they all just shook their heads.

I ended up checking the gym, and even went back to the pool, and didn't find him. Sick of searching, I headed back to my private quarters, and as soon as I entered, I called out to TODD to send a message to Ward letting him know I needed to speak with him.

But it wasn't until dinner that he finally resurfaced. Most of the steam had gone out of me by that point, as the odds of us heading down below this evening dwindled away. Even still, I marched over to him the second I spotted him over at the bar.

"Where have you been?" I demanded, by way of greeting.

"Captain," Ward turned lazily towards me, that smarmy grin on his face. The one I hated. "I was off ship for the afternoon."

I frowned at him, arms crossed. "Did you not get the message I sent you?"

"I did," he shrugged, looking somewhat contrite now. "Sorry about that, I was... in a meeting and couldn't respond."

"But you had time to stop here after, for a drink?" I raised an eyebrow at him. When he didn't respond, only glancing grimly down at the tumbler in his hand, I continued. "Meeting with who?"

Ward sighed. "The Admiral." He responded slowly.

The men surrounding Ward shrank back, visibly, as I glared at him. But he only took a sip of his drink, one eye on me over the rim of his glass.

"I need to speak with you. Now. In private." I ground out between clenched teeth.

Ward sighed, but he nodded, and leaned away from the bar, gesturing out into the room with a sweep of his arm, as though to say, *'after you'*.

I stalked away from him, not bothering to look back to check if he was following.

We walked in silence. At first, I was inclined to bring him down to Engineering. I didn't want to risk anyone overhearing us. Then I decided on my private quarters. But how did I know my room was safe? For all I knew, that was the worst possible place on board.

I came to an abrupt stop in the middle of the corridor, and Ward halted a moment later, at my back. I turned to him, "Take me to your private quarters."

His expression shifted, one eyebrow raising, as he grinned suggestively at me. "Now," I demanded, my expression hard as stone.

He flinched slightly, and let out a deep sigh, and nodded, turning and leading me down another corridor.

I waited until we were inside his quarters, the door closed behind us, before I spun towards him. "What the fuck is going on Ward?"

"Why don't you tell me, Kessler?" He asked archly. "Were you up late last night, calling your intrepid reporter?" His jaw was tight, muscles twitching.

I glared back at him. "You do know he's gay, right?" I asked, one eyebrow raised. When his expression softened, I snorted, shaking my head. "Idiot," I muttered, turning away from him.

I walked several paces away. His room was nice. Slightly larger than mine, with one wall made entirely of windows, a view of the curve of the earth far below. I stared out at the planet below. "Was that what you were meeting about, then? Did you turn me in?" I kept my voice nonchalant. But I also kept my back to him. I didn't want him to see my face when he said yes.

He chuckled darkly. "God Kessler, you still don't get it, do you?"

"Get what?" I asked, whirling back to him. He was standing just behind me now. He pulled me into his arms, his hands sliding behind my back. "Don't," I said, pressing my hands against his chest, holding him away. "I sent the Admiral an urgent message, the second I was back on base. I told him I needed to speak with him, and all I got back was a message saying he was too busy to meet with me. That he would have time in a few days." I paused for a breath and continued before Ward could retort. "Yet here you are, flying back to base to meet with him in person, this afternoon." I glared at him. "Do you know something that I don't, Ward? Because I'm sick of trying to figure out where your head is at. Tell me what's going on."

He shook his head, eyes heavy and full of some emotion I couldn't read. Pity? Sorrow? I couldn't tell.

"Were you meeting with him about me? What did you tell him?" I demanded again.

Ward pulled me closer, and I turned my face away, looking off to the side. He rested his forehead against my hair, his breath on my cheek. "I didn't tell him, Kessler. About Evans. And I won't." He paused for a moment. "I wish you could trust me. I won't let anything happen to you." I shook my head, and he reached up, one hand cupping the side of my face, turning me gently towards him. "I love you, you know. You infuriating, paradoxical, stubborn," I felt myself breaking, just a little, as he continued, my lips parting in a small smile that I couldn't quite stop, "stunning, intoxicating, determined," he was grinning now too, a hint of laughter in his voice, that faded away on his next words. "Recklessly brave, woman." I met his gaze then, and felt absurdly like I might cry.

I shook my head, but he held my cheek more firmly, pressing his forehead against mine, his voice low and deep. "I've loved you from the moment we met, and I'll go on loving you, despite your best efforts, and mine, to stop me." He kissed me then. And I let him.

He moved me over to his bed, slowly, and I didn't have it in me to protest. He was slower, more gentle, and deliberate this time. The urgency, his need for me, was still there, below the surface, but he took his time.

He climbed on top of me, pulling my clothes off and throwing them behind him, eyes locked on mine as he kissed me, easing into me.

He was so slow and deliberate, so steady for so long, that I was the one who lost control, this time, growing impatient. Desperate. I murmured in his ear, "Harder," my hands pressing against his back, holding him tighter to me, aching to feel him take me as he had the other night.

He let out a low, dark chuckle and murmured back to me, his voice making my toes curl. "I'm trying to make it last, this time."

I grinned against his shoulder. "We have all night, you know."

He laughed harder at that, and he gave me what I wanted.

35.

I woke suddenly, my heart racing, my limbs twisted in sheets, in an unfamiliar space. My head rested against Ward's chest. He jerked beneath me, the muscles in his abs rippling as we struggled to sit up.

I gazed around the room, disoriented, sure something had startled me awake, but the room was silent and dark. The window behind us was now covered by a shade that must have been set to close automatically.

"What was that?" Ward murmured groggily to me. I just shook my head, glancing around the room again.

"Captain Ward," TODD's voice rang out, causing me to jump, shattering the silence. "You are requested on the bridge, immediately. Emergency protocols. Contamination in the Lab. Contamination in the Lab."

"Jesus Christ," I murmured. I nearly fell off the bed as I tried to stand, one leg tied up in the tangled mass of sheets and

blankets. I managed to stagger to my feet, and we scrambled to search for our clothes in the dark.

"TODD, turn on the lights." Ward barked.

I managed to squeeze my eyes shut just in time as light flooded the room, too bright even through my eyelids. I forced them open a few seconds later, watching as Ward fumbled with his pants, pulling them on while walking over to retrieve his shirt.

I found my clothes in a pile at the foot of the bed and rushed to pull them on. I knew without looking in a mirror that my hair was a mess, but there was no time. We left his room, the door sliding shut behind us, and took off at a jog for the lab. I undid my braid as we went, running my fingers through my hair. Good enough. Hopefully, no one would question why we were arriving together or notice my disheveled state.

In our haste to leave, I hadn't even paused to note what time it was. But it felt late. The corridors were eerily empty and silent as we made our way through the maze of too-white hallways that seemed to merge into one unending loop. I was disoriented, given that I had no clue where our starting point was in the ship's schema. When we finally emerged into a wider corridor, the clinical white walls giving way to the familiar dull metal of the lab corridor, I breathed a sigh of relief.

We slowed our pace as we approached the lab. An alarm blared within, muted somewhat by the double doors. A red flashing light spilled out into the corridor through the windows, reflecting eerily off the metal walls.

We approached the door, and Ward held his arm out, hand splayed in front of me, as though he would shield me from whatever waited within. We peered through the windows.

There was no sight of Lindsay, or Topher, or anyone else. The lab appeared empty from here. But it was a vast space, as I knew from experience, and you couldn't see inside the Biohazard lab from the doorway.

"It could be the Biohazard Lab," I said breathlessly, putting a hand on Ward's arm. I pushed him gently aside and stepped forward, but the double doors remained closed.

We glanced sideways at each other. "TODD," Ward said, "open the doors to the lab." We waited, the red lights flashing on Ward's face, his expression grim.

"Unable to complete request." TODD's voice replied pleasantly. "Lockdown protocols are in effect."

"Fuck," I murmured, moving closer to the window, attempting to peer through the shadows in the far reaches of the lab. "TODD, patch me through on the comms to Dr. Lindsay Holloway."

"Location?" TODD's voice rang out instantly.

"For fuck's sake TODD, you tell me," I called out, my frustration and panic mounting.

"Location of Dr. Lindsay Holloway is unknown at this time," TODD replied.

"Check her private quarters, you useless–"

Ward cut me off. "TODD, relay the following message in all areas of the lab as well as Dr. Holloway's private quarters." He cleared his throat. "Containment breach reported in lab, Dr. Holloway, report to the lab entrance immediately."

"Yes, Captain Ward," TODD responded. In the background, I could already hear his voice echoing through the empty lab. "Message relayed."

We waited several minutes, my anxiety mounting, before I thought to add, "TODD, relay the previous message in Topher's private quarters as well."

Ward threw me a sideways grin, one eyebrow raised, and I just shook my head, grinning and rolling my eyes.

I leaned against the glass, both hands cupped around my forehead, attempting to peer into the shadows of the far reaches of the lab. I was just turning to Ward to ask whether he knew of a way to shut down TODD temporarily, so we could force the doors open, when the sound of running footsteps echoed down the corridor behind us.

I turned to see both Lindsay and Topher running in our direction, along with their lab tech, James.

"What the hell happened?" Lindsay sputtered as they came to a stop.

"No clue," Ward said dryly. "TODD relayed an alert to my private quarters that there was a containment breach, or something, in the lab. We ran straight here. Didn't know if you were in there, or what was going on." He gestured to the lab doors. "The doors are locked down; he won't let us in."

"Dammit," Lindsay muttered, shaking her head. "It's the middle of the night, and the lab's empty. What the heck could have happened?"

"I'm just glad you aren't trapped in there," I sighed, "I thought there had been some sort of accident."

"Maybe it's an error," Topher suggested. I stared at him for a moment, and it took me a second to figure out why he looked strange. He wasn't wearing his glasses. And his hair was even wilder than usual. "Maybe a bad sensor, or something. Tripped for no reason." He shrugged.

Ward turned back to the lab, nodding as he spoke. "Yeah, it must be. I don't know how, but there's gotta be a way to override the lockdown. We need to get in there and turn off the damn alarm." Ward turned to face the doors. "TODD, this is Captain Ward," he was interrupted by TODD's response.

"Good evening, Captain Ward."

"God..." Ward trailed off, pressing a hand to his forehead, shaking his head. "TODD, I'm ordering you to shut down the alarm protocols in the research lab. Shut off the alarms and release the main doors."

A long pause. "Per section 5.2 of the Emergency Protocol Code, I am unable to complete your request."

"Dammit," Ward grumbled, placing both hands on the doors. "We're going to have to call this in to base. I have no clue how to override this—" He paused, turning to Topher with a hopeful expression, as though he had suddenly remembered he was a hacker. "Any ideas?" He asked, "Can't you hack into the ship's system and shut everything down?"

Topher shrugged. "I mean, interfering with a Carrier's emergency protocols is probably like, at least a minor felony," shrugged, scratching his head, "but yeah, I'm sure I could. Only problem is, my computers are all in there." He pointed at the lab. "I'd have to try it from a ship terminal."

Ward nodded. "TODD, locate the closest ship terminal access point for us. Outside the lab." He added as an afterthought.

TODD was silent for a moment before barking out a random room number. "That's in Engineering," Ward turned to Topher. "Why don't you head down there and see what you can do? We'll wait here."

Topher nodded back, "Alright, I'll contact you through TODD if I hit a roadblock." He took off down the corridor at a jog.

We waited a moment or two in silence before Lindsay spoke up. "Listen, I don't see how it's possible for any sort of containment breach to have occurred, but maybe a vial burst, or some other odd accident happened. Either way, the fact that the biocontainment protocol was triggered is definitely concerning. We shouldn't just stroll in there without any sort of protective equipment."

I sighed, nodding. "You're right, but isn't most of that equipment inside the lab?"

Lindsay thought for a moment. "There's some PPE in the Med Bay. Surgical masks. Gloves and gowns. But there are chemical respirators just inside the lab, and those would be even better. They're in a cabinet on this first wall, just here." Lindsay peered to the right, pointing. We looked back at her blankly. "Gas masks." She clarified.

"I say we just duck in and grab them then. Put them on before we go check everything out." Ward glanced up and down the corridor. "I hate to put Med Bay on alert needlessly."

"We could do that. But we'll be at risk of inhaling any potential biomaterial that's airborne until we have our masks secured. Spores, specifically."

"Can't we just hold our breath?" Ward asked, shrugging.

Lindsay snorted a little. "We can try it. It's sloppy, but, again, I think the odds of an actual contamination are pretty low..."

It took Topher all of ten minutes to override TODD's protocols. Some of which must have been taken up by him simply making his way down to Engineering. Ward looked pleased and relieved when the doors slid open with a woosh, and the alarm cut off abruptly.

We followed Lindsay into the lab, and I tried not to breathe, as she grabbed masks and handed them out to Ward and me and the lab tech, who looked scared half to death to be here.

The masks were old and smelled of leather and must. I doubted whether they were actually functional anymore. The heavy respirator hung off my face, causing the mask to slide forward incrementally over my eyes as we searched the lab. The red lights were still flashing, rotating round and round, bathing the room in a red glow that alternated back to darkness.

Lindsay noted nothing out of place as she led us back towards the Biohazard lab, our voices muffled by the heavy masks.

She turned and called out to us. "We may have an issue getting into the Biohazard lab itself, although Topher has probably thought of that already." She swiveled towards the doors. "I think I should be the only one to enter, regardless. I'll need to put on the full suit and follow protocols."

"Go ahead," Ward nodded, "we'll wait here for you."

Lindsay was able to access the lab with no issues; the door slid open when she placed her hand on the sensor lock. We waited as she dressed in a full white suit and gloves, was sprayed down with some sort of chemical spray, and then entered the lab itself.

I watched at the window, moving closer, as she combed the lab. She didn't touch anything, moving from counter to counter, checking the samples inside the refrigeration units, and shaking her head. She turned back to me and shrugged at one point.

"I don't understand what triggered it," Ward said, sighing loudly. "There certainly doesn't seem to be anything out of place so far."

"I know," I replied, my eyes still on Lindsay, "it doesn't make any sense. Maybe it was just an error? I don't see–"

Lindsay was waving her arms at me now. Waving and gesturing wildly, then pointing behind me, jumping up and down. My blood ran cold, and I felt a shiver down my back as I turned.

The lab tech screamed; his voice oddly muffled through the gas mask. A loud crash rang out, and one of the metal tables slid towards me, hitting me in the stomach and knocking me back against the glass wall of the lab.

Ward was knocked off his feet as well. I peered over the table, pulling myself up, and stopped cold. James was flat on his back, a hunched figure on his chest, hands splayed, dripping with blood, sporting elongated nails, talons, on sinewed hands.

The thing leaned forward, spreading its jaws wide, sinking its teeth into the gaping hole that had opened in the tech's chest. He twitched, slightly, spasming, then went still.

The sickening crunch as the thing chewed on a glob of bloody flesh made my stomach twist. "Isla," I gasped, as she turned towards me, her eyes twin black pits, her nose merely a stump. A snarl and a skittering sound, almost a hiss, and her

470

head snapped backward, as a shot rang out from beside me, her body landing in a heap.

"Jesus Christ," Ward said, turning towards me, gun still trained on her body. He moved around the table, approaching her, and shooting her again in the chest. "Hopefully she doesn't get up again."

Lindsay exited the Biohazard lab behind us a moment later. She insisted Ward stop shooting Isla, after he'd put several rounds into her chest, where her heart should be. When he asked why it mattered, I already knew what her answer would be.

She dressed Ward in a full Biohazard suit, and gloves, and he helped her carry the bodies into the Biohazard lab. I watched in horror as she strapped both the poor lab tech, James, and Isla's body, to the specimen tables, double checking to make sure their arms and legs were secured.

When they exited the Biohazard lab again, she made us go out into the hall, outside the main lab. We found Topher there waiting for us. He had been peering through the lab windows.

Lindsay filled him in, but he seemed to have already surmised what had happened. She turned to us with a sigh, "I'll make sure we follow protocol, and get the lab cleaned up and sanitized again."

"We should call this in," Ward protested, shaking his head.

"No," Lindsay barked, a little harshly, then softened her tone. "Sorry," she winced, "but no, we can't do that. They'll order a full decontamination again. I can't risk them taking the bodies away. I need to study them. I need to–"

"Lindsay," I moved a step forward, "is that even... right? I mean, like, ethically? We don't have permission to... to... cut them open."

Lindsay shook her head. "I know, Jordan. But I'm not asking the Admiral for permission. I'm going to call my Captain and Major Tomlinson instead. I'll get the go-ahead I need from them." She sighed, "I'll ask them to send someone else out as well, to help me. We still understand so little about this disease. We need to know how to stop this before it gets to the point where there's no going back. We need a cure." She frowned.

"The EMP guns–" I said, but she interrupted.

"The EMP guns will be great, if they work," she added, with a hasty glance at Topher

Topher snorted. "Oh, it'll work." I turned to him eagerly. "I'm almost done," he said. "One more slight adjustment and I think we're ready to test it out." I gave him a broad smile and turned to Ward. He simply nodded back at me.

"Well, hopefully the EMP guns will allow us to fight back more effectively. But that alone may not be enough to stop this thing from spreading." Lindsay continued. "We need to combat this on more than one front, Jordan." She turned back to gaze at the lab. "Trust me, I don't want to do this. But I have to. We don't have any other choice. We need information. Answers. And this is going to help us get them."

I nodded my understanding and turned to see Ward give her a curt nod as well. "Do what you have to. The Admiral won't hear about it from me."

Lindsay nodded gratefully.

"How the hell did this happen?" He asked a moment later.

Lindsay shrugged. "There must have been some sort of slip-up. She must have been exposed, working in the lab. We weren't sure where she went. I hadn't seen her since we boarded."

Topher sighed. "I hacked into the health check database to see if maybe she was flagged, sent to Med Bay. But there was no record of her. It was like she never showed up. It seemed like she never left the ship, but we thought that wasn't possible. Now it's obvious that must have been exactly what happened." He shook his head.

"I saw a loose panel in the wall." Lindsay nodded towards the lab. "I bet she was in the walls, while they were sanitizing the ship."

"I'm surprised she didn't attack the cleaning crew," Ward said.

"Must not have been fully turned yet," Lindsay murmured, "I checked with the Med Bay here on board, and back on the base, and asked about her, but they didn't know anything either," Lindsay added. "I thought maybe she had gone to them. She had been complaining of a headache."

"Some headache," Ward muttered, peering back through the windows.

"But that seems crazy," I said slowly. "When did you see her last? She... transformed, that quickly? It was the night before last, right?"

Lindsay thought for a moment, then nodded. "Yes, it was. She had a headache that night, and I sent her back to get some sleep early."

"So, a little over 48 hours? She went from being a normal, walking, talking human being to that, in about 48 hours?" I stared at Lindsay incredulously.

"It would seem so," she said quietly, her face drawn.

"Jesus," Ward murmured. "Do whatever you need to do. Just let us know if you need anything."

Lindsay nodded wearily, and we headed back to our private quarters to get some sleep.

As we walked back, I was tempted to bring up planning a mission on the ground tomorrow, as soon as Topher was ready. But I decided to wait until morning to bring it up. I had a feeling after everything that had happened over the past two days, Ward wouldn't try to stand in my way.

36.

Topher felt confident that the gun was ready to test by noon. I was right about Ward. I didn't need to expend any energy convincing him. The men aboard *The Beagle* had managed to work themselves up into a frenzy over the events of the past 48 hours.

The fact that multiple people had turned on base during the night we spent there, and the news carrying the story Evans had broken 24/7 on every channel, was enough to cause a state of tension like I had never seen in my career.

Multiple fights had broken out by the time Topher asked to speak to me, and there were several men in the brig, cooling down. Ward had been peppered with questions from the moment he set foot in the Mess Hall at breakfast.

When I turned to him to make my pitch for my plans for the mission, he just waved a hand wearily at me. "Whatever you want. Just tell me what you need." He looked like he had aged overnight, dark circles bruised purple under his eyes. He was clearly on edge, just as much as his men, but at least it meant I wouldn't have to fight with him.

In the end, I decided on taking four of the small troop Carriers down, rather than the pods. Molton and Wren's units were to join Binson, McCullough, and me. The three of us would be in our flight suits.

I doubted we needed all the firepower for backup this time, given we weren't planning on collecting any samples. That was no longer necessary, thanks to Isla. I envisioned this being quick. Boots on the ground, locate a few Jumpers, test out the effects of the EMP gun, and get the heck out of dodge.

We had TODD help us select a location with known Jumper activity, that wasn't too close to a major city. Easy enough to do, unfortunately, at this point. The list of potential targets was far too long for my liking. Yet another indication of how widespread this thing had already become.

I took to the air, zooming up to just below the treeline. It wasn't entirely necessary, but for all I knew, this might be the last time, for a long time, that I would get a chance to fly in my flight suit. I scanned the fields up ahead, on the lookout for a stray Jumper or two.

It ended up being McCullough who spotted them first. A group of three, spreading out on the edge of a field to the west of our landing zone.

We headed in that direction. Binson and I flew ahead to meet him. I carried the EMP gun in a holster strapped to my thigh. I kept patting it with one hand, checking to make sure it was secure. Losing it now would be a mistake of potentially massive proportions.

The men had fanned out on foot to search, and they were heading towards the Jumpers now, equipped with face shields and gas masks. A few were in helmets. We had equipped them with anything we were able to find on board that might offer some protection against infection. The dark trails of moving figures in the twilight below reminded me ironically of ants.

We set down in the field beside McCullough. "Ready?" he asked, grinning through his face shield at me.

I removed the EMP gun from its holster. "It should still function essentially the same as before," Topher said suddenly in our ears. "I anticipate a direct hit shouldn't be necessary; something close enough, within a few feet, should, in theory, have an effect. But you might want to test out direct hits versus near misses."

I nodded as I listened. "Okay," I murmured back. I felt oddly nervous now that the moment was finally here. I checked the safety, making sure it was now off. Binson and McCullough had their rifles at the ready, in case it didn't work.

I moved closer to the first Jumper. He was one of those with elongated back legs, moving steadily closer to us as we made no effort to stay quiet over the comms.

I waited as the men chatted, until he was maybe ten feet away. Raising my arms, I locked on to him, aiming directly for his chest. He froze, almost as though he sensed he was in danger.

I stomped my foot on the ground. Once. Twice. A third time, and he began to move directly towards me. He emitted that odd chittering sound, the split halves of his jaw moving back and forth, as though he were tasting the air, searching for me.

"Come and get it," I murmured to him, and he let out a low snarl, scampering forward another few feet. When he was about seven feet away from me, I fired, hitting him directly in the chest.

The blast knocked him backwards, and he fell in a heap of limbs, scrambling, with a high-pitched screeching sound that made my skin crawl. No physical damage was obvious to the eye.

The Jumper seemed to shrink in on itself, as we watched, pulling its limbs in close, curling up. It sat there, trembling, shuddering for several seconds.

"It's working," Topher murmured in my ear. I watched in fascination as it turned away from us, moving on shaking, jittery limbs, stumbling and losing its footing.

The men had caught up to us now and watched at our backs. Some of them were clapping, letting out a few whoops as the Jumper retreated. The other two Jumpers were locked in our direction. One of them began to run at a loping pace, heading straight towards us.

"Try it on that one," Binson nodded in its direction. But I was already on it.

I waited another few seconds, as it moved closer, and shot off to the side, aiming about a foot away from it. It was rocked backwards, limbs shriveling up. It writhed and screeched for several seconds. The men were cheering in earnest now.

The first Jumper that had been hit seemed to be wandering aimlessly now. Despite the amount of noise we were making, it moved randomly through the field, heading in no particular direction.

"Fuck yeah!" Topher exclaimed in my ear. "We did it."

"*You* did it, Topher," I corrected him, grinning broadly. My chest filled with a lightness I hadn't felt in days. The return of a faint glimmer of hope.

"The real test will be to see if any others come." I heard Lindsay add in. "We need to see if the EMP blast managed to disrupt their communication via pheromones. It certainly seems like that one is just wandering around now. But will they still draw others to their location?"

"Shouldn't I hit the other one right away then?" I asked, swiveling back towards the remaining Jumper.

"Yes," Lindsay said, "take it out before it has a chance to sound the alarm."

I did. It was all too easy with the EMP gun. One hit, and the Jumper went down, just as the other two had.

All three now wandered through the fields, ignoring all of us, like we weren't even there.

The men were cheering, celebrating. I turned to see Ward approaching me, pulling his gas mask off as he went. He slid a hand behind my neck, pulling me to him, he pressed his forehead against mine. I grinned up at him, through the shield.

He moved away from me, after a brief pause, and began directing the men to form a perimeter and stay on guard, just in case they managed to release attack pheromones before we took them out.

I raised my face shield, glancing up at the sky above. Night was swiftly falling. The first visible stars above twinkled down at us, framed by a circle of tree limbs, stretching high into the sky. I breathed in deeply, relishing the scent of damp earth and the night wind.

"You did it." I turned to find Wren beside me, his blue eyes practically luminous in the twilight. "I knew you could do it," he murmured. He smiled at me, as I swallowed, my throat suddenly tight, nodding at him.

I had a hard time looking away; his gaze was so intense on mine, as Binson and McCullough approached us, clapping me on the back.

Binson lifted me up and spun me in a circle, while I laughed and kicked at him to put me down.

We spent another thirty minutes or so in that field, celebrating, as we waited for the first wave to arrive. But it never did.

37.

I was still grinning to myself as we rode back in the troop Carrier. I sat in the pilot's seat. I could have let the troop Carrier guide itself back to *The Beagle,* but I elected to fly it myself.

"Topher," I said suddenly, "are you still listening?"

A shuffling sound and a brief pause. "I'm still here, Captain, what's up?"

"Can you hail the base directly?" I asked.

"Hail the base?" I could hear the confusion in his voice. "Like, the general comms on base?"

"Yes," I said, "I want to send the Admiral a message."

"I mean, I can contact his office directly for you, Captain."

"No, I want this message to go through the general comms link on base, Topher. Can you patch me through to them?"

"Yeah, of course. Just give me a second." I waited until he gave me the go-ahead.

"This is Captain Kessler, of *The Beagle*," I began. "I have an urgent message for Admiral Martinez. Please tell the Admiral that our mission has been successful. We have identified the Jumpers' weaknesses and exploited them. We now have in our possession a weapon that can take them out."

A long silence on the other end of the comms. "Yes–yes, Captain. We will relay that message."

"Thank you," I said briskly. "Tell him to call me back as soon as possible."

I waited until we disconnected to speak to Topher again. "Topher, will you and Lindsay meet us back at the bridge, please?"

"We'll see you when you get back, Captain, over."

When we reached the hangar, we exited to a general cacophony, as the men poured off the troop Carriers, still celebrating.

I found Ward amongst the chaos. He was grinning broadly, striding towards me. "Well," he said, "this changes everything. We need to discuss what we do next."

I nodded up at him. "I just called and left a message for the Admiral, letting him know we were successful."

Ward's smile vanished in an instant, and he looked suddenly, oddly pale. "You did what? When?"

"Just now, from the troop Carrier." I jerked my head at the Carrier.

"Why did you do that?" Ward murmured; his brows creased.

"Why wouldn't I?" I asked, frowning at him. "He needs to know immediately. We need to get started right away; there's no time to waste."

"Get started with what?" Ward frowned, his voice dropping to a whisper as he moved closer to me.

"With manufacturing these, on a mass level," I gestured to the EMP gun strapped to my leg. "I've already talked it over with Topher. The North doesn't manufacture EMP guns at all. We're going to need to work with the South and coordinate this together. It's going to take a massive effort."

Ward was shaking his head, staring at me, eyes wide. "Those projections Evans broke the news about are accurate, Ward. We have three, maybe closer to only two, weeks until this thing spreads beyond the point where anyone can stop it. We're running out of time. If we don't find a way to get a hold of the stock of EMP guns the South has, and get them modified, we're dead in the water."

Ward just shook his head. "I really wish you hadn't done that. I wish you had waited to call him. I– we... I need to talk to you, Jordan. Alone."

I just stared back at him, my heart suddenly migrating to my throat.

"Let's head to the bridge," I said slowly. "I need to be there when the Admiral calls back."

We walked back with Wren and Molton trailing behind us. When we reached the bridge, Topher and Lindsay were already there waiting for us.

Ward sighed loudly. I muttered sideways to him. "I asked them to meet us here."

They were both grinning broadly, and Lindsay wrapped me in a hug, despite the bulky flight suit. Ward shook Topher's hand, thanking him for his hard work.

We entered the bridge, and I could tell that Ward wanted to ask them to leave, but they were all so excited, talking and laughing, joking around. Molton and Wren went straight to the mini bar, pouring drinks all around. They lifted their glasses and began a toast. Ward pulled me aside.

"Kessler, I need to talk to you, there's something you need to know."

My stomach flipped upside down. So, there was something. This was it. The something that nagged at the back of my mind. The something that stopped me from ever fully trusting him. Ever fully opening myself up to him.

He sighed, wiping a hand down his face, and he looked away from me, off towards the men celebrating. "The Admiral," he began, then stopped, "the Admiral gave me orders, Kessler. Orders regarding this mission, that was going to take place on board *The Beagle*."

I frowned, watching him. "I know, Ward, I was there, remember?"

"No," he chuckled slightly, and I realized this was the first time I had ever seen him look nervous. Scared. And my pulse ratcheted up another notch. "That was the second time."

He swallowed, shaking his head. "That was just for show. For your benefit." He met my eyes now. "He called me in the night before. That night, in the bar, when we met, I had to leave because he ordered me to come speak to him immediately. He gave me my orders then. My *real* orders. He told me there would be an officer assigned to *The Beagle* who would be investigating the Jumpers, trying to learn more about them, and put a stop to the spread." He waved his hand. "He didn't tell me who. I didn't know it would be you." He wiped a hand across his forehead. "I was ordered to stall them. Delay them. Cause friction. Cause issues, if I could. Make it difficult for them to do their job. To get the samples they needed. I was..." He trailed off.

I looked away, staring over at the men myself now, shaking my head. "Jordan," he continued. "When I realized it was you, the next day, I tried to get out of it; I didn't want anything to do with it. I–"

"I knew it," I murmured. "I knew there was something off. I knew you were hiding something from me. God," I shook my head. I had been so stupid not to see it. It was so obvious now. "I just thought you were sexist. Or an asshole."

"You don't know what it's been like, to try to choose between–"

"Why?" I snapped at him, whirling back to him. "Why did the Admiral do this? What possible–"

"Why do you think, Kessler?" Ward asked, chuckling darkly, "We're the closest we've ever been to ending the war. For the first time, we have a chance of winning. A real chance. And it's thanks to the Jumpers."

I shook my head at him, mouth gaping open. "No one in Command wants them stopped," he continued, "they wanted it to spread, to take out the enemy."

"It's going to take us out too," I hissed at him, "it's idiotic, asinine. What are they thinking? Did they think they could just flip a switch when the war ended, and everything would go back to normal? We are all fucked, because of what they did. Because of what *you* did."

He stared back at me, a shocked expression on his face. My own words sank in after I'd uttered them. Harsh, maybe. But true. He had deliberately tried to undermine the mission, tried to slow us down. That could be the difference between success and failure. "We were never sent down to the desert, were we? In Colorado? *You* sent us down there. You invented that mission to stall us for another few days."

Ward just looked away from me, his jaw clenched tight. "Damn it, Ward. Why didn't you just tell me? After everything–"

"I am telling you," he said forlornly.

"You waited until now. Until the last possible second, to tell me the truth. You–" My fists were clenched. I wanted to hit him now. I half wished I had taken him up on the offer when he'd asked me to.

"I'm sorry, Jordan, I really am. You have no idea how hard this has been for me."

I just shook my head. "Save it, Ward. I can't do this right now–"

"But you need to know," he said, moving closer and grabbing my arm. "You can't trust the Admiral; he will do whatever it takes to end this thing. We are so close. They're talking about a push into DC. He won't let anything stop him."

I shook my head, glaring back at him. I ripped my arm away and stalked across the bridge, back towards the far windows. "Jordan," he called out after me, his voice heavy with grief. But I ignored him. I needed space. I needed time. To breathe. To think.

An incoming call rang out, shrilly, plunging the bridge into silence. I turned slowly and stared up at the screen. At Admiral Martinez's face, looming over us all.

38.

Ward glanced sideways at me, his expression full of warning, as he strode over to stand beside his desk. "Admiral," he said with a nod and a salute. The rest of us snapped to attention.

"At ease," the Admiral said briskly.

Molton and Wren hid their glasses on the sideboard, while Topher glanced nervously in my direction.

"I hear you have some good news for me, Captain Kessler. I'm pleased to hear it. Although I'm not sure why you chose not to contact my office directly."

"My apologies, Sir," I said more calmly than I felt. "We hailed the base mid-flight. We were all so excited, it didn't occur to me to try to patch through directly."

The Admiral just frowned down at me, stroking his mustache. "Well, do tell. I would love to hear the details of this new weapon."

I swallowed, nodded, and moved a step or two forward. "Sir, I can't take any credit for the weapon; our team came up with the concept together, and Topher was the one who was able to modify an existing weapon to make it effective against the Jumpers." I cleared my throat. "Our field run tonight would indicate that it has the capability of rendering them a non-threat. They became docile, they... stopped attacking, wandered around aimlessly. This will be a major turning point, Sir."

"I'm thrilled to hear it, Captain." The Admiral nodded. "Thank you, and congratulations to your team on a successful mission." He smiled down at us now. "I would like to see you back on base for an immediate debriefing. We will need all the details."

"Sir," I nodded. "There is one catch, Sir." I took a deep breath. "The weapon we modified, it isn't one of ours. It was taken from the Southern Coalition. It's a model we don't manufacture currently, Sir. And I have to be honest with you, the odds of us somehow recreating and replicating this technology on the scale necessary seems close to impossible in the time we have left."

The Admiral was frowning now. "The time we have left?"

"Until we are overrun, Sir. This thing is going to spread out of control. Not just in the South, but in the North, as well. We are running out of time—"

"I am well aware of what they're saying in the news, Captain. But rest assured, the situation has been blown out of proportion."

"Not according to my calculations, Sir. I mean, Admiral." Topher added. He had stepped forward, his voice started out strong, but ended in a nervous sort of uptilt, as though he hadn't realized at first that he'd actually spoken out loud, and was now regretting it.

The Admiral stared at Topher, then glanced back in my direction, his brows creasing. My heart was thundering in my chest. Idiotic. We may as well come right out and tell him who leaked that story to the press. I waited for him to explode, but he only sighed deeply and gazed off into the distance.

"Captain, I'm more than grateful for your work and the work of your team. But you need to leave the tactical decisions and the planning of logistics to me to figure out. What happens next is between Command and Congress. It's none of your concern."

"None of my concern, Sir?" I frowned up at him, my heart in my throat. I could see, out of the corner of my eye, Ward shaking his head at me imperceptibly. "Sir, you might want to take a look at his projections," I said quietly. "This is all of our concern. If we don't find a way to mass produce these weapons in the next week, perhaps even the next few days, we're all dead." He glared down at me. "Sir." I added through gritted teeth.

"You certainly seem to think you know everything, Captain. But rest assured, you do not." He stared at me, his eyes lit with some inner fire. "Now, I'm not asking, I am ordering you to return to base immediately, with this modified weapon. You will hand it over, along with a detailed description of the exact modifications. Furthermore, I am ordering you not to speak of this. To anyone. Especially not reporters from the AP. Do I make myself clear?"

I swallowed, mind racing. But I was only stalling. Delaying the inevitable. The silence in the room was deafening, and I stared up into the Admiral's cold, hard eyes, and I knew. I knew he would take the technology away from us, and he would do nothing. Nothing, with it. He would delay. He would bury it. Until we'd made the final push into DC, minimally. Until we had all but won. Until it was too late.

I glanced once at Topher. I was banking everything on him being right. On his projections being correct. He only stared back at me, his eyes wide, full of fear.

I returned my gaze to the Admiral. "I can't do that." I heard myself say, in a small voice.

"Excuse me, Captain?" He said icily, leaning forward. "Did you just disobey a direct order? Because if so, that's very unfortunate. Incredibly unfortunate. Because that would make you insubordinate. Failure to return immediately to base and hand over the weapon would be considered a dereliction of duty, and I would be forced to declare you AWOL, at the minimum. And given the circumstances, I would say that declaring you an enemy of the state would be much more appropriate."

I swallowed thickly, my stomach sinking. My hands were tingling, as though all the blood had left my extremities. "Sir, the South has a stockpile of these weapons, if we can work with them to modify them—"

He cut me off with a deep, throaty laugh. "Work with them? If they have a stockpile of the weapons we need, then we'll take them, Captain. This is war. Not a tea party. You are to report immediately to base. This instant. Or I will declare you an enemy of the state, and I will authorize the use of lethal force to bring you in. You'll—"

"I don't think any of that will be necessary, Admiral," Ward said dryly.

I looked over to find him standing there, beside the desk. The drawer was pulled open. He held a handgun, aimed in my direction. I watched, frozen, my brows creasing in confusion, as he flicked the end of the gun upward, in an almost lazy motion, just as he had that first day on the bridge.

The force hit me square in the chest, and I went flying backwards. I heard Lindsay scream. My helmet cracked on the floor, bouncing up momentarily before slamming down again.

My muscles seized, as I attempted to suck in a deep, gasping breath. But my chest was too tight. My lungs too restricted. And I couldn't breathe. I couldn't get enough air. I let out a wheezing sound, and I heard the shuffling of footsteps across the room, and the Admiral's voice calling out.

"Thank you, Ward. I want her on a transport Carrier back to base. Now. Make sure the weapon and Topher travel with her."

"Yes, Sir," Ward replied, his tone nonchalant.

I struggled to breathe, forcing my lungs to expand in rapid, tiny movements. My limbs were starting to tingle now. The suit was locked into place. My body was on fire, with pins and needles.

I stared up at the ceiling. I would have flinched as Ward's face swam into view, but I still couldn't move. "I'm sorry, Kessler," he murmured. "Are you okay?"

"Dammit, Ward." I managed to choke out. "That's the last time you shoot me."

His face broke into a wide grin, and he let out a nervous chuckle. He glanced across me, over to my left. "Topher, can you hack into the navigation system from on board a troop Carrier? Make it look like it was hacked into from somewhere else?"

I heard Topher's voice, wearily, in the background. "I– I–" he stuttered, his voice unsteady. "I mean, yes. Yeah, I can technically hack into a system from on board, and I can route it through another server. Or bounce the signal around. I could make it look like it came from... basically anywhere I want."

"Good," Ward nodded at him, then glanced back down at me. "That's what we're going to do. We're going to carry you onto a troop Carrier, and we'll pre-program it to fly on autopilot back to base. Then, Topher, once you're in the air, you're going to hack into it, make it look like the signal is coming from somewhere else, and change the flight path mid-route."

He looked down at me, and his expression was wistful. "And you're going to call your mysterious friend. The one you called from the bridge, while we were in Atlanta." His gaze flickered back and forth over mine. "Arrange transport. Have them pick you up; get you somewhere safe."

"What?" I frowned up at him. "You knew about that?"

"Yeah," He shrugged. "I checked the comms logs after we got back." He shrugged again. "I've been keeping tabs on you. Turns out I was right to." He grinned wickedly at me. "You are an enemy of the state, after all."

"Fuck you, Ward," I managed to chuckle weakly. My lungs were able to expand more fully now, at least, but I still couldn't move. Perhaps a twitch, though, just then, in my toes.

"I'll stay here, Jordan," Lindsay said, leaning over me. "The Admiral doesn't need to know about the bodies in the lab? Right?" She looked up at Ward, and he nodded in confirmation. "I'm going to learn what I can, as fast as I can. I have a feeling we're going to need it."

"Thank you, Lindsay. I know it won't be easy. I–I'll get word back to you when I can. We'll figure out a way to communicate that they can't trace." My eyes locked onto Ward's as I uttered that last bit.

Topher cleared his throat. "That shouldn't be too much of a problem. I'll need to gather some of my things from the lab."

"Hurry," Ward nodded over to him. "Meet us in the hangar."

They carried me down to the hangar, awkwardly. Molton and Wren helped Ward, and Lindsay went ahead, clearing a path, but even still, they had to stop frequently. I could hear the murmured questions and whispers as we passed men in the corridors. They brought me aboard one of the small troop Carriers and worked on getting me out of the suit.

I was able to sit now, at least, reclining back against the seat. My muscles screamed in protest, and still felt locked up, as though my limbs had all fallen asleep, and were too stiff to bend. The pins and needles sensation was starting to wear off now, and I knew better range of movement would come next.

Molton walked over to me, setting a hand on my shoulder. He peered into my eyes from underneath his frames. "You give 'em hell, Captain." He said, grinning at me. I couldn't help but smile back. His voice dropped low. "No matter what the Admiral says, I'll make sure the men know the truth about what happened today." He lifted a finger to his lips and winked at me, squeezing my shoulder. "We'll all be rooting for you."

I fought the prickle of tears as I nodded to him. "Tell Binson and McCullough that I'm sorry, okay?" I didn't know what else to say.

He nodded back, his mouth set in a grim smile, before turning and exiting the Carrier. I caught a glimpse of Lindsay and Topher through the doorway; he reached out and grabbed her hand, holding it while she shook her head, murmuring something. My gut twisted a little. I didn't want to put Topher in any danger, but he would be invaluable. I didn't see any way around it. Besides, the Admiral had ordered Ward to send him with me. It would look suspicious if he remained behind.

Ward knelt beside me, taking my hand in his. "I'm sorry, Jordan," he swallowed, "that I didn't tell you sooner." His gaze dropped briefly to the floor. "Just make sure you're safe first, above anything else, okay?"

I nodded at him, my throat tight. We would have to discuss that later; there was no time now. "Thank you, Ward. For listening to me. To us This is the right thing to do. We'll have a chance now. I–" I paused, glancing away for a moment. Wren stood in the doorway, watching us. I couldn't look at either of them for a moment. "Just– thank you."

He squeezed my hand, and I squeezed his back. Then he leaned forward, resting his forehead against mine. "I'll find you, once things settle down. I'll figure out a way." I swallowed thickly, closing my eyes, nodding. We stayed that way for a moment, then he stood, backing away from me.

"I'll go with her," Wren said, his voice pitched low. My gaze snapped to him, but he was staring at Ward. Ward only stood there, staring down at me for several seconds. Then he turned towards Wren, his expression unreadable.

"He wouldn't expect you to send them alone, with no one on board to guard them. That makes no sense. I'll go with them. Make sure they're safe."

Ward shook his head slowly. "You'd be putting yourself at risk. He could have you declared AWOL as well, or worse." Ward's jaw was tight, that muscle clenching and unclenching, as he glanced from me to Wren.

Wren shrugged. "But if he buys the story about them being hacked from the outside, I can always come back. Say that's exactly what happened. Claim I had nothing to do with it."

Ward stared at him. And I thought he was going to say no. But then he nodded; one brisk tilt of his chin.

He reached out and grabbed Wren's hand, shaking it, then pulled him in for a hug. I watched as they patted each other on the back.

Ward turned back to me. "I won't say goodbye, Captain. I know how much you hate goodbyes." He winked.

"I'll see you soon, Ward." I managed. He stared back at me, his dark eyes full of something that looked like regret, until he disappeared through the doorway and was gone.

Wren was watching me. His blue eyes locked on mine; his expression solemn. I sighed deeply, then gave him a weak, half-hearted smile. "Help me over to the cockpit?" I asked him. I knew I couldn't trust my legs to carry me yet.

He put an arm around me and helped me sling my arm over his shoulders. We moved a few paces over to the pilot's chair. I leaned heavily on Wren, my legs still unable to bear any weight. I sat staring out the window at the hangar, eerily empty.

Wren spoke from behind me. "I'll go check and make sure Topher's on board, then we should get going. We don't want to delay too long, and cause him to get suspicious."

I nodded in agreement. "Thanks, Wren." I paused a beat. "You're sure you want to do this?"

"Yes." His voice came back firmly, without hesitation. "I am."

I only nodded again and listened as his footsteps receded.

I didn't have to wait long. We were ambling towards the middle of the hangar within moments. I was able to ease back in the chair, pressing my palms down and sliding myself backwards ever so slowly. I attempted to move my feet and was able to rotate my ankles in small circles. Almost there.

I watched as we took off into the night sky. The rumbling of the engines was comforting beneath me.

I felt strangely nostalgic, knowing my time on *The Beagle* was over. Possibly my time as a member of the Northern

Alliance, as well, in all reality. I fought against the tears that threatened to spring behind my eyes at the thought.

I had no choice, I reminded myself. No choice. We couldn't risk handing the technology over to the Admiral, only for him to sit on it. A delay of even a few days could make all the difference.

I didn't know if the Admiral was a rogue actor or in league with the rest of Command. Perhaps they all shared a similar mindset. But I refused to believe Congress would back any of his decisions.

If they knew he had ordered Ward to delay our mission, to try to slow us down, I had a feeling he would be the one facing dereliction of duty accusations. But that was an issue for another day. For now, I needed to focus on the task and the situation at hand.

I checked the time on the console. It was almost time for me to call. The timing was fortuitous. I prayed Billy would be waiting to hear from me as planned, with Captain Williams at his side.

I felt in my gut that I could trust them to direct us to safety. I knew minimally, they would want the cargo we carried. Knew they would want a solution as much as I did.

I sighed, leaning back in the seat as I felt the engines shudder, and the Carrier began to shift in its flight path.

I would speak with Topher about calling them securely on the comms. It would be vital that we made sure no one back at base could be listening in.

I was somewhat worried about Ward. He knew the location of the factory and all about the stockpile of EMP guns. What if the Admiral managed to get that out of him? Although maybe Captain Williams had been smart enough to move them after our failed mission. I had a feeling either way that Ward wouldn't break easily if questioned.

I sensed movement, a current of air, to my right, and I attempted to turn my head, gingerly, expecting to see Topher. A clear plastic mask clamped down over my mouth and nose, a hand pressing it firmly against my face, fingers cupping my jaw and chin.

I slammed my head back against the seat, attempting to jerk away, as an arm wrapped around my chest, pinning me back against the seat, holding my arms down. I let out a muffled cry, my muscles, still weak and tingling, felt like they were moving through molasses as I tried to raise my arms to fight back.

I shook my head back and forth, but the grip on my chin was like iron, and I was still far too weak. I breathed in, in my panic, and the scent, the taste of Nitrous filled my mouth, my lungs. *No.*

No. I held my breath as long as I could, as I struggled uselessly, trying desperately not to take in more of the intoxicating gas.

I managed to slide my head back, lifting my eyes towards the ceiling. I could feel myself growing weaker, and my lungs screamed for air. I took a deep, shuddering breath, and more of the fumes filled me as tears streamed from my eyes.

I continued to breathe, holding my breath for as long as possible each time, straining, until my body forced me to take another gulp of air.

I felt almost as though I were floating, now. Light. Lighter than air. As though I were flying on a soft current. Or maybe it was water. Maybe I was floating on a wave, lulled, as I rocked back and forth, back and forth. My eyes were growing heavy, closing against my will, and I fought to open them.

I turned my gaze to the right, eyes fluttering open and closed once more. I strained, attempting to get a glimpse of my attacker.

"I'm sorry, Jordan. I'm so sorry." He murmured softly to me, his voice heavy with sorrow. "I'm sorry." He squeezed me tighter, and I felt myself relax into his embrace. Going limp.

I peered up into those unnaturally blue eyes, and they stared back at me, piercing as always. As though they could see right through me, into the dark recesses of my mind. I laughed weakly, the muscles in my chest spasming, and he winced.

He was so close. His face, so close to mine. Only the mask between us, as he panted, his expression crumpling. I felt the strangest urge, as though I wanted to reach out to him.

Comfort him. I managed to lift my right hand, trembling, my fingers stretching.

"I'm sorry, Jordan," Wren repeated, as my eyelids, suddenly far too heavy, closed once more. His voice echoed to me through the darkness, and I clung to it as I began to fade. Clung to his arms, holding me down, the only thing stopping me from floating away. "I'm sorry. But I know you would understand."

THE END

Stay tuned for Volume II...

Visit A.C. Hessenauer's Author Website:

Sign up for A.C.'s monthly newsletter for updates on new releases, special content, ARC opportunities, free ebooks & more!

https://achessenauer
.wixsite.com/author